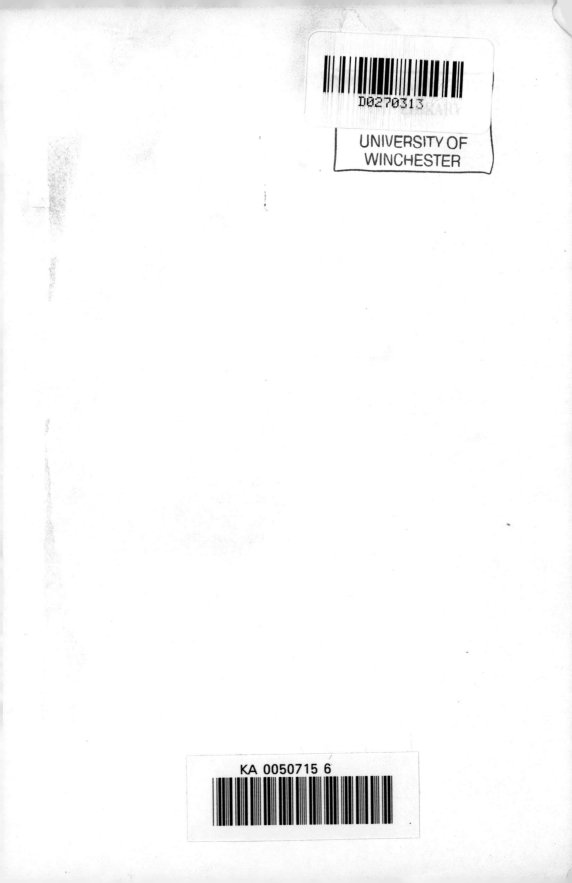

LITTLE NOVELS

LITTLE NOVELS

by

Wilkie Collins

DOVER PUBLICATIONS, INC.

NEW YORK

Published in Canada by General Publishing Company, Ltd., 30 Lesmill Road, Don Mills, Toronto, Ontario.

Published in the United Kingdom by Constable and Company, Ltd., 10 Orange Street, London WC2H 7EG.

This Dover edition, first published in 1977, is an unabridged republication of the text as published in three volumes by Chatto and Windus, Piccadilly, London, in 1887.

International Standard Book Number: 0-486-23506-8
Library of Congress Catalog Card Number: 77-074566

Manufactured in the United States of America
Dover Publications, Inc.
180 Varick Street
New York, N.Y. 10014

Contents

LITTLE NOVELS

Mrs. Zant and the Ghost

I.

THE course of this narrative describes the return of a disembodied spirit to earth, and leads the reader on new and strange ground.

Not in the obscurity of midnight, but in the searching light of day. did the supernatural influence assert itself. Neither revealed by a vision, nor announced by a voice, it reached mortal knowledge through the sense which is least easily self-deceived: the sense that feels.

The record of this event will of necessity produce conflicting impressions. It will raise, in some minds, the doubt which reason asserts ; it will invigorate, in other minds, the hope which faith justifies ; and it will leave the terrible question of the destinies of man, where centuries of vain investigation have left it—in the dark.

Having only undertaken in the present narrative to lead the way along a succession of events, the writer declines to follow modern examples by thrusting himself and his opinions on the public view. He returns to the shadow from which he has emerged, and leaves the opposing forces of incredulity and belief to fight the old battle over again, on the old ground.

II.

THE events happened soon after the first thirty years of the present century had come to an end.

On a fine morning, early in the month of April, a gentleman of middle age (named Rayburn) took his little daughter Lucy out for a walk, in the woodland pleasure-ground of Western London, called Kensington Gardens.

The few friends whom he possessed reported of Mr. Rayburn (not unkindly) that he was a reserved and solitary man. He might have been more accurately described as a widower devoted to his only surviving child. Although he was not more than forty years of age, the one pleasure which made life enjoyable to Lucy's father was offered by Lucy herself.

Playing with her ball, the child ran on to the southern limit of the Gardens, at that part of it which still remains nearest to the old Palace of Kensington. Observing close at hand one of those spacious covered seats, called in England 'alcoves,' Mr. Rayburn was reminded that he had the morning's newspaper in his pocket, and that he might do well to rest and read. At that early hour, the place was a solitude.

'Go on playing, my dear,' he said; 'but take care to keep where I can see you.'

Lucy tossed up her ball; and Lucy's father opened his newspaper. He had not been reading for more than ten minutes, when he felt a familiar little hand laid on his knee.

'Tired of playing?' he inquired—with his eyes still on the newspaper.

'I'm frightened, papa.'

He looked up directly. The child's pale face startled him. He took her on his knee and kissed her.

'You oughtn't to be frightened, Lucy, when I am with you,' he said gently. 'What is it?' He looked out of the alcove as he spoke, and saw a little dog among the trees. 'Is it the dog?' he asked.

Lucy answered:

'It's not the dog—it's the lady.'

The lady was not visible from the alcove.

'Has she said anything to you?' Mr. Rayburn inquired.

'No.'

'What has she done to frighten you?'

The child put her arms round her father's neck.

'Whisper, papa,' she said; 'I'm afraid of her hearing us. I think she's mad.'

'Why do you think so, Lucy?'

'She came near to me. I thought she was going to say something. She seemed to be ill.'

'Well? And what then?'

'She looked at me.'

There, Lucy found herself at a loss how to express what she had to say next—and took refuge in silence.

'Nothing very wonderful, so far,' her father suggested.

'Yes, papa—but she didn't seem to see me when she looked.'

'Well, and what happened then?'

'The lady was frightened — and that frightened me. I think,' the child repeated positively, 'she's mad.'

It occurred to Mr. Rayburn that the lady might be blind. He rose at once to set the doubt at rest.

'Wait here,' he said, 'and I'll come back to you.'

But Lucy clung to him with both hands; Lucy declared that she was afraid to be by herself. They left the alcove together.

The new point of view at once revealed the stranger, leaning against the trunk of a tree. She was dressed in the deep mourning of a widow. The pallor of her face, the glassy stare in her eyes, more than accounted for the child's terror—it excused the alarming conclusion at which she had arrived.

'Go nearer to her,' Lucy whispered.

They advanced a few steps. It was now easy to see that the lady was young, and wasted by illness — but (arriving at a doubtful conclusion perhaps under present circumstances) apparently possessed of rare personal attractions in happier days. As the father and daughter advanced a little, she discovered them. After some hesitation, she left the tree; approached with an evident intention of speaking; and suddenly paused. A change to astonishment and fear animated her vacant eyes. If it had not been plain before, it was now beyond all doubt that she was not a poor blind creature, deserted and helpless. At the same time, the expression of her face was not easy to understand. She could hardly have looked more amazed and bewildered, if the two strangers who were observing her had suddenly vanished from the place in which they stood.

Mr. Rayburn spoke to her with the utmost kindness of voice and manner.

'I am afraid you are not well,' he said. 'Is there anything that I can do——'

The next words were suspended on his lips. It was impossible to realize such a state of things ; but the strange impression that she had already produced on him was now confirmed. If he could believe his senses, her face did certainly tell him that he was invisible and inaudible to the woman whom he had just addressed ! She moved slowly away with a heavy sigh, like a person disappointed and distressed. Following her with his eyes, he saw the dog once more—a little smooth-coated terrier of the ordinary English breed. The dog showed none of the restless activity of his race. With his head down and his tail depressed, he crouched like a creature paralyzed by fear. His mistress roused him by a call. He followed her listlessly as she turned away.

After walking a few paces only, she suddenly stood still.

Mr. Rayburn heard her talking to herself.

'Did I feel it again ?' she said, as if perplexed by some doubt that awed or grieved her. After a while, her arms rose slowly, and opened with a gentle caressing action —an embrace strangely offered to the empty air ! 'No,' she said to herself sadly, after waiting a moment. 'More perhaps when to-morrow comes—-no more to-day.' She looked up at the clear blue sky. 'The beautiful sunlight ! the merciful sunlight !' she murmured. 'I should have died if it had happened in the dark.'

Once more she called to the dog ; and once more she walked slowly away.

'Is she going home, papa ?' the child asked.

'We will try and find out,' the father answered.

He was by this time convinced that the poor creature was in no condition to be permitted to go out without someone to take care of her. From motives of humanity, he was resolved on making the attempt to communicate with her friends.

III.

THE lady left the Gardens by the nearest gate ; stopping to lower her veil before she turned into the busy thoroughfare which leads to Kensington. Advancing a little way along the High Street, she entered a house of respectable appearance, with a card in one of the windows which announced that apartments were to let.

Mr. Rayburn waited a minute — then knocked at the door, and asked if he could see the mistress of the house. The servant showed him into a room on the ground floor, neatly but scantily furnished. One little white object varied the grim brown monotony of the empty table. It was a visiting-card.

With a child's unceremonious curiosity Lucy pounced on the card, and spelt the name, letter by letter :

'Z, A, N, T,' she repeated. 'What does that mean ?'

Her father looked at the card, as he took it away from her, and put it back on the table. The name was printed, and the address was added in pencil : 'Mr. John Zant, Purley's Hotel.'

The mistress made her appearance. Mr. Rayburn heartily wished himself out of the house again, the moment he saw her. The ways in which it is possible to cultivate the social virtues are more numerous and more varied than is generally supposed. This lady's way had apparently accustomed her to meet her fellow-creatures on the hard ground of justice without mercy. Something in her eyes, when she looked at Lucy, said :

' I wonder whether that child gets punished when she deserves it ?'

' Do you wish to see the rooms which I have to let ?' she began.

Mr. Rayburn at once stated the object of his visit—as clearly, as civilly, and as concisely as a man could do it. He was conscious (he added) that he had been guilty perhaps of an act of intrusion.

The manner of the mistress of the house showed that she entirely agreed with him. He suggested, however, that his motive might excuse him. The mistress's manner changed, and asserted a difference of opinion.

' I only know the lady whom you mention,' she said, ' as a person of the highest respectability, in delicate health. She has taken my first-floor apartments, with excellent references ; and she gives remarkably little trouble. I have no claim to interfere with her proceedings, and no reason to doubt that she is capable of taking care of herself.'

Mr. Rayburn unwisely attempted to say a word in his own defence.

' Allow me to remind you ——' he began.

' Of what, sir ?'

' Of what I observed, when I happened to see the lady in Kensington Gardens.'

' I am not responsible for what you observed in Kensington Gardens. If your time is of any value, pray don't let me detain you.'

Dismissed in those terms, Mr. Rayburn took Lucy's hand and withdrew. He had just reached the door, when it was opened from the outer side. The Lady of Kensington Gardens stood before him. In the position which he and his daughter now occupied, their backs were towards the window. Would she remember having seen them for a moment in the Gardens ?

' Excuse me for intruding on you,' she said to the landlady. ' Your servant tells me my brother-in-law called while I was out. He sometimes leaves a message on his card.'

She looked for the message, and appeared to be disappointed : there was no writing on the card.

Mr. Rayburn lingered a little in the doorway, on the chance of hearing something more. The landlady's vigilant eyes discovered him.

' Do you know this gentleman ?' she said maliciously to her lodger.

' Not that I remember.'

Replying in those words, the lady looked at Mr. Rayburn for the first time ; and suddenly drew back from him.

' Yes,' she said, correcting herself; ' I think we met——'

Her embarrassment overpowered her ; she could say no more.

Mr. Rayburn compassionately finished the sentence for her.

' We met accidentally in Kensington Gardens,' he said.

She seemed to be incapable of appreciating the kindness of his motive. After hesitating a little she addressed a proposal to him, which seemed to show distrust of the landlady.

' Will you let me speak to you upstairs in my own rooms ?' she asked.

Without waiting for a reply, she led the way to the stairs. Mr. Rayburn and Lucy followed. They were just beginning the ascent to the first floor, when the spiteful landlady left the lower room, and called to her lodger over their heads :

' Take care what you say to this man, Mrs. Zant! He thinks you're mad.'

Mrs. Zant turned round on the landing, and looked at him. Not a word fell from her lips. She suffered, she feared, in silence. Something in the sad submission of her face touched the springs of innocent pity in Lucy's heart. The child burst out crying.

That artless expression of sympathy drew

Mrs. Zant down the few stairs which separated her from Lucy.

'May I kiss your dear little girl?' she said to Mr. Rayburn. The landlady, standing on the mat below, expressed her opinion of the value of caresses, as compared with a sounder method of treating young persons in tears: 'If that child was mine,' she remarked, 'I would give her something to cry for.'

In the meantime, Mrs. Zant led the way to her rooms.

The first words she spoke showed that the landlady had succeeded but too well in prejudicing her against Mr. Rayburn.

'Will you let me ask your child,' she said to him, 'why you think me mad?'

He met this strange request with a firm answer.

'You don't know yet what I really do think. Will you give me a minute's attention?'

'No,' she said positively. 'The child pities me, I want to speak to the child. What did you see me do in the Gardens, my dear, that surprised you?' Lucy turned uneasily to her father; Mrs. Zant persisted. 'I first saw you by yourself, and then I saw you with your father,' she went on. 'When I came nearer to you, did I look very oddly—as if I didn't see you at all?'

Lucy hesitated again; and Mr. Rayburn interfered.

'You are confusing my little girl,' he said. 'Allow me to answer your questions —or excuse me if I leave you.'

There was something in his look, or in his tone, that mastered her. She put her hand to her head.

'I don't think I'm fit for it,' she answered vacantly. 'My courage has been sorely tried already. If I can get a little rest and sleep, you may find me a different person. I am left a great deal by myself; and I have reasons for trying to compose my mind.

Can I see you to-morrow? Or write to you? Where do you live?'

Mr. Rayburn laid his card on the table in silence. She had strongly excited his interest. He honestly desired to be of some service to this forlorn creature—abandoned so cruelly, as it seemed, to her own guidance. But he had no authority to exercise, no sort of claim to direct her actions, even if she consented to accept his advice. As a last resource he ventured on an allusion to the relative of whom she had spoken downstairs.

'When do you expect to see your brother-in-law again?' he said.

'I don't know,' she answered. 'I should like to see him—he is so kind to me.'

She turned aside to take leave of Lucy.

'Good-bye, my little friend. If you live to grow up, I hope you will never be such a miserable woman as I am.' She suddenly looked round at Mr. Rayburn. 'Have you got a wife at home?' she asked.

'My wife is dead.'

'And you have a child to comfort you! Please leave me; you harden my heart. Oh, sir, don't you understand? You make me envy you!'

Mr. Rayburn was silent when he and his daughter were out in the street again. Lucy, as became a dutiful child, was silent, too. But there are limits to human endurance—and Lucy's capacity for self-control gave way at last.

'Are you thinking of the lady, papa?' she said.

He only answered by nodding his head. His daughter had interrupted him at that critical moment in a man's reflections, when he is on the point of making up his mind. Before they were at home again Mr. Rayburn had arrived at a decision. Mrs. Zant's brother-in-law was evidently ignorant of any serious necessity for his interference—or he would have made arrangements for immediately repeating his visit. In this state of things, if any evil happened to Mrs. Zant, silence on Mr. Rayburn's part might be indirectly to blame for a serious misfortune. Arriving at that conclusion, he decided upon running the risk of being rudely received, for the second time, by another stranger.

Leaving Lucy under the care of her governess, he went at once to the address that had been written on the visiting-card left at the lodging-house, and sent in his name. A courteous message was returned. Mr. John Zant was at home, and would be happy to see him.

IV.

MR. RAYBURN was shown into one of the private sitting-rooms of the hotel.

He observed that the customary position of the furniture in a room had been, in some respects, altered. An armchair, a side-table, and a footstool had all been removed to one of the windows, and had been placed as close as possible to the light. On the table lay a large open roll of morocco leather, containing rows of elegant little instruments in steel and ivory. Waiting by the table, stood Mr. John Zant. He said 'Good-morning' in a bass voice, so profound and so melodious that those two commonplace words assumed a new importance, coming from his lips. His personal appearance was in harmony with his magnificent voice—he was a tall finely-made man of dark complexion; with big brilliant black eyes, and a noble curling beard, which hid the whole lower part of his face. Having bowed with a happy mingling of dignity and politeness, the conventional side of this gentleman's character suddenly vanished; and a crazy side, to all appearance, took its place. He dropped on his knees in front of the footstool. Had he forgotten to say his prayers that morning,

and was he in such a hurry to remedy the fault that he had no time to spare for consulting appearances ? The doubt had hardly suggested itself, before it was set at rest in a most unexpected manner. Mr. Zant looked at his visitor with a bland smile, and said:

'Please let me see your feet.'

For the moment, Mr. Rayburn lost his presence of mind. He looked at the instruments on the side-table.

'Are you a corn-cutter ?' was all he could say.

'Excuse me, sir,' returned the polite operator, 'the term you use is quite obsolete in our profession.' He rose from his knees, and added modestly : 'I am a Chiropodist.'

'I beg your pardon.'

'Don't mention it ! You are not, I imagine, in want of my professional services. To what motive may I attribute the honour of your visit ?'

By this time Mr. Rayburn had recovered himself.

'I have come here,' he answered, 'under circumstances which require apology as well as explanation.'

Mr. Zant's highly polished manner betrayed signs of alarm ; his suspicions pointed to a formidable conclusion—a conclusion that shook him to the innermost recesses of the pocket in which he kept his money.

'The numerous demands on me——' he began.

Mr. Rayburn smiled.

'Make your mind easy,' he replied. 'I don't want money. My object is to speak with you on the subject of a lady who is a relation of yours.'

'My sister-in-law !' Mr. Zant exclaimed. 'Pray, take a seat.'

Doubting if he had chosen a convenient time for his visit, Mr. Rayburn hesitated.

'Am I likely to be in the way of persons

who wish to consult you?' he asked.

'Certainly not. My morning hours of attendance on my clients are from eleven to one.' The clock on the mantelpiece struck the quarter-past one as he spoke. 'I hope you don't bring me bad news?' he said, very earnestly. 'When I called on Mrs. Zant this morning, I heard that she had gone out for a walk. Is it indiscreet to ask how you became acquainted with her?'

Mr. Rayburn at once mentioned what he had seen and heard in Kensington Gardens; not forgetting to add a few words, which described his interview afterwards with Mrs. Zant.

The lady's brother-in-law listened with an interest and sympathy, which offered the strongest possible contrast to the unprovoked rudeness of the mistress of the lodging-house. He declared that he could only do justice to his sense of obligation by following Mr. Rayburn's example, and expressing himself as frankly as if he had been speaking to an old friend.

'The sad story of my sister-in-law's life,' he said, 'will, I think, explain certain things which must have naturally perplexed you. My brother was introduced to her at the house of an Australian gentleman, on a visit to England. She was then employed as governess to his daughters. So sincere was the regard felt for her by the family that the parents had, at the entreaty of their children, asked her to accompany them when they returned to the Colony. The governess thankfully accepted the proposal.'

'Had she no relations in England?' Mr. Rayburn asked.

'She was literally alone in the world, sir. When I tell you that she had been brought up in the Foundling Hospital, you will understand what I mean. Oh, there is no romance in my sister-in-law's story! She never has known, or will know, who her parents were or why they deserted her. The happiest moment in her life was the moment when she and my brother first met. It was an instance, on both sides, of love at first sight. Though not a rich man, my brother had earned a sufficient income in mercantile pursuits. His character spoke for itself. In a word, he altered all the poor girl's prospects, as we then hoped and believed, for the better. Her employers deferred their return to Australia, so that she might be married from their house. After a happy life of a few weeks only——'

His voice failed him; he paused, and turned his face from the light.

'Pardon me,' he said; 'I am not able, even yet, to speak composedly of my brother's death. Let me only say that the poor young wife was a widow, before the happy days of the honeymoon were over. That dreadful calamity struck her down. Before my brother had been committed to the grave, her life was in danger from brain-fever.'

Those words placed in a new light Mr. Rayburn's first fear that her intellect might be deranged. Looking at him attentively, Mr. Zant seemed to understand what was passing in the mind of his guest.

'No!' he said. 'If the opinions of the medical men are to be trusted, the result of the illness is injury to her physical strength —not injury to her mind. I have observed in her, no doubt, a certain waywardness of temper since her illness; but that is a trifle. As an example of what I mean, I may tell you that I invited her, on her recovery, to pay me a visit. My house is not in London —the air doesn't agree with me—my place of residence is at St. Sallins-on-Sea. I am not myself a married man; but my excellent housekeeper would have received Mrs. Zant with the utmost kindness. She was resolved —obstinately resolved, poor thing—to remain in London. It is needless to say that, in her melancholy position, I am attentive to her slightest wishes. I took a lodging for her; and, at her special request, I chose a house which was near Kensington Gardens.'

' Is there any association with the Gardens which led Mrs. Zant to make that request ?'

' Some association, I believe, with the memory of her husband. By the way, I wish to be sure of finding her at home, when I call to-morrow. Did you say (in the course of your interesting statement) that she intended—as you supposed—to return to Kensington Gardens to-morrow ? Or has my memory deceived me ?'

' Your memory is perfectly accurate.'

' Thank you. I confess I am not only distressed by what you have told me of Mrs. Zant—I am at a loss to know how to act for the best. My only idea, at present, is to try change of air and scene. What do you think yourself ?'

' I think you are right.'

Mr. Zant still hesitated.

' It would not be easy for me, just now,' he said, ' to leave my patients and take her abroad.'

The obvious reply to this occurred to Mr. Rayburn. A man of larger worldly experience might have felt certain suspicions, and might have remained silent. Mr. Rayburn spoke.

' Why not renew your invitation and take her to your house at the seaside ?' he said.

In the perplexed state of Mr. Zant's mind, this plain course of action had apparently failed to present itself. His gloomy face brightened directly.

' The very thing !' he said. ' I will certainly take your advice. If the air of St. Sallins does nothing else, it will improve her health, and help her to recover her good looks. Did she strike you as having been (in happier days) a pretty woman ?'

This was a strangely familiar question to ask—almost an indelicate question, under the circumstances. A certain furtive expression in Mr. Zant's fine dark eyes seemed to imply that it had been put with a purpose. Was it possible that he suspected Mr. Rayburn's interest in his sister-in-law to be inspired by any motive which was not perfectly unselfish and perfectly pure ? To arrive at such a conclusion as this, might be to judge hastily and cruelly of a man who was perhaps only guilty of a want of delicacy of feeling. Mr. Rayburn honestly did his best to assume the charitable point of view. At the same time, it is not to be denied that his words, when he answered, were carefully guarded, and that he rose to take his leave.

Mr. John Zant hospitably protested.

' Why are you in such a hurry ? Must you really go ? I shall have the honour of returning your visit to-morrow, when I have made arrangements to profit by that excellent suggestion of yours. Good-bye. God bless you.'

He held out his hand: a hand with a smooth surface and a tawny colour, that fervently squeezed the fingers of a departing friend.

' Is that man a scoundrel ?' was Mr. Rayburn's first thought, after he had left the hotel. His moral sense set all hesitation at rest—and answered: ' You're a fool if you doubt it.'

V.

DISTURBED by presentiments, Mr. Rayburn returned to his house on foot, by way of trying what exercise would do towards composing his mind.

The experiment failed. He went upstairs and played with Lucy; he drank an extra glass of wine at dinner ; he took the child and her governess to a circus in the evening ; he ate a little supper, fortified by another glass of wine, before he went to bed—and still those vague forebodings of evil persisted in torturing him. Looking back through his past life, he asked himself if any woman (his late wife of course excepted!) had ever taken the predominant place in his thoughts which Mrs. Zant had assumed—without any discernible reason to account for it? If he had ventured to answer his own question, the reply would have been: Never!

All the next day he waited at home, in expectation of Mr. John Zant's promised visit, and waited in vain.

Towards evening the parlour-maid appeared at the family tea-table, and presented to her master an unusually large envelope sealed with black wax, and addressed in a strange handwriting. The absence of stamp and postmark showed that it had been left at the house by a messenger.

'Who brought this?' Mr. Rayburn asked.

'A lady, sir—in deep mourning.'

'Did she leave any message?'

'No, sir.'

Having drawn the inevitable conclusion, Mr. Rayburn shut himself up in his library. He was afraid of Lucy's curiosity and Lucy's questions, if he read Mrs. Zant's letter in his daughter's presence.

Looking at the open envelope after he had taken out the leaves of writing which it contained, he noticed these lines traced inside the cover:

'My one excuse for troubling you, when I might have consulted my brother-in-law, will be found in the pages which I enclose. To speak plainly, you have been led to fear that I am not in my right senses. For this very reason, I now appeal to you. Your dreadful doubt of me, sir, is my doubt too. Read what I have written about myself—and then tell me, I entreat you, which I am: A person who has been the object of a supernatural revelation? or an unfortunate creature who is only fit for imprisonment in a mad-house?'

Mr. Rayburn opened the manuscript. With steady attention, which soon quickened to breathless interest, he read what follows:

VI.

THE LADY'S MANUSCRIPT.

YESTERDAY morning, the sun shone in a clear blue sky—after a succession of cloudy days, counting from the first of the month.

The radiant light had its animating effect on my poor spirits. I had passed the night more peacefully than usual; undisturbed by the dream, so cruelly familiar to me, that my lost husband is still living—the dream from which I always wake in tears. Never, since the dark days of my sorrow, have I been so little troubled by the self-tormenting fancies and fears which beset miserable women, as when I left the house, and turned my steps towards Kensington Gardens—for the first time since my husband's death.

Attended by my only companion, the little dog who had been his favourite as well as mine, I went to the quiet corner of the Gardens which is nearest to Kensington.

On that soft grass, under the shade of those grand trees, we had loitered together in the days of our betrothal. It was his favourite walk; and he had taken me to see it in the early days of our acquaintance. There, he had first asked me to be his wife. There, we had felt the rapture of our first kiss. It was surely natural that I should wish to see once more a place sacred to such memories as these? I am only twenty-three years old; I have no child to comfort me, no companion of my own age, nothing to love but the dumb creature who is so faithfully fond of me.

I went to the tree under which we stood, when my dear one's eyes told his love before he could utter it in words. The sun of that vanished day shone on me again ; it was the same noontide hour; the same solitude was round me. I had feared the first effect of the dreadful contrast between past and present. No ! I was quiet and resigned. My thoughts, rising higher than earth, dwelt on the better life beyond the grave. Some tears came into my eyes. But I was not unhappy. My memory of all that happened may be trusted, even in trifles which relate only to myself—I was not unhappy.

The first object that I saw, when my eyes were clear again, was the dog. He crouched a few paces away from me, trembling pitiably, but uttering no cry. What had caused the fear that overpowered him?

I was soon to know.

I called to the dog ; he remained im-movable—conscious of some mysterious coming thing that held him spellbound. I tried to go to the poor creature, and fondle and comfort him.

At the first step forward that I took, something stopped me.

It was not to be seen, and not to be heard. It stopped me.

The still figure of the dog disappeared from my view: the lonely scene round me disappeared — excepting the light from heaven, the tree that sheltered me, and the grass in front of me. A sense of unutter-able expectation kept my eyes riveted on the grass. Suddenly, I saw its myriad blades rise erect and shivering. The fear came to me of something passing over them with the invisible swiftness of the wind. The shivering advanced. It was all round me. It crept into the leaves of the tree over my head ; they shuddered, without a sound to tell of their agitation : their pleasant natural rustling was struck dumb. The songs of the birds had ceased. The cries of the water-fowl on the pond were heard no more. There was a dreadful silence.

But the lovely sunshine poured down on me, as brightly as ever.

In that dazzling light, in that fearful silence, I felt an Invisible Presence near me.

It touched me gently.

At the touch, my heart throbbed with an overwhelming joy. Exquisite pleasure thrilled through every nerve in my body. I knew him! From the unseen world—himself unseen—he had returned to me. Oh, I knew him!

And yet, my helpless mortality longed for a sign that might give me assurance of the truth. The yearning in me shaped itself into words. I tried to utter the words. I would have said, if I could have spoken: 'Oh, my angel, give me a token that it is You!' But I was like a person struck dumb—I could only think it.

The Invisible Presence read my thought. I felt my lips touched, as my husband's lips used to touch them when he kissed me. And that was my answer. A thought came to me again. I would have said, if I could have spoken: 'Are you here to take me to the better world?'

I waited. Nothing that I could feel touched me.

I was conscious of thinking once more. I would have said, if I could have spoken: ' Are you here to protect me?'

I felt myself held in a gentle embrace, as my husband's arms used to hold me when he pressed me to his breast. And that was my answer.

The touch that was like the touch of his lips, lingered and was lost; the clasp that was like the clasp of his arms, pressed me and fell away. The garden-scene resumed its natural aspect. I saw a human creature near, a lovely little girl looking at me.

At that moment, when I was my own lonely self again, the sight of the child soothed and attracted me. I advanced, intending to speak to her. To my horror I suddenly ceased to see her. She disappeared as if I had been stricken blind.

And yet I could see the landscape round me; I could see the heaven above me. A time passed—only a few minutes, as I thought—and the child became visible to me again; walking hand-in-hand with her father. I approached them; I was close enough to see that they were looking at me with pity and surprise. My impulse was to ask if they saw anything strange in my face or my manner. Before I could speak, the horrible wonder happened again. They vanished from my view.

Was the Invisible Presence still near? Was it passing between me and my fellow-mortals; forbidding communication, in that place and at that time?

It must have been so. When I turned away in my ignorance, with a heavy heart, the dreadful blankness which had twice shut out from me the beings of my own race, was not between me and my dog. The poor little creature filled me with pity; I called him to me. He moved at the sound of my voice, and followed me languidly; not quite awakened yet from the trance of terror that had possessed him.

Before I had retired by more than a few steps, I thought I was conscious of the Presence again. I held out my longing arms to it. I waited in the hope of a touch to tell me that I might return. Perhaps I was answered by indirect means? I only know that a resolution to return to the same place, at the same hour, came to me, and quieted my mind.

The morning of the next day was dull and cloudy; but the rain held off. I set forth again to the Gardens.

My dog ran on before me into the street —and stopped: waiting to see in which direction I might lead the way. When I turned towards the Gardens, he dropped behind me. In a little while I looked back. He was following me no longer;

he stood irresolute. I called to him. He advanced a few steps—hesitated—and ran back to the house.

I went on by myself. Shall I confess my superstition? I thought the dog's desertion of me a bad omen.

Arrived at the tree, I placed myself under it. The minutes followed each other un-eventfully. The cloudy sky darkened. The dull surface of the grass showed no shuddering consciousness of an unearthly creature passing over it.

I still waited, with an obstinacy which was fast becoming the obstinacy of despair. How long an interval elapsed, while I kept watch on the ground before me, I am not able to say. I only know that a change came.

Under the dull gray light I saw the grass move—but not as it had moved, on the day before. It shrivelled as if a flame had scorched it. No flame appeared. The brown underlying earth showed itself winding onward in a thin strip—which might have been a footpath traced in fire. It frightened me. I longed for the protection of the Invisible Presence; I prayed for a warning of it, if danger was near.

A touch answered me. It was as if a hand unseen had taken my hand — had raised it, little by little—had left it, pointing to the thin brown path that wound towards me under the shrivelled blades of grass.

I looked to the far end of the path.

The unseen hand closed on my hand with a warning pressure: the revelation of the coming danger was near me—I waited for it; I saw it.

The figure of a man appeared, advancing towards me along the thin brown path. I looked in his face as he came nearer. It showed me dimly the face of my husband's brother—John Zant.

The consciousness of myself as a living creature left me. I knew nothing; I felt nothing; I was dead.

When the torture of revival made me open my eyes, I found myself on the grass. Gentle hands raised my head, at the moment when I recovered my senses. Who had brought me to life again? Who was taking care of me?

I looked upward, and saw—bending over me—John Zant.

VII.

There, the manuscript ended.

Some lines had been added on the last page; but they had been so carefully erased as to be illegible. These words of explanation appeared below the cancelled sentences:

'I had begun to write the little that remains to be told, when it struck me that I might, unintentionally, be exercising an unfair influence on your opinion. Let me only remind you that I believe absolutely in the supernatural revelation which I have endeavoured to describe. Remember this—and decide for me what I dare not decide for myself.'

There was no serious obstacle in the way of compliance with this request.

Judged from the point of view of the materialist, Mrs. Zant might no doubt be the victim of illusions (produced by a diseased state of the nervous system), which have been known to exist—as in the celebrated case of the bookseller, Nicolai, of Berlin—without being accompanied by derangement of the intellectual powers. But Mr. Rayburn was not asked to solve any such intricate problem as this. He had been merely instructed to read the manuscript, and to say what impression it had left on him of the mental condition of the writer; whose doubt of herself had been, in all probability, first suggested by remembrance of the illness from which she

had suffered—brain-fever.

Under these circumstances, there could be little difficulty in forming an opinion. The memory which had recalled, and the judgment which had arranged, the succession of events related in the narrative revealed a mind in full possession of its resources.

Having satisfied himself so far, Mr. Rayburn abstained from considering the more serious question suggested by what he had read.

At any time, his habits of life and his ways of thinking would have rendered him unfit to weigh the arguments, which assert or deny supernatural revelation among the creatures of earth. But his mind was now so disturbed by the startling record of experience which he had just read, that he was only conscious of feeling certain impressions—without possessing the capacity to reflect on them. That his anxiety on Mrs. Zant's account had been increased, and that his doubts of Mr. John Zant had been encouraged, were the only practical results of the confidence placed in him of which he was thus far aware. In the ordinary exigencies of life a man of hesitating disposition, his interest in Mrs. Zant's welfare, and his desire to discover what had passed between her brother-in-law and herself, after their meeting in the Gardens, urged him into instant action. In half an hour more, he had arrived at her lodgings. He was at once admitted.

VIII.

Mrs. Zant was alone, in an imperfectly lit room. 'I hope you will excuse the bad light,' she said; 'my head has been burning as if the fever had come back again. Oh, don't go away! After what I have suffered, you don't know how dreadful it is to be alone.'

The tone of her voice told him that she

had been crying. He at once tried the best means of setting the poor lady at ease, by telling her of the conclusion at which he had arrived, after reading her manuscript. The happy result showed itself instantly : her face brightened, her manner changed ; she was eager to hear more.

' Have I produced any other impression on you ?' she asked.

He understood the allusion. Expressing sincere respect for her own convictions, he told her honestly that he was not prepared to enter on the obscure and terrible question of supernatural interposition. Grateful for the tone in which he had answered her, she wisely and delicately changed the subject.

' I must speak to you of my brother-in-law,' she said. ' He has told me of your visit ; and I am anxious to know what you think of him. Do you like Mr. John Zant ?'

Mr. Rayburn hesitated.

The care-worn look appeared again in her face. ' If you had felt as kindly towards him as he feels towards you,' she said, ' I might have gone to St. Sallins with a lighter heart.'

Mr. Rayburn thought of the supernatural appearances, described at the close of her narrative. ' You believe in that terrible warning,' he remonstrated ; ' and yet, you go to your brother-in-law's house !'

' I believe,' she answered, ' in the spirit of the man who loved me in the days of his earthly bondage. I am under *his* protection. What have I to do but to cast away my fears, and to wait in faith and hope ? It might have helped my resolution if a friend had been near to encourage me.' She paused and smiled sadly. ' I must remember,' she resumed, ' that your way of understanding my position is not my way. I ought to have told you that Mr. John Zant feels needless anxiety about my health. He declares that he will not lose sight of me until his mind is at ease.

It is useless to attempt to alter his opinion. He says my nerves are shattered—and who that sees me can doubt it ? He tells me that my only chance of getting better is to try change of air and perfect repose—how can I contradict him ? He reminds me that I have no relation but himself, and no house open to me but his own—and God knows he is right !'

She said those last words in accents of melancholy resignation, which grieved the good man whose one merciful purpose was to serve and console her. He spoke impulsively with the freedom of an old friend.

' I want to know more of you and Mr. John Zant, than I know now,' he said. ' My motive is a better one than mere curiosity. Do you believe that I feel a sincere interest in you ?'

' With my whole heart.'

That reply encouraged him to proceed with what he had to say. ' When you recovered from your fainting-fit,' he began, ' Mr. John Zant asked questions, of course ?'

' He asked what could possibly have happened, in such a quiet place as Kensington Gardens, to make me faint.'

' And how did you answer ?'

' Answer ? I couldn't even look at him !'

' You said nothing ?'

' Nothing. I don't know what he thought of me ; he might have been surprised, or he might have been offended.'

' Is he easily offended?' Mr. Rayburn asked.

' Not in my experience of him.'

' Do you mean your experience of him before your illness ?'

' Yes. Since my recovery, his engagements with country patients have kept him away from London. I have not seen him since he took these lodgings for me. But he is always considerate. He has written more than once to beg that I will not think him neglectful, and to tell me (what I knew already through my poor husband) that he has no money of his own, and must live by his profession.'

'In your husband's lifetime, were the two brothers on good terms?'

'Always. The one complaint I ever heard my husband make of John Zant was that he didn't come to see us often enough, after our marriage. Is there some wickedness in him which we have never suspected? It may be—but *how* can it be? I have every reason to be grateful to the man against whom I have been supernaturally warned! His conduct to me has been always perfect. I can't tell you what I owe to his influence in quieting my mind, when a dreadful doubt arose about my husband's death.'

'Do you mean doubt if he died a natural death?'

'Oh, no! no! He was dying of rapid consumption—but his sudden death took the doctors by surprise. One of them thought that he might have taken an overdose of his sleeping drops, by mistake. The other disputed this conclusion, or there might have been an inquest in the house. Oh, don't speak of it any more! Let us talk of something else. Tell me when I shall see you again.'

'I hardly know. When do you and your brother-in-law leave London?'

'To-morrow.' She looked at Mr. Rayburn with a piteous entreaty in her eyes; she said timidly: 'Do you ever go to the seaside, and take your dear little girl with you?'

The request, at which she had only dared to hint, touched on the idea which was at that moment in Mr. Rayburn's mind.

Interpreted by his strong prejudice against John Zant, what she had said of her brother-in-law filled him with forebodings of peril to herself; all the more powerful in their influence, for this reason—that he shrank from distinctly realizing them. If

another person had been present at the interview, and had said to him afterwards: 'That man's reluctance to visit his sister-in-law, while her husband was living, is associated with a secret sense of guilt which her innocence cannot even imagine: he, and he alone, knows the cause of her husband's sudden death: his feigned anxiety about her health is adopted as the safest means of enticing her into his house'—if those formidable conclusions had been urged on Mr. Rayburn, he would have felt it his duty to reject them, as unjustifiable aspersions on an absent man. And yet, when he took leave that evening of Mrs. Zant, he had pledged himself to give Lucy a holiday at the seaside; and he had said, without blushing, that the child really deserved it, as a reward for general good conduct and attention to her lessons!

IX.

THREE days later, the father and daughter arrived towards evening at St. Sallins-on-Sea. They found Mrs. Zant at the station.

The poor woman's joy, on seeing them, expressed itself like the joy of a child. 'Oh, I am so glad! so glad!' was all she could say when they met. Lucy was half-smothered with kisses, and was made supremely happy by a present of the finest doll she had ever possessed. Mrs. Zant accompanied her friends to the rooms which had been secured at the hotel. She was able to speak confidentially to Mr. Rayburn, while Lucy was in the balcony hugging her doll, and looking at the sea.

The one event that had happened during Mrs. Zant's short residence at St. Sallins, was the departure of her brother-in-law that morning, for London. He had been called away to operate on the feet of a wealthy patient who knew the value of his time: his housekeeper expected that he would return to dinner.

As to his conduct towards Mrs. Zant, he was not only as attentive as ever—he was almost oppressively affectionate in his language and manner. There was no service that a man could render which he had not eagerly offered to her. He declared that he already perceived an improvement in her health ; he congratulated her on having decided to stay in his house ; and (as a proof, perhaps, of his sincerity) he had repeatedly pressed her hand. 'Have you any idea what all this means ?' she said simply.

Mr. Rayburn kept his idea to himself. He professed ignorance ; and asked next what sort of person the housekeeper was.

Mrs. Zant shook her head ominously.

'Such a strange creature,' she said, 'and in the habit of taking such liberties, that I begin to be afraid she is a little crazy.'

'Is she an old woman ?'

'No—only middle-aged. This morning, after her master had left the house, she actually asked me what I thought of my brother-in-law ! I told her, as coldly as possible, that I thought he was very kind. She was quite insensible to the tone in which I had spoken ; she went on from bad to worse. " Do you call him the sort of man who would take the fancy of a young woman ?" was her next question. She actually looked at me (I might have been wrong ; and I hope I was) as if the " young woman " she had in her mind was myself ! I said, " I don't think of such things, and I don't talk about them." Still, she was not in the least discouraged ; she made a personal remark next : " Excuse me—but you do look wretchedly pale." I thought she seemed to enjoy the defect in my complexion ; I really believe it raised me in her estimation. " We shall get on better in time," she said ; " I'm beginning to like you." She

walked out humming a tune. Don't you agree with me ? Don't you think she's crazy ?'

'I can hardly give an opinion until I have seen her. Does she look as if she might have been a pretty woman at one time of her life ?'

'Not the sort of pretty woman whom I admire !'

Mr. Rayburn smiled. 'I was thinking,' he resumed, ' that this person's odd conduct may perhaps be accounted for. She is probably jealous of any young lady who is invited to her master's house—and (till she noticed your complexion) she began by being jealous of you.'

Innocently at a loss to understand how *she* could become an object of the housekeeper's jealousy, Mrs. Zant looked at Mr. Rayburn in astonishment. Before she could give expression to her feeling of surprise, there was an interruption—a welcome interruption. A waiter entered the room, and announced a visitor ; described as ' a gentleman.'

Mrs. Zant at once rose to retire.

'Who is the gentleman ?' Mr. Rayburn asked—detaining Mrs. Zant as he spoke.

A voice which they both recognised answered gaily, from the outer side of the door :

'A friend from London.'

X.

'WELCOME to St. Sallins !' cried Mr. John Zant. 'I knew that you were expected, my dear sir, and I took my chance of finding you at the hotel.' He turned to his sister-in-law, and kissed her hand with an elaborate gallantry worthy of Sir Charles Grandison himself. 'When I reached home, my dear, and heard that you had gone out, I guessed that your object was to receive our excellent friend. You have not felt lonely while I have been away ? That's right ! that's right !' He looked towards the balcony, and discovered Lucy at the open window, staring at the magnificent stranger. 'Your little daughter, Mr. Rayburn ? Dear child ! Come, and kiss me.'

Lucy answered in one positive word: 'No.'

Mr. John Zant was not easily discouraged. 'Show me your doll, darling,' he said. 'Sit on my knee.'

Lucy answered in two positive words— 'I won't.'

Her father approached the window to administer the necessary reproof. Mr. John Zant interfered in the cause of mercy with his best grace. He held up his hands in cordial entreaty. 'Dear Mr. Rayburn ! The fairies are sometimes shy ; and *this* little fairy doesn't take to strangers at first sight. Dear child ! All in good time. And what stay do you make at St. Sallins ? May we hope that our poor attractions will tempt you to prolong your visit ?'

He put his flattering little question with an ease of manner which was rather too plainly assumed ; and he looked at Mr. Rayburn with a watchfulness which appeared to attach undue importance to the reply. When he said : 'What stay do you make at St. Sallins ?' did he really mean : 'How soon do you leave us ?' Inclining to adopt this conclusion, Mr. Rayburn answered cautiously, that his stay at the seaside would depend on circumstances. Mr. John Zant looked at his sister-in-law, sitting silent in a corner with Lucy on her lap. 'Exert your attractions,' he said ; 'make the circumstances agreeable to our good friend. Will you dine with us to-day, my dear sir, and bring your little fairy with you ?'

Lucy was far from receiving this complimentary allusion in the spirit in which it had been offered. 'I'm not a fairy,' she declared. 'I'm a child.'

'And a naughty child,' her father added,

with all the severity that he could assume.

'I can't help it, papa ; the man with the big beard puts me out.'

The man with the big beard was amused—amiably, paternally amused—by Lucy's plain speaking. He repeated his invitation to dinner ; and he did his best to look disappointed when Mr. Rayburn made the necessary excuses.

'Another day,' he said (without, however, fixing the day). 'I think you will find my house comfortable. My housekeeper may perhaps be eccentric — but in all essentials a woman in a thousand. Do you feel the change from London already ? Our air at St. Sallins is really worthy of its reputation. Invalids who come here are cured as if by magic. What do you think of Mrs. Zant ? How does she look ?'

Mr. Rayburn was evidently expected to say that she looked better. He said it. Mr. John Zant seemed to have anticipated a stronger expression of opinion.

'Surprisingly better !' he pronounced. 'Infinitely better ! We ought both to be grateful. Pray believe that we *are* grateful.'

'If you mean grateful to me,' Mr. Rayburn remarked, 'I don't quite understand——'

'You don't quite understand ? Is it possible that you have forgotten our conversation when I first had the honour of receiving you ? Look at Mrs. Zant again.'

Mr. Rayburn looked ; and Mrs. Zant's brother-in-law explained himself.

'You notice the return of her colour, the healthy brightness of her eyes. (No, my dear, I am not paying you idle compliments ; I am stating plain facts.) For that happy result, Mr. Rayburn, we are indebted to you.'

'Surely not ?'

'Surely yes ! It was at your valuable suggestion that I thought of inviting my sister-in-law to visit me at St. Sallins. Ah, you remember it now. Forgive me if I look at my watch ; the dinner hour is on my mind. Not, as your dear little daughter there seems to think, because I am greedy, but because I am always punctual, in justice to the cook. Shall we see you to-morrow ? Call early, and you will find us at home.'

He gave Mrs. Zant his arm, and bowed and smiled, and kissed his hand to Lucy, and left the room. Recalling their interview at the hotel in London, Mr. Rayburn now understood John Zant's object (on that occasion) in assuming the character of a helpless man in need of a sensible suggestion. If Mrs. Zant's residence under his roof became associated with evil consequences, he could declare that she would never have entered the house but for Mr. Rayburn's advice.

With the next day came the hateful necessity of returning this man's visit.

Mr. Rayburn was placed between two alternatives. In Mrs. Zant's interests he must remain, no matter at what sacrifice of his own inclinations, on good terms with her brother-in-law—or he must return to London, and leave the poor woman to her fate. His choice, it is needless to say, was never a matter of doubt. He called at the house, and did his innocent best—without in the least deceiving Mr. John Zant—to make himself agreeable during the short duration of his visit. Descending the stairs on his way out, accompanied by Mrs. Zant, he was surprised to see a middle-aged woman in the hall, who looked as if she was waiting there expressly to attract notice.

' The housekeeper,' Mrs. Zant whispered. ' She is impudent enough to try to make acquaintance with you.'

This was exactly what the housekeeper was waiting in the hall to do.

' I hope you like our watering-place, sir,' she began. ' If I can be of service to you, pray command me. Any friend of this lady's has a claim on me—and you are an old friend, no doubt. I am only the housekeeper ; but I presume to take a sincere interest in Mrs. Zant ; and I am indeed glad to see you here. We none of us know—do we ?—how soon we may want a friend. No offence, I hope ? Thank you, sir. Good morning.'

There was nothing in the woman's eyes which indicated an unsettled mind ; nothing in the appearance of her lips which suggested habits of intoxication. That her strange outburst of familiarity proceeded from some strong motive seemed to be more than probable. Putting together what Mrs. Zant had already told him, and what he had himself observed, Mr. Rayburn suspected that the motive might be found in the housekeeper's jealousy of her master.

XI.

REFLECTING in the solitude of his own room, Mr. Rayburn felt that the one prudent course to take would be to persuade Mrs. Zant to leave St. Sallins. He tried to prepare her for this strong proceeding, when she came the next day to take Lucy out for a walk.

' If you still regret having forced yourself to accept your brother-in-law's invitation,' was all he ventured to say, ' don't forget that you are perfect mistress of your own actions. You have only to come to me at the hotel, and I will take you back to London by the next train.'

She positively refused to entertain the idea.

' I should be a thankless creature indeed,' she said, ' if I accepted your proposal. Do you think I am ungrateful enough to involve you in a personal quarrel with John Zant ? No ! If I find myself forced to leave the house, I will go away alone.'

There was no moving her from this resolution. When she and Lucy had gone out together, Mr. Rayburn remained at the hotel, with a mind ill at ease. A man of readier mental resources might have felt at a loss how to act for the best, in the emergency that now confronted him. While he was still as far as ever from arriving at a decision, some person knocked at the door.

Had Mrs. Zant returned? He looked up as the door was opened, and saw to his astonishment — Mr. John Zant's housekeeper.

'Don't let me alarm you, sir,' the woman said. 'Mrs. Zant has been taken a little faint, at the door of our house. My master is attending to her.'

'Where is the child?' Mr. Rayburn asked.

'I was bringing her back to you, sir, when we met a lady and her little girl at the door of the hotel. They were on their way to the beach—and Miss Lucy begged hard to be allowed to go with them. The lady said the two children were playfellows, and she was sure you would not object.'

'The lady is quite right. Mrs. Zant's illness is not serious, I hope?'

'I think not, sir. But I should like to say something in her interests. May I? Thank you.' She advanced a step nearer to him, and spoke her next words in a whisper. 'Take Mrs. Zant away from this place, and lose no time in doing it.'

Mr. Rayburn was on his guard. He merely asked:

'Why?'

The housekeeper answered in a curiously indirect manner—partly in jest, as it seemed, and partly in earnest.

'When a man has lost his wife,' she said, 'there's some difference of opinion in Parliament, as I hear, whether he does right or wrong, if he marries his wife's sister. Wait a bit! I'm coming to the point. My master is one who has a long head on his shoulders; he sees consequences which escape the notice of people like me. In his

way of thinking, if one man may marry his wife's sister, and no harm done, where's the objection if another man pays a compliment to the family, and marries his brother's widow? My master, if you please, is that other man. Take the widow away before she marries him.'

This was beyond endurance.

'You insult Mrs. Zant,' Mr. Rayburn answered, 'if you suppose that such a thing is possible!'

'Oh! I insult her, do I? Listen to me. One of three things will happen. She will be entrapped into consenting to it—or frightened into consenting to it—or drugged into consenting to it——'

Mr. Rayburn was too indignant to let her go on.

'You are talking nonsense,' he said. 'There can be no marriage; the law forbids it.'

'Are you one of the people who see no farther than their noses?' she asked insolently. 'Won't the law take his money? Is he obliged to mention that he is related to her by marriage, when he buys the license?' She paused; her humour changed; she stamped furiously on the floor. The true motive that animated her showed itself in her next words, and warned Mr. Rayburn to grant a more favourable hearing than he had accorded to her yet. 'If you won't stop it,' she burst out, 'I will! If he marries anybody, he is bound to marry ME. Will you take her away? I ask you, for the last time—*will* you take her away?'

The tone in which she made that final appeal to him had its effect.

'I will go back with you to John Zant's house,' he said, 'and judge for myself.'

She laid her hand on his arm:

'I must go first—or you may not be let in. Follow me in five minutes; and don't knock at the street door.'

On the point of leaving him, she abruptly returned.

'We have forgotten something,' she said. 'Suppose my master refuses to see you. His temper might get the better of him; he might make it so unpleasant for you that you would be obliged to go.'

'*My* temper might get the better of *me*,' Mr. Rayburn replied; 'and—if I thought it was in Mrs. Zant's interests—I might refuse to leave the house unless she accompanied me.'

'That will never do, sir.'

'Why not?'

'Because I should be the person to suffer.'

'In what way?'

'In this way. If you picked a quarrel with my master, I should be blamed for it because I showed you upstairs. Besides, think of the lady. You might frighten her out of her senses, if it came to a struggle between you two men.'

The language was exaggerated; but there was a force in this last objection which Mr. Rayburn was obliged to acknowledge.

'And, after all,' the housekeeper continued, 'he has more right over her than you have. He is related to her, and you are only her friend.'

Mr. Rayburn declined to let himself be influenced by this consideration.

'Mr. John Zant is only related to her by marriage,' he said. 'If she prefers trusting in me—come what may of it, I will be worthy of her confidence.'

The housekeeper shook her head.

'That only means another quarrel,' she answered. 'The wise way, with a man like my master, is the peaceable way. We must manage to deceive him.'

'I don't like deceit.'

'In that case, sir, I'll wish you good-bye. We will leave Mrs. Zant to do the best she can for herself.'

Mr. Rayburn was unreasonable. He positively refused to adopt this alternative.

'Will you hear what I have got to say?'

the housekeeper asked.

'There can be no harm in that,' he admitted. 'Go on.'

She took him at his word.

'When you called at our house,' she began, 'did you notice the doors in the passage, on the first floor? Very well. One of them is the door of the drawing-room, and the other is the door of the library. Do you remember the drawing-room, sir?'

'I thought it a large well-lit room,' Mr. Rayburn answered. 'And I noticed a doorway in the wall, with a handsome curtain hanging over it.'

'That's enough for our purpose,' the housekeeper resumed. 'On the other side of the curtain, if you had looked in, you would have found the library. Suppose my master is as polite as usual, and begs to be excused for not receiving you, because it is an inconvenient time. And suppose you are polite on your side, and take yourself off by the drawing-room door. You will find me waiting downstairs, on the first landing. Do you see it now?'

'I can't say I do.'

'You surprise me, sir. What is to prevent us from getting back softly into the library, by the door in the passage? And why shouldn't we use that second way into the library as a means of discovering what may be going on in the drawing-room? Safe behind the curtain, you will see him if he behaves uncivilly to Mrs. Zant, or you will hear her if she calls for help. In either case, you may be as rough and ready with my master as you find needful; it will be he who has frightened her, and not you. And who can blame the poor housekeeper because Mr. Rayburn did his duty, and protected a helpless woman? There is my plan, sir. Is it worth trying?'

He answered, sharply enough: 'I don't like it.'

The housekeeper opened the door again,

and wished him good-bye.

If Mr. Rayburn had felt no more than an ordinary interest in Mrs. Zant, he would have let the woman go. As it was, he stopped her; and, after some further protest (which proved to be useless), he ended in giving way.

'You promise to follow my directions?' she stipulated.

He gave the promise. She smiled, nodded, and left him. True to his instructions, Mr. Rayburn reckoned five minutes by his watch, before he followed her.

XII.

THE housekeeper was waiting for him, with the street-door ajar.

'They are both in the drawing-room,' she whispered, leading the way upstairs. 'Step softly, and take him by surprise.'

A table of oblong shape stood midway between the drawing-room walls. At the end of it which was nearest to the window, Mrs. Zant was pacing to and fro across the breadth of the room. At the opposite end of the table, John Zant was seated. Taken completely by surprise, he showed himself in his true character. He started to his feet, and protested with an oath against the intrusion which had been committed on him.

Heedless of his action and his language, Mr. Rayburn could look at nothing; could think of nothing, but Mrs. Zant. She was still walking slowly to and fro, unconscious of the words of sympathy which he addressed to her, insensible even as it seemed to the presence of other persons in the room.

John Zant's voice broke the silence. His temper was under control again: he had his reasons for still remaining on friendly terms with Mr. Rayburn.

'I am sorry I forgot myself just now,' he said.

Mr. Rayburn's interest was concentrated on Mrs. Zant; he took no notice of the apology.

'When did this happen?' he asked.

'About a quarter of an hour ago. I was fortunately at home. Without speaking to me, without noticing me, she walked upstairs like a person in a dream.'

Mr. Rayburn suddenly pointed to Mrs. Zant.

'Look at her!' he said. 'There's a change!'

All restlessness in her movements had come to an end. She was standing at the farther end of the table which was nearest to the window, in the full flow of sunlight pouring at that moment over her face. Her eyes looked out straight before her— void of all expression. Her lips were a little parted; her head drooped slightly towards her shoulder, in an attitude which suggested listening for something or waiting for something. In the warm brilliant light, she stood before the two men, a living creature self-isolated in a stillness like the stillness of death.

John Zant was ready with the expression of his opinion.

'A nervous seizure,' he said. 'Something resembling catalepsy, as you see.'

'Have you sent for a doctor?'

'A doctor is not wanted.'

'I beg your pardon. It seems to me that medical help is absolutely necessary.'

'Be so good as to remember,' Mr. John Zant answered, 'that the decision rests with me, as the lady's relative. I am sensible of the honour which your visit confers on me. But the time has been unhappily chosen. Forgive me if I suggest that you will do well to retire.'

Mr. Rayburn had not forgotten the housekeeper's advice, or the promise which she had exacted from him. But the expression in John Zant's face was a serious trial to his self-control. He hesitated, and looked back at Mrs. Zant.

If he provoked a quarrel by remaining in the room, the one alternative would be the removal of her by force. Fear of the consequences to herself, if she was suddenly and roughly roused from her trance, was the one consideration which reconciled him to submission. He withdrew.

The housekeeper was waiting for him below, on the first landing. When the door of the drawing-room had been closed again, she signed to him to follow her, and returned up the stairs. After another struggle with himself, he obeyed. They entered the library from the corridor—and placed themselves behind the closed curtain which hung over the doorway. It was easy so to arrange the edge of the drapery as to observe, without exciting suspicion, whatever was going on in the next room.

Mrs. Zant's brother-in-law was approaching her, at the time when Mr. Rayburn saw him again.

In the instant afterwards, she moved—before he had completely passed over the space between them. Her still figure began to tremble. She lifted her drooping head. For a moment, there was a shrinking in her —as if she had been touched by something. She seemed to recognise the touch: she was still again.

John Zant watched the change. It suggested to him that she was beginning to recover her senses. He tried the experiment of speaking to her.

' My love, my sweet angel, come to the heart that adores you !'

He advanced again; he passed into the flood of sunlight pouring over her.

' Rouse yourself !' he said.

She still remained in the same position ; apparently at his mercy, neither hearing him nor seeing him.

' Rouse yourself !' he repeated. ' My darling, come to me !'

At the instant when he attempted to embrace her — at the instant when Mr. Rayburn rushed into the room — John Zant's arms, suddenly turning rigid, remained outstretched. With a shriek of horror, he struggled to draw them back— struggled, in the empty brightness of the sunshine, as if some invisible grip had seized him.

' What has got me ?' the wretch screamed. ' Who is holding my hands ? Oh, the cold of it ! the cold of it !'

His features became convulsed ; his eyes turned upwards until only the white eyeballs were visible. He fell prostrate with a crash that shook the room.

The housekeeper ran in. She knelt by her master's body. With one hand she loosened his cravat. With the other she pointed to the end of the table.

Mrs. Zant still kept her place ; but there was another change. Little by little, her eyes recovered their natural living expression — then slowly closed. She tottered backwards from the table, and lifted her hands wildly, as if to grasp at something which might support her. Mr. Rayburn hurried to her before she fell—lifted her in his arms—and carried her out of the room.

One of the servants met them in the hall. He sent her for a carriage. In a quarter of an hour more, Mrs. Zant was safe under his care at the hotel.

XIII.

THAT night a note, written by the housekeeper, was delivered to Mrs. Zant.

' The doctors give little hope. The paralytic stroke is spreading upwards to his face. If death spares him, he will live a helpless man. I shall take care of him to the last. As for you—forget him.'

Mrs. Zant gave the note to Mr. Rayburn.

' Read it, and destroy it,' she said. ' It is written in ignorance of the terrible truth.'

He obeyed—and looked at her in silence, waiting to hear more. She hid her face. The few words that she addressed to him, after a struggle with herself, fell slowly and reluctantly from her lips.

She said, ' No mortal hand held the hands of John Zant. The guardian spirit was with me. The promised protection was with me. I know it. I wish to know no more.'

Having spoken, she rose to retire. He opened the door for her, seeing that she needed rest in her own room.

Left by himself, he began to consider the prospect that was before him in the future. How was he to regard the woman who had just left him? As a poor creature weakened by disease, the victim of her own nervous delusion ? or as the chosen object of a supernatural revelation — unparalleled by any similar revelation that he had heard of, or had found recorded in books? His first discovery of the place that she really held in his estimation dawned on his mind, when he felt himself recoiling from the conclusion which presented her to his pity, and yielding to the nobler conviction which felt with her faith, and raised her to a place apart among other women.

XIV.

THEY left St. Sallins the next day.

Arrived at the end of the journey, Lucy held fast by Mrs. Zant's hand. Tears were rising in the child's eyes. ' Are we to bid her good-bye ?' she said sadly to her father.

He seemed to be unwilling to trust himself to speak ; he only said, ' My dear, ask her yourself.'

But the result justified him. Lucy was happy again.

Miss Morris and the Stranger

I.

WHEN I first saw him, he was lost in one of the Dead Cities of England—situated on the south coast, and called Sandwich.

Shall I describe Sandwich ? I think not. Let us own the truth ; descriptions of places, however nicely they may be written, are always more or less dull. Being a woman, I naturally hate dulness. Perhaps some description of Sandwich may drop out, as it were, from my report of our conversation when we first met as strangers in the street.

He began irritably. 'I've lost myself,' he said.

People who don't know the town often do that,' I remarked.

He went on : ' Which is my way to the Fleur de Lys Inn ?'

His way was, in the first place, to retrace his steps. Then to turn to the left. Then to go on until he found two streets meeting. Then to take the street on the right. Then to look out for the second turning on the left. Then to follow the turning until he smelt stables—and there was the inn. I put it in the clearest manner, and never stumbled over a word.

' How the devil am I to remember all that ?' he said.

This was rude. We are, naturally and properly, indignant with any man who is rude to us. But whether we turn our backs on him in contempt, or whether we are merciful and give him a lesson in politeness, depends entirely on the man. He may be a bear, but he may also have his redeeming qualities. This man had redeeming qualities. I cannot positively say that he was either handsome or ugly, young or old, well or ill dressed. But I can speak with certainty to the personal attractions which recommended him to notice. For instance, the tone of his voice was persuasive. (Did you ever read a story, written by one of *us*, in which we failed to dwell on our hero's voice ?) Then, again, his hair was reasonably long. (Are you acquainted with any woman who can endure a man with a cropped head ?) Moreover, he was of a good height. (It must be a very tall woman who can feel favourably inclined towards a short man.) Lastly, although his eyes were not more than fairly presentable in form and colour, the wretch had in some unaccountable manner become possessed of beautiful eyelashes.

They were even better eyelashes than mine. I write quite seriously. There is one woman who is above the common weakness of vanity—and she holds the present pen.

So I gave my lost stranger a lesson in politeness. The lesson took the form of a trap. I asked if he would like me to show him the way to the inn. He was still annoyed at losing himself. As I had anticipated, he bluntly answered : ' Yes.'

' When you were a boy, and you wanted something,' I said, ' did your mother teach you to say " Please " ?'

He positively blushed. ' She did,' he admitted ; ' and she taught me to say " Beg your pardon " when I was rude. I'll say it now : " Beg your pardon." '

This curious apology increased my belief in his redeeming qualities. · I led the way to the inn. He followed me in silence. No woman who respects herself can endure silence when she is in the company of a man. I made him talk.

' Do you come to us from Ramsgate ?' I began. He only nodded his head. ' We don't think much of Ramsgate here,' I went on. ' There is not an old building in the place. And their first Mayor was only elected the other day !'

This point of view seemed to be new to him. He made no attempt to dispute it ; he only looked round him, and said, ' Sandwich is a melancholy place, Miss.' He was so rapidly improving in politeness, that I encouraged him by a smile. As a citizen of Sandwich, I may say that we take it as a compliment when we are told that our town is a melancholy place. And why not ? Melancholy is connected with dignity. And dignity is associated with age. And *we* are old. I teach my pupils logic, among other things—there is a specimen. Whatever may be said to the contrary, women can reason. They can also wander ; and I must admit that *I* am wandering. Did I mention, at starting, that I was a governess ? If not,

that allusion to ' pupils ' must have come in rather abruptly. Let me make my excuses, and return to my lost stranger.

' Is there any such thing as a straight street in all Sandwich ?' he asked.

' Not one straight street in the whole town.'

' Any trade, Miss ?'

' As little as possible—and *that* is expiring.'

' A decayed place, in short ?'

' Thoroughly decayed.'

My tone seemed to astonish him. ' You speak as if you were proud of its being a decayed place,' he said.

I quite respected him ; this was such an intelligent remark to make. We do enjoy our decay : it is our chief distinction. Progress and prosperity everywhere else ; decay and dissolution here. As a necessary consequence, we produce our own impression, and we like to be original. The sea deserted us long ago : it once washed our walls, it is now two miles away from us —we don't regret the sea. We had sometimes ninety-five ships in our harbour, Heaven only knows how many centuries ago ; we now have one or two small coasting vessels, half their time aground in a muddy little river — we don't regret our harbour. But one house in the town is daring enough to anticipate the arrival of resident visitors, and announces furnished apartments to let. What a becoming contrast to our modern neighbour, Ramsgate ! Our noble market-place exhibits the laws made by the corporation ; and every week there are fewer and fewer people to obey the laws. How convenient ! Look at our one warehouse by the river side—with the crane generally idle, and the windows mostly boarded up ; and perhaps one man at the door, looking out for the job which his better sense tells him cannot possibly come. What a wholesome protest against the devastating hurry and over-work elsewhere, which has shattered the nerves of the nation! 'Far from me and from my friends' (to borrow the eloquent language of Doctor Johnson) 'be such frigid enthusiasm as shall conduct us indifferent and unmoved' over the bridge by which you enter Sandwich, and pay a toll if you do it in a carriage. 'That man is little to be envied' (Doctor Johnson again) who can lose himself in our labyrinthine streets, and not feel that he has reached the welcome limits of progress, and found a haven of rest in an age of hurry.

I am wandering again. Bear with the unpremeditated enthusiasm of a citizen who only attained years of discretion at her last birthday. We shall soon have done with Sandwich; we are close to the door of the inn.

'You can't mistake it now, sir,' I said. 'Good-morning.'

He looked down at me from under his beautiful eyelashes (have I mentioned that I am a little woman?), and he asked in his persuasive tones, 'Must we say good-bye?'

I made him a bow.

'Would you allow me to see you safe home?' he suggested.

Any other man would have offended me. This man blushed like a boy, and looked at the pavement instead of looking at me. By this time I had made up my mind about him. He was not only a gentleman beyond all doubt, but a shy gentleman as well. His bluntness and his odd remarks were, as I thought, partly efforts to disguise his shyness, and partly refuges in which he tried to forget his own sense of it. I answered his audacious proposal amiably and pleasantly. 'You would only lose your way again,' I said, 'and I should have to take you back to the inn for the second time.'

Wasted words! My obstinate stranger only made another proposal.

'I have ordered lunch here,' he said,

'and I am quite alone.' He stopped in confusion, and looked as if he rather expected me to box his ears. 'I shall be forty next birthday,' he went on; 'I am old enough to be your father.' I all but burst out laughing, and stepped across the street, on my way home. He followed me. 'We might invite the landlady to join us,' he said, looking the picture of a headlong man, dismayed by the consciousness of his own imprudence. 'Couldn't you honour me by lunching with me if we had the landlady?' he asked.

This was a little too much. 'Quite out of the question, sir—and you ought to know it,' I said with severity. He half put out his hand. 'Won't you even shake hands with me?' he inquired piteously. When we have most properly administered a reproof to a man, what *is* the perversity which makes us weakly pity him the minute afterwards? I was fool enough to shake hands with this perfect stranger. And, having done it, I completed the total loss of my dignity by running away. Our dear crooked little streets hid me from him directly.

As I rang at the door-bell of my employer's house, a thought occurred to me which might have been alarming to a better regulated mind than mine.

'Suppose he should come back to Sandwich?'

II.

BEFORE many more days passed I had troubles of my own to contend with, which put the eccentric stranger out of my head for the time.

Unfortunately, my troubles are part of my story; and my early life mixes itself up with them. In consideration of what is to follow, may I say two words relating to the period before I was a governess?

I am the orphan daughter of a shop-keeper of Sandwich. My father died, leaving to his widow and child an honest name and a little income of £80 a year. We kept on the shop—neither gaining nor losing by it. The truth is, nobody would buy our poor little business. I was thirteen years old at the time; and I was able to help my mother, whose health was then beginning to fail. Never shall I forget a certain bright summer's day, when I saw a new customer enter our shop. He was an elderly gentleman; and he seemed surprised to find so young a girl as myself in charge of the business, and, what is more, competent to support the charge. I answered his questions in a manner which seemed to please him. He soon discovered that my education (excepting my knowledge of the business) had been sadly neglected; and he inquired if he could see my mother. She was resting on the sofa in the back parlour—and she received him there. When he came out, he patted me on the cheek. 'I have taken a fancy to you,' he said, 'and perhaps I shall come back again.' He did come back again. My mother had referred him to the rector for our characters in the town, and he had heard what our clergyman could say for us. Our only relations had emigrated to Australia, and were not doing well there. My mother's death would leave me, so far as relatives were concerned, literally alone in the world. 'Give this girl a first-rate education,' said our elderly customer, sitting at our tea-table in the back parlour, 'and she will do. If you will send her to school, ma'am, I'll pay for her education.' My poor mother began to cry at the prospect of parting with me. The old gentleman said, 'Think of it,' and got up to go. He gave me his card as I opened the shop-door for him. 'If you find yourself in trouble,' he whispered, so that my mother could not hear him, 'be a wise child, and write and

tell me of it.' I looked at the card. Our kind-hearted customer was no less a person than Sir Gervase Damian, of Garrum Park, Sussex — with landed property in our county as well! He had made himself (through the rector, no doubt) far better acquainted than I was with the true state of my mother's health. In four months from the memorable day when the great man had taken tea with us, my time had come to be alone in the world. I have no courage to dwell on it; my spirits sink, even at this distance of time, when I think of myself in those days. The good rector helped me with his advice—I wrote to Sir Gervase Damian.

A change had come over his life as well as mine in the interval since we had met.

Sir Gervase had married for the second time—and, what was more foolish still, perhaps, at his age, had married a young woman. She was said to be consumptive, and of a jealous temper as well. Her husband's only child by his first wife, a son and heir, was so angry at his father's second marriage, that he left the house. The landed property being entailed, Sir Gervase could only express his sense of his son's conduct by making a new will, which left all his property in money to his young wife.

These particulars I gathered from the steward, who was expressly sent to visit me at Sandwich.

'Sir Gervase never makes a promise without keeping it,' this gentleman informed me. 'I am directed to take you to a first-rate ladies' school in the neighbourhood of London, and to make all the necessary arrangements for your remaining there until you are eighteen years of age. Any written communications in the future are to pass, if you please, through the hands of the rector of Sandwich. The delicate health of the new Lady Damian makes it only too likely that the lives of her husband and herself will be passed, for the most part, in a milder climate than the climate of England. I am instructed to say this, and to convey to you Sir Gervase's best wishes.'

By the rector's advice, I accepted the position offered to me in this unpleasantly formal manner — concluding (quite correctly, as I afterwards discovered) that I was indebted to Lady Damian for the arrangement which personally separated me from my benefactor. Her husband's kindness and my gratitude, meeting on the neutral ground of Garrum Park, were objects of conjugal distrust to this lady. Shocking! shocking! I left a sincerely grateful letter to be forwarded to Sir Gervase; and, escorted by the steward, I went to school—being then just fourteen years old.

I know I am a fool. Never mind. There is some pride in me, though I am only a small shopkeeper's daughter. My new life had its trials—my pride held me up.

For the four years during which I remained at the school, my poor welfare might be a subject of inquiry to the rector, and sometimes even to the steward—never to Sir Gervase himself. His winters were no doubt passed abroad; but in the summer time he and Lady Damian were at home again. Not even for a day or two in the holiday time was there pity enough felt for my lonely position to ask me to be the guest of the housekeeper (I expected nothing more) at Garrum Park. But for my pride, I might have felt it bitterly. My pride said to me, ' Do justice to yourself.' I worked so hard, I behaved so well, that the mistress of the school wrote to Sir Gervase to tell him how thoroughly I had deserved the kindness that he had shown to me. No answer was received. (Oh, Lady Damian!) No change varied the monotony of my life—except when one of my school-girl friends sometimes took me home with

her for a few days at vacation time. Never mind. My pride held me up.

As the last half-year of my time at school approached, I began to consider the serious question of my future life.

Of course, I could have lived on my eighty pounds a year; but what a lonely, barren existence it promised to be!—unless somebody married me; and where, if you please, was I to find him? My education had thoroughly fitted me to be a governess. Why not try my fortune, and see a little of the world in that way? Even if I fell among ill-conditioned people, I could be independent of them, and retire on my income.

The rector, visiting London, came to see me. He not only approved of my idea—he offered me a means of carrying it out. A worthy family, recently settled at Sandwich, were in want of a governess. The head of the household was partner in a business (the exact nature of which it is needless to mention) having ' branches ' out of London. He had become superintendent of a new ' branch'—tried as a commercial experiment, under special circumstances, at Sandwich. The idea of returning to my native place pleased me—dull as the place was to others. I accepted the situation.

When the steward's usual half-yearly letter arrived soon afterwards, inquiring what plans I had formed on leaving school, and what he could do to help them, acting on behalf of Sir Gervase, a delicious tingling filled me from head to foot when I thought of my own independence. It was not ingratitude towards my benefactor; it was only my little private triumph over Lady Damian. Oh, my sisters of the sex, can you not understand and forgive me?

So to Sandwich I returned; and there, for three years, I remained with the kindest people who ever breathed the breath of life. Under their roof I was still living when I met with my lost gentleman in the street.

Ah me! the end of that quiet, pleasant life was near. When I lightly spoke to the odd stranger of the expiring trade of the town, I never suspected that my employer's trade was expiring too. The speculation had turned out to be a losing one ; and all his savings had been embarked in it. He could no longer remain at Sandwich, or afford to keep a governess. His wife broke the sad news to me. I was so fond of the children, I proposed to her to give up my salary. Her husband refused even to consider the proposal. It was the old story of poor humanity over again. We cried, we kissed, we parted.

What was I to do next ?—write to Sir Gervase ?

I had already written, soon after my return to Sandwich ; breaking through the regulations by directly addressing Sir Gervase. I expressed my grateful sense of his generosity to a poor girl who had no family claim on him ; and I promised to make the one return in my power by trying to be worthy of the interest he had taken in me. The letter was written without any alloy of mental reserve. My new life as a governess was such a happy one, that I had forgotten my paltry bitterness of feeling against Lady Damian.

It was a relief to think of this change for the better, when the secretary at Garrum Park informed me that he had forwarded my letter to Sir Gervase, then at Madeira with his sick wife. She was slowly and steadily wasting away in a decline. Before another year had passed, Sir Gervase was left a widower for the second time, with no child to console him under his loss. No answer came to my grateful letter. I should have been unreasonable indeed if I had expected the bereaved husband to remember me in his grief and loneliness. Could I write to him again, in my own trumpery little interests, under these cir-

cumstances ? I thought (and still think) that the commonest feeling of delicacy forbade it. The only other alternative was to appeal to the ever-ready friends of the obscure and helpless public. I advertised in the newspapers.

The tone of one of the answers which I received impressed me so favourably, that I forwarded my references. The next post brought my written engagement, and the offer of a salary which doubled my income.

The story of the past is told ; and now we may travel on again, with no more stoppages by the way.

III.

THE residence of my present employer was in the north of England. Having to pass through London, I arranged to stay in town for a few days to make some necessary additions to my wardrobe. An old servant of the rector, who kept a lodging-house in the suburbs, received me kindly, and guided my choice in the serious matter of a dressmaker. On the second morning after my arrival, an event happened. The post brought me a letter forwarded from the rectory. Imagine my astonishment when my correspondent proved to be Sir Gervase Damian himself!

The letter was dated from his house in London. It briefly invited me to call and see him, for a reason which I should hear from his own lips. He naturally supposed that I was still at Sandwich, and requested me, in a postscript, to consider my journey as made at his expense.

I went to the house the same day. While I was giving my name, a gentleman came out into the hall. He spoke to me without ceremony.

' Sir Gervase,' he said, ' believes he is going to die. Don't encourage him in that idea. He may live for another year or more, if his friends will only persuade him to be hopeful about himself.'

With that, the gentleman left me ; the servant said it was the doctor.

The change in my benefactor, since I had seen him last, startled and distressed me. He lay back in a large arm-chair, wearing a grim black dressing-gown, and looking pitiably thin and pinched and worn. I do not think I should have known him again, if we had met by accident. He signed to me to be seated on a little chair by his side.

' I wanted to see you,' he said quietly, ' before I die. You must have thought me neglectful and unkind, with good reason. My child, you have not been forgotten. If years have passed without a meeting be-tween us, it has not been altogether my fault——'

He stopped. A pained expression passed over his poor worn face ; he was evidently thinking of the young wife whom he had lost. I repeated—fervently and sincerely repeated—what I had already said to him in writing. ' I owe everything, sir, to your fatherly kindness.' Saying this, I ventured a little further. I took his wan white hand, hanging over the arm of the chair, and re-spectfully put it to my lips.

He gently drew his hand away from me, and sighed as he did it. Perhaps *she* had sometimes kissed his hand.

' Now tell me about yourself,' he said.

I told him of my new situation, and how I had got it. He listened with evident in-terest.

' I was not self-deceived,' he said, ' when I first took a fancy to you in the shop. I admire your independent feeling ; it's the right kind of courage in a girl like you. But you must let me do something more for you—some little service, to remember me by when the end has come. What shall it be ?'

' Try to get better, sir ; and let me write

to you now and then,' I answered. ' Indeed, indeed, I want nothing more.'

' You will accept a little present, at least?' With those words he took from the breast-pocket of his dressing-gown an enamelled cross attached to a gold chain. ' Think of me sometimes,' he said, as he put the chain round my neck. He drew me to him gently, and kissed my forehead. It was too much for me. ' Don't cry, my dear,' he said ; ' don't remind me of another sad young face——'

Once more he stopped ; once more he was thinking of the lost wife. I pulled down my veil, and ran out of the room.

IV.

THE next day I was on my way to the north. My narrative brightens again—but let us not forget Sir Gervase Damian.

I ask permission to introduce some per-sons of distinction :—Mrs. Fosdyke, of Carsham Hall, widow of General Fosdyke ; also Master Frederick, Miss Ellen, and Miss Eva, the pupils of the new governess ; also two ladies and three gentlemen, guests stay-ing in the house.

Discreet and dignified ; handsome and well-bred—such was my impression of Mrs. Fosdyke, while she harangued me on the subject of her children, and communicated her views on education. Having heard the views before from others, I assumed a listening position, and privately formed my opinion of the schoolroom. It was large, lofty, perfectly furnished for the purpose ; it had a big window and a balcony looking out over the garden terrace and the park beyond—a wonderful schoolroom, in my limited experience. One of the two doors which it possessed was left open, and showed me a sweet little bedroom, with amber draperies and maplewood furniture, devoted to myself. Here were wealth and liberality, in that harmonious combination so seldom discovered by the spectator of small means. I controlled my first feeling of bewilderment just in time to answer Mrs. Fosdyke on the subject of reading and recitation—viewed as minor accomplishments which a good governess might be expected to teach.

' While the organs are young and pliable,' the lady remarked, ' I regard it as of great importance to practise children in the art of reading aloud, with an agreeable variety of tone and correctness of emphasis. Trained in this way, they will produce a favourable impression on others, even in ordinary conversation, when they grow up. Poetry, committed to memory and recited, is a valuable means towards this end. May I hope that your studies have enabled you to carry out my views ?'

Formal enough in language, but courteous and kind in manner. I relieved Mrs. Fosdyke from anxiety by informing her that we had a professor of elocution at school. And then I was left to improve my acquaintance with my three pupils.

They were fairly intelligent children ; the boy, as usual, being slower than the girls. I did my best—with many a sad remembrance of the far dearer pupils whom I had left—to make them like me and trust me ; and I succeeded in winning their confidence. In a week from the time of my arrival at Carsham Hall, we began to understand each other.

The first day in the week was one of our days for reciting poetry, in obedience to the instructions with which I had been favoured by Mrs. Fosdyke. I had done with the girls, and had just opened (perhaps I ought to say profaned) Shakespeare's ' Julius Cæsar,' in the elocutionary interests of Master Freddy. Half of Mark Antony's first glorious speech over Cæsar's dead body he had learnt by heart ; and it was now my duty to teach him, to the best of my small ability, how to speak it. The morning was warm. We had our big window open ; the delicious perfume of flowers in the garden beneath filled the room.

I recited the first eight lines, and stopped there, feeling that I must not exact too much from the boy at first. ' Now, Freddy,' I said, ' try if you can speak the poetry as I have spoken it.'

' Don't do anything of the kind, Freddy,' said a voice from the garden ; ' it's all spoken wrong.'

Who was this insolent person ? A man unquestionably—and, strange to say, there was something not entirely unfamiliar to me in his voice. The girls began to giggle. Their brother was more explicit. ' Oh,' says Freddy, ' it's only Mr. Sax.'

The one becoming course to pursue was to take no notice of the interruption. ' Go on,' I said. Freddy recited the lines, like a dear good boy, with as near an imitation of my style of elocution as could be expected from him.

' Poor devil !' cried the voice from the garden, insolently pitying my attentive pupil.

I imposed silence on the girls by a look —and then, without stirring from my chair, expressed my sense of the insolence of Mr. Sax in clear and commanding tones. ' I shall be obliged to close the window if this is repeated.' Having spoken to that effect, I waited in expectation of an apology. Silence was the only apology. It was enough for me that I had produced the right impression. I went on with my recitation.

' Here, under leave of Brutus, and the rest
(For Brutus is an honourable man ;
So are they all, all honourable men),
Come I to speak in Cæsar's funeral.
He was my friend, faithful and just to me—'

' Oh, good heavens, I can't stand that ! Why don't you speak the last line properly ? Listen to me.'

Dignity is a valuable quality, especially in a governess. But there are limits to the most highly trained endurance. I bounced out into the balcony—and there, on the terrace, smoking a cigar, was my lost stranger in the streets of Sandwich!

He recognised me, on his side, the instant I appeared. ' Oh, Lord !' he cried in tones of horror, and ran round the corner of the terrace as if my eyes had been mad bulls in close pursuit of him. By this time it is, I fear, useless for me to set myself up as a discreet person in emergencies. Another woman might have controlled herself. *I* burst into fits of laughter. Freddy and the girls joined me. For the time, it was plainly useless to pursue the business of education. I shut up Shakespeare, and allowed—no, let me tell the truth, encouraged—the children to talk about Mr. Sax.

They only seemed to know what Mr. Sax himself had told them. His father and mother and brothers and sisters had all died in course of time. He was the sixth and last of the children, and he had been christened ' Sextus ' in consequence, which is Latin (here Freddy interposed) for sixth. Also christened ' Cyril ' (here the girls recovered the lead) by his mother's request; ' Sextus ' being such a hideous name. And which of his Christian names does he use ? You wouldn't ask if you knew him ! ' Sextus ' of course, because it is the ugliest. Sextus Sax ? Not the romantic sort of name that one likes, when one is a woman. But I have no right to be particular. My own name (is it possible that I have not mentioned it in these pages yet ?) is only Nancy Morris. Do not despise me—and let us return to Mr. Sax.

Is he married ? The eldest girl thought not. She had heard mamma say to a lady, ' An old German family, my dear, and, in spite of his oddities, an excellent man ; but so poor—barely enough to live on—and blurts out the truth, if people ask his opinion, as if he had twenty thousand a

year !' Your mamma knows him well, of course ? I should think so, and so do we. He often comes here. They say he's not good company among grown-up people. *We* think him jolly. He understands dolls, and he's the best back at leap-frog in the whole of England.

Thus far we had advanced in the praise of Sextus Sax, when one of the maids came in with a note for me. She smiled mysteriously, and said, ' I'm to wait for an answer, Miss.'

I opened the note, and read these lines:—

' I am so ashamed of myself, I daren't attempt to make my apologies personally. Will you accept my written excuses ? Upon my honour, nobody told me when I got here yesterday that you were in the house. I heard the recitation, and—can you excuse my stupidity ?—I thought it was a stage-struck housemaid amusing herself with the children. May I accompany you when you go out with the young ones for your daily walk ? One word will do. Yes or no. Penitently yours,—S. S.'

In my position, there was but one possible answer to this. Governesses must not make appointments with strange gentlemen—even when the children are present in the capacity of witnesses. I said, No. Am I claiming too much for my readiness to forgive injuries, when I add that I should have preferred saying Yes ?

We had our early dinner, and then got ready to go out walking as usual. These pages contain a true confession. Let me own that I hoped Mr. Sax would understand my refusal, and ask Mrs. Fosdyke's leave to accompany us. Lingering a little as we went downstairs, I heard him in the hall—actually speaking to Mrs. Fosdyke! What was he saying ? That darling boy, Freddy, got into a difficulty with one of his boot-laces exactly at the right moment. I could help him, and listen—and be sadly disappointed by the result. Mr. Sax was offended with me.

'You needn't introduce me to the new governess,' I heard him say. 'We have met on a former occasion, and I produced a disagreeable impression on her. I beg you will not speak of me to Miss Morris.'

Before Mrs. Fosdyke could say a word in reply, Master Freddy changed suddenly from a darling boy to a detestable imp. 'I say, Mr. Sax!' he called out, 'Miss Morris doesn't mind you a bit—she only laughs at you.'

The answer to this was the sudden closing of a door. Mr. Sax had taken refuge from me in one of the ground-floor rooms. I was so mortified, I could almost have cried.

Getting down into the hall, we found Mrs. Fosdyke with her garden hat on, and one of the two ladies who were staying in the house (the unmarried one) whispering to her at the door of the morning-room. The lady — Miss Melbury — looked at me with a certain appearance of curiosity which I was quite at a loss to understand, and suddenly turned away towards the farther end of the hall.

'I will walk with you and the children,' Mrs. Fosdyke said to me. 'Freddy, you can ride your tricycle if you like.' She turned to the girls. 'My dears, it's cool under the trees. You may take your skipping-ropes.'

She had evidently something special to say to me; and she had adopted the necessary measures for keeping the children in front of us, well out of hearing. Freddy led the way on his horse on three wheels; the girls followed, skipping merrily. Mrs. Fosdyke opened her business by the most embarrassing remark that she could possibly have made under the circumstances.

'I find that you are acquainted with Mr. Sax,' she began; 'and I am surprised to hear that you dislike him.'

She smiled pleasantly, as it my supposed dislike of Mr. Sax rather amused her. What 'the ruling passion' may be among men, I cannot presume to consider. My own sex, however, I may claim to understand. The ruling passion among women is Conceit. My ridiculous notion of my own consequence was wounded in some way. I assumed a position of the loftiest indifference.

'Really, ma'am,' I said, 'I can't undertake to answer for any impression that Mr. Sax may have formed. We met by the merest accident. I know nothing about him.'

Mrs. Fosdyke eyed me slily, and appeared to be more amused than ever.

'He is a very odd man,' she admitted, 'but I can tell you there is a fine nature under that strange surface of his. However,' she went on, 'I am forgetting that he forbids me to talk about him in your presence. When the opportunity offers, I shall take my own way of teaching you two to understand each other: you will both be grateful to me when I have succeeded. In the meantime, there is a third person who will be sadly disappointed to hear that you know nothing about Mr. Sax.'

'May I ask, ma'am, who the person is?'

'Can you keep a secret, Miss Morris? Of course you can! The person is Miss Melbury.'

(Miss Melbury was a dark woman. It cannot be because I am a fair woman myself—I hope I am above such narrow prejudice as that—but it is certainly true that I don't admire dark women.)

'She heard Mr. Sax telling me that you particularly disliked him,' Mrs. Fosdyke proceeded. 'And just as you appeared in the hall, she was asking me to find out what your reason was. My own opinion of Mr. Sax, I ought to tell you, doesn't satisfy her; I am his old friend, and I present him of course from my own favourable point of view. Miss Melbury is anxious to be made acquainted with his faults—and she expected you to be a valuable witness against him.'

Thus far we had been walking on. We now stopped, as if by common consent, and looked at one another.

In my previous experience of Mrs. Fosdyke, I had only seen the more constrained and formal side of her character. Without being aware of my own success, I had won the mother's heart in winning the goodwill of her children. Constraint now seized its first opportunity of melting away ; the latent sense of humour in the great lady showed itself, while I was inwardly wondering what the nature of Miss Melbury's extraordinary interest in Mr. Sax might be. Easily penetrating my thoughts, she satisfied my curiosity without committing herself to a reply in words. Her large gray eyes sparkled as they rested on my face, and she hummed the tune of the old French song, '*C'est l'amour, l'amour, l'amour !*' There is no disguising it—something in this disclosure made me excessively angry. Was I angry with Miss Melbury ? or with Mr. Sax ? or with myself ? I think it must have been with myself.

Finding that I had nothing to say on my side, Mrs. Fosdyke looked at her watch, and remembered her domestic duties. To my relief, our interview came to an end.

' I have a dinner-party to-day,' she said, ' and I have not seen the housekeeper yet. Make yourself beautiful, Miss Morris, and join us in the drawing-room after dinner.'

V.

I wore my best dress; and, in all my life before, I never took such pains with my hair. Nobody will be foolish enough, I hope, to suppose that I did this on Mr.

Sax's account. How could I possibly care about a man who was little better than a stranger to me ? No ! the person I dressed at was Miss Melbury.

She gave me a look, as I modestly placed myself in a corner, which amply rewarded me for the time spent on my toilette. The gentlemen came in. I looked at Mr. Sax (mere curiosity) under shelter of my fan. His appearance was greatly improved by evening dress. He discovered me in my corner, and seemed doubtful whether to approach me or not. I was reminded of our first odd meeting ; and I could not help smiling as I called it to mind. Did he presume to think that I was encouraging him? Before I could decide that question, he took the vacant place on the sofa. In any other man—after what had passed in the morning —this would have been an audacious proceeding. *He* looked so painfully embarrassed, that it became a species of Christian duty to pity him.

' Won't you shake hands ?' he said, just as he had said it at Sandwich.

I peeped round the corner of my fan at Miss Melbury. She was looking at us. I shook hands with Mr. Sax.

' What sort of sensation is it,' he asked, ' when you shake hands with a man whom you hate ?'

' I really can't tell you,' I answered innocently; ' I have never done such a thing.'

' You would not lunch with me at Sandwich,' he protested; ' and, after the humblest apology on my part, you won't forgive me for what I did this morning. Do you expect me to believe that I am not the special object of your antipathy ? I wish I had never met with you ! At my age, a man gets angry when he is treated cruelly and doesn't deserve it. You don't understand that, I dare say.'

' Oh yes, I do. I heard what you said about me to Mrs. Fosdyke, and I heard you bang the door when you got out of my way.'

He received this reply with every appearance of satisfaction. 'So you listened, did you? I'm glad to hear that.'

'Why?'

'It shows you take some interest in me, after all.'

Throughout this frivolous talk (I only venture to report it because it shows that I bore no malice on my side) Miss Melbury was looking at us like the basilisk of the ancients. She owned to being on the wrong side of thirty; and she had a little money— but these were surely no reasons why she should glare at a poor governess. Had some secret understanding of the tender sort been already established between Mr. Sax and herself? She provoked me into trying to find out—especially as the last words he had said offered me the opportunity.

'I can prove that I feel a sincere interest in you,' I resumed. 'I can resign you to a lady who has a far better claim to your attention than mine. You are neglecting her shamefully.'

He stared at me with an appearance of bewilderment, which seemed to imply that the attachment was on the lady's side, so far. It was of course impossible to mention names; I merely turned my eyes in the right direction. He looked where I looked —and his shyness revealed itself, in spite of his resolution to conceal it. His face flushed; he looked mortified and surprised. Miss Melbury could endure it no longer. She rose, took a song from the music-stand, and approached us.

'I am going to sing,' she said, handing the music to him. 'Please turn over for me, Mr. Sax.'

I think he hesitated—but I cannot feel sure that I observed him correctly. It matters little. With or without hesitation, he followed her to the piano.

Miss Melbury sang—with perfect self-possession, and an immense compass of voice. A gentleman near me said she ought to be on the stage. I thought so too. Big as it was, our drawing-room was not large enough for her. The gentleman sang next. No voice at all—but so sweet, such true feeling! I turned over the leaves for him. A dear old lady, sitting near the piano, entered into conversation with me. She spoke of the great singers at the beginning of the present century. Mr. Sax hovered about, with Miss Melbury's eye on him. I was so entranced by the anecdotes of my venerable friend, that I could take no notice of Mr. Sax. Later, when the dinner-party was over, and we were retiring for the night, he still hovered about, and ended in offering me a bedroom candle. I immediately handed it to Miss Melbury. Really a most enjoyable evening!

VI.

THE next morning we were startled by an extraordinary proceeding on the part of one of the guests. Mr. Sax had left Carsham Hall, by the first train—nobody knew why.

Nature has laid—so at least philosophers say—some heavy burdens upon women. Do those learned persons include in their list the burden of hysterics? If so, I cordially agree with them. It is hardly worth speaking of in my case—a constitutional outbreak in the solitude of my own room, treated with eau-de-cologne and water, and quite forgotten afterwards in the absorbing employment of education. My favourite pupil, Freddy, had been up earlier than the rest of us—breathing the morning air in the fruit-garden. He had seen Mr. Sax and had asked when he was coming back again. And Mr. Sax had said, 'I shall be back again next month.' (Dear little Freddy!) In the meanwhile we, in the schoolroom, had the prospect before us of a dull time in an empty house. The remaining guests were to go away at the end of the week, their hostess being engaged to pay a visit to some old friends in Scotland.

During the next three or four days, though I was often alone with Mrs. Fosdyke, she never said one word on the subject of Mr. Sax. Once or twice I caught her looking at me with that unendurably significant smile of hers. Miss Melbury was equally unpleasant in another way. When we accidentally met on the stairs, her black eyes shot at me passing glances of hatred and scorn. Did these two ladies presume to think —— ?

No; I abstained from completing that inquiry at the time, and I abstain from completing it here.

The end of the week came, and I and the children were left alone at Carsham Hall.

I took advantage of the leisure hours at my disposal to write to Sir Gervase; respectfully inquiring after his health, and informing him that I had been again most fortunate in my engagement as a governess. By return of post an answer arrived. I eagerly opened it. The first lines informed me of Sir Gervase Damian's death.

The letter dropped from my hand. I looked at my little enamelled cross. It is not for me to say what I felt. Think of all that I owed to him; and remember how lonely my lot was in the world. I gave the children a holiday; it was only the truth to tell them that I was not well.

How long an interval passed before I could call to mind that I had only read the first lines of the letter, I am not able to say. When I did take it up I was surprised to see that the writing covered two pages. Beginning again where I had left off, my head, in a moment more, began to swim. A horrid fear overpowered me that I might not be in my right mind, after I had read the first three sentences. Here

they are, to answer for me that I exaggerate nothing:

'The will of our deceased client is not yet proved. But, with the sanction of the executors, I inform you confidentially that you are the person chiefly interested in it. Sir Gervase Damian bequeaths to you, absolutely, the whole of his personal property, amounting to the sum of seventy thousand pounds.'

If the letter had ended there, I really cannot imagine what extravagances I might not have committed. But the writer (head partner in the firm of Sir Gervase's lawyers) had something more to say on his own behalf. The manner in which he said it strung up my nerves in an instant. I cannot, and will not, copy the words here. It is quite revolting enough to give the substance of them.

The man's object was evidently to let me perceive that he disapproved of the will. So far I do not complain of him—he had, no doubt, good reason for the view he took. But, in expressing his surprise 'at this extraordinary proof of the testator's interest in a perfect stranger to the family,' he hinted his suspicion of an influence, on my part, exercised over Sir Gervase, so utterly shameful, that I cannot dwell on the subject. The language, I should add, was cunningly guarded. Even I could see that it would bear more than one interpretation, and would thus put me in the wrong if I openly resented it. But the meaning was plain; and part at least of the motive came out in the following sentences:

'The present Sir Gervase, as you are doubtless aware, is not seriously affected by his father's will. He is already more liberally provided for, as heir under the entail to the whole of the landed property. But, to say nothing of old friends who are forgotten, there is a surviving relative of the late Sir Gervase passed over, who is nearly akin to him by blood. In the event of this person disputing the will, you will of course hear from us again, and refer us to your legal adviser.'

The letter ended with an apology for delay in writing to me, caused by difficulty in discovering my address.

And what did I do?—Write to the rector, or to Mrs. Fosdyke, for advice? Not I!

At first I was too indignant to be able to think of what I ought to do. Our post-time was late, and my head ached as if it would burst into pieces. I had plenty of leisure to rest and compose myself. When I got cool again, I felt able to take my own part, without asking any one to help me.

Even if I had been treated kindly, I should certainly not have taken the money when there was a relative living with a claim to it. What did *I* want with a large fortune? To buy a husband with it, perhaps? No, no! from all that I have heard, the great Lord Chancellor was quite right when he said that a woman with money at her own disposal was ' either kissed out of it or kicked out of it, six weeks after her marriage.' The one difficulty before me was not to give up my legacy, but to express my reply with sufficient severity, and at the same time with due regard to my own self-respect. Here is what I wrote:

' Sir,—I will not trouble you by attempting to express my sorrow on hearing of Sir Gervase Damian's death. You would probably form your own opinion on that subject also ; and I have no wish to be judged by your unenviable experience of humanity for the second time.

' With regard to the legacy, feeling the sincerest gratitude to my generous benefactor, I nevertheless refuse to receive the money.

' Be pleased to send me the necessary document to sign, for transferring my fortune to that relative of. Sir Gervase

mentioned in your letter. The one condition on which I insist is, that no expression of thanks shall be addressed to me by the person in whose favour I resign the money. I do not desire (even supposing that justice is done to my motives on this occasion) to be made the object of expressions of gratitude for only doing my duty.'

So it ended. I may be wrong, but I call that strong writing.

In due course of post a formal acknowledgment arrived. I was requested to wait for the document until the will had been proved, and was informed that my name should be kept strictly secret in the interval. On this occasion, the executors were almost as insolent as the lawyer. They felt it their duty to give me time to reconsider a decision which had been evidently formed on impulse. Ah, how hard men are—at least, some of them! I locked up the acknowledgment in disgust, resolved to think no more of it until the time came for getting rid of my legacy. I kissed poor Sir Gervase's little keepsake. While I was still looking at it, the good children came in, of their own accord, to ask how I was. I was obliged to draw down the blind in my room, or they would have seen the tears in my eyes. For the first time since my mother's death, I felt the heartache. Perhaps the children made me think of the happier time when I was a child myself.

VII.

The will had been proved, and I was informed that the document was in course of preparation, when Mrs. Fosdyke returned from her visit to Scotland.

She thought me looking pale and worn.

' The time seems to me to have come,' she said, ' when I had better make you and Mr. Sax understand each other. Have you been thinking penitently of your own bad behaviour?'

I felt myself blushing. I *had* been thinking of my conduct to Mr. Sax—and I was heartily ashamed of it, too.

Mrs. Fosdyke went on, half in jest, half in earnest.

'Consult your own sense of propriety!' she said. 'Was the poor man to blame for not being rude enough to say No, when a lady asked him to turn over her music? Could *he* help it, if the same lady persisted in flirting with him? He ran away from her the next morning. Did you deserve to be told why he left us? Certainly not—after the vixenish manner in which you handed the bedroom candle to Miss Melbury. You foolish girl! Do you think I couldn't see that you were in love with him? Thank Heaven, he's too poor to marry you, and take you away from my children, for some time to come. There will be a long marriage engagement, even if he is magnanimous enough to forgive you. Shall I ask Miss Melbury to come back with him?'

She took pity on me at last, and sat down to write to Mr. Sax. His reply, dated from a country house some twenty miles distant, announced that he would be at Carsham Hall in three days' time.

On that third day the legal paper that I was to sign arrived by post. It was Sunday morning; I was alone in the schoolroom.

In writing to me, the lawyer had only alluded to 'a surviving relative of Sir Gervase, nearly akin to him by blood.' The document was more explicit. It described the relative as being a nephew of Sir Gervase, the son of his sister. The name followed.

It was Sextus Cyril Sax.

I have tried on three different sheets of paper to describe the effect which this discovery produced on me—and I have torn them up one after another. When I only

think of it, my mind seems to fall back into the helpless surprise and confusion of that time. After all that had passed between us —the man himself being then on his way to the house!—what would he think of me when he saw my name at the bottom of the document? what, in Heaven's name, was I to do?

How long I sat petrified, with the document on my lap, I never knew. Somebody knocked at the schoolroom door, and looked in and said something, and went out again. Then there was an interval. Then the door was opened again. A hand was laid kindly on my shoulder. I looked up—and there was Mrs. Fosdyke, asking, in the greatest alarm, what was the matter with me.

The tone of her voice roused me into speaking. I could think of nothing but Mr. Sax; I could only say, 'Has he come?'

'Yes—and waiting to see you.'

Answering in those terms, she glanced at the paper in my lap. In the extremity of my helplessness, I acted like a sensible creature at last. I told Mrs. Fosdyke all that I have told here.

She neither moved nor spoke until I had done. Her first proceeding, after that, was to take me in her arms and give me a kiss. Having so far encouraged me, she next spoke of poor Sir Gervase.

'We all acted like fools,' she announced, 'in needlessly offending him by protesting against his second marriage. I don't mean you—I mean his son, his nephew, and myself. If his second marriage made him happy, what business had we with the disparity of years between husband and wife? I can tell you this, Sextus was the first of us to regret what he had done. But for his stupid fear of being suspected of an interested motive, Sir Gervase might have known there was that much good in his sister's son.'

She snatched up a copy of the will, which I had not even noticed thus far.

'See what the kind old man says of you,' she went on, pointing to the words. I could not see them; she was obliged to read them for me. 'I leave my money to the one person living who has been more than worthy of the little I have done for her, and whose simple unselfish nature I know that I can trust.'

I pressed Mrs. Fosdyke's hand; I was not able to speak. She took up the legal paper next.

'Do justice to yourself, and be above contemptible scruples,' she said. 'Sextus is fond enough of you to be almost worthy of the sacrifice that you are making. Sign —and I will sign next as the witness.'

I hesitated.

'What will he think of me?' I said.

'Sign!' she repeated, 'and we will see to that.'

I obeyed. She asked for the lawyer's letter. I gave it to her, with the lines which contained the man's vile insinuation folded down, so that only the words above were visible, which proved that I had renounced my legacy, not even knowing whether the person to be benefited was a man or a woman. She took this, with the rough draft of my own letter, and the signed renunciation—and opened the door.

'Pray come back, and tell me about it!' I pleaded.

She smiled, nodded, and went out.

Oh, what a long time passed before I heard the long-expected knock at the door! 'Come in,' I cried impatiently.

Mrs. Fosdyke had deceived me. Mr. Sax had returned in her place. He closed the door. We two were alone.

He was deadly pale; his eyes, as they rested on me, had a wild startled look. With icy cold fingers he took my hand, and lifted it in silence to his lips. The sight of his agitation encouraged me—I don't to this day know why, unless it appealed in some way to my compassion. I was bold enough to look at him. Still silent, he placed the letters on the table—and then he laid the signed paper beside them. When I saw that, I was bolder still. I spoke first.

'Surely you don't refuse me?' I said.

He answered, 'I thank you with my whole heart; I admire you more than words can say. But I can't take it.'

'Why not?'

'The fortune is yours,' he said gently. 'Remember how poor I am, and feel for me if I say no more.'

His head sank on his breast. He stretched out one hand, silently imploring me to understand him. I could endure it no longer. I forgot every consideration which a woman, in my position, ought to have remembered. Out came the desperate words, before I could stop them.

'You won't take my gift by itself?' I said.

'No.'

'Will you take Me with it?'

That evening, Mrs. Fosdyke indulged her sly sense of humour in a new way. She handed me an almanack.

'After all, my dear,' she remarked, 'you needn't be ashamed of having spoken first. You have only used the ancient privilege of the sex. This is Leap Year.'

Mr. Cosway and the Landlady

I.

THE guests would have enjoyed their visit to Sir Peter's country house—but for Mr. Cosway.

And to make matters worse, it was not Mr. Cosway but the guests who were to blame. They repeated the old story of Adam and Eve, on a larger scale. The women were the first sinners ; and the men were demoralised by the women.

Mr. Cosway's bitterest enemy could not have denied that he was a handsome, well-bred, unassuming man. No mystery of any sort attached to him. He had adopted the Navy as a profession—had grown weary of it after a few years' service—and now lived on the moderate income left to him, after the death of his parents. Out of this unpromising material the lively imaginations of the women built up a romance. The men only noticed that Mr. Cosway was rather silent and thoughtful ; that he was not ready with his laugh ; and that he had a fancy for taking long walks by himself. Harmless peculiarities, surely ? And yet, they excited the curiosity of the women as signs of a mystery in Mr. Cosway's past life, in which some beloved object unknown must have played a chief part.

As a matter of course, the influence of the sex was tried, under every indirect and delicate form of approach, to induce Mr. Cosway to open his heart, and tell the tale of his sorrows. With perfect courtesy, he baffled curiosity, and kept his supposed secret to himself. The most beautiful girl in the house was ready to offer herself and her fortune as consolations, if this impenetrable bachelor would only have taken her into his confidence. He smiled sadly, and changed the subject.

Defeated so far, the women accepted the next alternative.

One of the guests staying in the house was Mr. Cosway's intimate friend—formerly his brother-officer on board ship. This gentleman was now subjected to the delicately directed system of investigation which had failed with his friend. With unruffled composure he referred the ladies, one after another, to Mr. Cosway. His name was Stone. The ladies decided that his nature was worthy of his name.

The last resource left to our fair friends was to rouse the dormant interest of the men, and to trust to the confidential intercourse of the smoking-room for the enlightenment which they had failed to obtain by other means.

In the accomplishment of this purpose, the degree of success which rewarded their efforts was due to a favouring state of affairs in the house. The shooting was not good for much; the billiard-table was under repair; and there were but two really skilled whist-players among the guests. In the atmosphere of dulness thus engendered, the men not only caught the infection of the women's curiosity, but were even ready to listen to the gossip of the servants' hall, repeated to their mistresses by the ladies'-maids. The result of such an essentially debased state of feeling as this was not slow in declaring itself. But for a lucky accident, Mr. Cosway would have discovered to what extremities of ill-bred curiosity idleness and folly can lead persons holding the position of ladies and gentlemen, when he joined the company at breakfast on the next morning.

The newspapers came in before the guests had risen from table. Sir Peter handed one of them to the lady who sat on his right hand.

She first looked, it is needless to say, at the list of births, deaths, and marriages; and then she turned to the general news—the fires, accidents, fashionable departures, and so on. In a few minutes, she indignantly dropped the newspaper in her lap.

'Here is another unfortunate man,' she exclaimed, ' sacrificed to the stupidity of women ! If I had been in his place, I would have used my knowledge of swimming to save myself, and would have left the women to go to the bottom of the river as they deserved !'

'A boat accident, I suppose?' said Sir Peter.

'Oh yes—the old story. A gentleman takes two ladies out in a boat. After a while they get fidgety, and feel an idiotic impulse to change places. The boat upsets as usual ; the poor dear man tries to save

them—and is drowned along with them for his pains. Shameful ! shameful !'

' Are the names mentioned ?'

' Yes. They are all strangers to me ; I speak on principle.' Asserting herself in those words, the indignant lady handed the newspaper to Mr. Cosway, who happened to sit next to her. ' When you were in the navy,' she continued, ' I dare say *your* life was put in jeopardy by taking women in boats. Read it yourself, and let it be a warning to you for the future.'

Mr. Cosway looked at the narrative of the accident—and revealed the romantic mystery of his life by a burst of devout exclamation, expressed in these words :

' Thank God, my wife's drowned !'

II.

To declare that Sir Peter and his guests were all struck speechless, by discovering in this way that Mr. Cosway was a married man, is to say very little. The general impression appeared to be that he was mad. His neighbours at the table all drew back from him, with the one exception of his friend. Mr. Stone looked at the newspaper : pressed Mr. Cosway's hand in silent sympathy—and addressed himself to his host.

' Permit me to make my friend's apologies,' he said, ' until he is composed enough to act for himself. The circumstances are so extraordinary that I venture to think they excuse him. Will you allow us to speak to you privately ?'

Sir Peter, with more apologies addressed to his visitors, opened the door which communicated with his study. Mr. Stone took Mr. Cosway's arm, and led him out of the room. He noticed no one, spoke to no one —he moved mechanically, like a man walking in his sleep.

After an unendurable interval of nearly

an hour's duration, Sir Peter returned alone to the breakfast-room. Mr. Cosway and Mr. Stone had already taken their departure for London, with their host's entire approval.

'It is left to my discretion,' Sir Peter proceeded, 'to repeat to you what I have heard in the study. I will do so, on one condition—that you all consider yourselves bound in honour not to mention the true names and the real places, when you tell the story to others.'

Subject to this wise reservation, the narrative is here repeated by one of the company. Considering how he may perform his task to the best advantage, he finds that the events which preceded and followed Mr. Cosway's disastrous marriage resolve themselves into certain well-marked divisions. Adopting this arrangement, he proceeds to relate:

The First Epoch in Mr. Cosway's Life.

The sailing of her Majesty's ship *Albicore* was deferred by the severe illness of the captain. A gentleman not possessed of political influence might, after the doctor's unpromising report of him, have been superseded by another commanding officer. In the present case, the Lords of the Admiralty showed themselves to be models of patience and sympathy. They kept the vessel in port, waiting the captain's recovery.

Among the unimportant junior officers, not wanted on board under these circumstances, and favoured accordingly by obtaining leave to wait for orders on shore, were two young men, aged respectively twenty-two and twenty-three years, and known by the names of Cosway and Stone. The scene which now introduces them opens at a famous seaport on the south coast of England, and discloses the two young gentlemen at dinner in a private room at their inn.

'I think that last bottle of champagne was corked,' Cosway remarked. 'Let's try another. You're nearest the bell, Stone. Ring.'

Stone rang, under protest. He was the elder of the two by a year, and he set an example of discretion.

'I am afraid we are running up a terrible bill,' he said. 'We have been here more than three weeks——'

'And we have denied ourselves nothing,' Cosway added. 'We have lived like princes. Another bottle of champagne, waiter. We have our riding-horses, and our carriage, and the best box at the theatre, and such cigars as London itself could not produce. I call that making the most of life. Try the new bottle. Glorious drink, isn't it? Why doesn't my father have champagne at the family dinner-table?'

'Is your father a rich man, Cosway?'

'I should say not. He didn't give me anything like the money I expected, when I said good-bye—and I rather think he warned me solemnly, at parting, to take the greatest care of it. "There's not a farthing more for you," he said, "till your ship returns from her South American station." *Your* father is a clergyman, Stone.'

'Well, and what of that?'

'And some clergymen are rich.'

'My father is not one of them, Cosway.'

'Then let us say no more about him. Help yourself, and pass the bottle.'

Instead of adopting this suggestion, Stone rose with a very grave face, and once more rang the bell. 'Ask the landlady to step up,' he said, when the waiter appeared.

'What do you want with the landlady?' Cosway inquired.

'I want the bill.'

The landlady—otherwise, Mrs. Pounce—entered the room. She was short, and old, and fat, and painted, and a widow. Students of character, as revealed in the face, would have discovered malice and cunning in her bright little black eyes, and a bitter vindictive temper in the lines about her thin red lips. Incapable of such subtleties of analysis as these, the two young officers differed widely, nevertheless, in their opinions of Mrs. Pounce. Cosway's reckless sense of humour delighted in pretending to be in love with her. Stone took a dislike to her from the first. When his friend asked for the reason, he made a strangely obscure answer. 'Do you remember that morning in the wood when you killed the snake?' he said. 'I took a dislike to the snake.' Cosway made no further inquiries.

'Well, my young heroes,' cried Mrs. Pounce (always loud, always cheerful, and always familiar with her guests), 'what do you want with me now?'

'Take a glass of champagne, my darling,' said Cosway; 'and let me try if I can get my arm round your waist. That's all *I* want with you.'

The landlady passed this over without notice. Though she had spoken to both of them, her cunning little eyes rested on Stone from the moment when she appeared in the room. She knew by instinct the man who disliked her—and she waited deliberately for Stone to reply.

'We have been here some time,' he said, 'and we shall be obliged, ma'am, if you will let us have our bill.'

Mrs. Pounce lifted her eyebrows with an expression of innocent surprise.

'Has the captain got well, and must you go on board to-night?' she asked.

'Nothing of the sort!' Cosway interposed. 'We have no news of the captain, and we are going to the theatre to-night.'

'But,' persisted Stone, 'we want, if you please, to have the bill.'

'Certainly, sir,' said Mrs. Pounce, with a sudden assumption of respect. 'But we are very busy downstairs, and we hope you will not press us for it to-night?'

'Of course not!' cried Cosway.

Mrs. Pounce instantly left the room, without waiting for any further remark from Cosway's friend.

'I wish we had gone to some other house,' said Stone. 'You mark my words —that woman means to cheat us.'

Cosway expressed his dissent from this opinion in the most amiable manner. He filled his friend's glass, and begged him not to say ill-natured things of Mrs. Pounce.

But Stone's usually smooth temper seemed to be ruffled: he insisted on his own view. 'She's impudent and inquisitive, if she is not downright dishonest,' he said. 'What right had she to ask you where we lived when we were at home; and what our Christian names were; and which of us was oldest, you or I? Oh, yes—it's all very well to say she only showed a flattering interest in us! I suppose she showed a flattering interest in my affairs, when I woke a little earlier than usual, and caught her in my bedroom with my pocket-book in her hand. Do you believe she was going to lock it up for safety's sake? She knows how much money we have got as well as we know it ourselves. Every halfpenny we have will be in her pocket to-morrow. And a good thing too—we shall be obliged to leave the house.'

Even this cogent reasoning failed in provoking Cosway to reply. He took Stone's hat, and handed it with the utmost politeness to his foreboding friend. 'There's only one remedy for such a state of mind as yours,' he said. 'Come to the theatre.'

At ten o'clock the next morning, Cosway found himself alone at the breakfast table. He was informed that Mr. Stone had gone out for a little walk, and would be back directly. Seating himself at the table, he perceived an envelope on his plate, which evidently enclosed the bill. He took up the envelope, considered a little, and put it back again unopened. At the same moment Stone burst into the room in a high state of excitement.

'News that will astonish you!' he cried. 'The captain arrived yesterday evening. His doctors say that the sea-voyage will complete his recovery. The ship sails to-day—and we are ordered to report ourselves on board in an hour's time. Where's the bill?'

Cosway pointed to it. Stone took it out of the envelope.

It covered two sides of a prodigiously long sheet of paper. The sum-total was brightly decorated with lines in red ink. Stone looked at the total, and passed it in silence to Cosway. For once, even Cosway was prostrated. In dreadful stillness, the two young men produced their pocket-books ; added up their joint stores of money, and compared the result with the bill. Their united resources amounted to a little more than one-third of their debt to the landlady of the inn.

The only alternative that presented itself was to send for Mrs. Pounce ; to state the circumstances plainly ; and to propose a compromise on the grand commercial basis of credit.

Mrs. Pounce presented herself superbly dressed in walking costume. Was she going out ? or had she just returned to the inn ? Not a word escaped her ; she waited gravely to hear what the gentlemen wanted. Cosway, presuming on his position as favourite, produced the contents of the two pocket-books, and revealed the melancholy truth.

'There is all the money we have,' he concluded. 'We hope you will not object to receive the balance in a bill at three months.'

Mrs. Pounce answered with a stern composure of voice and manner entirely new in the experience of Cosway and Stone.

'I have paid ready money, gentlemen, for the hire of your horses and carriages,' she said ; 'here are the receipts from the livery stables to vouch for me ; I never accept bills unless I am quite sure before-hand that they will be honoured. I defy you to find an overcharge in the account now rendered ; and I expect you to pay it before you leave my house.'

Stone looked at his watch. 'In three-quarters of an hour,' he said, 'we must be on board.'

Mrs. Pounce entirely agreed with him. 'And if you are not on board,' she remarked, 'you will be tried by court-martial, and dismissed the service with your characters ruined for life.'

'My dear creature, we haven't time to send home, and we know nobody in the town,' pleaded Cosway. 'For God's sake take our watches and jewelry, and our luggage—and let us go.'

'I am not a pawnbroker,' said the inflexible lady. 'You must either pay your lawful debt to me in honest money, or——'

She paused and looked at Cosway. Her fat face brightened—she smiled graciously for the first time.

Cosway stared at her in unconcealed perplexity. He helplessly repeated her last words. 'We must either pay the bill,' he said, 'or—what?'

'Or,' answered Mrs. Pounce, 'one of you must marry ME.'

Was she joking ? Was she intoxicated ? Was she out of her senses ? Neither of the three ; she was in perfect possession of herself ; her explanation was a model of lucid and convincing arrangement of facts.

'My position here has its drawbacks,' she began. 'I am a lone widow ; I am known to have an excellent business, and to have saved money. The result is that I am pestered to death by a set of needy vagabonds who want to marry me. In this position, I am exposed to slanders and insults. Even if I didn't know that the men were after my money, there is not one of them whom I would venture to marry. He might turn out a tyrant, and beat me; or a drunkard, and disgrace me; or a betting man, and ruin me. What I want, you see, for my own peace and protection, is to be able to declare myself married, and to produce the proof in the shape of a certificate. A born gentleman, with a character to lose, and so much younger in years than myself that he wouldn't think of living with me—there is the sort of husband who suits my book! I'm a reasonable woman, gentlemen. I would undertake to part with my husband at the church door—never to attempt to see him or write to him afterwards—and only to show my certificate when necessary, without giving any explanations. Your secret would be quite safe in my keeping. I don't care a straw for either of you, so long as you answer my purpose. What do you say to paying my bill (one or the other of you) in this way? I am ready dressed for the altar; and the clergyman has notice at the church. My preference is for Mr. Cosway,' proceeded this terrible woman with the cruellest irony, 'because he has been so particular in his attentions towards me. The license (which I provided on the chance a fortnight since) is made out in his name. Such is my weakness for Mr. Cosway. But that don't matter if Mr. Stone would like to take his place. He can hail by his friend's name. Oh yes, he can! I have consulted my lawyer. So long as the bride and bridegroom agree to it, they may be married in any name they like, and it stands good. Look at your watch again, Mr. Stone. The church is in the next street. By my calculation, you have just got five minutes to decide. I'm a punctual woman, my little dears; and I will be back to the moment.'

She opened the door, paused, and returned to the room.

'I ought to have mentioned,' she resumed, 'that I shall make you a present of the bill, receipted, on the conclusion of the ceremony. You will be taken to the ship in my own boat, with all your money in your pockets, and a hamper of good things for the mess. After that, I wash my hands of you. You may go to the devil your own way.'

With this parting benediction, she left them.

Caught in the landlady's trap, the two victims looked at each other in expressive silence. Without time enough to take legal advice; without friends on shore; without any claim on officers of their own standing in the ship, the prospect before them was literally limited to Marriage or Ruin. Stone made a proposal worthy of a hero.

'One of us must marry her,' he said; 'I'm ready to toss up for it.'

Cosway matched him in generosity. 'No,' he answered. 'It was I who brought you here; and I who led you into these infernal expenses. I ought to pay the penalty—and I will.'

Before Stone could remonstrate, the five minutes expired. Punctual Mrs. Pounce appeared again in the doorway.

'Well?' she inquired, 'which is it to be —Cosway, or Stone?'

Cosway advanced as reckless as ever, and offered his arm.

'Now then, Fatsides,' he said, 'come and be married!'

In five-and-twenty minutes more, Mrs. Pounce had become Mrs. Cosway; and the two officers were on their way to the ship.

The Second Epoch in Mr. Cosway's Life.

Four years elapsed before the *Albicore* returned to the port from which she had sailed.

In that interval, the death of Cosway's

parents had taken place. The lawyer who managed his affairs, during his absence from England, wrote to inform him that his inheritance from his late father's 'estate' was eight hundred a year. His mother only possessed a life interest in her fortune ; she had left her jewels to her son, and that was all.

Cosway's experience of the life of a naval officer on foreign stations (without political influence to hasten his promotion) had thoroughly disappointed him. He decided on retiring from the service when the ship was 'paid off.' In the meantime, to the astonishment of his comrades, he seemed to be in no hurry to make use of the leave granted him to go on shore. The faithful Stone was the only man on board who knew that he was afraid of meeting his ' wife.' This good friend volunteered to go to the inn, and make the necessary investigation with all needful prudence. ' Four years is a long time, at *her* age,' he said. ' Many things may happen in four years.'

An hour later, Stone returned to the ship, and sent a written message on board, addressed to his brother-officer, in these words : ' Pack up your things at once, and join me on shore.'

' What news ?' asked the anxious husband.

Stone looked significantly at the idlers on the landing-place. ' Wait,' he said, ' till we are by ourselves.'

' Where are we going?'

' To the railway station.'

They got into an empty carriage ; and Stone at once relieved his friend of all further suspense.

' Nobody is acquainted with the secret of your marriage but our two selves,' he began quietly. ' I don't think, Cosway, you need go into mourning.'

' You don't mean to say she's dead !'

' I have seen a letter (written by her own lawyer) which announces her death,' Stone replied. ' It was so short that I believe I can repeat it, word for word:—" Dear Sir,— I have received information of the death of my client. Please address your next and last payment, on account of the lease and goodwill of the inn, to the executors of the late Mrs. Cosway." There, that is the letter. " Dear Sir," means the present proprietor of the inn. He told me your wife's previous history in two words. After carrying on the business with her customary intelligence for more than three years, her health failed, and she went to London to consult a physician. There she remained under the doctor's care. The next event was the appearance of an agent, instructed to sell the business in consequence of the landlady's declining health. Add the death at a later time—and there is the beginning and the end of the story. Fortune owed you a good turn, Cosway— and Fortune has paid the debt. Accept my best congratulations.'

Arrived in London, Stone went on at once to his relations in the North. Cosway proceeded to the office of the family lawyer (Mr. Atherton), who had taken care of his interests in his absence. His father and Mr. Atherton had been schoolfellows and old friends. He was affectionately received, and was invited to pay a visit the next day to the lawyer's villa at Richmond.

' You will be near enough to London to attend to your business at the Admiralty,' said Mr. Atherton, 'and you will meet a visitor at my house, who is one of the most charming girls in England — the only daughter of the great Mr. Restall. Good heavens ! have you never heard of him ? My dear sir, he's one of the partners in the famous firm of Benshaw, Restall, and Benshaw.'

Cosway was wise enough to accept this last piece of information as quite conclusive. The next day, Mrs. Atherton presented him to the charming Miss

Restall; and Mrs. Atherton's young married daughter (who had been his playfellow when they were children) whispered to him, half in jest, half in earnest: 'Make the best use of your time; she isn't engaged yet.'

Cosway shuddered inwardly at the bare idea of a second marriage.

Was Miss Restall the sort of woman to restore his confidence?

She was small and slim and dark—a graceful, well-bred, brightly intelligent person, with a voice exquisitely sweet and winning in tone. Her ears, hands, and feet were objects to worship; and she had an attraction, irresistibly rare among the women of the present time—the attraction of a perfectly natural smile. Before Cosway had been an hour in the house, she discovered that his long term of service on foreign stations had furnished him with subjects of conversation which favourably contrasted with the commonplace gossip addressed to her by other men. Cosway at once became a favourite, as Othello became a favourite in his day.

The ladies of the household all rejoiced in the young officer's success, with the exception of Miss Restall's companion (supposed to hold the place of her lost mother, at a large salary), one Mrs. Margery.

Too cautious to commit herself in words, this lady expressed doubt and disapprobation by her looks. She had white hair, iron-gray eyebrows, and protuberant eyes; her looks were unusually expressive. One evening, she caught poor Mr. Atherton alone, and consulted him confidentially on the subject of Mr. Cosway's income. This was the first warning which opened the eyes of the good lawyer to the nature of the 'friendship' already established between his two guests. He knew Miss Restall's illustrious father well, and he feared that it might soon be his disagreeable duty to bring Cosway's visit to an end.

On a certain Saturday afternoon, while Mr. Atherton was still considering how he could most kindly and delicately suggest to Cosway that it was time to say good-bye, an empty carriage arrived at the villa. A note from Mr. Restall was delivered to Mrs. Atherton, thanking her with perfect politeness for her kindness to his daughter, 'Circumstances,' he added, 'rendered it necessary that Miss Restall should return home that afternoon.'

The 'circumstances' were supposed to refer to a garden-party to be given by Mr. Restall in the ensuing week. But why was his daughter wanted at home before the day of the party?

The ladies of the family, still devoted to Cosway's interests, entertained no doubt that Mrs. Margery had privately communicated with Mr. Restall, and that the appearance of the carriage was the natural result. Mrs. Atherton's married daughter did all that could be done: she got rid of Mrs. Margery for one minute, and so arranged it that Cosway and Miss Restall took leave of each other in her own sitting-room.

When the young lady appeared in the hall she had drawn her veil down. Cosway escaped to the road and saw the last of the carriage as it drove away. In little more than a fortnight, his horror of a second marriage had become one of the dead and buried emotions of his nature. He stayed at the villa until Monday morning, as an act of gratitude to his good friends and then accompanied Mr. Atherton to London. Business at the Admiralty was the excuse. It imposed on nobody. He was evidently on his way to Miss Restall.

'Leave your business in my hands,' said the lawyer, on the journey to town, 'and go and amuse yourself on the Continent. I can't blame you for falling in love with Miss Restall; I ought to have foreseen the danger, and waited till she had left us before I invited you to my house. But I may at least warn you to carry the matter no further. If you had eight thousand instead of eight hundred a year, Mr. Restall would think it an act of presumption on your part to aspire to his daughter's hand, unless you had a title to throw into the bargain. Look at it in the true light, my dear boy ; and one of these days you will thank me for speaking plainly.'

Cosway promised to 'look at it in the true light.'

The result, from his point of view, led him into a change of residence. He left his hotel and took a lodging in the nearest by-street to Mr. Restall's palace at Kensington.

On the same evening, he applied (with the confidence due to a previous arrangement) for a letter at the neighbouring post-office, addressed to E. C.—the initials of Edwin Cosway. 'Pray be careful,' Miss Restall wrote ; 'I have tried to get you a card for our garden-party. But that hateful creature, Margery, has evidently spoken to my father ; I am not trusted with any invitation cards. Bear it patiently, dear, as I do, and let me hear if you have succeeded in finding a lodging near us.'

Not submitting to this first disappointment very patiently, Cosway sent his reply to the post-office, addressed to A. R.—the initials of Adela Restall. The next day, the impatient lover applied for another letter. It was waiting for him, but it was not directed in Adela's handwriting. Had their correspondence been discovered? He opened the letter in the street ; and read, with amazement, these lines:—

'Dear Mr. Cosway, my heart sympathizes with two faithful lovers, in spite of my age and my duty. I enclose an invitation to the party to-morrow. Pray don't betray me, and don't pay too marked attention to Adela. Discretion is easy. There will be

twelve hundred guests. Your friend, in spite of appearances, Louisa Margery.'

How infamously they had all misjudged this excellent woman ! Cosway went to the party a grateful, as well as a happy, man. The first persons known to him, whom he discovered among the crowd of strangers, were the Athertons. They looked, as well they might, astonished to see him. Fidelity to Mrs. Margery forbade him to enter into any explanations. Where was that best and truest friend? With some difficulty he succeeded in finding her. Was there any impropriety in seizing her hand, and cordially pressing it ? The result of this expression of gratitude was, to say the least of it, perplexing.

Mrs. Margery behaved like the Athertons ! She looked astonished to see him, and she put precisely the same question, 'How did you get here ?' Cosway could only conclude that she was joking. 'Who should know that, dear lady, better than yourself ?' he rejoined. 'I don't understand you,' Mrs. Margery answered sharply. After a moment's reflection, Cosway hit on another solution of the mystery. Visitors were near them ; and Mrs. Margery had made her own private use of one of Mr. Restall's invitation cards. She might have serious reasons for pushing caution to its last extreme. Cosway looked at her significantly. 'The least I can do is not to be indiscreet,' he whispered—and left her.

He turned into a side walk; and there he met Adela at last!

It seemed like a fatality. *She* looked astonished ; and *she* said, 'How did you get here ?' No intrusive visitors were within hearing, this time. 'My dear!' Cosway remonstrated, 'Mrs. Margery must have told you, when she sent me my invitation.' Adela turned pale. 'Mrs. Margery ?' she repeated. 'Mrs. Margery has said nothing to me ; Mrs. Margery detests you. We

must have this cleared up. No; not now—
I must attend to our guests. Expect a
letter; and, for heaven's sake, Edwin, keep
out of my father's way. One of our visitors
whom he particularly wished to see has
sent an excuse—and he is dreadfully angry
about it.'

She left him before Cosway could explain
that he and Mr. Restall had thus far never
seen each other.

He wandered away towards the extremity
of the grounds, troubled by vague suspicions ; hurt at Adela's cold reception of
him. Entering a shrubbery, which seemed
intended to screen the grounds, at this point,
from a lane outside, he suddenly discovered
a pretty little summer-house among the trees.
A stout gentleman, of mature years, was
seated alone in this retreat. He looked up
with a frown. Cosway apologized for dis-
turbing him, and entered into conversation
as an act of politeness.

' A brilliant assembly to-day, sir.'

The stout gentleman replied by an in-
articulate sound—something between a grunt
and a cough.

' And a splendid house and grounds,'
Cosway continued.

The stout gentleman repeated the in-
articulate sound.

Cosway began to feel amused. Was this
curious old man deaf and dumb?

' Excuse my entering into conversation,'
he persisted. ' I feel like a stranger here.
There are so many people whom I don't
know.'

The stout gentleman suddenly burst into
speech. Cosway had touched a sympathetic
fibre at last.

' There are a good many people here
whom *I* don't know,' he said gruffly.
' You are one of them. What's your
name?'

' My name is Cosway, sir. What's
yours?'

The stout gentleman rose with fury in
his looks. He burst out with an oath ;
and added the intolerable question, already
three times repeated by others, ' How did
you get here?' The tone was even more
offensive than the oath. ' Your age pro-
tects you, sir,' said Cosway, with the loftiest
composure. ' I'm sorry I gave my name to
so rude a person.'

' Rude ?' shouted the old gentleman.
' You want my name in return, I suppose ?
You young puppy, you shall have it! My
name is Restall.'

He turned his back, and walked off.
Cosway took the only course now open to
him. He returned to his lodgings.

The next day, no letter reached him from
Adela. He went to the post-office. No
letter was there. The day wore on to
evening—and, with the evening, there appeared a woman who was a stranger to
him. She looked like a servant ; and she
was the bearer of a mysterious message.

' Please be at the garden-door that opens
on the lane, at ten o'clock to-morrow morning. Knock three times at the door—and
then say " Adela." Some one who wishes
you well will be alone in the shrubbery,
and will let you in. No, sir! I am not to
take anything ; and I am not to say a word
more.' She spoke—and vanished.

Cosway was punctual to his appointment.
He knocked three times ; he pronounced
Miss Restall's Christian name. Nothing
happened. He waited a while, and tried
again. This time, Adela's voice answered
strangely from the shrubbery in tones of
surprise: ' Edwin! is it really you?'

' Did you expect anyone else ?' Cosway
asked. ' My darling, your message said
ten o'clock—and here I am.'

The door was suddenly unlocked.

' I sent no message,' said Adela, as they
confronted each other on the threshold.

In the silence of utter bewilderment they
went together into the summer-house. At
Adela's request, Cosway repeated the mes-

sage that he had received, and described the woman who had delivered it. The description applied to no person known to Miss Restall. ' Mrs. Margery never sent you the invitation; and I repeat, I never sent you the message. This meeting has been arranged by some one who knows that I always walk in the shrubbery after breakfast. There is some underhand work going on——'

Still mentally in search of the enemy who had betrayed them, she checked herself, and considered a little. ' Is it possible——?' she began, and paused again. Her eyes filled with tears. ' My mind is so completely upset,' she said, ' that I can't think clearly of anything. Oh, Edwin, we have had a happy dream, and it has come to an end. My father knows more than we think for. Some friends of ours are going abroad to-morrow—and I am to go with them. Nothing I can say has the least effect upon my father. He means to part us for ever—and this is his cruel way of doing it !'

She put her arm round Cosway's neck, and lovingly laid her head on his shoulder. With tenderest kisses they reiterated their vows of eternal fidelity until their voices faltered and failed them. Cosway filled up the pause by the only useful suggestion which it was now in his power to make— he proposed an elopement.

Adela received this bold solution of the difficulty in which they were placed, exactly as thousands of other young ladies have received similar proposals before her time, and after.

She first said positively No. Cosway persisted. She began to cry, and asked if he had no respect for her. Cosway declared that his respect was equal to any sacrifice, except the sacrifice of parting with her for ever. He could, and would, if she preferred it, die for her, but while he was alive he must refuse to give her up. Upon this, she shifted her ground. Did he expect her to go away with him alone ? Certainly not. Her maid could go with her, or, if her maid was not to be trusted, he would apply to his landlady, and engage ' a respectable elderly person ' to attend on her until the day of their marriage. Would she have some mercy on him, and just consider it ? No : she was afraid to consider it. Did she prefer misery for the rest of her life ? Never mind *his* happiness : it was *her* happiness only that he had in his mind. Travelling with unsympathetic people ; absent from England, no one could say for how long ; married, when she did return, to some rich man whom she hated —would she, could she, contemplate that prospect ? She contemplated it through tears ; she contemplated it to an accompaniment of sighs, kisses, and protestations— she trembled, hesitated, gave way. At an appointed hour of the coming night, when her father would be in the smoking-room, and Mrs. Margery would be in bed, Cosway was to knock at the door in the lane once more ; leaving time to make all the necessary arrangements in the interval.

The one pressing necessity, under these circumstances, was to guard against the possibility of betrayal and surprise. Cosway discreetly alluded to the unsolved mysteries of the invitation and the message.

' Have you taken anybody into our confidence ?' he asked.

Adela answered with some embarrassment. ' Only one person,' she said—' dear Miss Benshaw.'

' Who is Miss Benshaw ?'

' Don't you really know, Edwin ? She is richer even than papa—she has inherited from her late brother one half-share in the great business in the City. Miss Benshaw is the lady who disappointed papa by not coming to the garden-party. You remember, dear, how happy we were, when we were together at Mr. Atherton's ? I was very miserable when they took me away.

Miss Benshaw happened to call the next day, and she noticed it. "My dear," she said (Miss Benshaw is quite an elderly lady now), "I am an old maid, who has missed the happiness of her life, through not having had a friend to guide and advise her when she was young. Are you suffering as I once suffered?" She spoke so nicely—and I was so wretched—that I really couldn't help it. I opened my heart to her.'

Cosway looked grave. 'Are you sure she is to be trusted?' he asked.

'Perfectly sure.'

'Perhaps, my love, she has spoken about us (not meaning any harm) to some friend of hers? Old ladies are so fond of gossip. It's just possible—don't you think so?'

Adela hung her head.

'I have thought it just possible myself,' she admitted. 'There is plenty of time to call on her to-day. I will set our doubts at rest, before Miss Benshaw goes out for her afternoon drive.'

On that understanding they parted.

Towards evening, Cosway's arrangements for the elopement were completed. He was eating his solitary dinner when a note was brought to him. It had been left at the door by a messenger. The man had gone away without waiting for an answer. The note ran thus:—

'Miss Benshaw presents her compliments to Mr. Cosway, and will be obliged if he can call on her at nine o'clock this evening, on business which concerns himself.'

This invitation was evidently the result of Adela's visit earlier in the day. Cosway presented himself at the house, troubled by natural emotions of anxiety and suspense. His reception was not of a nature to compose him. He was shown into a darkened room. The one lamp on the table was turned down low, and the little light thus given was still further obscured by a shade.

The corners of the room were in almost absolute darkness.

A voice out of one of the corners addressed him in a whisper:

'I must beg you to excuse the darkened room. I am suffering from a severe cold. My eyes are inflamed, and my throat is so bad that I can only speak in a whisper. Sit down, sir. I have got news for you.'

'Not bad news, I hope, ma'am?' Cosway ventured to inquire.

'The worst possible news,' said the whispering voice. 'You have an enemy striking at you in the dark.'

Cosway asked who it was, and received no answer. He varied the form of inquiry, and asked why the unnamed person struck at him in the dark. The experiment succeeded; he obtained a reply.

'It is reported to me,' said Miss Benshaw, 'that the person thinks it necessary to give you a lesson, and takes a spiteful pleasure in doing it as mischievously as possible. The person, as I happen to know, sent you your invitation to the party, and made the appointment which took you to the door in the lane. Wait a little, sir; I have not done yet. The person has put it into Mr. Restall's head to send his daughter abroad to-morrow.'

Cosway attempted to make her speak more plainly.

'Is this wretch a man or a woman?' he said.

Miss Benshaw proceeded without noticing the interruption.

'You needn't be afraid, Mr. Cosway; Miss Restall will not leave England. Your enemy is all-powerful. Your enemy's object could only be to provoke you into planning an elopement—and, your arrangements once completed, to inform Mr. Restall, and to part you and Miss Adela quite as effectually as if you were at opposite ends of the world. Oh, you will undoubtedly be parted! Spiteful, isn't it? And, what is worse, the mischief is as good as done already.'

Cosway rose from his chair.

' Do you wish for any further explanation?' asked Miss Benshaw.

' One thing more,' he replied. ' Does
Adela know of this?'

' No,' said Miss Benshaw ; ' it is left to
you to tell her.'

There was a moment of silence. Cosway
looked at the lamp. Once roused, as usual
with men of his character, his temper was
not to be trifled with.

' Miss Benshaw,' he said, ' I dare say you
think me a fool ; but I can draw my own
conclusion, for all that. *You* are my enemy.'

The only reply was a chuckling laugh.
All voices can be more or less effectually
disguised by a whisper—but a laugh carries
the revelation of its own identity with it.
Cosway suddenly threw off the shade over
the lamp, and turned up the wick.

The light flooded the room, and showed
him—His Wife.

The Third Epoch in Mr. Cosway's Life.

Three days had passed. Cosway sat
alone in his lodging—pale and worn: the
shadow already of his former self.

He had not seen Adela since the discovery. There was but one way in which
he could venture to make the inevitable
disclosure—he wrote to her; and Mr. Atherton's daughter took care that the letter
should be received. Inquiries made afterwards, by help of the same good friend,
informed him that Miss Restall was suffering from illness.

The mistress of the house came in

' Cheer up, sir,' said the good woman.
' There is better news of Miss Restall to-
day.'

He raised his head.

' Don't trifle with me!' he answered fret-
fully; ' tell me exactly what the servant
said.'

The mistress repeated the words. Miss

Restall had passed a quieter night, and had
been able for a few hours to leave her room.
He asked next if any reply to his letter had
arrived. No reply had been received.

If Adela definitely abstained from writing
to him, the conclusion would be too plain to
be mistaken. She had given him up—and
who could blame her?

There was a knock at the street-door.
The mistress looked out.

' Here's Mr. Stone come back, sir!' she
exclaimed joyfully—and hurried away to
let him in.

Cosway never looked up when his friend
appeared.

' I knew I should succeed,' said Stone. ' I
have seen your wife.'

' Don't speak of her,' cried Cosway. ' I
should have murdered her when I first saw
her face, if I had not instantly left the house.
I may be the death of the wretch yet, if you
persist in speaking of her!'

Stone put his hand kindly on his friend's
shoulder.

' Must I remind you that you owe something to your old comrade?' he asked. ' I
left my father and mother, the morning I
got your letter—and my one thought has
been to serve you. Reward me. Be a man,
and hear what it is your right and duty to
know. After that, if you like, we will
never refer to the woman again.'

Cosway took his hand, in silent acknowledgment that he was right. They sat
down together. Stone began.

' She is so entirely shameless,' he said,
' that I had no difficulty in getting her to
speak. And she so cordially hates you that
she glories in her own falsehood and
treachery.'

' Of course, she lies,' Cosway said bitterly,
' when she calls herself Miss Benshaw?'

' No; she is really the daughter of the
man who founded the great house in the
City. With every advantage that wealth
and position could give her, the perverse

creature married one of her father's clerks, who had been deservedly dismissed from his situation. From that moment her family discarded her. With the money procured by the sale of her jewels, her husband took the inn which we have such bitter cause to remember—and she managed the house after his death. So much for the past. Carry your mind on now to the time when our ship brought us back to England. At that date, the last surviving member of your wife's family—her elder brother—lay at the point of death. He had taken his father's place in the business, besides inheriting his father's fortune. After a happy married life, he was left a widower, without children; and it became necessary that he should alter his will. He deferred performing this duty. It was only at the time of his last illness that he had dictated instructions for a new will, leaving his wealth (excepting certain legacies to old friends) to the hospitals of Great Britain and Ireland. His lawyer lost no time in carrying out the instructions. The new will was ready for signature (the old will having been destroyed by his own hand), when the doctors sent a message to say that their patient was insensible, and might die in that condition.'

' Did the doctors prove to be right?'

' Perfectly right. Our wretched landlady, as next of kin, succeeded, not only to the fortune, but (under the deed of partnership) to her late brother's place in the firm: on the one easy condition of resuming the family name. She calls herself " Miss Benshaw." But as a matter of legal necessity she is set down in the deed as " Mrs. Cosway Benshaw." Her partners only now know that her husband is living, and that you are the Cosway whom she privately married. Will you take a little breathing-time? or shall I go on, and get done with it?'

Cosway signed to him to go on.

' She doesn't in the least care,' Stone proceeded, ' for the exposure. " I am the head partner," she says, " and the rich one of the firm ; they daren't turn their backs on Me." You remember the information I received—in perfect good faith on his part—from the man who now keeps the inn? The visit to the London doctor, and the assertion of failing health, were adopted as the best means of plausibly severing the lady's connection (the great lady now!) with a calling so unworthy of her as the keeping of an inn. Her neighbours at the seaport were all deceived by the stratagem, with two exceptions. They were both men—vagabonds who had pertinaciously tried to delude her into marrying them in the days when she was a widow. They refused to believe in the doctor and the declining health; they had their own suspicion of the motives which had led to the sale of the inn, under very unfavourable circumstances; and they decided on going to London, inspired by the same base hope of making discoveries which might be turned into a means of extorting money.'

' She escaped them, of course,' said Cosway. ' How?'

' By the help of her lawyer, who was not above accepting a handsome private fee. He wrote to the new landlord of the inn, falsely announcing his client's death, in the letter which I repeated to you in the railway carriage on our journey to London. Other precautions were taken to keep up the deception, on which it is needless to dwell. Your natural conclusion that you were free to pay your addresses to Miss Restall, and the poor young lady's innocent confidence in " Miss Benshaw's " sympathy, gave this unscrupulous woman the means of playing the heartless trick on you which is now exposed. Malice and jealousy—I have it, mind, from herself !—were not her only motives. " But for that Cosway," she said (I spare you the epithet which she put before your name), " with my money and position, I might have married a needy lord, and sunned myself in my old age in the full blaze of the peerage." Do you understand how she hated you, now? Enough of the subject! The moral of it, my dear Cosway, is to leave this place, and try what change of scene will do for you. I have time to spare; and I will go abroad with you. When shall it be?'

'Let me wait a day or two more,' Cosway pleaded.

Stone shook his head. 'Still hoping, my poor friend, for a line from Miss Restall? You distress me.'

'I am sorry to distress you, Stone. If I can get one pitying word from *her*, I can submit to the miserable life that lies before me.'

'Are you not expecting too much ?'

'You wouldn't say so, if you were as fond of her as I am.'

They were silent. The evening slowly darkened ; and the mistress came in as usual with the candles. She brought with her a letter for Cosway.

He tore it open ; read it in an instant ; and devoured it with kisses. His highly wrought feelings found their vent in a little allowable exaggeration. 'She has saved my life !' he said, as he handed the letter to Stone.

It only contained these lines :

'My love is yours, my promise is yours. Through all trouble, through all profanation, through the hopeless separation that may be before us in this world, I live yours —and die yours. My Edwin, God bless and comfort you.'

The Fourth Epoch in Mr. Cosway's Life.

The separation had lasted for nearly two years, when Cosway and Stone paid that visit to the country house which is recorded at the outset of the present narrative. In the interval, nothing had been heard of Miss Restall, except through Mr. Atherton.

He reported that Adela was leading a very quiet life. The one remarkable event had been an interview between 'Miss Benshaw' and herself. No other person had been present ; but the little that was reported placed Miss Restall's character above all praise. She had forgiven the woman who had so cruelly injured her !

The two friends, it may be remembered, had travelled to London, immediately after completing the fullest explanation of Cosway's startling behaviour at the breakfast-table. Stone was not by nature a sanguine man. 'I don't believe in our luck,' he said. 'Let us be quite sure that we are not the victims of another deception.'

The accident had happened on the Thames ; and the newspaper narrative proved to be accurate in every respect. Stone personally attended the inquest. From a natural feeling of delicacy towards Adela, Cosway hesitated to write to her on the subject. The ever-helpful Stone wrote in his place.

After some delay, the answer was received. It enclosed a brief statement (communicated officially by legal authority) of a last act of malice on the part of the late head-partner in the house of Benshaw and Company. She had not died intestate, like her brother. The first clause of her will contained the testator's grateful recognition of Adela Restall's Christian act of forgiveness. The second clause (after stating that there were neither relatives nor children to be benefited by the will) left Adela Restall mistress of Mrs. Cosway Benshaw's fortune —on the one merciless condition that she did *not* marry Edwin Cosway. The third clause—if Adela Restall violated the condition — handed over the whole of the money to the firm in the City, 'for the extension of the business, and the benefit of the surviving partners.'

Some months later, Adela came of age. To the indignation of Mr. Restall, and the astonishment of the 'Company,' the money actually went to the firm. The fourth epoch in Mr. Cosway's life witnessed his marriage to a woman who cheerfully paid half a million of money for the happiness of passing her life, on eight hundred a year, with the man whom she loved.

But Cosway felt bound in gratitude to make a rich woman of his wife, if work and resolution could do it. When Stone last heard of him, he was reading for the Bar; and Mr. Atherton was ready to give him his first brief.

NOTE.—That 'most improbable' part of the present narrative, which is contained in the division called The First Epoch, is founded on an adventure which actually occurred to no less a person than a cousin of Sir Walter Scott. In Lockhart's delightful 'Life,' the anecdote will be found as told by Sir Walter to Captain Basil Hall. The remainder of the present story is entirely imaginary. The writer wondered what such a woman as the landlady would do, under certain given circumstances, after her marriage to the young midshipman—and here is the result.

Mr. Medhurst and the Princess

I.

THE day before I left London, to occupy the post of second secretary of legation at a small German Court, I took leave of my excellent French singing-master, Monsieur Bonnefoy, and of his young and pretty daughter named Jeanne.

Our farewell interview was saddened by Monsieur Bonnefoy's family anxieties. His elder brother, known in the household as Uncle David, had been secretly summoned to Paris by order of a republican society. Anxious relations in London (whether reasonably or not, I am unable to say) were in some fear of the political consequences that might follow.

At parting, I made Mademoiselle Jeanne a present, in the shape of a plain gold brooch. For some time past, I had taken my lessons at Monsieur Bonnefoy's house; his daughter and I often sang together under his direction. Seeing much of Jeanne, under these circumstances, the little gift that I had offered to her was only the natural expression of a true interest in her welfare. Idle rumour asserted—quite falsely—that I was in love with her. I was sincerely the young lady's friend: no more, no less.

Having alluded to my lessons in singing, it may not be out of place to mention the circumstances under which I became Monsieur Bonnefoy's pupil, and to allude to the change in my life that followed in due course of time.

Our family property—excepting the sum of five thousand pounds left to me by my mother — is landed property, strictly entailed. The estates were inherited by my only brother, Lord Medhurst : the kindest, the best, and, I grieve to say it, the unhappiest of men. He lived separated from a bad wife ; he had no children to console him ; and he only enjoyed at rare intervals the blessing of good health. Having myself nothing to live on but the interest of my mother's little fortune, I had to make my own way in the world. Poor younger sons, not possessed of the commanding ability which achieves distinction, find the roads that lead to prosperity closed to them, with one exception. They can always apply themselves to the social arts which make a man agreeable in society. I had naturally a good voice, and I cultivated it. I was ready to sing, without being subject to the wretched vanity which makes objections and excuses — I pleased the ladies—the ladies spoke favourably of me to their husbands—and some of their husbands were persons of rank and influence. After no very long lapse of time, the result of this combination of circumstances declared itself. Monsieur Bonnefoy's lessons became the indirect means of starting me on a diplomatic career—and the diplomatic career made poor Ernest Medhurst, to his own unutterable astonishment, the hero of a love story!

The story being true, I must beg to be excused, if I abstain from mentioning names, places, and dates, when I enter on German ground. Let it be enough to say that I am writing of a bygone year in the present century, when no such thing as a German Empire existed, and when the revolutionary spirit of France was still an object of well-founded suspicion to tyrants by right divine on the continent of Europe.

II.

On joining the legation, I was not particularly attracted by my chief, the Minister. His manners were oppressively polite ; and his sense of his own importance was not sufficiently influenced by diplomatic reserve. I venture to describe him (mentally speaking) as an empty man, carefully trained to look full on public occasions.

My colleague, the first secretary, was a far more interesting person. Bright, unaffected, and agreeable, he at once interested me when we were introduced to each other. I pay myself a compliment, as I consider, when I add that he became my firm and true friend.

We took a walk together in the palace gardens on the evening of my arrival. Reaching a remote part of the grounds, we were passed by a lean sallow sour-looking old man, drawn by a servant in a chair on wheels. My companion stopped, whispered to me, ' Here is the Prince,' and bowed bareheaded. I followed his example as a matter of course. The Prince feebly returned our salutation. ' Is he ill ?' I asked, when we had put our hats on again.

' Shakespeare,' the secretary replied, ' tells us that " one man in his time plays many parts." Under what various aspects the Prince's character may have presented itself, in his younger days, I am not able to tell you. Since I have been here, he has played the part of a martyr to illness, misunderstood by his doctors.'

' And his daughter, the Princess—what do you say of her ?'

' Ah, she is not so easily described ! I can only appeal to your memory of other women like her, whom you must often have seen—women who are tall and fair, and fragile and elegant ; who have delicate aquiline noses and melting blue eyes— women who have often charmed you by their tender smiles and their supple graces of movement. As for the character of this popular young lady, I must not influence you either way ; study it for yourself.'

' Without a hint to guide me ?'

' With a suggestion,' he replied, ' which may be worth considering. If you wish to please the Princess, begin by endeavouring to win the good graces of the Baroness.'

' Who is the Baroness ?'

' One of the ladies in waiting—bosom friend of her Highness, and chosen repository of all her secrets. Personally, not likely to attract you ; short and fat, and ill-tempered and ugly. Just at this time, I happen myself to get on with her better than usual. We have discovered that we possess one sympathy in common—we are the only people at Court who don't believe in the Prince's new doctor.'

' Is the new doctor a quack ?'

The secretary looked round, before he

answered, to see that nobody was near us.

'It strikes me,' he said, 'that the Doctor is a spy. Mind! I have no right to speak of him in that way; it is only my impression—and I ought to add that appearances are all in his favour. He is in the service of our nearest royal neighbour, the Grand Duke; and he has been sent here expressly to relieve the sufferings of the Duke's good friend and brother, our invalid Prince. This is an honourable mission no doubt. And the man himself is handsome, well-bred, and (I don't quite know whether this is an additional recommendation) a countryman of ours. Nevertheless I doubt him, and the Baroness doubts him. You are an independent witness; I shall be anxious to hear if your opinion agrees with ours.'

I was presented at Court, towards the end of the week; and, in the course of the next two or three days, I more than once saw the Doctor. The impression that he produced on me surprised my colleague. It was my opinion that he and the Baroness had mistaken the character of a worthy and capable man.

The secretary obstinately adhered to his own view.

'Wait a little,' he answered, 'and we shall see.'

He was quite right. We did see.

III.

BUT the Princess — the gentle, gracious, beautiful Princess—what can I say of her Highness? I can only say that she enchanted me.

I had been a little discouraged by the reception that I met with from her father. Strictly confining himself within the limits of politeness, he bade me welcome to his Court in the fewest possible words, and then passed me by without further notice. He afterwards informed the English Minister

that I had been so unfortunate as to try his temper: 'Your new secretary irritates me, sir—he is a person in an offensively perfect state of health.' The Prince's charming daughter was not of her father's way of thinking; it is impossible to say how graciously, how sweetly I was received. She honoured me by speaking to me in my own language, of which she showed herself to be a perfect mistress. I was not only permitted, but encouraged, to talk of my family, and to dwell on my own tastes, amusements, and pursuits. Even when her Highness's attention was claimed by other persons waiting to be presented, I was not forgotten. The Baroness was instructed to invite me for the next evening to the Princess's tea-table; and it was hinted that I should be especially welcome if I brought my music with me, and sang.

My friend the secretary, standing near us at the time, looked at me with a mysterious smile. He had suggested that I should make advances to the Baroness—and here was the Baroness (under royal instructions) making advances to Me!

'We know what *that* means,' he whispered.

In justice to myself, I must declare that I entirely failed to understand him.

On the occasion of my second reception by the Princess, at her little evening party, I detected the Baroness, more than once, in the act of watching her Highness and myself, with an appearance of disapproval in her manner, which puzzled me. When I had taken my leave, she followed me out of the room.

'I have a word of advice to give you,' she said. 'The best thing you can do, sir, is to make an excuse to your Minister, and go back to England.'

I declare again, that I entirely failed to understand the Baroness.

IV.

BEFORE the season came to an end, the Court removed to the Prince's country-seat, in the interests of his Highness's health. Entertainments were given (at the Doctor's suggestion), with a view of raising the patient's depressed spirits. The members of the English legation were among the guests invited. To me it was a delightful visit. I had again every reason to feel gratefully sensible of the Princess's condescending kindness. Meeting the secretary one day in the library, I said that I thought her a perfect creature. Was this an absurd remark to make? I could see nothing absurd in it—and yet my friend burst out laughing.

'My good fellow, nobody is a perfect creature,' he said. 'The Princess has her faults and failings, like the rest of us.'

I denied it positively.

'Use your eyes,' he went on; 'and you will see, for example, that she is shallow and frivolous. Yesterday was a day of rain. We were all obliged to employ ourselves somehow, indoors. Didn't you notice that she had no resources in herself? She can't even read.'

'There you are wrong at any rate,' I declared. 'I saw her reading the newspaper.'

'You saw her with the newspaper in her hand. If you had not been deaf and blind to her defects, you would have noticed that she couldn't fix her attention on it. She was always ready to join in the chatter of the ladies about her. When even their stores of gossip were exhausted, she let the newspaper drop on her lap, and sat in vacant idleness smiling at nothing.'

I reminded him that she might have met with a dull number of the newspaper. He took no notice of this unanswerable reply.

'You were talking the other day of her warmth of feeling,' he proceeded. 'She has plenty of sentiment (German sentiment), I grant you, but no true feeling. What happened only this morning, when the Prince was in the breakfast-room, and when the Princess and her ladies were dressed to go out riding? Even *she* noticed the wretchedly depressed state of her father's spirits. A man of that hypochondriacal temperament suffers acutely, though he may only fancy himself to be ill. The Princess overflowed with sympathy, but she never proposed to stay at home, and try to cheer the old man. Her filial duty was performed to her own entire satisfaction, when she had kissed her hand to the Prince. The moment after, she was out of the room—eager to enjoy her ride. We all heard her laughing gaily among the ladies in the hall.'

I could have answered this also, if our discussion had not been interrupted at the moment. The Doctor came into the library in search of a book. When he had left us, my colleague's strong prejudice against him instantly declared itself.

'Be on your guard with that man,' he said.

'Why?' I asked.

'Haven't you noticed,' he replied, 'that when the Princess is talking to you, the Doctor always happens to be in that part of the room?'

'What does it matter where the Doctor is?'

My friend looked at me with an oddly mingled expression of doubt and surprise. 'Do you really not understand me?' he said.

'I don't indeed.'

'My dear Ernest, you are a rare and admirable example to the rest of us—you are a truly modest man.'

What did he mean?

V.

EVENTS followed, on the next day, which (as will presently be seen) I have a personal interest in relating.

The Baroness left us suddenly, on leave of absence. The Prince wearied of his residence in the country; and the Court returned to the capital. The charming Princess was reported to be 'indisposed,' and retired to the seclusion of her own apartments.

A week later, I received a note from the Baroness, marked ' private and confidential.' It informed me that she had resumed her duties as lady-in-waiting, and that she wished to see me at my earliest convenience. I obeyed at once; and naturally asked if there were better accounts of her Highness's health.

The Baroness's reply a little surprised me. She said, ' The Princess is perfectly well.'

' Recovered already!' I exclaimed.

' She has never been ill,' the Baroness answered. ' Her indisposition was a sham; forced on her by me, in her own interests. Her reputation is in peril; and you—you hateful Englishman—are the cause of it.'

Not feeling disposed to put up with such language as this, even when it was used by a lady, I requested that she would explain herself. She complied without hesitation. In another minute my eyes were opened to the truth. I knew—no; that is too positive—let me say I had reason to believe that the Princess loved me!

It is simply impossible to convey to the minds of others any idea of the emotions that overwhelmed me at that critical moment of my life. I was in a state of confusion at the time; and, when my memory tries to realize it, I am in a state of confusion now. The one thing I can do is to repeat what the Baroness said to me when I had in some degree recovered my composure.

' I suppose you are aware,' she began, ' of the disgrace to which the Princess's infatuation exposes her, if it is discovered? On my own responsibility I repeat what I said to you a short time since. Do you refuse to leave this place immediately?'

Does the man live, honoured as I was, who would have hesitated to refuse? Find him if you can!

' Very well,' she resumed. ' As the friend of the Princess, I have no choice now but to take things as they are, and to make the best of them. Let us realize your position to begin with. If you were (like your elder brother) a nobleman possessed of vast estates, my royal mistress might be excused. As it is, whatever you may be in the future, you are nothing now but an obscure young man, without fortune or title. Do you see your duty to the Princess? or must I explain it to you?'

I saw my duty as plainly as she did. ' Her Highness's secret is a sacred secret,' I said. ' I am bound to shrink from no sacrifice which may preserve it.'

The Baroness smiled maliciously. ' I may have occasion,' she answered, ' to remind you of what you have just said. In the meanwhile, the Princess's secret is in danger of discovery.'

' By her father?'

' No. By the Doctor.'

At first, I doubted whether she was in jest or in earnest. The next instant, I remembered that the secretary had expressly cautioned me against that man.

' It is evidently one of your virtues,' the Baroness proceeded, ' to be slow to suspect. Prepare yourself for a disagreeable surprise. The Doctor has been watching the Princess, on every occasion when she speaks to you, with some object of his own in view. During my absence, young sir, I have been engaged in discovering what that object is. My excellent mother lives at the Court of the Grand Duke, and enjoys the confidence of his Ministers. He is still a bachelor; and, in the interests of the succession to the throne, the time has arrived when he must marry. With my mother's assistance, I have found out that the Doctor's medical errand here is a pretence. Influenced by the Princess's beauty, the Grand Duke has thought of her first as his future Duchess. Whether he has heard slanderous stories, or whether he is only a cautious man, I can't tell you. But this I know: he has instructed his physician—if he had employed a professed diplomatist, his motive might have been suspected—to observe her Highness privately, and to communicate the result. The object of the report is to satisfy the Duke that the Princess's reputation is above the reach of scandal; that she is free from entanglements of a certain kind; and that she is in every respect a person to whom he can with propriety offer his hand in marriage. The Doctor, Mr. Ernest, is not disposed to allow you to prevent him from sending in a favourable report. He has drawn his conclusions from the Princess's extraordinary kindness to the second secretary of the English legation; and he is only waiting for a little plainer evidence to communicate his suspicions to the Prince. It rests with you to save the Princess.'

'Only tell me how I am to do it!' I said.

'There is but one way of doing it,' she answered; 'and that way has (comically enough) been suggested to me by the Doctor himself.'

Her tone and manner tried my patience.

'Come to the point!' I said.

She seemed to enjoy provoking me.

'No hurry, Mr. Ernest—no hurry! You shall be fully enlightened, if you will only wait a little. The Prince, I must tell you, believes in his daughter's indisposition. When he visited her this morning he was attended by his medical adviser. I was present at the interview. To do him justice, the Doctor is worthy of the trust reposed in him—he boldly attempted to verify his suspicions of the daughter, in the father's presence.'

'How?'

'Oh, in the well-known way that has been tried over and over again, under similar circumstances! He merely invented a report that you were engaged in a love-affair with some charming person in the town. Don't be angry; there's no harm done.'

'But there *is* harm done,' I insisted. 'What must the Princess think of me?'

'Do you suppose she is weak enough to believe the Doctor? Her Highness beat him at his own weapons; not the slightest sign of agitation on her part rewarded his ingenuity. All that you have to do is to help her to mislead this medical spy. It's as easy as lying, and easier. The Doctor's slander declares that you have a love-affair in the town. Take the hint—and astonish the Doctor by proving that he has hit on the truth.'

It was a hot day; the Baroness was beginning to get excited. She paused and fanned herself.

'Do I startle you?' she asked.

'You disgust me.'

She laughed.

'What a thick-headed man this is!' she said pleasantly. 'Must I put it more plainly still? Engage in what your English prudery calls a "flirtation," with some woman here—the lower in degree the better, or the Princess might be jealous—and let the affair be seen and known by everybody about the Court. Sly as he is, the Doctor is not prepared for that! At your age, and with your personal advantages, he will take appearances for granted; he will conclude that he has wronged you, and misinterpreted the motives of the Princess. The secret of her Highness's weakness will be preserved —thanks to that sacrifice, Mr. Ernest, which you are so willing and so eager to make.'

It was useless to remonstrate with such a woman as this. I simply stated my own objection to her artfully devised scheme.

'I don't wish to appear vain,' I said; 'but the woman to whom I am to pay these attentions may believe that I really admire her—and it is just possible that she may honestly return the feeling which I am only assuming.'

'Well—and what then?'

'It's hard on the woman, surely?'

The Baroness was shocked, unaffectedly shocked.

'Good heavens!' she exclaimed, 'how can anything that you do for the Princess be hard on a woman of the lower orders? There must be an end of this nonsense, sir! You have heard what I propose; and you know what the circumstances are. My mistress is waiting for your answer. What am I to say?'

'Let me see her Highness, and speak for myself,' I said.

'Quite impossible to-day, without running too great a risk. Your reply must be made through me.'

There was to be a Court concert at the end of the week. On that occasion I should be able to make my own reply. In the meanwhile I only told the Baroness I wanted time to consider.

'What time?' she asked.

'Until to-morrow. Do you object?'

'On the contrary, I cordially agree. Your base hesitation may lead to results which I have not hitherto dared to anticipate.'

'What do you mean?'

'Between this and to-morrow,' the horrid woman replied, 'the Princess may end in seeing you with my eyes. In that hope I wish you good-morning.'

VI.

My enemies say that I am a weak man, unduly influenced by persons of rank—because of their rank. If this were true, I should have found little difficulty in consenting to adopt the Baroness's suggestion. As it was, the longer I reflected on the scheme the less I liked it. I tried to think of some alternative that might be acceptably proposed. The time passed, and nothing occurred to me. In this embarrassing position my mind became seriously disturbed; I felt the necessity of obtaining some relief, which might turn my thoughts for a while into a new channel. The secretary called on me, while I was still in doubt what to do. He reminded me that a new prima-donna was advertised to appear on that night; and he suggested that we should go to the opera. Feeling as I did at the time, I readily agreed.

We found the theatre already filled, before the performance began. Two French gentlemen were seated in the row of stalls behind us. They were talking of the new singer.

'She is advertised as " Mademoiselle Fontenay," ' one of them said. 'That sounds like an assumed name.'

'It *is* an assumed name,' the other replied. 'She is the daughter of a French singing-master, named Bonnefoy.'

To my friend's astonishment I started to my feet, and left him without a word of apology. In another minute I was at the stage-door, and had sent in my card to 'Mademoiselle Fontenay.' While I was waiting, I had time to think. Was it possible that Jeanne had gone on the stage? Or were there two singing-masters in existence named Bonnefoy? My doubts were soon decided. The French woman-servant whom I remembered when I was Monsieur Bonnefoy's pupil, made her appearance, and conducted me to her young mistress's dressing-room. Dear good Jeanne, how glad she was to see me!

I found her standing before the glass, having just completed her preparations for appearing on the stage. Dressed in her picturesque costume, she was so charming that I expressed my admiration heartily, as became her old friend. 'Do you really like me?' she said, with the innocent familiarity which I recollected so well. 'See how I look in the glass—that is the great test.' It was not easy to apply the test. Instead of looking at her image in the glass, it was far more agreeable to look at herself. We were interrupted—too soon interrupted—by the call-boy. He knocked at the door, and announced that the overture had begun.

'I have a thousand things to ask you,' I told her. 'What has made this wonderful change in your life? How is it that I don't see your father——'

Her face instantly saddened; her hand trembled as she laid it on my arm to silence me.

'Don't speak of him now,' she said, ' or you will unnerve me! Come to me to-morrow when the stage will not be waiting; Annette will give you my address.' She opened the door to go out, and returned. 'Will you think me very unreasonable if I ask you not to make one of my audience to-night? You have reminded me of the dear old days that can never come again. If I feel that I am singing to *you*——' She left me to understand the rest, and turned away again to the door. As I followed her out, to say good-bye, she drew from her bosom the little brooch which had been my parting gift, and held it out to me. 'On the stage, or off,' she said, 'I always wear it. Good-night, Ernest.'

I was prepared to hear sad news, when we met the next morning.

My good old friend and master had died suddenly. To add to the bitterness of that affliction, he had died in debt to a dear and intimate friend. For his daughter's sake he had endeavoured to add to his little savings by speculating with borrowed money on the Stock Exchange. He had failed, and the loan advanced had not been repaid, when a fit of apoplexy struck him down. Offered the opportunity of trying her fortune on the operatic stage, Jeanne made the attempt, and was now nobly employed in earning the money to pay her father's debt.

'It was the only way in which I could do justice to his memory,' she said simply. 'I hope you don't object to my going on the stage?'

I took her hand, poor child—and let that simple action answer for me. I was too deeply affected to be able to speak.

'It is not in me to be a great actress,' she resumed; 'but you know what an admirable musician my father was. He has taught me to sing, so that I can satisfy the critics, as well as please the public. There was what they call a great success last night. It has earned me an engagement for another year to come, and an increase of salary. I have already sent some money to our good old friend at home, and I shall soon send more. It is my one consolation—I feel almost happy again when I am paying my poor father's debt. No more now of my sad story! I want to hear all that you can tell me of yourself.' She moved to the window, and looked out. 'Oh, the beautiful blue sky! We used sometimes to take a walk, when we were in London, on fine days like this. Is there a park here?'

I took her to the palace gardens, famous for their beauty in that part of Germany.

Arm in arm we loitered along the pleasant walks. The lovely flowers, the bright sun, the fresh fragrant breeze, all helped her to recover her spirits. She began to be like the happy Jeanne of my past experience, as easily pleased as a child. When we sat down to rest, the lap of her dress was full of daisies. 'Do you remember,' she said, 'when you first taught me to make a daisy-chain? Are you too great a man to help me again, now?'

We were still engaged with our chain, seated close together, when the smell of tobacco-smoke was wafted to us on the air.

I looked up and saw the Doctor passing us, enjoying his cigar. He bowed; eyed my pretty companion with a malicious smile; and passed on.

'Who is that man?' she asked.

'The Prince's physician,' I replied.

'I don't like him,' she said; 'why did he smile when he looked at me?'

'Perhaps,' I suggested, 'he thought we were lovers.'

She blushed. 'Don't let him think that! tell him we are only old friends.'

We were not destined to finish our flower chain on that day.

Another person interrupted us, whom I recognised as the elder brother of Monsieur Bonnefoy — already mentioned in these pages, under the name of Uncle David. Having left France for political reasons, the old republican had taken care of his niece after her father's death, and had accepted the position of Jeanne's business manager in her relations with the stage. Uncle David's object, when he joined us in the garden, was to remind her that she was wanted at rehearsal, and must at once return with him to the theatre. We parted, having arranged that I was to see the performance on that night.

Later in the day, the Baroness sent for me again.

'Let me apologize for having misunderstood you yesterday,' she said; 'and let me offer you my best congratulations. You have done wonders already in the way of misleading the Doctor. There is only one objection to that girl at the theatre—I

hear she is so pretty that she may possibly displease the Princess. In other respects, she is just in the public position which will make your attentions to her look like the beginning of a serious intrigue. Bravo, Mr. Ernest—bravo!'

I was too indignant to place any restraint on the language in which I answered her.

'Understand, if you please,' I said, 'that I am renewing an old friendship with Mademoiselle Jeanne — begun under the sanction of her father. Respect that young lady, madam, as I respect her.'

The detestable Baroness clapped her hands, as if she had been at the theatre.

'If you only say that to the Princess,' she remarked, 'as well as you have said it to me, there will be no danger of arousing her Highness's jealousy. I have a message for you. At the concert, on Saturday, you are to retire to the conservatory, and you may hope for an interview when the singers begin the second part of the programme. Don't let me detain you any longer. Go back to your young lady, Mr. Ernest—pray go back!'

VII.

On the second night of the opera the applications for places were too numerous to be received. Among the crowded audience, I recognised many of my friends. They persisted in believing an absurd report (first circulated, as I imagine, by the Doctor), which asserted that my interest in the new singer was something more than the interest of an old friend. When I went behind the scenes to congratulate Jeanne on her success, I was annoyed in another way --and by the Doctor again. He followed me to Jeanne's room, to offer *his* congratulations; and he begged that I would introduce him to the charming prima-donna. Having expressed his admiration, he looked at me with his insolently suggestive smile, and said he could not think of prolonging his intrusion. On leaving the room, he noticed Uncle David, waiting as usual to take care of Jeanne on her return from the theatre—looked at him attentively—bowed, and went out.

The next morning, I received a note from the Baroness, expressed in these terms :

'More news! My rooms look out on the wing of the palace in which the Doctor is lodged. Half an hour since, I discovered him at his window, giving a letter to a person who is a stranger to me. The man left the palace immediately afterwards. My maid followed him, by my directions. Instead of putting the letter in the post, he took a ticket at the railway-station—for what place the servant was unable to discover. Here, you will observe, is a letter important enough to be despatched by special messenger, and written at a time when we have succeeded in freeing ourselves from the Doctor's suspicions. It is at least possible that he has decided on sending a favourable report of the Princess to the Grand Duke. If this is the case, please consider whether you will not act wisely (in her Highness's interests) by keeping away from the concert.'

Viewing this suggestion as another act of impertinence on the part of the Baroness, I persisted in my intention of going to the concert. It was for the Princess to decide what course of conduct I was bound to follow. What did I care for the Doctor's report to the Duke ! Shall I own my folly? I do really believe I was jealous of the Duke.

VIII.

ENTERING the Concert Room, I found the Princess alone on the daïs, receiving the company. 'Nervous prostration' had made it impossible for the Prince to be present. He was confined to his bed-chamber ; and the Doctor was in attendance on him.

I bowed to the Baroness, but she was too seriously offended with me for declining to take her advice to notice my salutation. Passing into the conservatory, it occurred to me that I might be seen, and possibly suspected, in the interval between the first and second parts of the programme, when the music no longer absorbed the attention of the audience. I went on, and waited outside on the steps that led to the garden ; keeping the glass door open, so as to hear when the music of the second part of the concert began.

After an interval which seemed to be end-less, I saw the Princess approaching me.

She had made the heat in the Concert Room an excuse for retiring for a while ; and she had the Baroness in attendance on her to save appearances. Instead of leaving us to ourselves, the malicious creature persisted in paying the most respectful attentions to her mistress. It was impossible to make her understand that she was not wanted any longer until the Princess said sharply, 'Go back to the music !' Even then, the detestable woman made a low curtsey, and answered: 'I will return, Madam, in five minutes.'

I ventured to present myself in the conservatory.

The Princess was dressed with exquisite simplicity, entirely in white. Her only ornaments were white roses in her hair and in her bosom. To say that she looked lovely is to say nothing. She seemed to be the ethereal creature of some higher sphere ; too exquisitely delicate and pure to be approached by a mere mortal man like myself. I was awed ; I was silent. Her Highness's sweet smile encouraged me to venture a little nearer. She pointed to a footstool which the Baroness had placed for her. ' Are you afraid of me, Ernest ?' she asked softly.

Her divinely beautiful eyes rested on me with a look of encouragement. I dropped on my knees at her feet. She had asked if I was afraid of her. This, if I may use such an expression, roused my manhood. My own boldness astonished me. I answered: ' Madam, I adore you.'

She laid her fair hand on my head, and looked at me thoughtfully. ' Forget my rank,' she whispered—' have I not set you the example ? Suppose that I am nothing but an English Miss. What would you say to Miss ?'

' I should say, I love you.'

' Say it to Me.'

My lips said it on her hand. She bent forward. My heart beats fast at the bare remembrance of it. Oh, Heavens, her Highness kissed me !

' There is your reward,' she murmured, ' for all that you have sacrificed for my sake. What an effort it must have been to offer the pretence of love to an obscure stranger ! The Baroness tells me this actress—this singer—what is she ?—is pretty. Is it true ?'

The Baroness was quite mischievous enough to have also mentioned the false impression, prevalent about the Court, that I was in love with Jeanne. I attempted to explain. The gracious Princess refused to hear me.

' Do you think I doubt you?' she said. ' Distinguished by me, could you waste a look on a person in *that* rank of life ?' She laughed softly, as if the mere idea of such a thing amused her. It was only for a moment: her thoughts took a new direction — they contemplated the uncertain future. ' How is this to end ?' she asked. ' Dear Ernest, we are not in Paradise ; we are in a hard cruel world which insists on distinctions in rank. To what unhappy destiny does the fascination which you

exercise over me condemn us both ?'

She paused—took one of the white roses out of her bosom—touched it with her lips —and gave it to me.

' I wonder whether you feel the burden of life as I feel it ?' she resumed. ' It is immaterial to me, whether we are united in this world or in the next. Accept my rose, Ernest, as an assurance that I speak with perfect sincerity. I see but two alternatives before us. One of them (beset with dangers) is elopement. And the other,' she added, with truly majestic composure ' is suicide.'

Would Englishmen in general have rightly understood such fearless confidence in them as this language implied ? I am afraid they might have attributed it to, what my friend the secretary called, ' German sentiment.' Perhaps they might even have suspected the Princess of quoting from some old-fashioned German play. Under the irresistible influence of that glorious creature, I contemplated with such equal serenity the perils of elopement and the martyrdom of love, that I was for the moment at a loss how to reply. In that moment, the evil genius of my life appeared in the conservatory. With haste in her steps, with alarm in her face, the Baroness rushed up to her royal mistress, and said, ' For God's sake, Madam, come away ! The Prince desires to speak with you instantly.'

Her Highness rose, calmly superior to the vulgar excitement of her lady in waiting. ' Think of it to-night,' she said to me, ' and let me hear from you to-morrow.'

She pressed my hand ; she gave me a farewell look. I sank into the chair that she had just left. Did I think of elopement ? Did I think of suicide ? The elevating influence of the Princess no longer sustained me ; my nature became degraded. Horrid doubts rose in my mind. Did her father suspect us ?

IX.

NEED I say that I passed a sleepless night ?

The morning found me with my pen in my hand, confronting the serious responsibility of writing to the Princess, and not knowing what to say. I had already torn up two letters, when Uncle David presented himself with a message from his niece. Jeanne was in trouble, and wanted to ask my advice.

My state of mind, on hearing this, became simply inexplicable. Here was an interruption which ought to have annoyed me. It did nothing of the kind—it inspired me with a feeling of relief !

I naturally expected that the old Frenchman would return with me to his niece, and tell me what had happened. To my surprise, he begged that I would excuse him, and left me without a word of explanation. I found Jeanne walking up and down her little sitting-room, flushed and angry. Fragments of torn paper and heaps of flowers littered the floor ; and three unopened jewel-cases appeared to have been thrown into the empty fireplace. She caught me excitedly by the hand the moment I entered the room.

'You are my true friend,' she said; 'you were present the other night when I sang. Was there anything in my behaviour on the stage which could justify men who call themselves gentlemen in insulting me ?'

'My dear, how can you ask the question?'

'I must ask it. Some of them send flowers, and some of them send jewels ; and every one of them writes letters—infamous abominable letters—saying they are in love with me, and asking for appointments as if I was——'

She could say no more. Poor dear Jeanne—her head dropped on my shoulder; she burst out crying. Who could see her so cruelly humiliated—the faithful loving daughter, whose one motive for appearing on the stage had been to preserve her father's good name—and not feel for her as I did ? I forgot all considerations of prudence; I thought of nothing but consoling her; I took her in my arms ; I dried her tears ; I kissed her ; I said, 'Tell me the name of any one of the wretches who has written to you, and I will make him an example to the rest !' She shook her head, and pointed to the morsels of paper on the floor. 'Oh, Ernest, do you think I asked you to come here for any such purpose as that ? Those jewels, those hateful jewels, tell me how I can send them back! spare me the sight of them!'

So far, it was easy to console her. I sent the jewels at once to the manager of the theatre—with a written notice to be posted at the stage door, stating that they were waiting to be returned to the persons who could describe them.

'Try, my dear, to forget what has happened,' I said. 'Try to find consolation and encouragement in your art.'

'I have lost all interest in my success on the stage,' she answered, 'now I know the penalty I must pay for it. When my father's memory is clear of reproach, I shall leave the theatre never to return to it again.'

'Take time to consider, Jeanne.'

'I will do anything you ask of me.'

For a while we were silent. Without any influence to lead to it that I could trace, I found myself recalling the language that the Princess had used in alluding to Jeanne. When I thought of them now, the words and the tone in which they had been spoken jarred on me. There is surely something mean in an assertion of superiority which depends on nothing better than the accident of birth. I don't know why I took Jeanne's hand ; I don't know why I said, 'What a good girl you are ! how glad I am to have been of some little use to you !' Is my friend the secretary right, when he reproaches me with acting on impulse, like a woman ? I don't like to think so ; and yet, this I must own—it was well for me that I was obliged to leave her, before I had perhaps said other words which might have been alike unworthy of Jeanne, of the Princess, and of myself. I was called away to speak to my servant. He brought with him the secretary's card, having a line written on it : ' I am waiting at your rooms, on business which permits of no delay.'

As we shook hands, Jeanne asked me if I knew where her uncle was. I could only tell her that he had left me at my own door. She made no remark ; but she seemed to be uneasy on receiving that reply.

X.

WHEN I arrived at my rooms, my colleague hurried to meet me the moment I opened the door.

' I am going to surprise you,' he said ; ' and there is no time to prepare you for it. Our chief, the Minister, has seen the Prince this morning, and has been officially informed of an event of importance in the life of the Princess. She is engaged to be married to the Grand Duke.'

Engaged to the Duke—and not a word from her to warn me of it ! Engaged—after what she had said to me no longer ago than the past night ! Had I been made a plaything to amuse a great lady? Oh, what degradation ! I was furious ; I snatched up my hat to go to the palace—to force my way to her — to overwhelm her with reproaches. My friend stopped me. He put an official document into my hand.

' There is your leave of absence from the legation,' he said ; ' beginning from to-day. I have informed the Minister, in strict confidence, of the critical position in which you

are placed. He agrees with me that the Princess's inexcusable folly is alone to blame. Leave us, Ernest, by the next train. There is some intrigue going on, and I fear you may be involved in it. You know that the rulers of these little German States can exercise despotic authority when they choose?'

' Yes ! yes !'

' Whether the Prince has acted of his own free will—or whether he has been influenced by some person about him—I am not able to tell you. He has issued an order to arrest an old Frenchman, known to be a republican, and suspected of associating with one of the secret societies in this part of Germany. The conspirator has taken to flight ; having friends, as we suppose, who warned him in time. But this, Ernest, is not the worst of it. That charming singer, that modest pretty girl——'

' You don't mean Jeanne?'

' I am sorry to say I do. Advantage has been taken of her relationship to the old man, to include that innocent creature in political suspicions which it is simply absurd to suppose that she has deserved. She is ordered to leave the Prince's dominions immediately.—Are you going to her?'

' Instantly !' I replied.

Could I feel a moment's hesitation, after the infamous manner in which the Princess had sacrificed me to the Grand Duke? Could I think of the poor girl, friendless, helpless—with nobody near her but a stupid woman-servant, unable to speak the language of the country—and fail to devote myself to the protection of Jeanne? Thank God, I reached her lodgings in time to tell her what had happened, and to take it on myself to receive the police.

XI.

In three days more, Jeanne was safe in London; having travelled under my escort. I was fortunate enough to find a home for her, in the house of a lady who had been my mother's oldest and dearest friend.

We were separated, a few days afterwards, by the distressing news which reached me of the state of my brother's health. I went at once to his house in the country. His medical attendants had lost all hope of saving him : they told me plainly that his release from a life of suffering was near at hand.

While I was still in attendance at his bedside, I heard from the secretary. He enclosed a letter, directed to me in a strange handwriting. I opened the envelope and looked for the signature. My friend had been entrapped into sending me an anonymous letter.

Besides addressing me in French (a language seldom used in my experience at the legation), the writer disguised the identity of the persons mentioned by the use of classical names. In spite of these precautions, I felt no difficulty in arriving at a conclusion. My correspondent's special knowledge of Court secrets, and her malicious way of communicating them, betrayed the Baroness.

I translate the letter ; restoring to the persons who figure in it the names under which they are already known. The writer began in these satirically familiar terms :

' When you left the Prince's dominions, my dear sir, you no doubt believed yourself to be a free agent. Quite a mistake ! You were a mere puppet ; and the strings that moved you were pulled by the Doctor.

' Let me tell you how.

' On a certain night, which you well remember, the Princess was unexpectedly summoned to the presence of her father. His physician's skill had succeeded in re- lieving the illustrious Prince, prostrate under nervous miseries. He was able to attend to a state affair of importance, revealed to him by the Doctor—who then for the first time acknowledged that he had presented himself at Court in a diplomatic, as well as in a medical capacity.

' This state affair related to a proposal for the hand of the Princess, received from the Grand Duke through the authorised medium of the Doctor. Her Highness, being consulted, refused to consider the proposal. The Prince asked for her reason. She answered, " I have no wish to be married." Naturally irritated by such a ridiculous excuse, her father declared positively that the marriage should take place.

' The impression produced on the Grand Duke's favourite and emissary was of a different kind.

' Certain suspicions of the Princess and yourself, which you had successfully contrived to dissipate, revived in the Doctor's mind when he heard the lady's reason for refusing to marry his royal master. It was now too late to regret that he had suffered himself to be misled by cleverly managed appearances. He could not recall the favourable report which he had addressed to the Duke—or withdraw the proposal of marriage which he had been commanded to make.

' In this emergency, the one safe course open to him was to get rid of You—and, at the same time, so to handle circumstances as to excite against you the pride and anger of the Princess. In the pursuit of this latter object he was assisted by one of the ladies in waiting, sincerely interested in the welfare of her gracious mistress, and therefore ardently desirous of seeing her Highness married to the Duke.

' A wretched old French conspirator was made the convenient pivot on which the intrigue turned.

' An order for the arrest of this foreign

republican having been first obtained, the Prince was prevailed on to extend his distrust of the Frenchman to the Frenchman's niece. You know this already; but you don't know why it was done. Having believed from the first that you were really in love with the young lady, the Doctor reckoned confidently on your devoting yourself to the protection of a friendless girl, cruelly exiled at an hour's notice.

'The one chance against us was that tender considerations, associated with her Highness, might induce you to hesitate. The lady in waiting easily moved this obstacle out of the way. She abstained from delivering a letter addressed to you, entrusted to her by the Princess. When the great lady asked why she had not received your reply, she was informed (quite truly) that you and the charming opera singer had taken your departure together. You may imagine what her Highness thought of you, and said of you, when I mention in conclusion that she consented, the same day, to marry the Duke.

'So, Mr. Ernest, these clever people tricked you into serving their interests, blindfold. In relating how it was done, I hope I may have assisted you in forming a correct estimate of the state of your own intelligence. You have made a serious mistake in adopting your present profession. Give up diplomacy—and get a farmer to employ you in keeping his sheep.'

*　　*　　*　　*　　*

Do I sometimes think regretfully of the Princess?

Permit me to mention a circumstance, and to leave my answer to be inferred. Jeanne is Lady Medhurst.

Mr. Lismore and the Widow

LATE in the autumn, not many years since, a public meeting was held at the Mansion House, London, under the direction of the Lord Mayor.

The list of gentlemen invited to address the audience had been chosen with two objects in view. Speakers of celebrity, who would rouse public enthusiasm, were supported by speakers connected with commerce, who would be practically useful in explaining the purpose for which the meeting was convened. Money wisely spent in advertising had produced the customary result—every seat was occupied before the proceedings began.

Among the late arrivals, who had no choice but to stand or to leave the hall, were two ladies. One of them at once decided on leaving the hall. 'I shall go back to the carriage,' she said, 'and wait for you at the door.' Her friend answered, 'I shan't keep you long. He is advertised to support the second Resolution; I want to see him—and that is all.'

An elderly gentleman, seated at the end of a bench, rose and offered his place to the lady who remained. She hesitated to take advantage of his kindness, until he reminded her that he had heard what she said to her friend. Before the third Resolution was proposed, his seat would be at his own disposal again. She thanked him, and without further ceremony took his place. He was provided with an opera-glass, which he more than once offered to her, when famous orators appeared on the platform; she made no use of it until a speaker—known in the City as a shipowner—stepped forward to support the second Resolution.

His name (announced in the advertisements) was Ernest Lismore.

The moment he rose, the lady asked for the opera-glass. She kept it to her eyes for such a length of time, and with such evident interest in Mr. Lismore, that the curiosity of her neighbours was aroused. Had he anything to say in which a lady (evidently a stranger to him) was personally interested? There was nothing in the address that he delivered which appealed to the enthusiasm of women. He was undoubtedly a handsome man, whose appearance proclaimed him to be in the prime of life—midway perhaps between thirty and forty years of age. But why a lady should persist in keeping an opera-glass fixed on him all through his speech, was a question which found the general ingenuity at a loss for a reply.

Having returned the glass with an apology, the lady ventured on putting a question next. 'Did it strike you, sir, that Mr. Lismore seemed to be out of spirits ?' she asked.

'I can't say it did, ma'am.'

'Perhaps you noticed that he left the platform the moment he had done ?'

This betrayal of interest in the speaker did not escape the notice of a lady, seated on the bench in front. Before the old gentleman could answer, she volunteered an explanation.

'I am afraid Mr. Lismore is troubled by anxieties connected with his business,' she said. 'My husband heard it reported in the City yesterday that he was seriously embarrassed by the failure——'

A loud burst of applause made the end of the sentence inaudible. A famous member of Parliament had risen to propose the third Resolution. The polite old man took his seat, and the lady left the hall to join her friend.

*   *   *   *   *

'Well, Mrs. Callender, has Mr. Lismore disappointed you ?'

'Far from it ! But I have heard a report about him which has alarmed me: he is said to be seriously troubled about money matters. How can I find out his address in the City ?'

'We can stop at the first stationer's shop we pass, and ask to look at the Directory. Are you going to pay Mr. Lismore a visit ?'

'I am going to think about it.'

II.

THE next day a clerk entered Mr. Lismore's private room at the office, and presented a visiting-card. Mrs. Callender had reflected, and had arrived at a decision. Underneath her name she had written these explanatory words : 'On important business.'

'Does she look as if she wanted money ?' Mr. Lismore inquired.

'Oh dear, no! She comes in her carriage.'

'Is she young or old ?'

'Old, sir.'

To Mr. Lismore—conscious of the disastrous influence occasionally exercised over busy men by youth and beauty—this was a recommendation in itself. He said:

'Show her in.'

Observing the lady, as she approached him, with the momentary curiosity of a stranger, he noticed that she still preserved the remains of beauty. She had also escaped the misfortune, common to persons at her time of life, of becoming too fat. Even to a man's eye, her dressmaker appeared to have made the most of that favourable circumstance. Her figure had its defects concealed, and its remaining merits set off to advantage. At the same time she evidently held herself above the common deceptions by which some women seek to conceal their age. She wore her own gray hair; and her complexion bore the test of daylight. On entering the room, she made her apologies with some embarrassment. Being the embarrassment of a stranger (and not of a youthful stranger), it failed to impress Mr. Lismore favourably.

'I am afraid I have chosen an inconvenient time for my visit,' she began.

'I am at your service,' he answered a little stiffly; 'especially if you will be so kind as to mention your business with me in few words.'

She was a woman of some spirit, and that reply roused her.

'I will mention it in one word,' she said smartly. 'My business is—gratitude.'

He was completely at a loss to understand what she meant, and he said so plainly. Instead of explaining herself, she put a question.

'Do you remember the night of the

eleventh of March, between five and six years since?'

He considered for a moment.

'No,' he said, 'I don't remember it. Excuse me, Mrs. Callender, I have affairs of my own to attend to which cause me some anxiety——'

'Let me assist your memory, Mr. Lismore; and I will leave you to your affairs. On the date that I have referred to you were on your way to the railway-station at Bexmore, to catch the night express from the North to London.'

As a hint that his time was valuable the shipowner had hitherto remained standing. He now took his customary seat, and began to listen with some interest. Mrs. Callender had produced her effect on him already.

'It was absolutely necessary,' she proceeded, 'that you should be on board your ship in the London Docks at nine o'clock the next morning. If you had lost the express, the vessel would have sailed without you.'

The expression of his face began to change to surprise.

'Who told you that?' he asked.

'You shall hear directly. On your way into the town, your carriage was stopped by an obstruction on the highroad. The people of Bexmore were looking at a house on fire.'

He started to his feet.

'Good heavens! are you the lady?'

She held up her hand in satirical protest.

'Gently, sir! You suspected me just now of wasting your valuable time. Don't rashly conclude that I am the lady, until you find that I am acquainted with the circumstances.'

'Is there no excuse for my failing to recognise you?' Mr. Lismore asked. 'We were on the dark side of the burning house; you were fainting, and I——'

'And you,' she interposed, 'after saving me at the risk of your own life, turned a deaf ear to my poor husband's entreaties,

when he asked you to wait till I had recovered my senses.'

'Your poor husband? Surely, Mrs. Callender, he received no serious injury from the fire?'

'The firemen rescued him under circumstances of peril,' she answered, 'and at his great age he sank under the shock. I have lost the kindest and best of men. Do you remember how you parted from him—burnt and bruised in saving me? He liked to talk of it in his last illness. "At least" (he said to you) "tell me the name of the man who has preserved my wife from a dreadful death." You threw your card to him out of the carriage window, and away you went at a gallop to catch your train! In all the years that have passed I have kept that card, and have vainly inquired for my brave sea-captain. Yesterday I saw your name on the list of speakers at the Mansion House. Need I say that I attended the meeting? Need I tell you now why I come here and interrupt you in business-hours?'

She held out her hand. Mr. Lismore took it in silence, and pressed it warmly.

'You have not done with me yet,' she resumed with a smile. 'Do you remember what I said of my errand, when I first came in?'

'You said it was an errand of gratitude.'

'Something more than the gratitude which only says 'Thank you,'' she added. 'Before I explain myself, however, I want to know what you have been doing, and how it was that my inquiries failed to trace you after that terrible night.'

The appearance of depression which Mrs. Callender had noticed at the public meeting showed itself again in Mr. Lismore's face. He sighed as he answered her.

'My story has one merit,' he said; 'it is soon told. I cannot wonder that you failed to discover me. In the first place, I was not captain of my ship at that time; I was only mate. In the second place, I inherited some money, and ceased to lead a sailor's life, in less than a year from the night of the fire. You will now understand what obstacles were in the way of your tracing me. With my little capital I started successfully in business as a ship-owner. At the time, I naturally congratulated myself on my own good fortune. We little know, Mrs. Callender, what the future has in store for us.'

He stopped. His handsome features hardened—as if he was suffering (and concealing) pain. Before it was possible to speak to him, there was a knock at the door. Another visitor, without an appointment, had called; the clerk appeared again, with a card and a message.

'The gentleman begs you will see him, sir. He has something to tell you which is too important to be delayed.'

Hearing the message, Mrs. Callender rose immediately.

'It is enough for to-day that we understand each other,' she said. 'Have you any engagement to-morrow, after the hours of business?'

'None.'

She pointed to her card on the writing-table. 'Will you come to me to-morrow evening at that address? I am like the gentleman who has just called; I too have my reason for wishing to see you.

He gladly accepted the invitation. Mrs. Callender stopped him as he opened the door for her.

'Shall I offend you,' she said, 'if I ask a strange question before I go? I have a better motive, mind, than mere curiosity. Are you married?'

'No.'

'Forgive me again,' she resumed. 'At my age, you cannot possibly misunderstand me; and yet——'

She hesitated. Mr. Lismore tried to give her confidence. 'Pray don't stand on ceremony, Mrs. Callender. Nothing that *you* can ask me need be prefaced by an apology.'

Thus encouraged, she ventured to proceed.

'You may be engaged to be married?' she suggested. 'Or you may be in love?'

He found it impossible to conceal his surprise. But he answered without hesitation.

'There is no such bright prospect in *my* life,' he said. 'I am not even in love.'

She left him with a little sigh. It sounded like a sigh of relief.

Ernest Lismore was thoroughly puzzled. What could be the old lady's object in ascertaining that he was still free from a matrimonial engagement? If the idea had occurred to him in time, he might have alluded to her domestic life, and might have asked if she had children? With a little tact he might have discovered more than this. She had described her feeling towards him as passing the ordinary limits of gratitude; and she was evidently rich enough to be above the imputation of a mercenary motive. Did she propose to brighten those dreary prospects to which he had alluded in speaking of his own life? When he presented himself at her house the next evening, would she introduce him to a charming daughter?

He smiled as the idea occurred to him. 'An appropriate time to be thinking of my chances of marriage!' he said to himself. 'In another month I may be a ruined man.'

III.

THE gentleman who had so urgently requested an interview was a devoted friend —who had obtained a means of helping Ernest at a serious crisis in his affairs.

It had been truly reported that he was in a position of pecuniary embarrassment, owing to the failure of a mercantile house with which he had been intimately connected. Whispers affecting his own solvency had followed on the bankruptcy of the firm. He had already endeavoured to obtain advances of money on the usual conditions, and had been met by excuses for delay. His friend had now arrived with a letter of introduction to a capitalist, well known in commercial circles for his daring speculations, and for his great wealth.

Looking at the letter, Ernest observed that the envelope was sealed. In spite of that ominous innovation on established usage, in cases of personal introduction, he presented the letter. On this occasion, he was not put off with excuses. The capitalist flatly declined to discount Mr. Lismore's bills, unless they were backed by responsible names.

Ernest made a last effort.

He applied for help to two mercantile men whom he had assisted in *their* difficulties, and whose names would have satisfied the money-lender. They were most sincerely sorry — but they too refused.

The one security that he could offer was open, it must be owned, to serious objections on the score of risk. He wanted an advance of twenty thousand pounds, secured on a homeward-bound ship and cargo. But the vessel was not insured ; and, at that stormy season, she was already more than a month overdue. Could grateful colleagues be blamed if they forgot their obligations when they were asked to offer pecuniary help to a merchant in this situation? Ernest returned to his office, without money and without credit.

A man threatened by ruin is in no state of mind to keep an engagement at a lady's tea-table. Ernest sent a letter of apology to Mrs. Callender, alleging extreme pressure of business as the excuse for breaking his engagement.

'Am I to wait for an answer, sir?' the messenger asked.

'No ; you are merely to leave the letter.'

IV.

In an hour's time—to Ernest's astonishment—the messenger returned with a reply.

'The lady was just going out, sir, when I rang at the door,' he explained, 'and she took the letter from me herself. She didn't appear to know your handwriting, and she asked me who I came from. When I mentioned your name, I was ordered to wait.'

Ernest opened the letter.

'Dear Mr. Lismore,

'One of us must speak out, and your letter of apology forces me to be that one. If you are really so proud and so distrustful as you seem to be, I shall offend you. If not, I shall prove myself to be your friend.

'Your excuse is " pressure of business." The truth (as I have good reason to believe) is " want of money." I heard a stranger, at that public meeting, say that you were seriously embarrassed by some failure in the City.

'Let me tell you what my own pecuniary position is in two words. I am the childless widow of a rich man——'

Ernest paused. His anticipated discovery of Mrs. Callender's 'charming daughter' was in his mind for the moment. 'That little romance must return to the world of dreams,' he thought—and went on with the letter.

'After what I owe to you, I don't regard it as repaying an obligation—I consider myself as merely performing a duty when I offer to assist you by a loan of money.

'Wait a little before you throw my letter into the wastepaper-basket.

'Circumstances (which it is impossible for me to mention before we meet) put it out of my power to help you—unless I attach to my most sincere offer of service a very unusual and very embarrassing condition. If you are on the brink of ruin, that misfortune will plead my excuse—and your excuse too, if you accept the loan on my terms. In any case, I rely on the sympathy and forbearance of the man to whom I owe my life.

'After what I have now written, there is only one thing to add. I beg to decline accepting your excuses ; and I shall expect to see you to-morrow evening, as we arranged. I am an obstinate old woman— but I am also your faithful friend and servant,

'MARY CALLENDER.'

Ernest looked up from the letter. 'What can this possibly mean ?' he wondered.

But he was too sensible a man to be content with wondering—he decided on keeping his engagement.

V.

WHAT Doctor Johnson called 'the insolence of wealth' appears far more frequently in the houses of the rich than in the manners of the rich. The reason is plain enough. Personal ostentation is, in the very nature of it, ridiculous. But the ostentation which exhibits magnificent pictures, priceless china, and splendid furniture, can purchase good taste to guide it, and can assert itself without affording the smallest opening for a word of depreciation, or a look of contempt. If I am worth a million of money, and if I am dying to show it, I don't ask you to look at me—I ask you to look at my house.

Keeping his engagement with Mrs. Callender, Ernest discovered that riches might be lavishly and yet modestly used.

In crossing the hall and ascending the stairs, look where he might, his notice was insensibly won by proofs of the taste which is not to be purchased, and the wealth which uses but never exhibits its purse. Conducted by a man-servant to the landing on the first floor, he found a maid at the door of the boudoir waiting to announce him. Mrs. Callender advanced to welcome her guest, in a simple evening dress perfectly suited to her age. All that had looked worn and faded in her fine face, by daylight, was now softly obscured by shaded lamps. Objects of beauty surrounded her, which glowed with subdued radiance from their background of sober colour. The influence of appearances is the strongest of all outward influences, while it lasts. For the moment, the scene produced its impression on Ernest, in spite of the terrible anxieties which consumed him. Mrs. Callender, in his office, was a woman who had stepped out of her appropriate sphere. Mrs. Callender, in her own house, was a woman who had risen to a new place in his estimation.

'I am afraid you don't thank me for forcing you to keep your engagement,' she said, with her friendly tones and her pleasant smile.

'Indeed I do thank you,' he replied. 'Your beautiful house and your gracious welcome have persuaded me into forgetting my troubles—for a while.'

The smile passed away from her face. 'Then it is true ?' she said gravely.

'Only too true.'

She led him to a seat beside her, and waited to speak again until her maid had brought in the tea.

'Have you read my letter in the same

friendly spirit in which I wrote it?' she asked when they were alone again.

'I have read your letter gratefully, but——'

'But you don't know yet what I have to say. Let us understand each other before we make any objections on either side. Will you tell me what your present position is—at its worst? I can, and will, speak plainly when my turn comes, if you will honour me with your confidence. Not if it distresses you,' she added, observing him attentively.

He was ashamed of his hesitation—and he made amends for it.

'Do you thoroughly understand me?' he asked, when the whole truth had been laid before her without reserve.

She summed up the result in her own words.

'If your overdue ship returns safely, within a month from this time, you can borrow the money you want, without difficulty. If the ship is lost, you have no alternative (when the end of the month comes) but to accept a loan from me or to suspend payment. Is that the hard truth?'

'It is.'

'And the sum you require is—twenty thousand pounds?'

'Yes.'

'I have twenty times as much money as that, Mr. Lismore, at my sole disposal—on one condition.'

'The condition alluded to in your letter?'

'Yes.'

'Does the fulfilment of the condition depend in some way on any decision of mine?'

'It depends entirely on you.'

That answer closed his lips.

With a composed manner and a steady hand she poured herself out a cup of tea.

'I conceal it from you,' she said; 'but I want confidence. Here' (she pointed to the cup) 'is the friend of women, rich or poor, when they are in trouble. What I have now to say obliges me to speak in praise of myself. I don't like it—let me get it over as soon as I can. My husband was very fond of me: he had the most absolute confidence in my discretion, and in my sense of duty to him and to myself. His last words, before he died, were words that thanked me for making the happiness of his life. As soon as I had in some degree recovered, after the affliction that had fallen on me, his lawyer and executor produced a copy of his will, and said there were two clauses in it which my husband had expressed a wish that I should read. It is needless to say that I obeyed.'

She still controlled her agitation—but she was now unable to conceal it. Ernest made an attempt to spare her.

'Am I concerned in this?' he asked.

'Yes. Before I tell you why, I want to know what you would do—in a certain case which I am unwilling even to suppose. I have heard of men, unable to pay the demands made on them, who began business again, and succeeded, and in course of time paid their creditors.'

'And you want to know if there is any likelihood of my following their example?' he said. 'Have you also heard of men who have made that second effort—who have failed again—and who have doubled the debts they owed to their brethren in business who trusted them? I knew one of those men myself. He committed suicide.'

She laid her hand for a moment on his.

'I understand you,' she said. 'If ruin comes——'

'If ruin comes,' he interposed, 'a man without money and without credit can make but one last atonement. Don't speak of it now.'

She looked at him with horror.

'I didn't mean *that!*' she said.

'Shall we go back to what you read in the will?' he suggested.

'Yes—if you will give me a minute to compose myself.'

VI.

IN less than the minute she had asked for, Mrs. Callender was calm enough to go on.

'I now possess what is called a life-interest in my husband's fortune,' she said. 'The money is to be divided, at my death, among charitable institutions; excepting a certain event——'

'Which is provided for in the will?' Ernest added, helping her to go on.

'Yes. I am to be absolute mistress of the whole of the four hundred thousand pounds——' her voice dropped, and her eyes looked away from him as she spoke the next words—'on this one condition, that I marry again.'

He looked at her in amazement.

'Surely I have mistaken you,' he said. 'You mean on this one condition, that you do *not* marry again?'

'No, Mr. Lismore; I mean exactly what I have said. You now know that the recovery of your credit and your peace of mind rests entirely with yourself.'

After a moment of reflection he took her hand, and raised it respectfully to his lips.

'You are a noble woman!' he said.

She made no reply. With drooping head and downcast eyes she waited for his decision. He accepted his responsibility.

'I must not, and dare not, think of the hardship of my own position,' he said; 'I owe it to you to speak without reference to the future that may be in store for me. No man can be worthy of the sacrifice which your generous forgetfulness of yourself is willing to make. I respect you; I admire you; I thank you with my whole heart.

Leave me to my fate, Mrs. Callender—and let me go.'

He rose. She stopped him by a gesture.

'A *young* woman,' she answered, 'would shrink from saying—what I, as an old woman, mean to say now. I refuse to leave you to your fate. I ask you to prove that you respect me, admire me, and thank me with your whole heart. Take one day to think—and let me hear the result. You promise me this?'

He promised.

'Now go,' she said.

VII.

THE next morning Ernest received a letter from Mrs. Callender. She wrote to him as follows:—

'There are some considerations which I ought to have mentioned yesterday evening, before you left my house.

'I ought to have reminded you—if you consent to reconsider your decision—that the circumstances do not require you to pledge yourself to me absolutely.

'At my age, I can with perfect propriety assure you that I regard our marriage simply and solely as a formality which we must fulfil, if I am to carry out my intention of standing between you and ruin.

'Therefore—if the missing ship appears in time, the only reason for the marriage is at an end. We shall be as good friends as ever; without the encumbrance of a formal tie to bind us.

'In the other event, I should ask you to submit to certain restrictions which, remembering my position, you will understand and excuse.

'We are to live together, it is unnecessary to say, as mother and son. The marriage ceremony is to be strictly private; and you are so to arrange your affairs that, immediately afterwards, we leave England for any foreign place which you prefer. Some of my friends, and (perhaps) some of your friends, will certainly misinterpret our motives—if we stay in our own country—in a manner which would be unendurable to a woman like me.

‘ As to our future lives, I have the most perfect confidence in you, and I should leave you in the same position of independence which you occupy now. When you wish for my company, you will always be welcome. At other times, you are your own master. I live on my side of the house, and you live on yours—and I am to be allowed my hours of solitude every day, in the pursuit of musical occupations, which have been happily associated with all my past life, and which I trust confidently to your indulgence.

‘ A last word, to remind you of what you may be too kind to think of yourself.

‘ At my age, you cannot, in the course of Nature, be troubled by the society of a grateful old woman for many years. You are young enough to look forward to another marriage, which shall be something more than a mere form. Even if you meet with the happy woman in my lifetime, honestly tell me of it—and I promise to tell her that she has only to wait.

‘ In the meantime, don’t think, because I write composedly, that I write heartlessly. You pleased and interested me, when I first saw you, at the public meeting. I don’t think I could have proposed, what you call this sacrifice of myself, to a man who had personally repelled me—though I might have felt my debt of gratitude as sincerely as ever. Whether your ship is saved, or whether your ship is lost, old Mary Callender likes you—and owns it without false shame.

‘ Let me have your answer this evening, either personally or by letter—whichever you like best.’

VIII.

Mrs. Callender received a written answer long before the evening. It said much in few words:—

‘ A man impenetrable to kindness might be able to resist your letter. I am not that man. Your great heart has conquered me.’

The few formalities which precede marriage by special license were observed by Ernest. While the destiny of their future lives was still in suspense, an unacknowledged feeling of embarrassment, on either side, kept Ernest and Mrs. Callender apart. Every day brought the lady her report of the state of affairs in the City, written always in the same words : ‘ No news of the ship.’

IX.

On the day before the shipowner’s liabilities became due, the terms of the report from the City remained unchanged—and the special license was put to its contemplated use. Mrs. Callender’s lawyer and Mrs. Callender’s maid were the only persons trusted with the secret. Leaving the chief clerk in charge of the business, with every pecuniary demand on his employer satisfied in full, the strangely married pair quitted England.

They arranged to wait for a few days in Paris, to receive any letters of importance which might have been addressed to Ernest in the interval. On the evening of their arrival, a telegram from London was waiting at their hotel. It announced that the missing ship had passed up Channel—undiscovered in a fog, until she reached the Downs—on the day before Ernest’s liabilities fell due.

‘ Do you regret it?’ Mrs. Lismore said to her husband.

'Not for a moment!' he answered.

They decided on pursuing their journey as far as Munich.

Mrs. Lismore's taste for music was matched by Ernest's taste for painting. In his leisure hours he cultivated the art, and delighted in it. The picture galleries of Munich were almost the only galleries in Europe which he had not seen. True to the engagements to which she had pledged herself, his wife was willing to go wherever it might please him to take her. The one suggestion she made was, that they should hire furnished apartments. If they lived at an hotel, friends of the husband or the wife (visitors like themselves to the famous city) might see their names in the book, or might meet them at the door.

They were soon established in a house large enough to provide them with every accommodation which they required.

Ernest's days were passed in the galleries ; Mrs. Lismore remaining at home, devoted to her music, until it was time to go out with her husband for a drive. Living together in perfect amity and concord, they were nevertheless not living happily. Without any visible reason for the change, Mrs. Lismore's spirits were depressed. On the one occasion when Ernest noticed it she made an effort to be cheerful, which it distressed him to see. He allowed her to think that she had relieved him of any further anxiety. Whatever doubts he might feel were doubts delicately concealed from that time forth.

But when two people are living together in a state of artificial tranquillity, it seems to be a law of Nature that the elements of disturbance gather unseen, and that the outburst comes inevitably with the lapse of time.

In ten days from the date of their arrival at Munich the crisis came. Ernest returned later than usual from the picture-gallery, and—for the first time in his wife's ex-

perience—shut himself up in his own room.

He appeared at the dinner-hour with a futile excuse. Mrs. Lismore waited until the servant had withdrawn.

'Now, Ernest,' she said, 'it's time to tell me the truth.'

Her manner, when she said those few words, took him by surprise. She was unquestionably confused ; and, instead of looking at him, she trifled with the fruit on her plate. Embarrassed on his side, he could only answer:

'I have nothing to tell.'

'Were there many visitors at the gallery?' she asked.

'About the same as usual.'

'Any that you particularly noticed?' she went on. 'I mean, among the ladies.'

He laughed uneasily.

'You forget how interested I am in the pictures,' he said.

There was a pause. She looked up at him—and suddenly looked away again. But he saw it plainly ; there were tears in her eyes.

'Do you mind turning down the gas?' she said. 'My eyes have been weak all day.'

He complied with her request—the more readily, having his own reasons for being glad to escape the glaring scrutiny of the light.

'I think I will rest a little on the sofa,' she resumed. In the position which he occupied, his back would have been now turned on her. She stopped him when he tried to move his chair. 'I would rather not look at you, Ernest,' she said, 'when you have lost confidence in me.'

Not the words, but the tone, touched all that was generous and noble in his nature. He letf his place, and knelt beside her—and opened to her his whole heart.

'Am I not unworthy of you?' he asked when it was over.

She pressed his hand in silence.

'I should be the most ungrateful wretch living,' he said, 'if I did not think of you, and you only, now that my confession is made. We will leave Munich to-morrow—and, if resolution can help me, I will only remember the sweetest woman my eyes ever looked on as the creature of a dream.'

She hid her face on his breast, and reminded him of that letter of her writing, which had decided the course of their lives.

'When I thought you might meet the happy woman in my lifetime, I said to you, "Tell me of it—and I promise to tell *her* that she has only to wait." Time must pass, Ernest, before it can be needful to perform my promise. But you might let me see her. If you find her in the gallery to-morrow, you might bring her here.'

Mrs. Lismore's request met with no refusal. Ernest was only at a loss to know how to grant it.

'You tell me she is a copyist of pictures,' his wife reminded him. 'She will be interested in hearing of the portfolio of drawings by the great French artists which I bought for you in Paris. Ask her to come and see them, and to tell you if she can make some copies. And say, if you like, that I shall be glad to become acquainted with her.'

He felt her breath beating fast on his bosom. In the fear that she might lose all control over herself, he tried to relieve her by speaking lightly. 'What an invention yours is!' he said. 'If my wife ever tries to deceive me, I shall be a mere child in her hands.'

She rose abruptly from the sofa—kissed him on the forehead—and said wildly, 'I shall be better in bed!' Before he could move or speak, she had left him.

X.

THE next morning he knocked at the door of his wife's room, and asked how she had passed the night.

'I have slept badly,' she answered, 'and I must beg you to excuse my absence at breakfast-time.' She called him back as he was about to withdraw. 'Remember,' she said, 'when you return from the gallery to-day, I expect that you will not return alone.'

*   *   *   *   *

Three hours later he was at home again. The young lady's services as a copyist were at his disposal; she had returned with him to look at the drawings.

The sitting-room was empty when they entered it. He rang for his wife's maid—and was informed that Mrs. Lismore had gone out. Refusing to believe the woman, he went to his wife's apartments. She was not to be found.

When he returned to the sitting-room, the young lady was not unnaturally offended. He could make allowances for her being a little out of temper at the slight that had been put on her; but he was inexpressibly disconcerted by the manner—almost the coarse manner — in which she expressed herself.

'I have been talking to your wife's maid, while you have been away,' she said. 'I find you have married an old lady for her money. She is jealous of me, of course?'

'Let me beg you to alter your opinion,' he answered. 'You are wronging my wife; she is incapable of any such feeling as you attribute to her.'

The young lady laughed. 'At any rate you are a good husband,' she said satirically. 'Suppose you own the truth? Wouldn't you like her better if she was young and pretty like me?'

He was not merely surprised — he was disgusted. Her beauty had so completely fascinated him, when he first saw her, that the idea of associating any want of refinement and good breeding with such a charming creature never entered his mind. The disenchantment of him was already so complete that he was even disagreeably affected by the tone of her voice : it was almost as repellent to him as the exhibition of unrestrained bad temper which she seemed perfectly careless to conceal.

'I confess you surprise me,' he said coldly.

The reply produced no effect on her. On the contrary, she became more insolent than ever.

'I have a fertile fancy,' she went on, 'and your absurd way of taking a joke only encourages me! Suppose you could transform this sour old wife of yours, who has insulted me, into the sweetest young creature that ever lived, by only holding up your finger—wouldn't you do it?'

This passed the limits of his endurance. 'I have no wish,' he said, 'to forget the consideration which is due to a woman. You leave me but one alternative.' He rose to go out of the room.

She ran to the door as he spoke, and placed herself in the way of his going out.

He signed to her to let him pass.

She suddenly threw her arms round his neck, kissed him passionately, and whispered, with her lips at his ear, 'Oh, Ernest, forgive me! Could I have asked you to marry me for my money if I had not taken refuge in a disguise?'

XI.

WHEN he had sufficiently recovered to think, he put her back from him. 'Is there an end of the deception now ?' he asked sternly. 'Am I to trust you in your new character ?'

'You are not to be harder on me than I deserve,' she answered gently. 'Did you ever hear of an actress named Miss Max ?'

He began to understand her. 'Forgive me if I spoke harshly,' he said. 'You have put me to a severe trial.'

She burst into tears. 'Love,' she murmured, 'is my only excuse.'

From that moment she had won her pardon. He took her hand, and made her sit by him.

'Yes,' he said, 'I have heard of Miss Max, and of her wonderful powers of personation—and I have always regretted not having seen her while she was on the stage.'

'Did you hear anything more of her, Ernest ?'

'I heard that she was a pattern of modesty and good conduct, and that she gave up her profession, at the height of her success, to marry an old man.'

'Will you come with me to my room ?' she asked. 'I have something there which I wish to show you.'

It was the copy of her husband's will.

'Read the lines, Ernest, which begin at the top of the page. Let my dead husband speak for me.'

The lines ran thus :—

'My motive in marrying Miss Max must be stated in this place, in justice to her—and, I will venture to add, in justice to myself. I felt the sincerest sympathy for her position. She was without father, mother, or friends ; one of the poor forsaken children, whom the mercy of the Foundling Hospital provides with a home. Her after-life on the stage was the life of a virtuous woman: persecuted by profligates ; insulted by some of the baser creatures associated with her, to whom she was an object of envy. I offered her a home, and the protection of a father—on the only terms which the world would recognise as worthy of us. My experience of her since our marriage has been the experience of unvarying goodness, sweetness, and sound sense. She has behaved so nobly, in a trying position, that I wish her (even in this life) to have her reward. I entreat her to make a second choice in marriage, which shall not be a mere form. I firmly believe that she will choose well and wisely—that she will make the happiness of a man who is worthy of her—and that, as wife and mother, she will set an example of inestimable value in the social sphere that she occupies. In proof of the heartfelt sincerity with which I pay my tribute to her virtues, I add to this my will the clause that follows.'

With the clause that followed, Ernest was already acquainted.

'Will you now believe that I never loved till I saw your face for the first time?' said his wife. 'I had no experience to place me on my guard against the fascination— the madness some people might call it— which possesses a woman when all her heart is given to a man. Don't despise me, my dear! Remember that I had to save you from disgrace and ruin. Besides, my old stage remembrances tempted me. I had acted in a play in which the heroine did— what I have done! It didn't end with me, as it did with her in the story. *She* was

represented as rejoicing in the success of her disguise. *I* have known some miserable hours of doubt and shame since our marriage. When I went to meet you in my own person at the picture-gallery—oh, what relief, what joy I felt, when I saw how you admired me —it was not because I could no longer carry on the disguise. I was able to get hours of rest from the effort ; not only at night but in the daytime, when I was shut up in my retirement in the music-room ; and when my maid kept watch against discovery. No, my love! I hurried on the disclosure, because I could no longer endure the hateful triumph of my own deception. Ah, look at that witness against me! I can't bear even to see it !'

She abruptly left him. The drawer that she had opened to take out the copy of the will also contained the false gray hair which she had discarded. It had only that moment attracted her notice. She snatched it up, and turned to the fireplace.

Ernest took it from her, before she could destroy it. 'Give it to me,' he said.

'Why?'

He drew her gently to his bosom, and answered, 'I must not forget my old wife.'

Miss Jeromette and the Clergyman

I.

My brother, the clergyman, looked over my shoulder before I was aware of him, and discovered that the volume which completely absorbed my attention was a collection of famous Trials, published in a new edition and in a popular form.

He laid his finger on the Trial which I happened to be reading at the moment. I looked up at him; his face startled me. He had turned pale. His eyes were fixed on the open page of the book with an expression which puzzled and alarmed me.

'My dear fellow,' I said, 'what in the world is the matter with you?'

He answered in an odd absent manner, still keeping his finger on the open page.

'I had almost forgotten,' he said. 'And this reminds me.'

'Reminds you of what?' I asked. 'You don't mean to say you know anything about the Trial?'

'I know this,' he said. 'The prisoner was guilty.'

'Guilty?' I repeated. 'Why, the man was acquitted by the jury, with the full approval of the judge! What can you possibly mean?'

'There are circumstances connected with that Trial,' my brother answered, 'which were never communicated to the judge or the jury—which were never so much as hinted or whispered in court. *I* know them—of my own knowledge, by my own personal experience. They are very sad, very strange, very terrible. I have mentioned them to no mortal creature. I have done my best to forget them. You—quite innocently—have brought them back to my mind. They oppress, they distress me. I wish I had found you reading any book in your library, except *that* book!'

My curiosity was now strongly excited. I spoke out plainly.

'Surely,' I suggested, 'you might tell your brother what you are unwilling to mention to persons less nearly related to you. We have followed different professions, and have lived in different countries, since we were boys at school. But you know you can trust me.'

He considered a little with himself.

'Yes,' he said. 'I know I can trust you.' He waited a moment; and then he surprised me by a strange question.

'Do you believe,' he asked, 'that the

spirits of the dead can return to earth, and show themselves to the living?'

I answered cautiously—adopting as my own the words of a great English writer, touching the subject of ghosts.

' You ask me a question,' I said, ' which, after five thousand years, is yet undecided. On that account alone, it is a question not to be trifled with.'

My reply seemed to satisfy him.

' Promise me,' he resumed, ' that you will keep what I tell you a secret as long as I live. After my death I care little what happens. Let the story of my strange experience be added to the published experience of those other men who have seen what I have seen, and who believe what I believe. The world will not be the worse, and may be the better, for knowing one day what I am now about to trust to your ear alone.'

My brother never again alluded to the narrative which he had confided to me, until the later time when I was sitting by his death-bed. He asked if I still remembered the story of Jéromette. ' Tell it to others,' he said, ' as I have told it to you.'

I repeat it, after his death—as nearly as I can in his own words.

II.

On a fine summer evening, many years since, I left my chambers in the Temple, to meet a fellow-student, who had proposed to me a night's amusement in the public gardens at Cremorne.

You were then on your way to India; and I had taken my degree at Oxford. I had sadly disappointed my father by choosing the Law as my profession, in preference to the Church. At that time, to own the truth, I had no serious intention of following any special vocation. I simply wanted an excuse for enjoying the pleasures of a London life. The study of the Law sup-

plied me with that excuse. And I chose the Law as my profession accordingly.

On reaching the place at which we had arranged to meet, I found that my friend had not kept his appointment. After waiting vainly for ten minutes, my patience gave way, and I went into the Gardens by myself.

I took two or three turns round the platform devoted to the dancers, without discovering my fellow-student, and without seeing any other person with whom I happened to be acquainted at that time.

For some reason which I cannot now remember, I was not in my usual good spirits that evening. The noisy music jarred on my nerves, the sight of the gaping crowd round the platform irritated me, the blandishments of the painted ladies of the profession of pleasure saddened and disgusted me. I opened my cigar-case, and turned aside into one of the quiet by-walks of the Gardens.

A man who is habitually careful in choosing his cigar has this advantage over a man who is habitually careless. He can always count on smoking the best cigar in his case, down to the last. I was still absorbed in choosing *my* cigar, when I heard these words behind me—spoken in a foreign accent and in a woman's voice :

' Leave me directly, sir! I wish to have nothing to say to you.'

I turned round and discovered a little lady very simply and tastefully dressed, who looked both angry and alarmed as she rapidly passed me on her way to the more frequented part of the Gardens. A man (evidently the worse for the wine he had drunk in the course of the evening) was following her, and was pressing his tipsy attentions on her with the coarsest insolence of speech and manner. She was young and pretty, and she cast one entreating look at me as she went by, which it was not in manhood—perhaps I ought to say, in young-manhood—to resist.

I instantly stepped forward to protect her, careless whether I involved myself in a discreditable quarrel with a blackguard or not. As a matter of course, the fellow resented my interference, and my temper gave way. Fortunately for me, just as I lifted my hand to knock him down, a policeman appeared who had noticed that he was drunk, and who settled the dispute officially by turning him out of the Gardens.

I led her away from the crowd that had collected. She was evidently frightened— I felt her hand trembling on my arm—but she had one great merit: she made no fuss about it.

'If I can sit down for a few minutes,' she said in her pretty foreign accent, 'I shall soon be myself again, and I shall not trespass any farther on your kindness. I thank you very much, sir, for taking care of me.'

We sat down on a bench in a retired part of the Gardens, near a little fountain. A row of lighted lamps ran round the outer rim of the basin. I could see her plainly.

I have said that she was 'a little lady.' I could not have described her more correctly in three words.

Her figure was slight and small: she was a well-made miniature of a woman from head to foot. Her hair and her eyes were both dark. The hair curled naturally; the expression of the eyes was quiet, and rather sad; the complexion, as I then saw it, very pale; the little mouth perfectly charming. I was especially attracted, I remember, by the carriage of her head; it was strikingly graceful and spirited; it distinguished her, little as she was and quiet as she was, among the thousands of other women in the Gardens, as a creature apart. Even the one marked defect in her —a slight 'cast' in the left eye—seemed to add, in some strange way, to the quaint attractiveness of her face. I have already

spoken of the tasteful simplicity of her dress. I ought now to add that it was not made of any costly material, and that she wore no jewels or ornaments of any sort. My little lady was not rich: even a man's eye could see that.

She was perfectly unembarrassed and unaffected. We fell as easily into talk as if we had been friends instead of strangers.

I asked how it was that she had no companion to take care of her. 'You are too young and too pretty,' I said in my blunt English way, 'to trust yourself alone in such a place as this.'

She took no notice of the compliment. She calmly put it away from her as if it had not reached her ears.

'I have no friend to take care of me,' she said simply. 'I was sad and sorry this evening, all by myself, and I thought I would go to the Gardens and hear the music, just to amuse me. It is not much to pay at the gate; only a shilling.'

'No friend to take care of you?' I repeated. 'Surely there must be one happy man who might have been here with you to-night?'

'What man do you mean?' she asked.

'The man,' I answered thoughtlessly, 'whom we call, in England, a Sweetheart.'

I would have given worlds to have recalled those foolish words the moment they passed my lips. I felt that I had taken a vulgar liberty with her. Her face saddened; her eyes dropped to the ground. I begged her pardon.

'There is no need to beg my pardon,' she said. 'If you wish to know, sir—yes, I had once a sweetheart, as you call it in England. He has gone away and left me. No more of him, if you please. I am rested now. I will thank you again, and go home.'

She rose to leave me.

I was determined not to part with her in that way. I begged to be allowed to see her safely back to her own door. She hesitated. I took a man's unfair advantage of her, by appealing to her fears. I said, ' Suppose the blackguard who annoyed you should be waiting outside the gates ?' That decided her. She took my arm. We went away together by the bank of the Thames, in the balmy summer night.

A walk of half an hour brought us to the house in which she lodged—a shabby little house in a by-street, inhabited evidently by very poor people.

She held out her hand at the door, and wished me good-night. I was too much interested in her to consent to leave my little foreign lady without the hope of seeing her again. I asked permission to call on her the next day. We were standing under the light of the street-lamp. She studied my face with a grave and steady attention before she made any reply.

' Yes,' she said at last. ' I think I do know a gentleman when I see him. You may come, sir, if you please, and call upon me to-morrow.'

So we parted. So I entered—doubting nothing, foreboding nothing—on a scene in my life, which I now look back on with unfeigned repentance and regret.

III.

I AM speaking at this later time in the position of a clergyman, and in the character of a man of mature age. Remember that ; and you will understand why I pass as rapidly as possible over the events of the next year of my life—why I say as little as I can of the errors and the delusions of my youth.

I called on her the next day. I repeated my visits during the days and weeks that followed, until the shabby little house in the by-street had become a second and (I say it with shame and self-reproach) a dearer home to me.

All of herself and her story which she thought fit to confide to me under these circumstances may be repeated to you in few words.

The name by which letters were addressed to her was ' Mademoiselle Jéromette.' Among the ignorant people of the house and the small tradesmen of the neighbourhood—who found her name not easy of pronunciation by the average English tongue—she was known by the friendly nickname of ' The French Miss.' When I knew her, she was resigned to her lonely life among strangers. Some years had elapsed since she had lost her parents, and had left France. Possessing a small, very small, income of her own, she added to it by colouring miniatures for the photographers. She had relatives still living in France ; but she had long since ceased to correspond with them. ' Ask me nothing more about my family,' she used to say. ' I am as good as dead in my own country and among my own people.'

This was all—literally all—that she told me of herself. I have never discovered more of her sad story from that day to this.

She never mentioned her family name— never even told me what part of France she came from, or how long she had lived in England. That she was, by birth and breeding, a lady, I could entertain no doubt ; her manners, her accomplishments, her ways of thinking and speaking, all proved it. Looking below the surface, her character showed itself in aspects not common among young women in these days. In her quiet way, she was an incurable fatalist, and a firm believer in the ghostly reality of apparitions from the dead. Then again, in the matter of money, she had strange views of her own. Whenever my purse was in my hand, she held me resolutely at a distance from first to last. She refused to move into better apartments ; the shabby little house was clean inside, and the poor people who lived in it were kind to her—and that was enough. The most expensive present that she ever permitted me to offer her was a little enamelled ring, the plainest and cheapest thing of the kind in the jeweller's shop. In all her relations with me she was sincerity itself. On all occasions, and under all circumstances, she spoke her mind (as the phrase is) with the same uncompromising plainness.

'I like you,' she said to me; 'I respect you; I shall always be faithful to you while you are faithful to me. But my love has gone from me. There is another man who has taken it away with him, I know not where.'

Who was the other man?

She refused to tell me. She kept his rank and his name strict secrets from me. I never discovered how he had met with her, or why he had left her, or whether the guilt was his of making her an exile from her country and her friends. She despised herself for still loving him; but the passion was too strong for her—she owned it and lamented it with the frankness which was so pre-eminently a part of her character. More than this, she plainly told me, in the early days of our acquaintance, that she believed he would return to her. It might be to-morrow, or it might be years hence. Even if he failed to repent of his own cruel conduct, the man would still miss her, as something lost out of his life; and, sooner or later, he would come back.

'And will you receive him if he does come back?' I asked.

'I shall receive him,' she replied, 'against my own better judgment—in spite of my own firm persuasion that the day of his return to me will bring with it the darkest days of my life.'

I tried to remonstrate with her.

'You have a will of your own,' I said. 'Exert it, if he attempts to return to you.'

'I have no will of my own,' she answered quietly, 'where *he* is concerned. It is my misfortune to love him.' Her eyes rested for a moment on mine, with the utter self-abandonment of despair. 'We have said enough about this,' she added abruptly. 'Let us say no more.'

From that time we never spoke again of the unknown man. During the year that followed our first meeting, she heard nothing of him directly or indirectly. He might be living, or he might be dead. There came no word of him, or from him. I was fond enough of her to be satisfied with this—he never disturbed us.

IV.

THE year passed—and the end came. Not the end as you may have anticipated it, or as I might have foreboded it.

You remember the time when your letters from home informed you of the fatal termination of our mother's illness? It is the time of which I am now speaking. A few hours only before she breathed her last, she called me to her bedside, and desired that we might be left together alone. Reminding me that her death was near, she spoke of my prospects in life; she noticed my want of interest in the studies which were then supposed to be engaging my attention, and she ended by entreating me to reconsider my refusal to enter the Church.

'Your father's heart is set upon it,' she said. 'Do what I ask of you, my dear, and you will help to comfort him when I am gone.'

Her strength failed her: she could say no more. Could I refuse the last request she would ever make to me? I knelt at the bedside, and took her wasted hand in mine, and solemnly promised her the respect which a son owes to his mother's last wishes.

Having bound myself by this sacred engagement, I had no choice but to accept the sacrifice which it imperatively exacted from me. The time had come when I must tear myself free from all unworthy associations. No matter what the effort cost me, I must separate myself at once and for ever from the unhappy woman who was not, who never could be, my wife.

At the close of a dull foggy day I set forth with a heavy heart to say the words which were to part us for ever.

Her lodging was not far from the banks of the Thames. As I drew near the place the darkness was gathering, and the broad surface of the river was hidden from me in a chill white mist. I stood for a while, with my eyes fixed on the vaporous shroud that brooded over the flowing water—I stood, and asked myself in despair the one dreary question : ' What am I to say to her ?'

The mist chilled me to the bones. I turned from the river-bank, and made my way to her lodgings hard by. ' It must be done!' I said to myself, as I took out my key and opened the house door.

She was not at her work, as usual, when I entered her little sitting-room. She was standing by the fire, with her head down, and with an open letter in her hand.

The instant she turned to meet me, I saw in her face that something was wrong. Her ordinary manner was the manner of an unusually placid and self-restrained person. Her temperament had little of the liveliness which we associate in England with the French nature. She was not ready with her laugh ; and, in all my previous experience, I had never yet known her to cry. Now, for the first time, I saw the quiet face disturbed ; I saw tears in the pretty brown eyes. She ran to meet me, and laid her head on my breast, and burst into a passionate fit of weeping that shook her from head to foot.

Could she by any human possibility have heard of the coming change in my life ? Was she aware, before I had opened my lips, of the hard necessity which had brought me to the house ?

It was simply impossible ; the thing could not be.

I waited until her first burst of emotion had worn itself out. Then I asked—with an uneasy conscience, with a sinking heart —what had happened to distress her.

She drew herself away from me, sighing heavily, and gave me the open letter which I had seen in her hand.

' Read that,' she said. ' And remember I told you what might happen when we first met.'

I read the letter.

It was signed in initials only ; but the writer plainly revealed himself as the man who had deserted her. He had repented ; he had returned to her. In proof of his penitence he was willing to do her the justice which he had hitherto refused—he was willing to marry her; on the condition that she would engage to keep the marriage a secret, so long as his parents lived. Submitting this proposal, he waited to know whether she would consent, on her side, to forgive and forget.

I gave her back the letter in silence. This unknown rival had done me the service of paving the way for our separation. In offering her the atonement of marriage, he had made it, on my part, a matter of duty to *her*, as well as to myself, to say the parting words. I felt this instantly. And yet, I hated him for helping me !

She took my hand, and led me to the sofa. We sat down, side by side. Her face was composed to a sad tranquillity. She was quiet ; she was herself again.

' I have refused to see him,' she said, ' until I had first spoken to you. You have read his letter. What do you say ?'

I could make but one answer. It was my duty to tell her what my own position

was in the plainest terms.   I did my duty
—leaving her free to decide on the future
for herself.   Those sad words said, it was
useless to prolong the wretchedness of our
separation.   I rose, and took her hand for
the last time.

I see her again now, at that final moment,
as plainly as if it had happened yesterday.
She had been suffering from an affection of
the throat ; and she had a white silk handkerchief tied loosely round her neck.   She
wore a simple dress of purple merino, with
a black-silk apron over it.   Her face was
deadly pale ; her fingers felt icily cold as
they closed round my hand.

' Promise me one thing,' I said, ' before I
go.   While I live, I am your friend—if I am
nothing more.   If you are ever in trouble,
promise that you will let me know it.'

She started, and drew back from me as
if I had struck her with a sudden terror.

' Strange !' she said, speaking to herself.
' He feels as I feel.   *He* is afraid of what
may happen to me, in my life to come.'

I attempted to reassure her.   I tried to
tell her what was indeed the truth—that I
had only been thinking of the ordinary
chances and changes of life, when I spoke.

She paid no heed to me ; she came back
and put her hands on my shoulders, and
thoughtfully and sadly looked up in my face.

' My mind is not your mind in this
matter,' she said.   ' I once owned to you
that I had my forebodings, when we first
spoke of this man's return.   I may tell you
now, more than I told you then.   I believe
I shall die young, and die miserably.   If I
am right, have you interest enough still
left in me to wish to hear of it ?'

She paused, shuddering—and added these
startling words :

' You *shall* hear of it.'

The tone of steady conviction in which
she spoke alarmed and distressed me.   My
face showed her how deeply and how painfully I was affected.

' There, there !' she said, returning to her
natural manner ; ' don't take what I say too
seriously.   A poor girl who has led a lonely
life like mine thinks strangely and talks
strangely—sometimes.   Yes ; I give you
my promise.   If I am ever in trouble, I
will let you know it.   God bless you—you
have been very kind to me—good-bye !'

A tear dropped on my face as she kissed
me.   The door closed between us.   The
dark street received me.

It was raining heavily.   I looked up at
her window, through the drifting shower.
The curtains were parted : she was standing
in the gap, dimly lit by the lamp on the
table behind her, waiting for our last look
at each other.   Slowly lifting her hand, she
waved her farewell at the window, with the
unsought native grace which had charmed
me on the night when we first met.
The curtains fell again—she disappeared—
nothing was before me, nothing was round
me, but the darkness and the night.

V.

In two years from that time, I had redeemed
the promise given to my mother on her
deathbed.   I had entered the Church.

My father's interest made my first step in
my new profession an easy one.   After
serving my preliminary apprenticeship as a
curate, I was appointed, before I was thirty
years of age, to a living in the West of
England.

My new benefice offered me every advantage that I could possibly desire—with
the one exception of a sufficient income.
Although my wants were few, and although
I was still an unmarried man, I found it
desirable, on many accounts, to add to my
resources.   Following the example of other
young clergymen in my position, I determined to receive pupils who might stand in
need of preparation for a career at the

Universities. My relatives exerted themselves ; and my good fortune still befriended me. I obtained two pupils to start with. A third would complete the number which I was at present prepared to receive. In course of time, this third pupil made his appearance, under circumstances sufficiently remarkable to merit being mentioned in detail.

It was the summer vacation ; and my two pupils had gone home. Thanks to a neighbouring clergyman, who kindly undertook to perform my duties for me, I too obtained a fortnight's holiday, which I spent at my father's house in London.

During my sojourn in the metropolis, I was offered an opportunity of preaching in a church, made famous by the eloquence of one of the popular pulpit-orators of our time. In accepting the proposal, I felt naturally anxious to do my best, before the unusually large and unusually intelligent congregation which would be assembled to hear me.

At the period of which I am now speaking, all England had been startled by the discovery of a terrible crime, perpetrated under circumstances of extreme provocation. I chose this crime as the main subject of my sermon. Admitting that the best among us were frail mortal creatures, subject to evil promptings and provocations like the worst among us, my object was to show how a Christian man may find his certain refuge from temptation in the safeguards of his religion. I dwelt minutely on the hardship of the Christian's first struggle to resist the evil influence—on the help which his Christianity inexhaustibly held out to him in the worst relapses of the weaker and viler part of his nature—on the steady and certain gain which was the ultimate reward of his faith and his firmness—and on the blessed sense of peace and happiness which accompanied the final triumph. Preaching to this effect, with the fervent conviction which I really felt, I may say for myself, at least, that I did no discredit to the choice which had placed me in the pulpit. I held the attention of my congregation, from the first word to the last.

While I was resting in the vestry on the conclusion of the service, a note was brought to me written in pencil. A member of my congregation—a gentleman—wished to see me, on a matter of considerable importance to himself. He would call on me at any place, and at any hour, which I might choose to appoint. If I wished to be satisfied of his respectability, he would beg leave to refer me to his father, with whose name I might possibly be acquainted.

The name given in the reference was undoubtedly familiar to me, as the name of a man of some celebrity and influence in the world of London. I sent back my card, appointing an hour for the visit of my correspondent on the afternoon of the next day.

VI.

THE stranger made his appearance punctually. I guessed him to be some two or three years younger than myself. He was undeniably handsome ; his manners were the manners of a gentleman—and yet, without knowing why, I felt a strong dislike to him the moment he entered the room.

After the first preliminary words of politeness had been exchanged between us, my visitor informed me as follows of the object which he had in view.

' I believe you live in the country, sir ?' he began.

' I live in the West of England,' I answered.

' Do you make a long stay in London ?'

' No. I go back to my rectory to-morrow.'

' May I ask if you take pupils ?'

' Yes.'

' Have you any vacancy?'

' I have one vacancy.'

' Would you object to let me go back with you to-morrow, as your pupil?'

The abruptness of the proposal took me by surprise. I hesitated.

In the first place (as I have already said), I disliked him. In the second place, he was too old to be a fit companion for my other two pupils—both lads in their teens. In the third place, he had asked me to receive him at least three weeks before the vacation came to an end. I had my own pursuits and amusements in prospect during that interval, and saw no reason why I should inconvenience myself by setting them aside.

He noticed my hesitation, and did not conceal from me that I had disappointed him.

' I have it very much at heart,' he said, ' to repair without delay the time that I have lost. My age is against me, I know. The truth is—I have wasted my opportunities since I left school, and I am anxious, honestly anxious, to mend my ways, before it is too late. I wish to prepare myself for one of the Universities—I wish to show, if I can, that I am not quite unworthy to inherit my father's famous name. You are the man to help me, if I can only persuade you to do it. I was struck by your sermon yesterday; and, if I may venture to make the confession in your presence, I took a strong liking to you. Will you see my father, before you decide to say No? He will be able to explain whatever may seem strange in my present application; and he will be happy to see you this afternoon, if you can spare the time. As to the question of terms, I am quite sure it can be settled to your entire satisfaction.'

He was evidently in earnest—gravely, vehemently in earnest. I unwillingly consented to see his father.

Our interview was a long one. All my questions were answered fully and frankly.

The young man had led an idle and desultory life. He was weary of it, and ashamed of it. His disposition was a peculiar one. He stood sorely in need of a guide, a teacher, and a friend, in whom he was disposed to confide. If I disappointed the hopes which he had centred in me, he would be discouraged, and he would relapse into the aimless and indolent existence of which he was now ashamed. Any terms for which I might stipulate were at my disposal if I would consent to receive him, for three months to begin with, on trial.

Still hesitating, I consulted my father and my friends.

They were all of opinion (and justly of opinion so far) that the new connection would be an excellent one for me. They all reproached me for taking a purely capricious dislike to a well-born and well-bred young man, and for permitting it to influence me, at the outset of my career, against my own interests. Pressed by these considerations, I allowed myself to be persuaded to give the new pupil a fair trial. He accompanied me, the next day, on my way back to the rectory.

VII.

LET me be careful to do justice to a man whom I personally disliked. My senior pupil began well: he produced a decidedly favourable impression on the persons attached to my little household.

The women, especially, admired his beautiful light hair, his crisply-curling beard, his delicate complexion, his clear blue eyes, and his finely-shaped hands and feet. Even the inveterate reserve in his manner, and the downcast, almost sullen, look which had prejudiced *me* against him, aroused a common feeling of romantic enthusiasm in my servants' hall. It was decided, on the high authority of the housekeeper herself, that 'the new gentleman' was in love—and, more interesting still, that he was the victim of an unhappy attachment which had driven him away from his friends and his home.

For myself, I tried hard, and tried vainly, to get over my first dislike to the senior pupil.

I could find no fault with him. All his habits were quiet and regular ; and he devoted himself conscientiously to his reading. But, little by little, I became satisfied that his heart was not in his studies. More than this, I had my reasons for suspecting that he was concealing something from me, and that he felt painfully the reserve on his own part which he could not, or dared not, break through. There were moments when I almost doubted whether he had not chosen my remote country rectory, as a safe place of refuge from some person or persons of whom he stood in dread.

For example, his ordinary course of proceeding, in the matter of his correspondence, was, to say the least of it, strange.

He received no letters at my house. They waited for him at the village post-office. He invariably called for them himself, and invariably forbore to trust any of my servants with his own letters for the post. Again, when we were out walking together, I more than once caught him looking furtively over his shoulder, as if he suspected some person of following him, for some evil purpose. Being constitutionally a hater of mysteries, I determined, at an early stage of our intercourse, on making an effort to clear matters up. There might be just a chance of my winning the senior pupil's confidence, if I spoke to him while the last days of the summer vacation still left us alone together in the house.

' Excuse me for noticing it,' I said to him one morning, while we were engaged over our books—'I cannot help observing that you appear to have some trouble on your mind. Is it indiscreet, on my part, to ask if I can be of any use to you ?'

He changed colour—looked up at me quickly—looked down again at his book —struggled hard with some secret fear or secret reluctance that was in him—and suddenly burst out with this extraordinary question :

' I suppose you were in earnest when you preached that sermon in London ?'

' I am astonished that you should doubt it,' I replied.

He paused again ; struggled with himself again ; and startled me by a second outbreak, even stranger than the first.

' I am one of the people you preached at in your sermon,' he said. ' That's the true reason why I asked you to take me for your pupil. Don't turn me out ! When you talked to your congregation of tortured and tempted people, you talked of Me.'

I was so astonished by the confession, that I lost my presence of mind. For the moment, I was unable to answer him.

' Don't turn me out !' he repeated. ' Help me against myself. I am telling you the truth. As God is my witness, I am telling you the truth !'

' Tell me the *whole* truth,' I said ; 'and rely on my consoling and helping you—rely on my being your friend.'

In the fervour of the moment, I took his hand. It lay cold and still in mine : it mutely warned me that I had a sullen and a secret nature to deal with.

' There must be no concealment between us,' I resumed. ' You have entered my house, by your own confession, under false pretences. It is your duty to me, and your duty to yourself, to speak out.'

The man's inveterate reserve—cast off for the moment only—renewed its hold on him. He considered, carefully considered, his next words before he permitted them to pass his lips.

' A person is in the way of my prospects

in life,' he began slowly, with his eyes cast down on his book. 'A person provokes me horribly. I feel dreadful temptations (like the man you spoke of in your sermon) when I am in the person's company. Teach me to resist temptation! I am afraid of myself, if I see the person again. You are the only man who can help me. Do it while you can.'

He stopped, and passed his handkerchief over his forehead.

'Will that do?' he asked—still with his eyes on his book.

'It will *not* do,' I answered. 'You are so far from really opening your heart to me, that you won't even let me know whether it is a man or a woman who stands in the way of your prospects in life. You use the word "person," over and over again—rather than say "he" or "she" when you speak of the provocation which is trying you. How can I help a man who has so little confidence in me as that?'

My reply evidently found him at the end of his resources. He tried, tried desperately, to say more than he had said yet. No! The words seemed to stick in his throat. Not one of them would pass his lips.

'Give me time,' he pleaded piteously. 'I can't bring myself to it, all at once. I mean well. Upon my soul, I mean well. But I am slow at this sort of thing. Wait till to-morrow.'

To-morrow came—and again he put it off.

'One more day!' he said. 'You don't know how hard it is to speak plainly. I am half afraid; I am half ashamed. Give me one more day.'

I had hitherto only disliked him. Try as I might (and did) to make merciful allowance for his reserve, I began to despise him now.

VIII.

THE day of the deferred confession came, and brought an event with it, for which both he and I were alike unprepared. Would he really have confided in me but for that event? He must either have done it, or have abandoned the purpose which had led him into my house.

We met as usual at the breakfast-table. My housekeeper brought in my letters of the morning. To my surprise, instead of leaving the room again as usual, she walked round to the other side of the table, and laid a letter before my senior pupil—the first letter, since his residence with me, which had been delivered to him under my roof.

He started, and took up the letter. He looked at the address. A spasm of suppressed fury passed across his face; his breath came quickly; his hand trembled as it held the letter. So far, I said nothing. I waited to see whether he would open the envelope in my presence or not.

He was afraid to open it, in my presence. He got on his feet; he said, in tones so low that I could barely hear him: 'Please excuse me for a minute'—and left the room.

I waited for half an hour—for a quarter of an hour, after that—and then I sent to ask if he had forgotten his breakfast.

In a minute more, I heard his footstep in the hall. He opened the breakfast-room door, and stood on the threshold, with a small travelling-bag in his hand.

'I beg your pardon,' he said, still standing at the door. 'I must ask for leave of absence for a day or two. Business in London.'

'Can I be of any use?' I asked. 'I am afraid your letter has brought you bad news?'

'Yes,' he said shortly. 'Bad news. I have no time for breakfast.'

'Wait a few minutes,' I urged. 'Wait long enough to treat me like your friend —to tell me what your trouble is before you go.'

He made no reply. He stepped into the hall, and closed the door—then opened it again a little way, without showing himself.

'Business in London,' he repeated—as if he thought it highly important to inform me of the nature of his errand. The door closed for the second time. He was gone.

I went into my study, and carefully considered what had happened.

The result of my reflections is easily described. I determined on discontinuing my relations with my senior pupil. In writing to his father (which I did, with all due courtesy and respect, by that day's post), I mentioned as my reason for arriving at this decision :—First, that I had found it impossible to win the confidence of his son. Secondly, that his son had that morning suddenly and mysteriously left my house for London, and that I must decline accepting any further responsibility towards him, as the necessary consequence.

I had put my letter in the post-bag, and was beginning to feel a little easier after having written it, when my housekeeper appeared in the study, with a very grave face, and with something hidden apparently in her closed hand.

'Would you please look, sir, at what we have found in the gentleman's bedroom, since he went away this morning ?'

I knew the housekeeper to possess a woman's full share of that amiable weakness of the sex which goes by the name of 'Curiosity.' I had also, in various indirect ways, become aware that my senior pupil's strange departure had largely increased the disposition among the women of my household to regard him as the victim of an unhappy attachment. The time was ripe, as it seemed to me, for checking any further gossip about him, and any renewed attempts at prying into his affairs in his absence.

'Your only business in my pupil's bedroom,' I said to the housekeeper, 'is to see that it is kept clean, and that it is properly aired. There must be no interference, if you please, with his letters, or his papers, or with anything else that he has left behind him. Put back directly whatever you may have found in his room.'

The housekeeper had her full share of a woman's temper as well as of a woman's curiosity. She listened to me with a rising colour, and a just perceptible toss of the head.

'Must I put it back, sir, on the floor, between the bed and the wall ?' she inquired, with an ironical assumption of the humblest deference to my wishes. '*That's* where the girl found it when she was sweeping the room. Anybody can see for themselves,' pursued the housekeeper indignantly, 'that the poor gentleman has gone away broken-hearted. And there, in my opinion, is the hussy who is the cause of it!'

With those words, she made me a low curtsey, and laid a small photographic portrait on the desk at which I was sitting.

I looked at the photograph.

In an instant, my heart was beating wildly—my head turned giddy—the housekeeper, the furniture, the walls of the room, all swayed and whirled round me.

The portrait that had been found in my senior pupil's bedroom was the portrait of Jéromette !

IX.

I HAD sent the housekeeper out of my study. I was alone, with the photograph of the Frenchwoman on my desk.

There could surely be little doubt about the discovery that had burst upon me.

The man who had stolen his way into my house, driven by the terror of a temptation that he dared not reveal, and the man who had been my unknown rival in the by-gone time, were one and the same !

Recovering self-possession enough to realize this plain truth, the inferences that followed forced their way into my mind as a matter of course. The unnamed person who was the obstacle to my pupil's prospects in life, the unnamed person in whose company he was assailed by temptations which made him tremble for himself, stood revealed to me now as being, in all human probability, no other than Jéromette. Had she bound him in the fetters of the marriage which he had himself proposed ? Had she discovered his place of refuge in my house ? And was the letter that had been delivered to him of her writing ? Assuming these questions to be answered in the affirmative, what, in that case, was his 'business in London ?' I remembered how he had spoken to me of his temptations, I recalled the expression that had crossed his face when he recognised the handwriting on the letter—and the conclusion that followed literally shook me to the soul. Ordering my horse to be saddled, I rode instantly to the railway-station.

The train by which he had travelled to London had reached the terminus nearly an hour since. The one useful course that I could take, by way of quieting the dreadful misgivings crowding one after another on my mind, was to telegraph to Jéromette at the address at which I had last seen her. I sent the subjoined message—prepaying the reply :

'If you are in any trouble, telegraph to me. I will be with you by the first train. Answer, in any case.'

There was nothing in the way of the immediate despatch of my message. And yet the hours passed, and no answer was received. By the advice of the clerk, I sent a second telegram to the London office, requesting an explanation. The reply came back in these terms :

'Improvements in street. Houses pulled down. No trace of person named in telegram.'

I mounted my horse, and rode back slowly to the rectory.

'The day of his return to me will bring with it the darkest days of my life.' . . . 'I shall die young, and die miserably. Have you interest enough still left in me to wish to hear of it ?' . . . 'You *shall* hear of it.' Those words were in my memory while I rode home in the cloudless moonlight night. They were so vividly present to me that I could hear again her pretty foreign accent, her quiet clear tones, as she spoke them. For the rest, the emotions of that memorable day had worn me out. The answer from the telegraph-office had struck me with a strange and stony despair. My mind was a blank. I had no thoughts. I had no tears.

I was about half-way on my road home, and I had just heard the clock of a village church strike ten, when I became conscious, little by little, of a chilly sensation slowly creeping through and through me to the bones. The warm balmy air of a summer night was abroad. It was the month of July. In the month of July, was it possible that any living creature (in good health) could feel cold ? It was *not* possible—and yet, the chilly sensation still crept through and through me to the bones.

I looked up. I looked all round me.

My horse was walking along an open high-road. Neither trees nor waters were near me. On either side, the flat fields stretched away bright and broad in the moonlight.

I stopped my horse, and looked round me again.

Yes : I saw it. With my own eyes I saw it. A pillar of white mist—between five and six feet high, as well as I could judge—was moving beside me at the edge of the road, on my left hand. When I stopped, the white mist stopped. When I went on, the white mist went on. I pushed my horse to a trot—the pillar of mist was with me. I urged him to a gallop—the pillar of mist was with me. I stopped him again—the pillar of mist stood still.

The white colour of it was the white colour of the fog which I had seen over the river—on the night when I had gone to bid her farewell. And the chill which had then crept through me to the bones was the chill that was creeping through me now.

I went on again slowly. The white mist went on again slowly—with the clear bright night all round it.

I was awed rather than frightened. There was one moment, and one only, when the fear came to me that my reason might be shaken. I caught myself keeping time to the slow tramp of the horse's feet with the slow utterance of these words, repeated over and over again : 'Jéromette is dead. Jéromette is dead.' But my will was still my own : I was able to control myself, to impose silence on my own muttering lips. And I rode on quietly. And the pillar of mist went quietly with me.

My groom was waiting for my return at the rectory gate. I pointed to the mist, passing through the gate with me.

'Do you see anything there?' I said.

The man looked at me in astonishment.

I entered the rectory. The housekeeper met me in the hall. I pointed to the mist, entering with me.

'Do you see anything at my side?' I asked.

The housekeeper looked at me as the groom had looked at me.

'I am afraid you are not well, sir,' she said. 'Your colour is all gone—you are shivering. Let me get you a glass of wine.'

I went into my study, on the ground-floor, and took the chair at my desk. The photograph still lay where I had left it The pillar of mist floated round the table, and stopped opposite to me, behind the photograph.

The housekeeper brought in the wine. I put the glass to my lips, and set it down again. The chill of the mist was in the wine. There was no taste, no reviving spirit in it. The presence of the house-keeper oppressed me. My dog had followed her into the room. The presence of the animal oppressed me. I said to the woman, 'Leave me by myself, and take the dog with you.'

They went out, and left me alone in the room.

I sat looking at the pillar of mist, hovering opposite to me.

It lengthened slowly, until it reached to the ceiling. As it lengthened, it grew bright and luminous. A time passed, and a shadowy appearance showed itself in the centre of the light. Little by little, the shadowy appearance took the outline of a human form. Soft brown eyes, tender and melancholy, looked at me through the unearthly light in the mist. The head and the rest of the face broke next slowly on my view. Then the figure gradually revealed itself, moment by moment, downward and downward to the feet. She stood before me as I had last seen her, in her purple-merino dress, with the black-silk apron, with the white handkerchief tied loosely round her neck. She stood before me, in the gentle beauty that I remembered so well ; and looked at me as she had looked when she gave me her last kiss—when her tears had dropped on my cheek.

I fell on my knees at the table. I stretched out my hands to her imploringly. I said, 'Speak to me—O, once again speak to me, Jéromette.'

Her eyes rested on me with a divine compassion in them. She lifted her hand,

and pointed to the photograph on my desk, with a gesture which bade me turn the card. I turned it. The name of the man who had left my house that morning was inscribed on it, in her own handwriting.

I looked up at her again, when I had read it. She lifted her hand once more, and pointed to the handkerchief round her neck. As I looked at it, the fair white silk changed horribly in colour—the fair white silk became darkened and drenched in blood.

A moment more—and the vision of her began to grow dim. By slow degrees, the figure, then the face, faded back into the shadowy appearance that I had first seen. The luminous inner light died out in the white mist. The mist itself dropped slowly downwards—floated a moment in airy circles on the floor—vanished. Nothing was before me but the familiar wall of the room, and the photograph lying face downwards on my desk.

X.

THE next day, the newspapers reported the discovery of a murder in London. A Frenchwoman was the victim. She had been killed by a wound in the throat. The crime had been discovered between ten and eleven o'clock on the previous night.

I leave you to draw your conclusion from what I have related. My own faith in the reality of the apparition is immovable. I say, and believe, that Jéromette kept her word with me. She died young, and died miserably. And I heard of it from herself.

Take up the Trial again, and look at the circumstances that were revealed during the investigation in court. His motive for murdering her is there.

You will see that she did indeed marry him privately; that they lived together contentedly, until the fatal day when she discovered that his fancy had been caught by another woman; that violent quarrels took place between them, from that time to the time when my sermon showed him his own deadly hatred towards her, reflected in the case of another man; that she discovered his place of retreat in my house, and threatened him by letter with the public assertion of her conjugal rights; lastly, that a man, variously described by different witnesses, was seen leaving the door of her lodgings on the night of the murder. The Law—advancing no farther than this—may have discovered circumstances of suspicion, but no certainty. The Law, in default of direct evidence to convict the prisoner, may have rightly decided in letting him go free.

But *I* persist in believing that the man was guilty. *I* declare that he, and he alone, was the murderer of Jéromette. And now, you know why.

Miss Mina and the Groom

I.

I HEAR that the 'shocking story of my conduct' was widely circulated at the ball, and that public opinion (among the ladies), in every part of the room, declared I had disgraced myself.

But there was one dissentient voice in this chorus of general condemnation. You spoke, Madam, with all the authority of your wide celebrity and your high rank. You said: 'I am personally a stranger to the young lady who is the subject of remark. If I venture to interfere, it is only to remind you that there are two sides to every question. May I ask if you have waited to pass sentence, until you have heard what the person accused has to say in her own defence?'

These just and generous words produced, if I am correctly informed, a dead silence. Not one of the women who had condemned me had heard me in my own defence. Not one of them ventured to answer you.

How I may stand in the opinions of such persons as these, is a matter of perfect indifference to me. My one anxiety is to show that I am not quite unworthy of your considerate interference in my favour.

Will you honour me by reading what I have to say for myself in these pages?

I will pass as rapidly as I can over the subject of my family; and I will abstain (in deference to motives of gratitude and honour) from mentioning surnames in my narrative.

My father was the second son of an English nobleman. A German lady was his first wife, and my mother. Left a widower, he married for the second time; the new wife being of American birth. She took a stepmother's dislike to me— which, in some degree at least, I must own that I deserved.

When the newly-married pair went to the United States they left me in England, by my own desire, to live under the protection of my uncle — a General in the army. This good man's marriage had been childless; and his wife (Lady Claudia) was, perhaps on that account, as kindly ready as her husband to receive me in the character of an adopted daughter. I may add here, that I bear my German mother's Christian name, Wilhelmina. All my friends, in the days when I had friends, used to shorten this to Mina. Be my friend so far, and call me Mina, too.

After these few words of introduction, will your patience bear with me, if I try to make you better acquainted with my uncle and aunt, and if I allude to circumstances connected with my new life which had, as I fear, some influence in altering my character for the worse ?

II.

WHEN I think of the good General's fatherly kindness to me, I really despair of writing about him in terms that do justice to his nature. To own the truth, the tears get into my eyes, and the lines mingle in such confusion that I cannot read them myself. As for my relations with my aunt, I only tell the truth when I say that she performed her duties towards me without the slightest pretension, and in the most charming manner.

At nearly fifty years old, Lady Claudia was still admired, though she had lost the one attraction which distinguished her before my time — the attraction of a perfectly beautiful figure. With fine hair and expressive eyes, she was otherwise a plain woman. Her unassuming cleverness and her fascinating manners were the qualities no doubt which made her popular everywhere. We never quarrelled. Not because I was always amiable, but because my aunt would not allow it. She managed me, as she managed her husband, with perfect tact. With certain occasional checks, she absolutely governed the General. There were eccentricities in his character which made him a man easily ruled by a clever woman. Deferring to his opinion, so far as appearances went, Lady Claudia generally contrived to get her own way in the end. Except when he was at his club, happy in his gossip, his good dinners, and his whist, my excellent uncle lived under a despotism, in the happy delusion that he was master in his own house.

Prosperous and pleasant as it appeared on the surface, my life had its sad side for a young woman.

In the commonplace routine of our existence, as wealthy people in the upper rank, there was nothing to ripen the growth of any better capacities which may have been in my nature. Heartily as I loved and admired my uncle, he was neither of an age nor of a character to be the chosen depositary of my most secret thoughts, the friend of my inmost heart who could show me how to make the best and the most of my life. With friends and admirers in plenty, I had found no one who could hold this position towards me. In the midst of society I was, unconsciously, a lonely woman.

As I remember them, my hours of happiness were the hours when I took refuge in my music and my books. Out of the house, my one diversion, always welcome and always fresh, was riding. Without any false modesty, I may mention that I had lovers as well as admirers ; but not one of them produced an impression on my heart. In all that related to the tender passion, as it is called, I was an undeveloped being. The influence that men have on women, *because* they are men, was really and truly a mystery to me. I was ashamed of my own coldness — I tried, honestly tried, to copy other girls ; to feel my heart beating in the presence of the one chosen man. It was not to be done. When a man pressed my hand, I felt it in my rings, instead of my heart.

These confessions made, I have done with the past, and may now relate the events which my enemies, among the ladies, have described as presenting a shocking story.

III.

WE were in London for the season. One morning, I went out riding with my uncle, as usual, in Hyde Park.

The General's service in the army had been in a cavalry regiment—service distinguished by merits which justified his rapid rise to the high places in his profession. In the hunting-field, he was noted as one of the most daring and most accomplished riders in our county. He had always delighted in riding young and high-spirited horses; and the habit remained with him after he had quitted the active duties of his profession in later life. From first to last he had met with no accidents worth remembering, until the unlucky morning when he went out with me.

His horse, a fiery chestnut, ran away with him, in that part of the Park-ride called Rotten Row. With the purpose of keeping clear of other riders, he spurred his runaway horse at the rail which divides the Row from the grassy enclosure at its side. The terrified animal swerved in taking the leap, and dashed him against a tree. He was dreadfully shaken and injured; but his strong constitution carried him through to recovery—with the serious drawback of an incurable lameness in one leg.

The doctors, on taking leave of their patient, united in warning him (at his age, and bearing in mind his weakened leg) to ride no more restive horses. ' A quiet cob, General,' they all suggested. My uncle was sorely mortified and offended. ' If I am fit for nothing but a quiet cob,' he said bitterly, ' I will ride no more.' He kept his word. No one ever saw the General on horseback again.

Under these sad circumstances (and my aunt being no horsewoman), I had apparently no other choice than to give up riding also. But my kind-hearted uncle was not the man to let me be sacrificed to

his own disappointment. His riding-groom had been one of his soldier-servants in the cavalry regiment—a quaint sour-tempered old man, not at all the sort of person to attend on a young lady taking her riding-exercise alone. ' We must find a smart fellow who can be trusted,' said the General. ' I shall inquire at the club.'

For a week afterwards, a succession of grooms, recommended by friends, applied for the vacant place.

The General found insurmountable objections to all of them. ' I'll tell you what I have done,' he announced one day, with the air of a man who had hit on a grand discovery; ' I have advertised in the papers.'

Lady Claudia looked up from her embroidery with the placid smile that was peculiar to her. ' I don't quite like advertising for a servant,' she said. ' You are at the mercy of a stranger; you don't know that you are not engaging a drunkard or a thief.'

' Or you may be deceived by a false character,' I added, on my side. I seldom ventured, at domestic consultations, on giving my opinion unasked—but the new groom represented a subject in which I felt a strong personal interest. In a certain sense, he was to be *my* groom.

' I'm much obliged to you both for warning me that I am so easy to deceive,' the General remarked satirically. ' Unfortunately, the mischief is done. Three men have answered my advertisement already. I expect them here to-morrow to be examined for the place.'

Lady Claudia looked up from her embroidery again. ' Are you going to see them yourself ?' she asked softly. ' I thought the steward——'

' I have hitherto considered myself a better judge of a groom than my steward,' the General interposed. ' However, don't be alarmed ; I won't act on my own sole responsibility, after the hint you have given me. You and Mina shall lend me your valuable assistance, and discover whether they are thieves, drunkards, and what not, before I feel the smallest suspicion of it, myself.'

IV.

WE naturally supposed that the General was joking. No. This was one of those rare occasions on which Lady Claudia's tact —infallible in matters of importance— proved to be at fault in a trifle. My uncle's self-esteem had been touched in a tender place ; and he had resolved to make us feel it. The next morning a polite message came, requesting our presence in the library, to see the grooms. My aunt (always ready with her smile, but rarely tempted into laughing outright) did for once laugh heartily. ' It is really too ridiculous!' she said. However, she pursued her policy of always yielding, in the first instance. We went together to the library.

The three grooms were received in the order in which they presented themselves for approval. Two of them bore the ineffaceable mark of the public-house so plainly written on their villainous faces, that even I could see it. My uncle ironically asked us to favour him with our opinions. Lady Claudia answered with her sweetest smile : ' Pardon me, General—we are here to learn.' The words were nothing; but the manner in which they were spoken was perfect. Few men could have resisted that gentle influence—and the General was not one of the few. He stroked his moustache, and returned to his petticoat government. The two grooms were dismissed.

The entry of the third and last man took me completely by surprise.

If the stranger's short coat and tight trousers had not proclaimed his vocation in life, I should have taken it for granted that there had been some mistake, and that we were favoured with a visit from a gentleman unknown. He was between dark and light in complexion, with frank clear blue eyes ; quiet and intelligent, if appearances were to be trusted ; easy in his movements ; respectful in his manner, but perfectly free from servility. ' I say !' the General blurted out, addressing my aunt confidentially, ' he looks as if he would do, doesn't he ?'

The appearance of the new man seemed to have had the same effect on Lady Claudia which it had produced on me. But she got over her first feeling of surprise sooner than I did. ' You know best,' she answered, with the air of a woman who declined to trouble herself by giving an opinion.

' Step forward, my man,' said the General. The groom advanced from the door, bowed, and stopped at the foot of the table—my uncle sitting at the head, with my aunt and myself on either side of him. The inevitable questions began.

' What is your name ?'

' Michael Bloomfield.'

' Your age ?'

' Twenty-six.'

My aunt's want of interest in the proceedings expressed itself by a little weary sigh. She leaned back resignedly in her chair.

The General went on with his questions : ' What experience have you had as a groom ?'

' I began learning my work, sir, before I was twelve years old.'

' Yes! yes! I mean, what private families have you served in ?'

' Two, sir.'

' How long have you been in your two situations ?'

' Four years in the first ; and three in the second.'

The General looked agreeably surprised.

'Seven years in only two situations is a good character in itself,' he remarked. 'Who are your references?'

The groom laid two papers on the table.

'I don't take written references,' said the General.

'Be pleased to read my papers, sir,' answered the groom.

My uncle looked sharply across the table. The groom sustained the look with respectful but unshaken composure. The General took up the papers, and seemed to be once more favourably impressed as he read them. 'Personal references in each case if required, in support of strong written recommendations from both his employers,' he informed my aunt. 'Copy the addresses, Mina. Very satisfactory, I must say. Don't you think so yourself?' he resumed, turning again to my aunt.

Lady Claudia replied by a courteous bend of her head. The General went on with his questions. They related to the management of horses ; and they were answered to his complete satisfaction.

'Michael Bloomfield, you know your business,' he said, 'and you have a good character. Leave your address. When I have consulted your references, you shall hear from me.'

The groom took out a blank card, and wrote his name and address on it. I looked over my uncle's shoulder when he received the card. Another surprise ! The handwriting was simply irreproachable — the lines running perfectly straight, and every letter completely formed. As this perplexing person made his modest bow, and withdrew, the General, struck by an afterthought, called him back from the door.

'One thing more,' said my uncle. 'About friends and followers? I consider it my duty to my servants to allow them to see their relations ; but I expect them to submit to certain conditions in return——'

'I beg your pardon, sir,' the groom interposed. 'I shall not give you any trouble on that score. I have no relations.'

'No brothers or sisters?' asked the General.

'None, sir.'

'Father and mother both dead?'

'I don't know, sir.'

'You don't know ! What does that mean ?'

'I am telling you the plain truth, sir. I never heard who my father and mother were—and I don't expect to hear now.'

He said those words with a bitter composure which impressed me painfully. Lady Claudia was far from feeling it as I did. Her languid interest in the engagement of the groom seemed to be completely exhausted—and that was all. She rose, in her easy graceful way, and looked out of window at the courtyard and fountain, the house-dog in his kennel, and the box of flowers in the coachman's window.

In the meanwhile, the groom remained near the table, respectfully waiting for his dismissal. The General spoke to him sharply, for the first time. I could see that my good uncle had noticed the cruel tone of that passing reference to the parents, and thought of it as I did.

'One word more, before you go,' he said. 'If I don't find you more mercifully inclined towards my horses than you seem to be towards your father and mother, you won't remain long in my service. You might have told me you had never heard who your parents were, without speaking as if you didn't care to hear.'

'May I say a bold word, sir, in my own defence ?'

He put the question very quietly, but, at the same time, so firmly that he even surprised my aunt. She looked round from the window—then turned back again, and stretched out her hand towards the curtain, intending, as I supposed, to alter the arrangement of it. The groom went on.

' May I ask, sir, why I should care about a father and mother who deserted me ? Mind what you are about, my lady !' he cried — suddenly addressing my aunt. ' There's a cat in the folds of that curtain; she might frighten you.'

He had barely said the words, before the housekeeper's large tabby cat, taking its noonday siesta in the looped-up fold of the curtain, leaped out and made for the door.

Lady Claudia was, naturally enough, a little perplexed by the man's discovery of an animal completely hidden in the curtain. She appeared to think that a person who was only a groom had taken a liberty in presuming to puzzle her. Like her husband, she spoke to Michael sharply.

' Did you see the cat ?' she asked.

' No, my lady.'

' Then how did you know the creature was in the curtain ?'

For the first time since he had entered the room, the groom looked a little confused.

' It's a sort of presumption for a man in my position to be subject to a nervous infirmity,' he answered. ' I am one of those persons (the weakness is not uncommon, as your ladyship is aware) who know by their own unpleasant sensations when a cat is in the room. It goes a little farther than that with me. The " antipathy," as the gentlefolks call it, tells me in what part of the room the cat is.'

My aunt turned to her husband, without attempting to conceal that she took no sort of interest in the groom's antipathies.

' Haven't you done with the man yet ?' she asked.

The General gave the groom his dismissal.

' You shall hear from me in three days' time. Good-morning.'

Michael Bloomfield seemed to have noticed my aunt's ungracious manner. He looked at her for a moment with steady attention, before he left the room.

V.

' You don't mean to engage that man ?' said Lady Claudia as the door closed.

' Why not ?' asked my uncle.

' I have taken a dislike to him.'

This short answer was so entirely out of the character of my aunt, that the General took her kindly by the hand, and said:

' I am afraid you are not well.'

She irritably withdrew her hand.

' I don't feel well. It doesn't matter.'

' It does matter, Claudia. What can I do for you ?'

' Write to the man——' She paused and smiled contemptuously. ' Imagine a groom with an antipathy to cats !' she said, turning to me. ' I don't know what you think, Mina. I have a strong objection, myself, to servants who hold themselves above their position in life. Write,' she resumed, addressing her husband, ' and tell him to look for another place.'

' What objection can I make to him ?' the General asked helplessly.

' Good heavens ! . can't you make an excuse ? Say he is too young.'

My uncle looked at me in expressive silence—walked slowly to the writing-table —and glanced at his wife, in the faint hope that she might change her mind. Their eyes met—and she seemed to recover the command of her temper. She put her hand caressingly on the General's shoulder.

' I remember the time,' she said softly, ' when any caprice of mine was a command to you. Ah, I was younger then !'

The General's reception of this little advance was thoroughly characteristic of him. He first kissed Lady Claudia's hand, and then he wrote the letter. My aunt rewarded him by a look, and left the library.

' What the deuce is the matter with her ?' my uncle said to me, when we were alone. ' Do you dislike the man too ?'

' Certainly not. So far as I can judge, he appears to be just the sort of person we want.'

' And knows thoroughly well how to manage horses, my dear. What *can* be your aunt's objection to him ?'

As the words passed his lips, Lady Claudia opened the library door.

' I am so ashamed of myself,' she said sweetly. ' At my age, I have been behaving like a spoilt child. How good you are to me, General ! Let me try to make amends for my misconduct. Will you permit me ?'

She took up the General's letter, without waiting for permission ; tore it to pieces, smiling pleasantly all the while ; and threw the fragments into the waste-paper basket. ' As if you didn't know better than I do !' she said, kissing him on the forehead. ' Engage the man by all means.'

She left the room for the second time. For the second time my uncle looked at me in blank perplexity—and I looked back at him in the same condition of mind. The sound of the luncheon bell was equally a relief to both of us. Not a word more was spoken on the subject of the new groom. His references were verified ; and he entered the General's service in three days' time.

VI.

ALWAYS careful in anything that concerned my welfare, no matter how trifling it might be, my uncle did not trust me alone with the new groom when he first entered our service. Two old friends of the General accompanied me at his special request, and reported the man to be perfectly competent and trustworthy. After that, Michael rode out with me alone ; my friends among young ladies seldom caring to accompany me, when I abandoned the Park for the quiet country roads, on the north and west of London. Was it wrong in me to talk

to him on these expeditions ? It would surely have been treating a man like a brute never to take the smallest notice of him— especially as his conduct was uniformly respectful towards me. Not once, by word or look, did he presume on the position which my favour permitted him to occupy.

Ought I to blush, when I confess (though he was only a groom) that he interested me ?

In the first place, there was something romantic in the very blankness of the story of his life.

He had been left, in his infancy, in the stables of a gentleman living in Kent, near the high-road between Gravesend and Rochester. The same day, the stable-boy had met a woman running out of the yard, pursued by the dog. She was a stranger and was not well dressed. While the boy was protecting her by chaining the dog to his kennel, she was quick enough to place herself beyond the reach of pursuit.

The infant's clothing proved, on examination, to be of the finest linen. He was warmly wrapt in a beautiful shawl of some foreign manufacture, entirely unknown to all the persons present, including the master and mistress of the house. Among the folds of the shawl there was discovered an open letter, without date, signature, or address, which it was presumed the woman must have forgotten.

Like the shawl, the paper was of foreign manufacture. The handwriting presented a strongly marked character ; and the composition plainly revealed the mistakes of a person imperfectly acquainted with the English language. The contents of the letter, after alluding to the means supplied for the support of the child, announced that the writer had committed the folly of enclosing a sum of a hundred pounds in a bank-note, ' to pay expenses.' In a postscript, an appointment was made for a meeting, in six months' time, on the eastward side of London Bridge.

The stable-boy's description of the woman who had passed him showed that she belonged to the lower class. To such a person a hundred pounds would be a fortune. She had, no doubt, abandoned the child, and made off with the money.

No trace of her was ever discovered. On the day of the appointment the police watched the eastward side of London Bridge without obtaining any result. Through the kindness of the gentleman in whose stable he had been found, the first ten years of the boy's life were passed under the protection of a charitable asylum. They gave him the name of one of the little inmates who had died; and they sent him out to service before he was eleven years old. He was harshly treated, and ran away; wandered to some training-stables near Newmarket; attracted the favourable notice of the head-groom, was employed among the other boys, and liked the occupation. Growing up to manhood, he had taken service in private families as a groom. This was the story of twenty-six years of Michael's life!

But there was something in the man himself which attracted attention, and made one think of him in his absence.

I mean by this, that there was a spirit of resistance to his destiny in him, which is very rarely found in serving-men of his order. I remember accompanying the General 'on one of his periodical visits of inspection to the stable.' He was so well satisfied, that he proposed extending his investigations to the groom's own room.

'If you don't object, Michael?' he added, with his customary consideration for the self-respect of all persons in his employment. Michael's colour rose a little; he looked at me. 'I am afraid the young lady will not find my room quite so tidy as it ought to be,' he said as he opened the door for us.

The only disorder in the groom's room was produced, to our surprise, by the groom's books and papers.

Cheap editions of the English poets, translations of Latin and Greek 'classics, handbooks for teaching French and German 'without a master,' carefully written 'exercises' in both languages, manuals of short-hand, with more 'exercises' in that art, were scattered over the table, round the central object of a reading-lamp, which spoke plainly of studies by night. 'Why, what is all this?' cried the General. 'Are you going to leave me, Michael, and set up a school?' Michael answered in sad sub-missive tones. 'I try to improve myself, sir—though I sometimes lose heart and hope.' 'Hope of what?' asked my uncle. 'Are you not content to be a servant? Must you rise in the world, as the saying is?' The groom shrank a little at that abrupt question. 'If I had relations to care for me and help me along the hard ways of life,' he said, 'I might be satisfied, sir, to remain as I am. As it is, I have no one to think about but myself—and I am foolish enough sometimes to look beyond myself.'

So far, I had kept silence; but I could no longer resist giving him a word of encouragement—his confession was so sadly and so patiently made. 'You speak too harshly of yourself,' I said; 'the best and greatest men have begun like you by looking beyond themselves.' For a moment our eyes met. I admired the poor lonely fellow trying so modestly and so bravely to teach himself—and I did not care to conceal it. He was the first to look away; some suppressed emotion turned him deadly pale. Was I the cause of it? I felt myself tremble as that bold question came into my mind. The General, with one sharp glance at me, diverted the talk (not very delicately, as I thought) to the misfortune of Michael's birth.

'I have heard of your being deserted in your infancy by some woman unknown,' he said. 'What has become of the things you were wrapped in, and the letter that was found on you? They might lead to a discovery, one of these days.' The groom smiled. 'The last master I served thought of it as you do, sir. He was so good as to write to the gentleman who was first burdened with the care of me—and the things were sent to me in return.'

He took up an unlocked leather bag, which opened by touching a brass knob, and showed us the shawl, the linen (sadly faded by time), and the letter. We were puzzled by the shawl. My uncle, who had served in the East, thought it looked like a very rare kind of Persian work. We examined with interest the letter, and the fine linen. When Michael quietly remarked, as we handed them back to him, 'They keep the secret, you see,' we could only look at each other, and own there was nothing more to be said.

VII.

THAT night, lying awake thinking, I made my first discovery of a great change that had come over me. I felt like a new woman.

Never yet had my life been so enjoyable to me as it was now. I was conscious of a delicious lightness of heart. The simplest things pleased me ; I was ready to be kind to everybody, and to admire everything. Even the familiar scenery of my rides in the Park developed beauties which I had never noticed before. The enchantments of music affected me to tears. I was absolutely in love with my dogs and my birds—and, as for my maid, I bewildered the girl with presents, and gave her holidays almost before she could ask for them. In a bodily sense, I felt an extraordinary accession of strength and activity. I romped with the dear old General, and actually kissed Lady Claudia, one morning, instead of letting her kiss me as usual. My friends noticed my

new outburst of gaiety and spirit—and wondered what had produced it. I can honestly say that I wondered too ! Only on that wakeful night which followed our visit to Michael's room, did I arrive at something like a clear understanding of myself. The next morning completed the process of enlightenment. I went out riding as usual. The instant when Michael put his hand under my foot as I sprang into the saddle, his touch flew all over me like a flame. I knew who had made a new woman of me from that moment.

As to describing the first sense of confusion that overwhelmed me, even if I were a practised writer I should be incapable of doing it. I pulled down my veil, and rode on in a sort of trance. Fortunately for me, our house looked on the Park, and I had only to cross the road. Otherwise, I should have met with some accident if I had ridden through the streets. To this day, I don't know where I rode. The horse went his own way quietly—and the groom followed me.

The groom ! Is there any human creature so free from the hateful and anti-Christian pride of rank as a woman who loves with all her heart and soul, for the first time in her life ? I only tell the truth (in however unfavourable a light it may place me) when I declare that my confusion was entirely due to the discovery that I was in love. I was not ashamed of myself for being in love with the groom. I had given my heart to the *man*. What did the accident of his position matter? Put money into his pocket and a title before his name—by another accident : in speech, manners, and attainments, he would be a gentleman worthy of his wealth and worthy of his rank.

Even the natural dread of what my relations and friends might say, if they discovered my secret, seemed to be a sensation so unworthy of me and of him, that I looked round, and called to him to speak to me, and asked him questions about himself which kept him riding nearly side by side with me. Ah, how I enjoyed the gentle deference and respect of his manner as he answered me! He was hardly bold enough to raise his eyes to mine, when I looked at him. Absorbed in the Paradise of my own making, I rode on slowly, and was only aware that friends had passed and had recognised me, by seeing him touch his hat. I looked round and discovered the women smiling ironically as they rode by. That one circumstance roused me rudely from my dream. I let Michael fall back again to his proper place, and quickened my horse's pace; angry with myself, angry with the world in general—then suddenly changing, and being fool enough and child enough to feel ready to cry. How long these varying moods lasted, I don't know. On returning, I slipped off my horse without waiting for Michael to help me, and ran into the house without even wishing him 'Good-day.'

VIII.

AFTER taking off my riding-habit, and cooling my hot face with eau-de-cologne and water, I went down to the room which we called the morning-room. The piano there was my favourite instrument—and I had the idea of trying what music would do towards helping me to compose myself.

As I sat down before the piano, I heard the opening of the door of the breakfast room (separated from me by a curtained archway), and the voice of Lady Claudia asking if Michael had returned to the stable. On the servant's reply in the affirmative, she desired that he might be sent to her immediately.

No doubt, I ought either to have left the morning-room, or to have let my aunt know of my presence there. I did neither the one nor the other. Her first dislike of Michael had, to all appearance, subsided. She had once or twice actually taken opportunities of speaking to him kindly. I believed this was due to the caprice of the moment. The tone of her voice too suggested, on this occasion, that she had some spiteful object in view, in sending for him. I knew it was unworthy of me—and yet, I deliberately waited to hear what passed between them.

Lady Claudia began.

'You were out riding to-day with Miss Mina?'

'Yes, my lady.'

'Turn to the light. I wish to see people when I speak to them. You were observed by some friends of mine; your conduct excited remark. Do you know your business as a lady's groom?'

'I have had seven years' experience, my lady.'

'Your business is to ride at a certain distance behind your mistress. Has your experience taught you that?'

'Yes, my lady.'

'You were not riding behind Miss Mina —your horse was almost side by side with hers. Do you deny it?'

'No, my lady.'

'You behaved with the greatest impropriety—you were seen talking to Miss Mina. Do you deny that?'

'No, my lady.'

'Leave the room. No! come back. Have you any excuse to make?'

'None, my lady.'

'Your insolence is intolerable! I shall speak to the General.'

The sound of the closing door followed.

I knew now what the smiles meant on the false faces of those women-friends of mine who had met me in the Park. An ordinary man, in Michael's place, would have mentioned my own encouragement of him as a sufficient excuse. *He,* with the inbred delicacy and reticence of a gentleman, had taken all the blame on himself. Indignant and ashamed, I advanced to the breakfast-room, bent on instantly justifying him. Drawing aside the curtain, I was startled by a sound as of a person sobbing. I cautiously looked in. Lady Claudia was prostrate on the sofa, hiding her face in her hands, in a passion of tears.

I withdrew, completely bewildered. The extraordinary contradictions in my aunt's conduct were not at an end yet. Later in the day, I went to my uncle, resolved to set Michael right in *his* estimation, and to leave him to speak to Lady Claudia. The General was in the lowest spirits ; he shook his head ominously the moment I mentioned the groom's name. ' I dare say the man meant no harm—but the thing has been observed. I can't have you made the subject of scandal, Mina. My wife makes a point of it—Michael must go.'

' You don't mean to say that she has insisted on your sending Michael away?'

Before he could answer me, a footman appeared with a message. ' My lady wishes to see you, sir.'

The General rose directly. My curiosity had got, by this time, beyond all restraint. I was actually indelicate enough to ask if I might go with him ! He stared at me, as well he might. I persisted ; I said I particularly wished to see Lady Claudia. My uncle's punctilious good breeding still resisted me. ' Your aunt may wish to speak to me in private,' he said. ' Wait a moment, and I will send for you.'

I was incapable of waiting; my obstinacy was something superhuman. The bare idea that Michael might lose his place, through my fault, made me desperate, I suppose. ' I won't trouble you to send for me,' I persisted ; ' I will go with you at once as far as the door, and wait to hear if I may come in.' The footman was still

present, holding the door open ; the General gave way. I kept so close behind him, that my aunt saw me as her husband entered the room. ' Come in, Mina,' she said, speaking and looking like the charming Lady Claudia of every-day life. Was this the woman whom I had seen crying her heart out on the sofa hardly an hour ago ?

' On second thoughts,' she continued, turning to the General, ' I fear I may have been a little hasty. Pardon me for troubling you about it again—have you spoken to Michael yet ? No? Then let us err on the side of kindness ; let us look over his misconduct this time.'

My uncle was evidently relieved. I seized the opportunity of making my confession, and taking the whole blame on myself. Lady Claudia stopped me with the perfect grace of which she was mistress.

' My good child, don't distress yourself ! don't make mountains out of molehills !' She patted me on the cheek with two plump white fingers which felt deadly cold. ' I was not always prudent, Mina, when I was your age. Besides, your curiosity is naturally excited about a servant who is— what shall I call him ?—a foundling.'

She paused and fixed her eyes on me attentively. ' What did he tell you ?' she asked. ' Is it a very romantic story ?'

The General began to fidget in his chair. If I had kept my attention on him, I should have seen in his face a warning to me to be silent. But my interest at the moment was absorbed in my aunt. Encouraged by her amiable reception, I was not merely unsuspicious of the trap that she had set for me—I was actually foolish enough to think that I could improve Michael's position in her estimation (remember that I was in love with him !) by telling his story exactly as I have already told it in these pages. I spoke with fervour. Will you believe it ? —her humour positively changed again ! She flew into a passion with me for the first time in her life.

'Lies !' she cried. 'Impudent lies on the face of them—invented to appeal to your interest. How dare you repeat them? General ! if Mina had not brought it on herself, this man's audacity would justify you in instantly dismissing him. Don't you agree with me ?'

The General's sense of fair play roused him for once into openly opposing his wife. 'You are completely mistaken,' he said. 'Mina and I have both had the shawl and the letter in our hands—and (what was there besides ?)—ah, yes, the very linen the child was wrapped in.'

What there was in those words to check Lady Claudia's anger in its full flow, I was quite unable to understand. If her husband had put a pistol to her head, he could hardly have silenced her more effectually. She did not appear to be frightened, or ashamed of her outbreak of rage—she sat vacant and speechless, with her eyes on the General and her hands crossed on her lap. After waiting a moment (wondering as I did what it meant) my uncle rose with his customary resignation and left her. I followed him. He was unusually silent and thoughtful ; not a word passed between us. I afterwards discovered that he was beginning to fear, poor man, that his wife's mind must be affected in some way, and was meditating a consultation with the physician who helped us in cases of need.

As for myself, I was either too stupid or too innocent to feel any positive forewarning of the truth, so far. After luncheon, while I was alone in the conservatory, my maid came to me from Michael, asking if I had any commands for him in the afternoon. I thought this rather odd ; but it occurred to me that he might want some hours to himself. I made the inquiry.

To my astonishment, the maid announced that Lady Claudia had employed Michael to go on an errand for her. The nature of the errand was to take a letter to her book-seller, and to bring back the books which she had ordered. With three idle footmen in the house, whose business it was to perform such service as this, why had she taken the groom away from his work ? The question obtained such complete possession of my mind, that I actually summoned courage enough to go to my aunt. I said I had thought of driving out in my pony-carriage that afternoon, and I asked if she objected to sending one of the three indoor servants for her books in Michael's place.

She received me with a strange hard stare, and answered with obstinate self-possession, 'I wish Michael to go.' No explanation followed. With reason or without it, agreeable to me or not agreeable to me, she wished Michael to go.

I begged her pardon for interfering, and replied that I would give up the idea of driving on that day. She made no further remark. I left the room, determining to watch her. There is no defence for my conduct ; it was mean and unbecoming, no doubt. I was drawn on, by some force in me which I could not even attempt to resist. Indeed, indeed I am not a mean person by nature !

At first, I thought of speaking to Michael ; not with any special motive, but simply because I felt drawn towards him as the guide and helper in whom my heart trusted at this crisis in my life. A little considera-tion, however, suggested to me that I might be seen speaking to him, and might so do him an injury. While I was still hesitating, the thought came to me that my aunt's motive for sending him to her bookseller might be to get him out of her way.

Out of her way in the house ? No : his place was not in the house. Out of her way in the stable ? The next instant, the idea flashed across my mind of watching the stable door.

The best bedrooms, my room included, were all in front of the house. I went up to my maid's room, which looked on the court-yard; ready with my excuse, if she happened to be there. She was not there. I placed myself at the window, in full view of the stable opposite.

An interval elapsed—long or short, I cannot say which; I was too much excited to look at my watch. All I know is that I discovered her! She crossed the yard, after waiting to make sure that no one was there to see her; and she entered the stable by the door which led to that part of the building occupied by Michael. This time I looked at my watch.

Forty minutes passed before I saw her again. And then, instead of appearing at the door, she showed herself at the window of Michael's room; throwing it wide open. I concealed myself behind the window curtain, just in time to escape discovery, as she looked up at the house. She next appeared in the yard, hurrying back. I waited a while, trying to compose myself in case I met anyone on the stairs. There was little danger of a meeting at that hour. The General was at his club; the servants were at their tea. I reached my own room without being seen by anyone, and locked myself in.

What had my aunt been doing for forty minutes in Michael's room? And why had she opened the window?

I spare you my reflections on these perplexing questions. A convenient head-ache saved me from the ordeal of meeting Lady Claudia at the dinner-table. I passed a restless and miserable night; conscious that I had found my way blindly, as it were, to some terrible secret which might have its influence on my whole future life, and not knowing what to think, or what to do next. Even then, I shrank instinctively from speaking to my uncle. This was not wonderful. But I felt afraid to speak to Michael—and that perplexed and alarmed me. Considera-

tion for Lady Claudia was certainly not the motive that kept me silent, after what I had seen.

The next morning, my pale face abundantly justified the assertion that I was still ill.

My aunt, always doing her maternal duty towards me, came herself to inquire after my health before I was out of my room. So certain was she of not having been observed on the previous day—or so prodigious was her power of controlling herself—that she actually advised me to go out riding before lunch, and try what the fresh air and the exercise would do to relieve me! Feeling that I must end in speaking to Michael, it struck me that this would be the one safe way of consulting him in private. I accepted her advice, and had another approving pat on the cheek from her plump white fingers. They no longer struck cold on my skin; the customary vital warmth had returned to them. Her ladyship's mind had recovered its tranquillity.

IX.

I LEFT the house for my morning ride.

Michael was not in his customary spirits. With some difficulty, I induced him to tell me the reason. He had decided on giving notice to leave his situation in the General's employment. As soon as I could command myself, I asked what had happened to justify this incomprehensible proceeding on his part. He silently offered me a letter. It was written by the master whom he had served before he came to us; and it announced that an employment as secretary was offered to him, in the house of a gentleman who was 'interested in his creditable efforts to improve his position in the world.'

What it cost me to preserve the outward appearance of composure as I handed back the letter, I am ashamed to tell. I spoke to him with some bitterness. ' Your wishes are gratified,' I said ; ' I don't wonder that you are eager to leave your place.' He reined back his horse, and repeated my words. ' Eager to leave my place ? I am heart-broken at leaving it.' I was reckless enough to ask why. His head sank. ' I daren't tell you,' he said. I went on from one imprudence to another. ' What are you afraid of ?' I asked. He suddenly looked up at me. His eyes answered : ' *You.*'

Is it possible to fathom the folly of a woman in love ? Can any sensible person imagine the enormous importance which the veriest trifles assume in her poor little mind ? I was perfectly satisfied—even perfectly happy, after that one look. I rode on briskly for a minute or two—then the forgotten scene at the stable recurred to my memory. I resumed a foot-pace and beckoned to him to speak to me.

' Lady Claudia's bookseller lives in the City, doesn't he ?' I began.

' Yes, Miss.'

' Did you walk both ways ?'

' Yes.'

' You must have felt tired when you got back ?'

' I hardly remember what I felt when I got back—I was met by a surprise.'

' May I ask what it was ?'

' Certainly, Miss. Do you remember a black bag of mine ?'

' Perfectly.'

' When I returned from the City, I found the bag open ; and the things I kept in it— the shawl, the linen, and the letter——'

' Gone ?'

' Gone.'

My heart gave one great leap in me, and broke into vehement throbbings, which made it impossible for me to say a word more. I reined up my horse, and fixed my eyes on Michael. He was startled ; he asked if I felt faint. I could only sign to

him that I was waiting to hear more.

' My own belief,' he proceeded, ' is that some person burnt the things in my absence, and opened the window to prevent any suspicion being excited by the smell. I am certain I shut the window before I left my room. When I closed it on my return, the fresh air had not entirely removed the smell of burning ; and, what is more, I found a heap of ashes in the grate. As to the person who has done me this injury, and why it has been done, those are mysteries beyond my fathoming.—I beg your pardon, Miss, I am sure you are not well. Might I advise you to return to the house ?'

I accepted his advice, and turned back.

In the tumult of horror and amazement that filled my mind, I could still feel a faint triumph stirring in me through it all, when I saw how alarmed and how anxious he was about me. Nothing more passed between us on the way back. Confronted by the dreadful discovery that I had now made, I was silent and helpless. Of the guilty persons concerned in the concealment of the birth, and in the desertion of the infant, my nobly-born, highly-bred, irreproachable aunt now stood revealed before me as one ! An older woman than I was might have been hard put to it to preserve her presence of mind, in such a position as mine. Instinct, not reason, served me in my sore need. Instinct, not reason, kept me passively and stupidly silent when I got back to the house. ' We will talk about it to-morrow,' was all I could say to Michael, when he gently lifted me from my horse.

I excused myself from appearing at the luncheon-table ; and I drew down the blinds in my sitting-room, so that my face might not betray me when Lady Claudia's maternal duty brought her upstairs to make inquiries. The same excuse served in both cases—my ride had failed to relieve me of my headache. My aunt's brief visit led to one result which is worth mentioning. The indescribable horror of her that I felt, forced the conviction on my mind that we two could live no longer under the same roof. While I was still trying to face this alternative with the needful composure, my uncle presented himself, in some anxiety about my continued illness. I should certainly have burst out crying, when the kind and dear old man condoled with me, if he had not brought news with him which turned back all my thoughts on myself and my aunt. Michael had shown the General his letter, and had given notice to leave. Lady Claudia was present at the time. To her husband's amazement, she abruptly interfered with a personal request to Michael to think better of it, and to remain in his place !

'I should not have troubled you, my dear, on this unpleasant subject,' said my uncle, 'if Michael had not told me that you were aware of the circumstances under which he feels it his duty to leave us. After your aunt's interference (quite incomprehensible to _me_), the man hardly knows what to do. Being your groom, he begs me to ask if there is any impropriety in his leaving the difficulty to your decision. I tell you of his request, Mina; but I strongly advise you to decline taking any responsibility on yourself.'

I answered mechanically, accepting my uncle's suggestion, while my thoughts were wholly absorbed in this last of the many extraordinary proceedings on Lady Claudia's part since Michael had entered the house. There are limits—out of books and plays—to the innocence of a young unmarried woman. After what I had just heard, the doubts which had thus far perplexed me were suddenly and completely cleared up. I said to my secret self : 'She has some human feeling left. If her son goes away, she knows that they may never meet again !'

From the moment when my mind emerged from the darkness, I recovered the use of such intelligence and courage as I naturally possessed. From this point, you will find that, right or wrong, I saw my way before me, and took it.

To say that I felt for the General with my whole heart, is merely to own that I could be commonly grateful. I sat on his knee, and laid my cheek against his cheek, and thanked him for his long, long years of kindness to me. He stopped me in his simple generous way. 'Why, Mina, you talk as if you were going to leave us !' I started up, and went to the window, opening it and complaining of the heat, and so concealing from him that he had unconsciously anticipated the event that was indeed to come. When I returned to my chair, he helped me to recover myself by alluding once more to his wife. He feared that her health was in some way impaired. In the time when they had first met, she was subject to nervous maladies, having their origin in a 'calamity' which was never mentioned by either of them in later days. She might possibly be suffering again, from some other form of nervous derangement, and he seriously thought of persuading her to send for medical advice.

Under ordinary circumstances, this vague reference to a 'calamity' would not have excited any special interest in me. But my mind was now in a state of morbid suspicion. I had not heard how long my uncle and aunt had been married; but I remembered that Michael had described himself as being twenty-six years old. Bearing these circumstances in . mind, it struck me that I might be acting wisely (in Michael's interest) if I persuaded the General to speak further of what had happened, at the time when he met the woman whom an evil destiny had bestowed on him for a wife. Nothing but the consideration of serving the man I loved, would have reconciled me to making my own secret use of the recollections which my uncle might innocently confide to me. As it was, I thought the means would, in this case, be for once justified by the end. Before we part, I have little doubt that you will think so too.

I found it an easier task than I had anticipated to turn the talk back again to the days when the General had seen Lady Claudia for the first time. He was proud of the circumstances under which he had won his wife. Ah, how my heart ached for him as I saw his eyes sparkle, and the colour mount in his fine rugged face!

This is the substance of what I heard from him. I tell it briefly, because it is still painful to me to tell it at all.

My uncle had met Lady Claudia at her father's country house. She had then re-appeared in society, after a period of seclusion, passed partly in England, partly on the Continent. Before the date of her retirement, she had been engaged to marry a French nobleman, equally illustrious by his birth, and by his diplomatic services in the East. Within a few weeks of the wedding-day, he was drowned by the wreck of his yacht. This was the calamity to which my uncle had referred.

Lady Claudia's mind was so seriously affected by the dreadful event, that the doctors refused to answer for the conse-quences, unless she was at once placed in the strictest retirement. Her mother, and a French maid devotedly attached to her, were the only persons whom it was con-sidered safe for the young lady to see, until time and care had in some degree composed her. Her return to her friends and admirers, after the necessary interval of seclusion, was naturally a subject of sincere rejoicing among the guests assembled in her father's house. My uncle's interest in Lady Claudia soon developed into love. They were equals in rank, and well suited to each other in

age. The parents raised no obstacles ; but they did not conceal from their guest that the disaster which had befallen their daughter was but too likely to disincline her to receive his addresses, or any man's addresses, favourably. To their surprise, they proved to be wrong. The young lady was touched by the simplicity and the delicacy with which her lover urged his suit. She had lived among worldly people. This was a man whose devotion she could believe to be sincere. They were married.

Had no unusual circumstances occurred ? Had nothing happened which the General had forgotten ? Nothing.

X.

IT is surely needless that I should stop here, to draw the plain inferences from the events just related.

Any person who remembers that the shawl in which the infant was wrapped came from those Eastern regions which were associated with the French nobleman's diplomatic services—also, that the faults of composition in the letter found on the child were exactly the faults likely to have been committed by the French maid—any person who follows these traces can find his way to the truth as I found mine.

Returning for a moment to the hopes which I had formed of being of some service to Michael, I have only to say that they were at once destroyed, when I heard of the death by drowning of the man to whom the evidence pointed as his father. The pros-pect looked equally barren when I thought of the miserable mother. That she should openly acknowledge her son in her position, was perhaps not to be expected of any woman. Had she courage enough, or, in plainer words, heart enough to acknowledge him privately ?

I called to mind again some of the

apparent caprices and contradictions in Lady Claudia's conduct, on the memorable day when Michael had presented himself to fill the vacant place. Look back with me to the record of what she said and did on that occasion, by the light of your present knowledge, and you will see that his likeness to his father must have struck her when he entered the room, and that his statement of his age must have correctly described the age of her son. Recall the actions that followed, after she had been exhausted by her first successful efforts at self-control—the withdrawal to the window to conceal her face ; the clutch at the curtain when she felt herself sinking ; the harshness of manner under which she concealed her emotions when she ventured to speak to him ; the reiterated inconsistencies and vacillations of conduct that followed, all alike due to the protest of Nature, desperately resisted to the last—and say if I did her injustice when I believed her to be incapable of running the smallest risk of discovery at the prompting of maternal love.

There remained, then, only Michael to think of. I remembered how he had spoken of the unknown parents whom he neither expected nor cared to discover. Still, I could not reconcile it to my conscience to accept a chance outbreak of temper, as my sufficient justification for keeping him in ignorance of a discovery which so nearly concerned him. It seemed at least to be my duty to make myself acquainted with the true state of his feelings, before I decided to bear the burden of silence with me to my grave.

What I felt it my duty to do in this serious matter, I determined to do at once. Besides, let me honestly own that I felt lonely and desolate, oppressed by the critical situation in which I was placed, and eager for the relief that it would be to me only to hear the sound of Michael's voice. I sent my maid to say that I wished to speak to him immediately. The crisis was already hanging over my head. That one act brought it down.

XI.

He came in, and stood modestly waiting at the door.

After making him take a chair, I began by saying that I had received his message, and that, acting on my uncle's advice, I must abstain from interfering in the question of his leaving, or not leaving, his place. Having in this way established a reason for sending for him, I alluded next to the loss that he had sustained, and asked if he had any prospect of finding out the person who had entered his room in his absence. On his reply in the negative, I spoke of the serious results to him of the act of destruction that had been committed. 'Your last chance of discovering your parents,' I said, ' has been cruelly destroyed.'

He smiled sadly. ' You know already, Miss, that I never expected to discover them.'

I ventured a little nearer to the object I had in view.

' Do you never think of your mother?' I asked. ' At your age, she might be still living. Can you give up all hope of finding her, without feeling your heart ache?'

' If I have done her wrong, in believing that she deserted me,' he answered, 'the heart-ache is but a poor way of expressing the remorse that I should feel.'

I ventured nearer still. 'Even if you were right,' I began—' even if she did desert you——'

He interrupted me sternly. ' I would not cross the street to see her,' he said. ' A woman who deserts her child is a monster. Forgive me for speaking so, Miss ! When I see good mothers and their children, it maddens me when I think of what *my* childhood was.'

Hearing those words, and watching him attentively while he spoke, I could see that my silence would be a mercy, not a crime. I hastened to speak of other things. ' If you decide to leave us,' I said, ' when shall you go?'

His eyes softened instantly. Little by little the colour faded out of his face as he answered me.

' The General kindly said, when I spoke of leaving my place——' His voice faltered, and he paused to steady it. ' My master,' he resumed, ' said that I need not keep my new employer waiting by staying for the customary month, provided—provided you were willing to dispense with my services.'

So far, I had succeeded in controlling myself. At that reply I felt my resolution failing me. I saw how he suffered ; I saw how manfully he struggled to conceal it.

' I am not willing,' I said. ' I am sorry —very, very sorry to lose you. But I will do anything that is for your good. I can say no more.'

He rose suddenly, as if to leave the room ; mastered himself ; stood for a moment silently looking at me—then looked away again, and said his parting words.

' If I succeed, Miss Mina, in my new employment—if I get on perhaps to higher things—is it—is it presuming too much, to ask if I might, some day—perhaps when you are out riding alone—if I might speak to you—only to ask if you are well and happy——'

He could say no more. I saw the tears in his eyes ; saw him shaken by the convulsive breathings which break from men in the rare moments when they cry. He forced it back even then. He bowed to me —oh, God, he bowed to me, as if he were only my servant ! as if he were too far below me to take my hand, even at that moment ! I could have endured anything else ; I believe I could still have restrained myself

under any other circumstances. It matters little now ; my confession must be made, whatever you may think of me. I flew to him like a frenzied creature—I threw my arms round his neck—I said to him, 'Oh, Michael, don't you know that I love you?' And then I laid my head on his breast, and held him to me, and said no more.

In that moment of silence, the door of the room was opened. I started, and looked up. Lady Claudia was standing on the threshold.

I saw in her face that she had been listening—she must have followed him when he was on his way to my room. That conviction steadied me. I took his hand in mine, and stood side by side with him, waiting for her to speak first. She looked at Michael, not at me. She advanced a step or two, and addressed him in these words : ' It is just possible that *you* have some sense of decency left. Leave the room.'

That deliberate insult was all I wanted to make me completely mistress of myself. I told Michael to wait a moment, and opened my writing-desk. I wrote on an envelope the address in London of a faithful old servant, who had attended my mother in her last moments. I gave it to Michael. 'Call there to-morrow morning,' I said. ' You will find me waiting for you.'

He looked at Lady Claudia, evidently unwilling to leave me alone with her. ' Fear nothing,' I said ; ' I am old enough to take care of myself. I have only a word to say to this lady before I leave the house.' With that, I took his arm, and walked with him to the door, and said good-bye almost as composedly as if we had been husband and wife already.

Lady Claudia's eyes followed me as I shut the door again, and crossed the room to a second door which led into my bed-chamber. She suddenly stepped up to me, just as I was entering the room, and laid her hand on my arm.

'What do I see in your face?' she asked, as much of herself as of me—with her eyes fixed in keen inquiry on mine.

'You shall know directly,' I answered. 'Let me get my bonnet and cloak first.'

'Do you mean to leave the house?'

'I do.'

She rang the bell. I quietly dressed myself, to go out.—The servant answered the bell, as I returned to the sitting-room.

'Tell your master I wish to see him instantly,' said Lady Claudia.

'My master has gone out, my lady.'

'To his club?'

'I believe so, my lady.'

'I will send you with a letter to him. Come back when I ring again.' She turned to me as the man withdrew. 'Do you refuse to stay here until the General returns?'

'I shall be happy to see the General, if you will enclose my address in your letter to him.'

Replying in those terms, I wrote the address for the second time. Lady Claudia knew perfectly well, when I gave it to her, that I was going to a respectable house kept by a woman who had nursed me when I was a child.

'One last question,' she said. 'Am I to tell the General that it is your intention to marry your groom?'

Her tone stung me into making an answer which I regretted the moment it had passed my lips.

'You can put it more plainly, if you like,' I said. 'You can tell the General that it is my intention to marry *your son*.'

She was near the door, on the point of leaving me. As I spoke, she turned with a ghastly stare of horror—felt about her with her hands as if she was groping in darkness—and dropped on the floor.

I instantly summoned help. The women-servants carried her to my bed. While they were restoring her to herself, I wrote a few lines telling the miserable woman how I had discovered her secret.

'Your husband's tranquillity,' I added, 'is as precious to me as my own. As for your son, you know what he thinks of the mother who deserted him. Your secret is safe in my keeping—safe from your husband, safe from your son, to the end of my life.'

I sealed up those words, and gave them to her when she had come to herself again. I never heard from her in reply. I have never seen her from that time to this. She knows she can trust me.

And what did my good uncle say, when we next met? I would rather report what he did, when he had got the better of his first feelings of anger and surprise on hearing of my contemplated marriage. He consented to receive us on our wedding-day; and he gave my husband the appointment which places us both in an independent position for life.

But he had his misgivings. He checked me when I tried to thank him.

'Come back in a year's time,' he said. 'I will wait to be thanked till the experience of your married life tells me that I have deserved it.'

The year passed; and the General received the honest expression of my gratitude. He smiled and kissed me; but there was something in his face which suggested that he was not quite satisfied yet.

'Do you believe that I have spoken sincerely?' I asked.

'I firmly believe it,' he answered—and there he stopped.

A wiser woman would have taken the hint and dropped the subject. My folly persisted in putting another question:—

'Tell me, uncle. Haven't I proved that I was right when I married my groom?'

'No, my dear. You have only proved that you are a lucky woman!'

Mr. Lepel and the Housekeeper

FIRST EPOCH.

THE Italians are born actors.

At this conclusion I arrived, sitting in a Roman theatre — now many years since. My friend and travelling companion, Rothsay, cordially agreed with me. Experience had given us some claim to form an opinion. We had visited, at that time, nearly every city in Italy. Wherever a theatre was open, we had attended the performances of the companies which travel from place to place ; and we had never seen bad acting from first to last. Men and women, whose names are absolutely unknown in England, played (in modern comedy and drama for the most part) with a general level of dramatic ability which I have never seen equalled in the theatres of other nations. Incapable Italian actors there must be, no doubt. For my own part I have only discovered them, by ones and twos, in England ; appearing among the persons engaged to support Salvini and Ristori before the audiences of London.

On the occasion of which I am now writing, the night's performances consisted of two plays. An accident, to be presently related, prevented us from seeing more than the introductory part of the second piece. That one act—in respect of the influence which the remembrance of it afterwards exercised over Rothsay and myself—claims a place of its own in the opening pages of the present narrative.

The scene of the story was laid in one of the principalities of Italy, in the bygone days of the Carbonaro conspiracies. The chief persons were two young noblemen, friends affectionately attached to each other, and a beautiful girl born in the lower ranks of life.

On the rising of the curtain, the scene before us was the courtyard of a prison. We found the beautiful girl (called Celia as well as I can recollect) in great distress ; confiding her sorrows to the gaoler's daughter. Her father was pining in the prison, charged with an offence of which he was innocent ; and she herself was suffering the tortures of hopeless love. She was on the point of confiding her secret to her friend, when the appearance of the young noblemen closed her lips. The girls at once withdrew; and the two friends—whom I now only remember as The Marquis and The Count—

began the dialogue which prepared us for the story of the play.

The Marquis has been tried for conspiracy against the reigning Prince and his government ; has been found guilty, and is condemned to be shot that evening. He accepts his sentence with the resignation of a man who is weary of his life. Young as he is, he has tried the round of pleasures without enjoyment ; he has no interests, no aspirations, no hopes ; he looks on death as a welcome release. His friend the Count, admitted to a farewell interview, has invented a stratagem by which the prisoner may escape and take to flight. The Marquis expresses a grateful sense of obligation, and prefers being shot. ' I don't value my life,' he says ; ' I am not a happy man like you.' Upon this the Count mentions circumstances which he has hitherto kept secret. He loves the charming Celia, and loves in vain. Her reputation is unsullied ; she possesses every good quality that a man can desire in a wife —but the Count's social position forbids him to marry a woman of low birth. He is heartbroken ; and he too finds life without hope a burden that is not to be borne. The Marquis at once sees a way of devoting himself to his friend's interests. He is rich ; his money is at his own disposal ; he will bequeath a marriage portion to Celia which will make her one of the richest women in Italy. The Count receives this proposal with a sigh. ' No money,' he says, ' will remove the obstacle that still remains. My father's fatal objection to Celia is her rank in life.' The Marquis walks apart—considers a little—consults his watch—and returns with a new idea. ' I have nearly two hours of life still left,' he says. ' Send for Celia : she was here just now, and she is probably in her father's cell.' The Count is at a loss to understand what this proposal means. The Marquis explains himself. ' I ask your permission,' he resumes, ' to offer marriage to Celia—for your sake.

The chaplain of the prison will perform the ceremony. Before dark, the girl you love will be my widow. My widow is a lady of title — a fit wife for the greatest nobleman in the land.' The Count protests and refuses in vain. The gaoler is sent to find Celia. She appears. Unable to endure the scene, the Count rushes out in horror. The Marquis takes the girl into his confidence, and makes his excuses. If she becomes a widow of rank, she may not only marry the Count, but will be in a position to procure the liberty of the innocent old man, whose strength is failing him under the rigours of imprisonment. Celia hesitates. After a struggle with herself, filial love prevails, and she consents. The gaoler announces that the chaplain is waiting ; the bride and bridegroom withdraw to the prison chapel. Left on the stage, the gaoler hears a distant sound in the city, which he is at a loss to understand. It sinks, increases again, travels nearer to the prison, and now betrays itself as the sound of multitudinous voices in a state of furious uproar. Has the conspiracy broken out again ? Yes ! The whole population has risen ; the soldiers have refused to fire on the people ; the terrified Prince has dismissed his ministers, and promises a constitution. The Marquis, returning from the ceremony which has just made Celia his wife, is presented with a free pardon, and with the offer of a high place in the reformed ministry. A new life is opening before him — and he has innocently ruined his friend's prospects ! On this striking situation the drop-curtain falls.

While we were still applauding the first act, Rothsay alarmed me : he dropped from his seat at my side, like a man struck dead. The stifling heat in the theatre had proved too much for him. We carried him out at once into the fresh air. When he came to his senses, my friend entreated me to leave him, and see the end of the play. To my mind, he looked as if he might faint again.

I insisted on going back with him to our hotel.

On the next day I went to the theatre, to ascertain if the play would be repeated. The box-office was closed. The dramatic company had left Rome.

My interest in discovering how the story ended led me next to the booksellers' shops—in the hope of buying the play. Nobody knew anything about it. Nobody could tell me whether it was the original work of an Italian writer, or whether it had been stolen (and probably disfigured) from the French. As a fragment I had seen it. As a fragment it has remained from that time to this.

SECOND EPOCH.

ONE of my objects in writing these lines is to vindicate the character of an innocent woman (formerly in my service as housekeeper) who has been cruelly slandered. Absorbed in the pursuit of my purpose, it has only now occurred to me that strangers may desire to know something more than they know now of myself and my friend. 'Give us some idea,' they may say, 'of what sort of persons you are, if you wish to interest us at the outset of your story.'

A most reasonable suggestion, I admit. Unfortunately, I am not the right man to comply with it.

In the first place, I cannot pretend to pronounce judgment on my own character. In the second place, I am incapable of writing impartially of my friend. At the imminent risk of his own life, Rothsay rescued me from a dreadful death by accident, when we were at college together. Who can expect me to speak of his faults? I am not even capable of seeing them.

Under these embarrassing circumstances—and not forgetting, at the same time, that a servant's opinion of his master and his

master's friends may generally be trusted not to err on the favourable side—I am tempted to call my valet as a witness to character.

I slept badly on our first night at Rome; and I happened to be awake while the man was talking of us confidentially in the courtyard of the hotel—just under my bedroom window. Here, to the best of my recollection, is a faithful report of what he said to some friend among the servants who understood English:

'My master's well connected, you must know—though he's only plain Mr. Lepel. His uncle's the great lawyer, Lord Lepel; and his late father was a banker. Rich, did you say? I should think he *was* rich—and be hanged to him! No; not married, and not likely to be. Owns he was forty last birthday; a regular old bachelor. Not a bad sort, taking him altogether. The worst of him is, he is one of the most indiscreet persons I ever met with. Does the queerest things, when the whim takes him, and doesn't care what other people think of it. They say the Lepels have all got a slate loose in the upper story. Oh, no; not a very old family—I mean, nothing compared to the family of his friend, young Rothsay. *They* count back, as I have heard, to the ancient Kings of Scotland. Between ourselves, the ancient Kings haven't left the Rothsays much money. They would be glad, I'll be bound, to get my rich master for one of their daughters. Poor as Job, I tell you. This young fellow, travelling with us, has never had a spare five-pound note since he was born. Plenty of brains in his head, I grant you; and a little too apt sometimes to be suspicious of other people. But liberal—oh, give him his due—liberal in a small way. Tips me with a sovereign now and then. I take it—Lord bless you, I take it. What do you say? Has he got any employment? Not he! Dabbles in chemistry (experiments, and that sort of thing) by way of amusing himself ; and tells the most infernal lies about it. The other day he showed me a bottle about as big as a thimble, with what looked like water in it, and said it was enough to poison everybody in the hotel. What rot ! Isn't that the clock striking again ? Near about bedtime, I should say. Wish you good-night.'

There are our characters—drawn on the principle of justice without mercy, by an impudent rascal who is the best valet in England. Now you know what sort of persons we are ; and now we may go on again.

Rothsay and I parted, soon after our night at the theatre. He went to Civita Vecchia to join a friend's yacht, waiting for him in the harbour. I turned homeward, travelling at a leisurely rate through the Tyrol and Germany.

After my arrival in England, certain events in my life occurred, which did not appear to have any connection at the time. They led nevertheless to consequences which seriously altered the relations of happy past years between Rothsay and myself.

The first event took place on my return to my house in London. I found among the letters waiting for me, an invitation from Lord Lepel to spend a few weeks with him at his country seat in Sussex.

- I had made so many excuses, in past years, when I received invitations from my uncle, that I was really ashamed to plead engagements in London again. There was no unfriendly feeling between us. My only motive for keeping away from him took its rise in dislike of the ordinary modes of life in an English country-house. A man who feels no interest in politics, who cares nothing for field sports, who is impatient of amateur music and incapable of small talk, is a man out of his element in country society. This was my unlucky case. I went to Lord

Lepel's house sorely against my will ; longing already for the day when it would be time to say good-bye.

The routine of my uncle's establishment had remained unaltered since my last experience of it.

I found my lord expressing the same pride in his collection of old masters, and telling the same story of the wonderful escape of his picture-gallery from fire—I renewed my acquaintance with the same members of Parliament among the guests, all on the same side in politics—I joined in the same dreary amusements — I saluted the same resident priest (the Lepels are all born and bred Roman Catholics)—I submitted to the same rigidly early breakfast hour ; and inwardly cursed the same peremptory bell, ringing as a means of reminding us of our meals. The one change that presented itself was a change out of the house. Death had removed the lodge-keeper at the park-gate. His widow and daughter (Mrs. Rymer and little Susan) remained in their pretty cottage. They had been allowed by my lord's kindness to take charge of the gate.

Out walking, on the morning after my arrival, I was caught in a shower on my way back to the park, and took shelter in the lodge.

In the bygone days, I had respected Mrs. Rymer's husband as a thoroughly worthy man—but Mrs. Rymer herself was no great favourite of mine. She had married beneath her, as the phrase is, and she was a little too conscious of it. A woman with a sharp eye to her own interests ; selfishly discontented with her position in life, and not very scrupulous in her choice of means when she had an end in view: that is how I describe Mrs. Rymer. Her daughter, whom I only remembered as a weakly child, astonished me when I saw her again after the interval that had elapsed. The backward flower had bloomed into perfect health. Susan was now a lovely little modest girl of seventeen—with a natural delicacy and refinement of manner, which marked her to my mind as one of Nature's gentlewomen. When I entered the lodge she was writing at a table in a corner, having some books on it, and rose to withdraw. I begged that she would proceed with her employment, and asked if I might know what it was. She answered me with a blush, and a pretty brightening of her clear blue eyes. ' I am trying, sir, to teach myself French,' she said. The weather showed no signs of improving—I volunteered to help her, and found her such an attentive and intelligent pupil that I looked in at the lodge from time to time afterwards, and continued my instructions. The younger men among my uncle's guests set their own stupid construction on my attentions to ' the girl at the gate,' as they called her—rather too familiarly, according to my notions of propriety. I contrived to remind them that I was old enough to be Susan's father, in a manner which put an end to their jokes ; and I was pleased to hear, when I next went to the lodge, that Mrs. Rymer had been wise enough to keep these facetious gentlemen at their proper distance.

The day of my departure arrived. Lord Lepel took leave of me kindly, and asked for news of Rothsay. ' Let me know when your friend returns,' my uncle said ; ' he belongs to a good old stock. Put me in mind of him when I next invite you to come to my house.'

On my way to the train I stopped of course at the lodge to say good-bye. Mrs. Rymer came out alone. I asked for Susan.

' My daughter is not very well to-day.'

' Is she confined to her room ?'

' She is in the parlour.'

I might have been mistaken, but I thought Mrs. Rymer answered me in no very friendly way. Resolved to judge for myself, I entered the lodge, and found my poor little pupil sitting in a corner, crying.

When I asked her what was the matter, the excuse of a ' bad headache ' was the only reply that I received. The natures of young girls are a hopeless puzzle to me. Susan seemed, for some reason which it was impossible to understand, to be afraid to look at me.

' Have you and your mother been quarrelling ?' I asked.

' Oh, no !'

She denied it with such evident sincerity that I could not for a moment suspect her of deceiving me. Whatever the cause of her distress might be, it was plain that she had her own reasons for keeping it a secret.

Her French books were on the table. I tried a little allusion to her lessons.

' I hope you will go on regularly with your studies,' I said.

' I will do my best, sir—without you to help me.'

She said it so sadly that I proposed— purely from the wish to encourage her— a continuation of our lessons through the post.

' Send your exercises to me once a week,' I suggested ; ' and I will return them corrected.'

She thanked me in low tones, with a shyness of manner which I had never noticed in her before. I had done my best to cheer her—and I was conscious, as we shook hands at parting, that I had failed. A feeling of disappointment overcomes me when I see young people out of spirits. I was sorry for Susan.

THIRD EPOCH.

ONE of my faults (which has not been included in the list set forth by my valet) is a disinclination to occupy myself with my own domestic affairs. The proceedings of my footman, while I had been away from home, left me no alternative but to dismiss him on my return. With this exertion of authority my interference as chief of the household came to an end. I left it to my excellent housekeeper, Mrs. Mozeen, to find a sober successor to the drunken vagabond who had been sent away. She discovered a respectable young man—tall, plump, and rosy—whose name was Joseph, and whose character was beyond reproach. I have but one excuse for noticing such a trifling event as this. It took its place, at a later period, in the chain which was slowly winding itself round me.

My uncle had asked me to prolong my visit ; and I should probably have consented, but for anxiety on the subject of a near and dear relative—my sister. Her health had been failing since the death of her husband, to whom she was tenderly attached. I heard news of her while I was in Sussex, which hurried me back to town. In a month more, her death deprived me of my last living relation. She left no children ; and my two brothers had both died unmarried while they were still young men.

This affliction placed me in a position of serious embarrassment, in regard to the disposal of my property after my death.

I had hitherto made no will ; being well aware that my fortune (which was entirely in money) would go in due course of law to the person of all others who would employ it to the best purpose—that is to say, to my sister as my nearest of kin. As I was now situated, my property would revert to my uncle if I died intestate. He was a richer man than I was. Of his two children, both sons, the eldest would inherit his estates : the youngest had already succeeded to his mother's ample fortune. Having literally no family claims on me, I felt bound to recognise the wider demands of poverty and

misfortune, and to devote my superfluous wealth to increasing the revenues of charitable institutions. As to minor legacies, I owed it to my good housekeeper, Mrs. Mozeen, not to forget the faithful services of past years. Need I add—if I had been free to act as I pleased—that I should have gladly made Rothsay the object of a handsome bequest ? But this was not to be. My friend was a man morbidly sensitive on the subject of money. In the early days of our intercourse, we had been for the first and only time on the verge of a quarrel, when I had asked (as a favour to myself) to be allowed to provide for him in my will.

' It is because I am poor,' he explained, ' that I refuse to profit by your kindness— though I feel it gratefully.'

I failed to understand him—and said so plainly.

' You will understand this,' he resumed ; ' I should never recover my sense of degradation, if a mercenary motive on my side was associated with our friendship. Don't say it's impossible ! You know as well as I do that appearances would be against me, in the eyes of the world. Besides, I don't want money ; my own small income is enough for me. Make me your executor if you like, and leave me the customary present of five hundred pounds. If you exceed that sum I declare on my word of honour that I will not touch one farthing of it.' He took my hand, and pressed it fervently. ' Do me a favour,' he said. ' Never let us speak of this again !'

I understood that I must yield—or lose my friend.

In now making my will, I accordingly appointed Rothsay one of my executors, on the terms that he had prescribed. The minor legacies having been next duly reduced to writing, I left the bulk of my fortune to public charities.

My lawyer laid the fair copy of the will

on my table.

'A dreary disposition of property for a man of your age,' he said. 'I hope to receive a new set of instructions before you are a year older.'

'What instructions?' I asked.

'To provide for your wife and children,' he answered.

My wife and children! The idea seemed to be so absurd that I burst out laughing. It never occurred to me that there could be any absurdity in my own point of view.

I was sitting alone, after my legal adviser had taken his leave, looking absently at the newly-engrossed will, when I heard a sharp knock at the house-door which I thought I recognised. In another minute Rothsay's bright face enlivened my dull room. He had returned from the Mediterranean that morning.

'Am I interrupting you?' he asked, pointing to the leaves of manuscript before me. 'Are you writing a book?'

'I am making my will.'

His manner changed; he looked at me seriously.

'Do you remember what I said, when we once talked of your will?' he asked. I set his doubts at rest immediately—but he was not quite satisfied yet. 'Can't you put your will away?' he suggested. 'I hate the sight of anything that reminds me of death.'

'Give me a minute to sign it,' I said—and rang to summon the witnesses.

Mrs. Mozeen answered the bell. Rothsay looked at her, as if he wished to have my housekeeper put away as well as my will. From the first moment when he had seen her, he conceived a great dislike to that good creature. There was nothing, I am sure, personally repellent about her. She was a little slim quiet woman, with a pale complexion and bright brown eyes. Her movements were gentle; her voice was low;

her decent gray dress was adapted to her age. Why Rothsay should dislike her was more than he could explain himself. He turned his unreasonable prejudice into a joke—and said he hated a woman who wore slate-coloured cap-ribbons!

I explained to Mrs. Mozeen that I wanted witnesses to the signature of my will. Naturally enough—being in the room at the time—she asked if she could be one of them.

I was obliged to say No; and not to mortify her, I gave the reason.

'My will recognises what I owe to your good services,' I said. 'If you are one of the witnesses, you will lose your legacy. Send up the men-servants.'

With her customary tact, Mrs. Mozeen expressed her gratitude silently, by a look, —and left the room.

'Why couldn't you tell that woman to send the servants, without mentioning her legacy?' Rothsay asked. 'My friend Lepel, you have done a very foolish thing.'

'In what way?'

'You have given Mrs. Mozeen an interest in your death.'

It was impossible to make a serious reply to this ridiculous exhibition of Rothsay's prejudice against poor Mrs. Mozeen.

'When am I to be murdered?' I asked. 'And how is it to be done? Poison?'

'I'm not joking,' Rothsay answered. 'You are infatuated about your housekeeper. When you spoke of her legacy, did you notice her eyes?'

'Yes.'

'Did nothing strike you?'

'It struck me that they were unusually well preserved eyes for a woman of her age.'

The appearance of the valet and the footman put an end to this idle talk. The will was executed, and locked up. Our conversation turned on Rothsay's travels by sea. The cruise had been in every way successful. The matchless shores of the Mediterranean defied description; the sailing of the famous yacht had proved to be worthy of her reputation; and, to crown all, Rothsay had come back to England, in a fair way, for the first time is his life, of making money.

'I have discovered a treasure,' he announced.

'What is it?'

'It *was* a dirty little modern picture, picked up in a by-street at Palermo. It *is* a Virgin and Child, by Guido.'

On further explanation it appeared that the picture exposed for sale was painted on copper. Noticing the contrast between the rare material and the wretchedly bad painting that covered it, Rothsay had called to mind some of the well-known stories of valuable works of art that had been painted over for purposes of disguise. The price asked for the picture amounted to little more than the value of the metal. Rothsay bought it. His knowledge of chemistry enabled him to put his suspicion successfully to the test; and one of the guests on board the yacht—a famous French artist—had declared his conviction that the picture now revealed to view was a genuine work by Guido. Such an opinion as this convinced me that it would be worth while to submit my friend's discovery to the judgment of other experts. Consulted independently, these critics confirmed the view taken by the celebrated personage who had first seen the work. This result having been obtained, Rothsay asked my advice next on the question of selling his picture. I at once thought of my uncle. An undoubted work by Guido would surely be an acquisition to his gallery. I had only (in accordance with his own request) to let him know that my friend had returned to England. We might take the picture with us, when we received our invitation to Lord Lepel's house.

FOURTH EPOCH.

MY uncle's answer arrived by return of post. Other engagements obliged him to defer receiving us for a month. At the end of that time, we were cordially invited to visit him, and to stay as long as we liked.

In the interval that now passed, other events occurred—still of the trifling kind.

One afternoon, just as I was thinking of taking my customary ride in the Park, the servant appeared charged with a basket of flowers, and with a message from Mrs. Rymer, requesting me to honour her by accepting a little offering from her daughter. Hearing that she was then waiting in the hall, I told the man to show her in. Susan (as I ought to have already mentioned) had sent her exercises to me regularly every week. In returning them corrected, I had once or twice added a word of well-deserved approval. The offering of flowers was evidently intended to express my pupil's grateful sense of the interest taken in her by her teacher.

I had no reason, this time, to suppose that Mrs. Rymer entertained an unfriendly feeling towards me. At the first words of greeting that passed between us I perceived a change in her manner, which ran into the opposite extreme. She overwhelmed me with the most elaborate demonstrations of politeness and respect; dwelling on her gratitude for my kindness in receiving her, and on her pride at seeing her daughter's flowers on my table, until I made a resolute effort to stop her by asking (as if it was actually a matter of importance to me!) whether she was in London on business or on pleasure.

'Oh, on business, sir! My poor husband invested his little savings in bank stock, and I have just been drawing my dividend. I do hope you don't think my girl over-bold in venturing to send you a few flowers. She wouldn't allow me to interfere. I do assure you she would gather and arrange them with her own hands. In themselves I know they are hardly worth accepting; but if you will allow the motive to plead——'

I made another effort to stop Mrs. Rymer; I said her daughter could not have sent me a prettier present.

The inexhaustible woman only went on more fluently than ever.

'She is so grateful, sir, and so proud of your goodness in looking at her exercises. The difficulties of the French language seem as nothing to her, now her motive is to please you. She is so devoted to her studies that I find it difficult to induce her to take the exercise necessary to her health; and, as you may perhaps remember, Susan was always rather weakly as a child. She inherits her father's constitution, Mr. Lepel —not mine.'

Here, to my infinite relief, the servant appeared, announcing that my horse was at the door.

Mrs. Rymer opened her mouth. I saw a coming flood of apologies on the point of pouring out—and seized my hat on the spot. I declared I had an appointment; I sent kind remembrances to Susan (pitying her for having such a mother with my whole heart); I said I hoped to return to my uncle's house soon, and to continue the French lessons. The one thing more that I remember was finding myself safe in the saddle, and out of the reach of Mrs. Rymer's tongue.

Reflecting on what had passed, it was plain to me that this woman had some private end in view, and that my abrupt departure had prevented her from finding the way to it. What motive could she possibly have for that obstinate persistence in presenting poor Susan under a favourable aspect, to a man who had already shown that he was honestly interested in her pretty modest daughter? I tried hard to penetrate the mystery—and gave it up in despair.

Three days before the date at which Rothsay and I were to pay our visit to Lord Lepel, I found myself compelled to undergo one of the minor miseries of human life. In other words, I became one of the guests at a large dinner-party. It was a rainy day in October. My position at the table placed me between a window that was open, and a door that was hardly ever shut. I went to bed shivering; and woke the next morning with a headache and a difficulty in breathing. On consulting the doctor, I found that I was suffering from an attack of bronchitis. There was no reason to be alarmed. If I remained indoors, and submitted to the necessary treatment, I might hope to keep my engagement with my uncle in ten days or a fortnight.

There was no alternative but to submit. I accordingly arranged with Rothsay that he should present himself at Lord Lepel's house (taking the picture with him), on the date appointed for our visit, and that I should follow as soon as I was well enough to travel.

On the day when he was to leave London, my friend kindly came to keep me company for awhile. He was followed into my room by Mrs. Mozeen, with a bottle of medicine in her hand. This worthy creature, finding that the doctor's directions occasionally escaped my memory, devoted herself to the duty of administering the remedies at the prescribed intervals of time. When she left the room, having performed her duties as usual, I saw Rothsay's eyes follow her to the door with an expression of sardonic curiosity. He put a strange question to me as soon as we were alone.

'Who engaged that new servant of yours?' he asked. 'I mean the fat fellow, with the curly flaxen hair.'

'Hiring servants,' I replied, 'is not much in my way. I left the engagement of the new man to Mrs. Mozeen.'

Rothsay walked gravely up to my bed-side.

'Lepel,' he said, 'your respectable house-keeper is in love with the fat young foot-man.'

It is not easy to amuse a man suffering from bronchitis. But this new outbreak of absurdity was more than I could resist, even with a mustard-plaster on my chest.

'I thought I should raise your spirits,' Rothsay proceeded. 'When I came to your house this morning, the valet opened the door to me. I expressed my surprise at his condescending to take that trouble. He informed me that Joseph was otherwise engaged. "With anybody in particular?" I asked, humouring the joke. "Yes, sir, with the housekeeper. She's teaching him how to brush his hair, so as to show off his good looks to the best advantage." Make up your mind, my friend, to lose Mrs. Mozeen—especially if she happens to have any money.'

'Nonsense, Rothsay! The poor woman is old enough to be Joseph's mother.'

'My good fellow, that won't make any difference to Joseph. In the days when we were rich enough to keep a manservant, our footman—as handsome a fellow as ever you saw, and no older than I am—married a witch with a lame leg. When I asked him why he had made such a fool of himself he looked quite indignant, and said, "Sir! she has got six hundred pounds." He and the witch keep a public-house. What will you bet me that we don't see your housekeeper drawing beer at the bar, and Joseph getting drunk in the parlour, before we are a year older?'

I was not well enough to prolong my enjoyment of Rothsay's boyish humour. Besides, exaggeration to be really amusing must have some relation, no matter how slender it may be, to the truth. My house-keeper belonged to a respectable family, and was essentially a person accustomed to re-spect herself. Her brother occupied a posi-tion of responsibility in the establishment of a firm of chemists whom I had employed for years past. Her late husband had farmed his own land, and had owed his ruin to calamities for which he was in no way responsible. Kind-hearted Mrs. Mozeen was just the woman to take a motherly interest in a well-disposed lad like Joseph; and it was equally characteristic of my valet—especially when Rothsay was thoughtless enough to encourage him—to pervert an innocent action for the sake of indulging in a stupid jest. I took advan-tage of my privilege as an invalid, and changed the subject.

A week passed. I had expected to hear from Rothsay. To my surprise and disap-pointment no letter arrived.

Susan was more considerate. She wrote, very modestly and prettily, to say that she and her mother had heard of my illness from Mr. Rothsay, and to express the hope that I should soon be restored to health. A few days later, Mrs. Rymer's politeness carried her to the length of taking the journey to London, to make inquiries at my door. I did not see her, of course. She left word that she would have the honour of calling again.

The second week followed. I had by that time perfectly recovered from my attack of bronchitis—and yet I was too ill to leave the house.

The doctor himself seemed to be at a loss to understand the symptoms that now presented themselves. A vile sensation of nausea tried my endurance, and an incom-prehensible prostration of strength depressed my spirits. I felt such a strange reluctance to exert myself, that I actually left it to Mrs. Mozeen to write to my uncle in my name, and say that I was not yet well enough to visit him. My medical adviser tried various methods of treatment; my housekeeper administered the prescribed medicines with unremitting care; but nothing came of it. A physician of great authority was called into consultation. Being completely puzzled, he retreated to the last refuge of bewildered doctors. I asked him what was the matter with me. And he answered:

'Suppressed gout.'

FIFTH EPOCH.

MIDWAY in the third week, my uncle wrote to me as follows:

'I have been obliged to request your friend Rothsay to bring his visit to a conclusion. Although he refuses to confess it, I have reason to believe that he has committed the folly of falling seriously in love with the young girl at my lodge gate. I have tried remonstrance in vain; and I write to his father at the same time that I write to you. There is much more that I might say. I reserve it for the time when I hope to have the pleasure of seeing you, restored to health.'

Two days after the receipt of this alarming letter, Rothsay returned to me.

Ill as I was, I forgot my sufferings the moment I looked at him. Wild and haggard, he stared at me with bloodshot eyes like a man demented.

'Do you think I am mad? I dare say I am. I can't live without her.' Those were the first words he said when we shook hands.

But I had more influence over him than any other person; and, weak as I was, I exerted it. Little by little, he became more reasonable; he began to speak like his old self again.

To have expressed any surprise, on my part, at what had happened, would have been not only imprudent, but unworthy of

him and of me. My first inquiry was suggested by the fear that he might have been hurried into openly confessing his passion to Susan—although his position forbade him to offer marriage. I had done him an injustice. His honourable nature had shrunk from the cruelty of raising hopes, which, for all he knew to the contrary, might never be realized. At the same time, he had his reasons for believing that he was at least personally acceptable to her.

'She was always glad to see me,' said poor Rothsay. 'We constantly talked of you. She spoke of your kindness so prettily and so gratefully. Oh, Lepel, it is not her beauty only that has won my heart! Her nature is the nature of an angel.'

His voice failed him. For the first time in my remembrance of our long companionship, he burst into tears.

I was so shocked and distressed that I had the greatest difficulty in preserving my own self-control. In the effort to comfort him, I asked if he had ventured to confide in his father.

'You are the favourite son,' I reminded him. 'Is there no gleam of hope in the future?'

He had written to his father. In silence he gave me the letter in reply.

It was expressed with a moderation which I had hardly dared to expect. Mr. Rothsay the elder admitted that he had himself married for love, and that his wife's rank in the social scale (although higher than Susan's) had not been equal to his own.

'In such a family as ours,' he wrote— perhaps with pardonable pride—'we raise our wives to our own degree. But this young person labours under a double disadvantage. She is obscure, and she is poor. What have you to offer her? Nothing. And what have I to give you? Nothing'

This meant, as I interpreted it, that the

main obstacle in the way was Susan's poverty. And I was rich! In the excitement that possessed me, I followed the impulse of the moment headlong, like a child.

'While you were away from me,' I said to Rothsay, 'did you never once think of your old friend? Must I remind you that I can make Susan your wife with one stroke of my pen?' He looked at me in silent surprise. I took my cheque-book from the drawer of the table, and placed the inkstand within reach. 'Susan's marriage portion,' I said, 'is a matter of a line of writing, with my name at the end of it.'

He burst out with an exclamation that stopped me, just as my pen touched the paper.

'Good heavens!' he cried, 'you are thinking of that play we saw at Rome! Are we on the stage? Are you performing the part of the Marquis—and am I the Count?'

I was so startled by this wild allusion to the past—I recognised with such astonishment the reproduction of one of the dramatic situations in the play, at a crisis in his life and mine—that the use of the pen remained suspended in my hand. For the first time in my life, I was conscious of a sensation which resembled superstitious dread.

Rothsay recovered himself first. He misinterpreted what was passing in my mind.

'Don't think me ungrateful,' he said. 'You dear, kind, good fellow, consider for a moment, and you will see that it can't be. What would be said of her and of me, if you made Susan rich with your money, and if I married her? The poor innocent would be called your cast-off mistress. People would say, "He has behaved liberally to her, and his needy friend has taken advantage of it."'

The point of view which I had failed to see was put with terrible directness of expression: the conviction that I was wrong was literally forced on me. What reply could I make? Rothsay evidently felt for me.

'You are ill,' he said gently; 'let me leave you to rest.'

He held out his hand to say good-bye. I insisted on his taking up his abode with me, for the present at least. Ordinary persuasion failed to induce him to yield. I put it on selfish grounds next.

'You have noticed that I am ill,' I said; 'I want you to keep me company.'

He gave way directly.

Through the wakeful night, I tried to consider what moral remedies might be within our reach. The one useful conclusion at which I could arrive was to induce Rothsay to try what absence and change might do to compose his mind. To advise him to travel alone was out of the question. I wrote to his one other old friend besides myself—the friend who had taken him on a cruise in the Mediterranean.

The owner of the yacht had that very day given directions to have his vessel laid up for the winter season. He at once countermanded the order by telegraph. "I am an idle man," he said, "and I am as fond of Rothsay as you are. I will take him wherever he likes to go." It was not easy to persuade the object of these kind intentions to profit by them. Nothing that I could say roused him. I spoke to him of his picture. He had left it at my uncle's house, and neither knew nor cared to know whether it had been sold or not. The one consideration which ultimately influenced Rothsay was presented by the doctor; speaking as follows (to quote his own explanation) in the interests of my health:—

'I warned your friend,' he said, 'that his conduct was causing anxiety which you were not strong enough to bear. On hearing this he at once promised to follow the advice which you had given to him, and to join the yacht. As you know, he has kept his word. May I ask if he has ever followed the medical profession?'

Replying in the negative, I begged the doctor to tell me why he had put his question.

He answered, ' Mr. Rothsay requested me to tell him all that I knew about your illness. I complied, of course ; mentioning that I had lately adopted a new method of treatment, and that I had every reason to feel confident of the results. He was so interested in the symptoms of your illness, and in the remedies being tried, that he took notes in his pocket-book of what I had said. When he paid me that compliment, I thought it possible that I might be speaking to a colleague.'

I was pleased to hear of my friend's anxiety for my recovery. If I had been in better health, I might have asked myself what reason he could have had for making those entries in his pocket-book.

Three days later, another proof reached me of Rothsay's anxiety for my welfare.

The owner of the yacht wrote to beg that I would send him a report of my health, addressed to a port on the south coast of England, to which they were then bound. ' If we don't hear good news,' he added, ' I have reason to fear that Rothsay will overthrow our plans for the recovery of his peace of mind by leaving the vessel, and making his own inquiries at your bedside.'

With no small difficulty I roused myself sufficiently to write a few words with my own hand. They were words that lied—for my poor friend's sake. In a postscript, I begged my correspondent to let me hear if the effect produced on Rothsay had answered to our hopes and expectations.

SIXTH EPOCH.

THE weary days followed each other—and

time failed to justify the doctor's confidence in his new remedies. I grew weaker and weaker.

My uncle came to see me. He was so alarmed that he insisted on a consultation being held with his own physician. Another great authority was called in, at the same time, by the urgent request of my own medical man. These distinguished persons held more than one privy council, before they would consent to give a positive opinion. It was an evasive opinion (encumbered with hard words of Greek and Roman origin) when it was at last pronounced. I waited until they had taken their leave, and then appealed to my own doctor. ' What do those men really think?' I asked. ' Shall I live, or die ?'

The doctor answered for himself as well as for his illustrious colleagues. ' We have great faith in the new prescriptions,' he said.

I understood what that meant. They were afraid to tell me the truth. I insisted on the truth.

' How long shall I live ?' I said. ' Till the end of the year ?'

The reply followed in one terrible word : ' Perhaps.'

It was then the first week in December. I understood that I might reckon—at the utmost—on three weeks of life. What I felt, on arriving at this conclusion, I shall not say. It is the one secret I keep from the readers of these lines.

The next day, Mrs. Rymer called once more to make inquiries. Not satisfied with the servant's report, she entreated that I would consent to see her. My housekeeper, with her customary kindness, undertook to convey the message. If she had been a wicked woman, would she have acted in this way ? ' Mrs. Rymer seems to be sadly distressed,' she pleaded. ' As I understand, sir, she is suffering under some domestic anxiety which can only be mentioned to yourself.'

Did this anxiety relate to Susan ? The bare doubt of it decided me. I consented to see Mrs. Rymer. Feeling it necessary to control her in the use of her tongue, I spoke the moment the door was opened.

' I am suffering from illness ; and I must ask you to spare me as much as possible. What do you wish to say to me ?'

The tone in which I addressed Mrs. Rymer would have offended a more sensitive woman. The truth is, she had chosen an unfortunate time for her visit. There were fluctuations in the progress of my malady : there were days when I felt better, and days when I felt worse—and this was a bad day. Moreover, my uncle had tried my temper that morning. He had called to see me, on his way to winter in the south of France by his physician's advice ; and he recommended a trial of change of air in my case also. His country house (only thirty miles from London) was entirely at my disposal ; and the railway supplied beds for invalids. It was useless to answer that I was not equal to the effort. He reminded me that I had exerted myself to leave my bedchamber for my arm-chair in the next room, and that a little additional resolution would enable me to follow his advice. We parted in a state of irritation on either side which, so far as I was concerned, had not subsided yet.

' I wish to speak to you, sir, about my daughter,' Mrs. Rymer answered.

The mere allusion to Susan had its composing effect on me. I said kindly that I hoped she was well.

' Well in body,' Mrs. Rymer announced. ' Far from it, sir, in mind.'

Before I could ask what this meant, we were interrupted by the appearance of the servant, bringing the letters which had arrived for me by the afternoon post. I

told the man, impatiently, to put them on the table at my side.

' What is distressing Susan ?' I inquired, without stopping to look at the letters.

' She is fretting, sir, about your illness. Oh, Mr. Lepel, if you would only try the sweet country air ! If you only had my good little Susan to nurse you !'

She too taking my uncle's view ! And talking of Susan as my nurse !

' What are you thinking of ?' I asked her. ' A young girl like your daughter nursing Me ! You ought to have more regard for Susan's good name !'

' I know what *you* ought to do !' She made that strange reply with a furtive look at me ; half in anger, half in alarm.

' Go on,' I said.

' Will you turn me out of your house for my impudence ?' she asked.

' I will hear what you have to say to me. What ought I to do ?'

' Marry Susan.'

I heard the woman plainly—and yet, I declare I doubted the evidence of my senses.

' She's breaking her heart for you,' Mrs. Rymer burst out. ' She's been in love with you, since you first darkened our doors— and it will end in the neighbours finding it out. I did my duty to her ; I tried to stop it ; I tried to prevent you from seeing her, when you went away. Too late ; the mischief was done. When I see my girl fading day by day—crying about you in secret, talking about you in her dreams—I can't stand it ; I must speak out. Oh, yes, I know how far beneath you she is—the daughter of your uncle's servant. But she's your equal, sir, in the sight of Heaven. My lord's priest converted her only last year —and my Susan is as good a Papist as yourself.'

How could I let this go on ? I felt that I ought to have stopped it before.

' It's possible,' I said, ' that you may not be deliberately deceiving me. If you are yourself deceived, I am bound to tell you the truth. Mr. Rothsay loves your daughter, and, what is more, Mr. Rothsay has reason to know that Susan——'

' That Susan loves him ?' she interposed, with a mocking laugh. ' Oh, Mr. Lepel, is it possible that a clever man like you can't see clearer than that ? My girl in love with Mr. Rothsay! She wouldn't have looked at him a second time if he hadn't talked to her about *you*. When I complained privately to my lord of Mr. Rothsay hanging about the lodge, do you think she turned as pale as ashes, and cried when *he* passed through the gate, and said good-bye ?'

She had complained of Rothsay to Lord Lepel—I understood her at last ! She knew that my friend and all his family were poor. She had put her own construction on the innocent interest that I had taken in her daughter. Careless of the difference in rank, blind to the malady that was killing me, she was now bent on separating Rothsay and Susan, by throwing the girl into the arms of a rich husband like myself!

' You are wasting your breath,' I told her ; ' I don't believe one word you say to me.'

' Believe Susan, then !' cried the reckless woman. ' Let me bring her here. If she's too shamefaced to own the truth, look at her—that's all I ask—look at her, and judge for yourself !'

This was intolerable. In justice to Susan, in justice to Rothsay, I insisted on silence. ' No more of it !' I said. ' Take care how you provoke me. Don't you see that I am ill ? don't you see that you are irritating me to no purpose ?'

She altered her tone. ' I'll wait,' she said quietly, ' while you compose yourself.'

With those words, she walked to the window, and stood there with her back towards me. Was the wretch taking advantage of my helpless condition ? I stretched out my hand to ring the bell, and have her

sent away—and hesitated to degrade Susan's mother, for Susan's sake. In my state of prostration, how could I arrive at a decision ? My mind was dreadfully disturbed ; I felt the imperative necessity of turning my thoughts to some other subject. Looking about me, the letters on the table attracted my attention. Mechanically, I took them up ; mechanically, I put them down again. Two of them slipped from my trembling fingers ; my eyes fell on the uppermost of the two. The address was in the hand-writing of the good friend with whom Rothsay was sailing.

Just as I had been speaking of Rothsay, here was the news of him for which I had been waiting.

I opened the letter and read these words:

' There is, I fear, but little hope for our friend—unless this girl on whom he has set his heart can (by some lucky change of circumstances) become his wife. He has tried to master his weakness ; but his own infatuation is too much for him. He is really and truly in a state of despair. Two evenings since—to give you a melancholy example of what I mean—I was in my cabin, when I heard the alarm of a man overboard. The man was Rothsay. My sailing-master, seeing that he was unable to swim, jumped into the sea and rescued him, as I got on deck. Rothsay declares it to have been an accident ; and everybody believes him but myself. I know the state of his mind. Don't be alarmed ; I will have him well looked after ; and I won't give him up just yet. We are still bound southward, with a fair wind. If the new scenes which I hope to show him prove to be of no avail, I must reluctantly take him back to England. In that case, which I don't like to contemplate, you may see him again—perhaps in a month's time.'

He might return in a month's time—
return to hear of the death of the one
friend, on whose power and will to help
him he might have relied. If I failed to
employ in his interests the short interval
of life still left to me, could I doubt (after
what I had just read) what the end would
be? How could I help him? Oh, God!
how could I help him?

Mrs. Rymer left the window, and returned to the chair which she had occupied
when I first received her.

'Are you quieter in your mind now?'
she asked.

I neither answered her nor looked at
her.

Still determined to reach her end, she
tried again to force her unhappy daughter
on me. 'Will you consent,' she persisted,
'to see Susan?'

If she had been a little nearer to me, I
am afraid I should have struck her. 'You
wretch!' I said, 'do you know that I am
a dying man?'

'While there's life there's hope,' Mrs.
Rymer remarked.

I ought to have controlled myself; but
it was not to be done.

'Hope of your daughter being my rich
widow?' I asked.

Her bitter answer followed instantly.

'Even then,' she said, 'Susan wouldn't
marry Rothsay.'

A lie! If circumstances favoured her, I
knew, on Rothsay's authority, what Susan
would do.

The thought burst on my mind, like light
bursting on the eyes of a man restored to
sight. If Susan agreed to go through the
form of marriage with a dying bridegroom,
my rich widow could (and would) become
Rothsay's wife. Once more, the remembrance of the play at Rome returned, and
set the last embers of resolution which sick-
ness and suffering had left to me, in a flame.
The devoted friend of that imaginary story

had counted on death to complete his
generous purpose in vain : *he* had been
condemned by the tribunal of man, and
had been reprieved. I—in his place, and
with his self-sacrifice in my mind—might
found a firmer trust in the future ; for I
had been condemned by the tribunal of
God.

Encouraged by my silence, the obstinate
woman persisted. 'Won't you even send
a message to Susan?' she asked.

Rashly, madly, without an instant's
hesitation, I answered :

'Go back to Susan, and say I leave it to
her.'

Mrs. Rymer started to her feet. 'You
leave it to Susan to be your wife, if she
likes?'

'I do.'

'And if she consents?'

'*I* consent.'

In two weeks and a day from that time,
the deed was done. When Rothsay returned
to England, he would ask for Susan—and
he would find my virgin-widow rich and
free.

SEVENTH EPOCH.

WHATEVER may be thought of my conduct,
let me say this in justice to myself—I was
resolved that Susan should not be deceived.

Half an hour after Mrs. Rymer had left
my house, I wrote to her daughter, plainly
revealing the motive which led me to offer
marriage, solely in the future interest of
Rothsay and herself. 'If you refuse,' I
said, in conclusion, 'you may depend on
my understanding you and feeling for you.
But, if you consent—then I have a favour
to ask. Never let us speak to one another
of the profanation that we have agreed to
commit, for your faithful lover's sake.'

I had formed a high opinion of Susan—

too high an opinion as it seemed. Her reply surprised and disappointed me. In other words, she gave her consent.

I stipulated that the marriage should be kept strictly secret, for a certain period. In my own mind I decided that the interval should be held to expire, either on the day of my death, or on the day when Rothsay returned.

My next proceeding was to write in confidence to the priest whom I have already mentioned, in an earlier part of these pages. He has reasons of his own for not permitting me to disclose the motive which induced him to celebrate my marriage privately in the chapel at Lord Lepel's house. My uncle's desire that I should try change of air, as offering a last chance of recovery, was known to my medical attendant, and served as a sufficient reason (although he protested against the risk) for my removal to the country. I was carried to the station, and placed on a bed—slung by ropes to the ceiling of a saloon carriage, so as to prevent me from feeling the vibration when the train was in motion. Faithful Mrs. Mozeen entreated to be allowed to accompany me. I was reluctantly compelled to refuse compliance with this request, in justice to the claims of my lord's housekeeper ; who had been accustomed to exercise undivided authority in the household, and who had made every preparation for my comfort. With her own hands, Mrs. Mozeen packed everything that I required, including the medicines prescribed for the occasion. She was deeply affected, poor soul, when we parted.

I bore the journey—happily for me, it was a short one—better than had been anticipated. For the first few days that followed, the purer air of the country seemed, in some degree, to revive me. But the deadly sense of weakness, the slow sinking of the vital power in me, returned as the time drew near for the marriage. The ceremony was performed at night. Only Susan and her mother were present. No persons in the house but ourselves had the faintest suspicion of what had happened.

I signed my new will (the priest and Mrs. Rymer being the witnesses) in my bed that night. It left everything that I possessed, excepting a legacy to Mrs. Mozeen, to my wife.

Obliged, it is needless to say, to preserve appearances, Susan remained at the lodge as usual. But it was impossible to resist her entreaty to be allowed to attend on me, for a few hours daily, as assistant to the regular nurse. When she was alone with me, and had no inquisitive eyes to dread, the poor girl showed a depth of feeling, which I was unable to reconcile with the motives that could alone have induced her (as I then supposed) to consent to the mockery of our marriage. On occasions when I was so far able to resist the languor that oppressed me as to observe what was passing at my bedside—I saw Susan look at me, as if there were thoughts in her pressing for utterance which she hesitated to express. Once, she herself acknowledged this. 'I have so much to say to you,' she owned, 'when you are stronger and fitter to hear me.' At other times, her nerves seemed to be shaken by the spectacle of my sufferings. Her kind hands trembled and made mistakes, when they had any nursing duties to perform near me. The servants, noticing her, used to say, 'That pretty girl seems to be the most awkward person in the house.' On the day that followed the ceremony in the chapel, this want of self-control brought about an accident which led to serious results.

In removing the small chest which held my medicines from the shelf on which it was placed, Susan let it drop on the floor. The two full bottles still left were so completely shattered that not even a tea-spoonful of the contents was saved.

Shocked at what she had done, the poor girl volunteered to go herself to my chemist in London, by the first train. I refused to allow it. What did it matter to me now, if my death from exhaustion was hastened by a day or two? Why need my life be prolonged artificially by drugs, when I had nothing left to live for? An excuse for me which would satisfy others was easily found. I said that I had been long weary of physic, and that the accident had decided me on refusing to take more.

That night I did not wake quite so often as usual. When she came to me the next day, Susan noticed that I looked better. The day after, the other nurse made the same observation. At the end of the week, I was able to leave my bed, and sit by the fireside, while Susan read to me. Some mysterious change in my health had completely falsified the prediction of the medical men. I sent to London for my doctor—and told him that the improvement in me had begun on the day when I left off taking my remedies. 'Can you explain it?' I asked.

He answered that no such 'resurrection from the dead' (as he called it) had ever happened in his long experience. On leaving me, he asked for the latest prescriptions that had been written. I inquired what he was going to do with them. 'I mean to go to the chemist,' he replied, 'and to satisfy myself that your medicines have been properly made up.'

I owed it to Mrs. Mozeen's true interest in me, to tell her what had happened. The same day I wrote to her. I also mentioned what the doctor had said, and asked her to call on him, and ascertain if the prescriptions had been shown to the chemist, and if any mistake had been made.

A more innocently intended letter than this never was written. And yet, there are people who have declared that it was inspired by suspicion of Mrs. Mozeen!

EIGHTH EPOCH.

WHETHER I was so weakened by illness as to be incapable of giving my mind to more than one subject for reflection at a time (that subject being now the extraordinary recovery of my health) — or whether I was preoccupied by the effort, which I was in honour bound to make, to resist the growing attraction to me of Susan's society—I cannot presume to say. This only I know : when the discovery of the terrible position towards Rothsay in which I now stood suddenly overwhelmed me, an interval of some days had passed. I cannot account for it. I can only say—so it was.

Susan was in the room. I was wholly unable to hide from her the sudden change of colour which betrayed the horror that had overpowered me. She said anxiously : 'What has frightened you ?'

I don't think I heard her. The play was in my memory again—the fatal play, which had wound itself into the texture of Rothsay's life and mine. In vivid remembrance, I saw once more the dramatic situation of the first act, and shrank from the reflection of it in the disaster which had fallen on my friend and myself.

'What has frightened you ?' Susan repeated.

I answered in one word—I whispered his name : ' Rothsay !'

She looked at me in innocent surprise. ' Has he met with some misfortune ?' she asked quietly.

' Misfortune '—did she call it ? Had I not said enough to disturb her tranquillity in mentioning Rothsay's name ? 'I am living !' I said. ' Living—and likely to live !'

Her answer expressed fervent gratitude. ' Thank God for it !'

I looked at her, astonished as she had been astonished when she looked at me.

'Susan, Susan,' I cried—'must I own it? I love you!'

She came nearer to me with timid pleasure in her eyes—with the first faint light of a smile playing round her lips.

'You say it very strangely,' she murmured. 'Surely, my dear one, you ought to love me? Since the first day when you gave me my French lesson—haven't I loved You?'

'*You* love *me?*' I repeated. 'Have you read——?' My voice failed me; I could say no more.

She turned pale. 'Read—what?' she asked.

'My letter.'

'What letter?'

'The letter I wrote to you before we were married.'

Am I a coward? The bare recollection of what followed that reply makes me tremble. Time has passed. I am a new man now; my health is restored; my happiness is assured: I ought to be able to write on. No: it is not to be done. How can I think coolly? how force myself to record the suffering that I innocently, most innocently, inflicted on the sweetest and truest of women? Nothing saved us from a parting as absolute as the parting that follows death, but the confession that had been wrung from me at a time when my motive spoke for itself. The artless avowal of her affection had been justified, had been honoured, by the words which laid my heart at her feet when I said 'I love you.'

*　　*　　*　　*　　*

She had risen to leave me. In a last look, we had silently resigned ourselves to wait, apart from each other, for the day of reckoning that must follow Rothsay's return, when we heard the sound of carriage-wheels

on the drive that led to the house. In a minute more, the man himself entered the room.

He looked first at Susan—then at me. In both of us he saw the traces that told of agitation endured, but not yet composed. Worn and weary he waited, hesitating, near the door.

'Am I intruding?' he asked.

'We were thinking of you, and speaking of you,' I replied, 'just before you came in.'

'*We?*' he repeated, turning towards Susan once more. After a pause, he offered me his hand—and drew it back.

'You don't shake hands with me,' he said.

'I am waiting, Rothsay, until I know that we are the same firm friends as ever.'

For the third time he looked at Susan.

'Will *you* shake hands?' he asked.

She gave him her hand cordially. 'May I stay here?' she said, addressing herself to me.

In my situation at that moment, I understood the generous purpose that animated her. But she had suffered enough already—I led her gently to the door. 'It will be better,' I whispered, 'if you will wait down stairs in the library.' She hesitated. 'What will they say in the house?' she objected, thinking of the servants, and of the humble position which she was still supposed to occupy. 'It matters nothing what they say, now,' I told her. She left us.

'There seems to be some private understanding between you,' Rothsay said, when we were alone.

'You shall hear what it is,' I answered. 'But I must beg you to excuse me if I speak first of myself.'

'Are you alluding to your health?'

'Yes.'

'Quite needless, Lepel. I met your doctor this morning. I know that a council of physicians decided you would die before the year was out.'

He paused there.

'And they proved to be wrong,' I added.

'They might have proved to be right,' Rothsay rejoined, 'but for the accident which spilt your medicine, and the despair of yourself which decided you on taking no more.'

I could hardly believe that I understood him. 'Do you assert,' I said, 'that my medicine would have killed me, if I had taken the rest of it ?'

'I have no doubt that it would.'

'Will you explain what you mean ?'

'Let me have your explanation first. I was not prepared to find Susan in your room. I was surprised to see traces of tears in her face. Something has happened in my absence. Am I concerned in it ?'

'You are.'

I said it quietly—in full possession of myself. The trial of fortitude through which I had already passed seemed to have blunted my customary sense of feeling. I approached the disclosure which I was now bound to make with steady resolution, resigned to the worst that could happen when the truth was known.

'Do you remember the time,' I resumed, 'when I was so eager to serve you that I proposed to make Susan your wife by making her rich ?'

'Yes.'

'Do you remember asking me if I was thinking of the play we saw together at Rome ? Is the story as present to your mind now, as it was then ?'

'Quite as present.'

'You asked if I was performing the part of the Marquis—and if you were the Count. Rothsay ! the devotion of that ideal character to his friend has been *my* devotion ; his conviction that his death would justify what he had done for his friend's sake, has been *my* conviction ; and as it ended with him, so it has ended with me—his terrible position is *my* terrible position towards you, at this moment.'

'Are you mad ?' Rothsay asked sternly.

I passed over that first outbreak of his anger in silence.

'Do you mean to tell me you have married Susan ?' he went on.

'Bear this in mind,' I said. 'When I married her, I was doomed to death. Nay more. In your interests—as God is my witness—I welcomed death.'

He stepped up to me, in silence, and raised his hand with a threatening gesture.

That action at once deprived me of my self-possession. I spoke with the ungovernable rashness of a boy.

'Carry out your intention,' I said. 'Insult me.'

His hand dropped.

'Insult me,' I repeated ; 'it is one way out of the unendurable situation in which we are placed. You may trust me to challenge you. Duels are still fought on the Continent ; I will follow you abroad ; I will choose pistols ; I will take care that we fight on the fatal foreign system ; and I will purposely miss you. Make her what I intended her to be—my rich widow.'

He looked at me attentively.

'Is *that* your refuge ?' he asked scornfully. 'No ! I won't help you to commit suicide.'

God forgive me ! I was possessed by a spirit of reckless despair ; I did my best to provoke him.

'Reconsider your decision,' I said ; 'and remember — you tried to commit suicide yourself.'

He turned quickly to the door, as if he distrusted his own powers of self-control.

'I wish to speak to Susan,' he said, keeping his back turned on me.

'You will find her in the library.'

He left me.

I went to the window. I opened it, and let the cold wintry air blow over my burning head. I don't know how long I sat at the window. There came a time when I saw Rothsay on the house steps. He walked rapidly towards the park gate. His head was down ; he never once looked back at the room in which he had left me.

As he passed out of my sight, I felt a hand laid gently on my shoulder. Susan had returned to me.

' He will not come back,' she said. ' Try still to remember him as your old friend. He asks you to forgive and forget.'

She had made the peace between us. I was deeply touched ; my eyes filled with tears as I looked at her. She kissed me on the forehead and went out. I afterwards asked what had passed between them when Rothsay spoke with her in the library. She never has told me what they said to each other ; and she never will. She is right.

Later in the day, I was told that Mrs. Rymer had called, and wished to ' pay her respects.'

I refused to see her. Whatever claim she might have otherwise had on my consideration had been forfeited by the infamy of her conduct, when she intercepted my letter to Susan. Her sense of injury, on receiving my message, was expressed in writing, and was sent to me the same evening. The last sentence in her letter was characteristic of the woman.

' However your pride may despise me,' she wrote, ' I am indebted to you for the rise in life that I have always desired. You may refuse to see me—but you can't prevent my being the mother-in-law of a gentleman.'

Soon afterwards, I received a visit which I had hardly ventured to expect. Busy as he was in London, my doctor came to see me. He was not in his usual good spirits.

' I hope you don't bring me any bad news,' I said.

' You shall judge for yourself,' he replied. ' I come from Mr. Rothsay, to say for him what he is not able to say for himself.'

' Where is he ?'

' He has left England.'

' For any purpose that you know of ?'

' Yes. He has sailed to join the expedition of rescue—I ought rather to call it the forlorn hope—which is to search for the lost explorers in Central Australia.'

In other words, he had gone to seek death in the fatal footsteps of Burke and Wills. I could not trust myself to speak.

The doctor saw that there was a reason for my silence, and that he would do well not to notice it. He changed the subject.

' May I ask,' he said, ' if you have heard from the servants left in charge at your house in London ?'

' Has anything happened ?'

' Something has happened which they are evidently afraid to tell you ; knowing the high opinion which you have of Mrs. Mozeen. She has suddenly quitted your service, and has gone, nobody knows where. I have taken charge of a letter which she left for you.'

He handed me the letter. As soon as I had recovered myself, I looked at it.

There was this inscription on the address : —' For my good master, to wait until he returns home.'

The few lines in the letter itself ran thus :—

" Distressing circumstances oblige me to leave you, sir, and do not permit me to enter into particulars. In asking your pardon, I offer my sincere thanks for your kindness, and my fervent prayers for your welfare.'

That was all. The date had a special interest for me. Mrs. Mozeen had written on the day when she must have received my letter—the letter which has already appeared in these pages.

'Is there really nothing known of the poor woman's motives?' I asked.

'There are two explanations suggested,' the doctor informed me. 'One of them, which is offered by your female servants, seems to me absurd. They declare that Mrs. Mozeen, at her mature age, was in love with the young man who is your footman! It is even asserted that she tried to recommend herself to him, by speaking of the money which she expected to bring to the man who would make her his wife. The footman's reply, informing her that he was already engaged to be married, is alleged to be the cause which has driven her from your house.'

I begged that the doctor would not trouble himself to repeat more of what my women servants had said. 'If the other explanation,' I added, 'is equally unworthy of notice——'

'The other explanation,' the doctor interposed, 'comes from Mr. Rothsay, and is of a very serious kind.'

Rothsay's opinion demanded my respect. 'What view does he take?' I inquired.

'A view that startles me,' the doctor said. 'You remember my telling you of the interest he took in your symptoms, and in the remedies I had employed? Well! Mr. Rothsay accounts for the incomprehensible recovery of your health by asserting that poison—probably administered in small quantities, and intermitted at intervals in fear of discovery—has been mixed with your medicine; and he asserts that the guilty person is Mrs. Mozeen.'

It was impossible that I could openly express the indignation that I felt on hearing this. My position towards Rothsay forced me to restrain myself.

'May I ask,' the doctor continued, 'if Mrs. Mozeen was aware that she had a legacy to expect at your death?'

'Certainly.'

'Has she a brother who is one of the dispensers employed by your chemists?'

'Yes.'

'Did she know that I doubted if my prescriptions had been properly prepared, and that I intended to make inquiries?'

'I wrote to her myself on the subject.'

'Do you think her brother told her that I was referred to *him*, when I went to the chemists?'

'I have no means of knowing what her brother did.'

'Can you at least tell me when she received your letter?'

'She must have received it on the day when she left my house.'

The doctor rose with a grave face. 'These are rather extraordinary coincidences,' he remarked.

I merely replied, 'Mrs. Mozeen is as incapable of poisoning as I am.'

The doctor wished me good morning.

I repeat here my conviction of my housekeeper's innocence. I protest against the cruelty which accuses her. And, whatever may have been her motive in suddenly leaving my service, I declare that she still possesses my sympathy and esteem, and I invite her to return to me if she ever sees these lines.

I have only to add, by way of postscript, that we have heard of the safe return of the expedition of rescue. Time, as my wife and I both hope, may yet convince Rothsay that he will not be wrong in counting on Susan's love—the love of a sister.

In the meanwhile, we possess a memorial of our absent friend. We have bought his picture.

Mr. Captain and the Nymph

I.

'THE Captain is still in the prime of life,' the widow remarked. 'He has given up his ship; he possesses a sufficient income, and he has nobody to live with him. I should like to know why he doesn't marry.'

'The Captain was excessively rude to Me,' the widow's younger sister added, on her side. 'When we took leave of him in London, I asked if there was any chance of his joining us at Brighton this season. He turned his back on me as if I had mortally offended him; and he made me this extraordinary answer: "Miss! I hate the sight of the sea." The man has been a sailor all his life. What does he mean by saying that he hates the sight of the sea?'

These questions were addressed to a third person present—and the person was a man. He was entirely at the mercy of the widow and the widow's sister. The other ladies of the family—who might have taken him under their protection—had gone to an evening concert. He was known to be the Captain's friend, and to be well acquainted with events in the Captain's later life. As it happened, he had reasons for hesitating to revive associations connected with those events. But what polite alternative was left to him? He must either inflict disappointment, and, worse still, aggravate curiosity—or he must resign himself to circumstances, and tell the ladies why the Captain would never marry, and why (sailor as he was) he hated the sight of the sea. They were both young women and handsome women—and the person to whom they had appealed (being a man) followed the example of submission to the sex, first set in the garden of Eden. He enlightened the ladies, in the terms that follow:

II.

THE British merchantman, *Fortuna*, sailed from the port of Liverpool (at a date which it is not necessary to specify) with the morning tide. She was bound for certain islands in the Pacific Ocean, in search of a cargo of sandal-wood—a commodity which, in those days, found a ready and profitable market in the Chinese Empire.

A large discretion was reposed in the Captain by the owners, who knew him to be not only trustworthy, but a man of rare ability, carefully cultivated during the leisure hours of a seafaring life. Devoted heart and soul to his professional duties, he was a hard reader and an excellent linguist as well. Having had considerable experience among the inhabitants of the Pacific Islands, he had attentively studied their characters, and had mastered their language in more than one of its many dialects. Thanks to the valuable information thus obtained, the Captain was never at a loss to conciliate the islanders. He had more than once succeeded in finding a cargo, under circumstances in which other captains had failed.

Possessing these merits, he had also his fair share of human defects. For instance, he was a little too conscious of his own good looks—of his bright chestnut hair and whiskers, of his beautiful blue eyes, of his fair white skin, which many a woman had looked at with the admiration that is akin to envy. His shapely hands were protected by gloves; a broad-brimmed hat sheltered his complexion in fine weather from the sun. He was nice in the choice of his perfumes; he never drank spirits, and the smell of tobacco was abhorrent to him. New men among his officers and his crew, seeing him in his cabin, perfectly dressed, washed, and brushed until he was an object speckless to look upon—a merchant-captain soft of voice, careful in his choice of words, devoted to study in his leisure hours—were apt to conclude that they had trusted themselves at sea under a commander who was an anomalous mixture of a schoolmaster and a dandy. But if the slightest infraction of discipline took place, or if the storm rose and the vessel proved to be in peril, it was soon discovered that the gloved hands held a rod of iron; that the soft voice could make itself heard through wind and sea from one end of the deck to the other; and that it issued orders which the greatest fool on board discovered to be orders that had

saved the ship. Throughout his professional life, the general impression that this variously gifted man produced on the little world about him was always the same. Some few liked him; everybody respected him; nobody understood him. The Captain accepted these results. He persisted in reading his books and protecting his complexion, with this result : his owners shook hands with him, and put up with his gloves.

The *Fortuna* touched at Rio for water, and for supplies of food which might prove useful in case of scurvy. In due time the ship rounded Cape Horn, favoured by the finest weather ever known in those latitudes by the oldest hand on board. The mate— one Mr. Duncalf—a boozing, wheezing, self-confident old sea-dog, with a flaming face and a vast vocabulary of oaths, swore that he didn't like it. ' The foul weather's coming, my lads,' said Mr. Duncalf. ' Mark my words, there'll be wind enough to take the curl out of the Captain's whiskers before we are many days older !'

For one uneventful week, the ship cruised in search of the islands to which the owners had directed her. At the end of that time the wind took the predicted liberties with the Captain's whiskers; and Mr. Duncalf stood revealed to an admiring crew in the character of a true prophet.

For three days and three nights the *Fortuna* ran before the storm, at the mercy of wind and sea. On the fourth morning the gale blew itself out, the sun appeared again towards noon, and the Captain was able to take an observation. The result informed him that he was in a part of the Pacific Ocean with which he was entirely unacquainted. Thereupon, the officers were called to a council in the cabin.

Mr. Duncalf, as became his rank, was consulted first. His opinion possessed the merit of brevity. ' My lads, this ship's bewitched. Take my word for it, we shall wish ourselves back in our own latitudes before we are many days older.' Which, being interpreted, meant that Mr. Duncalf was lost, like his superior officer, in a part of the ocean of which he knew nothing.

The remaining members of the council, having no suggestions to offer, left the Captain to take his own way. He decided (the weather being fine again) to stand on under an easy press of sail for four-and-twenty hours more, and to see if anything came of it.

Soon after night-fall, something did come of it. The look-out forward hailed the quarter-deck with the dreadful cry, 'Breakers ahead!' In less than a minute more, everybody heard the crash of the broken water. The *Fortuna* was put about, and came round slowly in the light wind. Thanks to the timely alarm and the fine weather, the safety of the vessel was easily provided for. They kept her under short sail; and they waited for the morning.

The dawn showed them in the distance a glorious green island, not marked in the ship's charts—an island girt about by a coral-reef, and having in its midst a high-peaked mountain which looked, through the telescope, like a mountain of volcanic origin. Mr. Duncalf, taking his morning draught of rum and water, shook his groggy old head, and said (and swore): 'My lads, I don't like the look of that island.' The Captain was of a different opinion. He had one of the ship's boats put into the water; he armed himself and four of his crew who accompanied him; and away he went in the morning sunlight to visit the island.

Skirting round the coral-reef, they found a natural breach, which proved to be broad enough and deep enough not only for the passage of the boat, but of the ship herself if needful. Crossing the broad inner belt of smooth water, they approached the golden sands of the island, strewed with magnificent shells, and crowded by the dusky islanders—men, women, and children, all waiting in breathless astonishment to see the strangers land.

The Captain kept the boat off, and examined the islanders carefully. The innocent simple people danced, and sang, and ran into the water, imploring their wonderful white visitors by gestures to come on shore. Not a creature among them carried arms of any sort; a hospitable curiosity animated the entire population. The men cried out, in their smooth musical language, 'Come and eat!' and the plump black-eyed women, all laughing together, added their own invitation, 'Come and be kissed!' Was it in mortals to resist such temptations as these? The Captain led the way on shore, and the women surrounded him in an instant, and screamed for joy at the glorious spectacle of his whiskers, his complexion, and his gloves. So, the mariners from the far north were welcomed to the newly-discovered island.

III.

THE morning wore on. Mr. Duncalf, in charge of the ship, cursing the island over his rum and water, as a 'beastly green strip of a place, not laid down in any Christian chart,' was kept waiting four mortal hours before the Captain returned to his command, and reported himself to his officers as follows:

He had found his knowledge of the Polynesian dialects sufficient to make himself in some degree understood by the natives of the new island. Under the guidance of the chief he had made a first journey of exploration, and had seen for himself that the place was a marvel of natural beauty and fertility. The one barren spot in it was the peak of the volcanic mountain, composed of crumbling rock; originally no doubt lava and ashes, which had cooled and consolidated with the lapse of time. So far as he could see, the crater at the top was now an extinct crater. But, if he had understood rightly, the chief had spoken of earthquakes and eruptions at certain bygone periods, some of which lay within his own earliest recollections of the place.

Adverting next to considerations of practical utility, the Captain announced that he had seen sandal-wood enough on the island to load a dozen ships, and that the natives were willing to part with it for a few toys and trinkets generally distributed amongst them. To the mate's disgust, the *Fortuna* was taken inside the reef that day, and was anchored before sunset in a natural harbour. Twelve hours of recreation, beginning with the next morning, were granted to the men, under the wise restrictions in such cases established by the Captain. That interval over, the work of cutting the precious wood and loading the ship was to be unremittingly pursued.

Mr. Duncalf had the first watch after the *Fortuna* had been made snug. He took the boatswain aside (an ancient sea-dog like himself), and he said in a gruff whisper : ' My lad, this here ain't the island laid down in our sailing orders. See if mischief don't come of disobeying orders before we are many days older.'

Nothing in the shape of mischief happened that night. But at sunrise the next morning a suspicious circumstance occurred ; and Mr. Duncalf whispered to the boatswain : ' What did I tell you ?' The Captain and the chief of the islanders held a private conference in the cabin ; and the Captain, after first forbidding any communication with the shore until his return, suddenly left the ship,

alone with the chief, in the chief's own canoe.

What did this strange disappearance mean ? The Captain himself, when he took his seat in the canoe, would have been puzzled to answer that question. He asked, in the nearest approach that his knowledge could make to the language used in the island, whether he would be a long time or a short time absent from his ship.

The chief answered mysteriously (as the Captain understood him) in these words : ' Long time or short time, your life depends on it, and the lives of your men.'

Paddling his light little boat in silence over the smooth water inside the reef, the chief took his visitor ashore at a part of the island which was quite new to the Captain. The two crossed a ravine, and ascended an eminence beyond. There the chief stopped, and silently pointed out to sea.

The Captain looked in the direction indicated to him, and discovered a second and a smaller island, lying away to the south-west. Taking out his telescope from the case by which it was slung at his back, he narrowly examined the place. Two of the native canoes were lying off the shore of the new island ; and the men in them appeared to be all kneeling or crouching in curiously chosen attitudes. Shifting the range of his glass, he next beheld a white-robed figure, tall and solitary—the one inhabitant of the island whom he could discover. The man was standing on the highest point of a rocky cape. A fire was burning at his feet. Now he lifted his arms solemnly to the sky ; now he dropped some invisible fuel into the fire, which made a blue smoke ; and now he cast other invisible objects into the canoes floating beneath him, which the islanders reverently received with bodies that crouched in abject submission. Lowering his telescope, the Captain looked round at the chief for an explanation. The chief gave the explanation readily. His language was in-terpreted by the English stranger in these terms :

'Wonderful white man! the island you see yonder is a Holy Island. As such it is *Taboo* — an island sanctified and set apart. The honourable person whom you notice on the rock is an all-powerful favourite of the gods. He is by vocation a Sorcerer, and by rank a Priest. You now see him casting charms and blessings into the canoes of our fishermen, who kneel to him for fine weather and great plenty of fish. If any profane person, native or stranger, presumes to set foot on that island, my otherwise peaceful subjects will (in the performance of a religious duty) put that person to death. Mention this to your men. They will be fed by my male people, and fondled by my female people, so long as they keep clear of the Holy Isle. As they value their lives, let them respect this prohibition. Is it understood between us? Wonderful white man! my canoe is waiting for you. Let us go back.'

Understanding enough of the chief's language (illustrated by his gestures) to receive in the right spirit the communica-tion thus addressed to him, the Captain repeated the warning to the ship's company in the plainest possible English. The officers and men then took their holiday on shore, with the exception of Mr. Dun-calf, who positively refused to leave the ship. For twelve delightful hours they were fed by the male people, and fondled by the female people, and then they were mercilessly torn from the flesh-pots and the arms of their new friends, and set to work on the sandal-wood in good earnest. Mr. Duncalf superintended the loading, and waited for the mischief that was to come of disobeying the owners' orders with a confidence worthy of a better cause.

IV.

STRANGELY enough, chance once more declared itself in favour of the mate's point of view. The mischief did actually come ; and the chosen instrument of it was a hand-some young islander, who was one of the sons of the chief.

The Captain had taken a fancy to the sweet-tempered intelligent lad. Pursuing his studies in the dialect of the island, at leisure hours, he had made the chief's son his tutor, and had instructed the youth in English by way of return. More than a month had passed in this intercourse, and the ship's lading was being rapidly com-pleted—when, in an evil hour, the talk between the two turned on the subject of the Holy Island.

'Does nobody live on the island but the Priest ?' the Captain asked.

The chief's son looked round him sus-piciously. 'Promise me you won't tell anybody !' he began very earnestly.

The Captain gave his promise.

'There is one other person on the island,' the lad whispered ; 'a person to feast your eyes upon, if you could only see her! She is the Priest's daughter. Removed to the island in her infancy, she has never left it since. In that sacred solitude she has only looked on two human beings—her father and her mother. I once saw her from my canoe, taking care not to attract her notice, or to approach too near the holy soil. Oh, so young, dear master, and, oh, so beauti-ful !' The chief's son completed the description by kissing his own hands as an expression of rapture.

The Captain's fine blue eyes sparkled. He asked no more questions ; but, later on that day, he took his telescope with him, and paid a secret visit to the eminence which overlooked the Holy Island. The next day, and the next, he privately returned to the same place. On the fourth day,

fatal Destiny favoured him.   He discovered
the nymph of the island.

Standing alone upon the cape on which
he had already seen her father, she was
feeding some tame birds which looked like
turtle-doves.   The glass showed the Captain
her white robe, fluttering in the sea-breeze ;
her long black hair falling to her feet ; her
slim and supple young figure ; her simple
grace of attitude, as she turned this way
and that, attending to the wants of her
birds.   Before her was the blue ocean ;
behind her rose the lustrous green of the
island forest.   He looked and looked until
his eyes and arms ached.   When she
disappeared among the trees, followed by
her favourite birds, the Captain shut up
his telescope with a sigh, and said to himself : ' I have seen an angel !'

From that hour he became an altered
man ; he was languid, silent, interested
in nothing.   General opinion, on board his
ship, decided that he was going to be taken ill.

A week more elapsed, and the officers
and crew began to talk of the voyage to
their market in China.   The Captain
refused to fix a day for sailing.   He even
took offence at being asked to decide.
Instead of sleeping in his cabin, he went
ashore for the night.

Not many hours afterwards (just before
daybreak), Mr. Duncalf, snoring in his
cabin on deck, was aroused by a hand laid
on his shoulder.   The swinging lamp, still
alight, showed him the dusky face of the
chief's son, convulsed with terror.   By
wild signs, by disconnected words in the
little English which he had learnt, the lad
tried to make the mate understand him.
Dense Mr. Duncalf, understanding nothing,
hailed the second officer, on the opposite
side of the deck.   The second officer was
young and intelligent ; he rightly interpreted the terrible news that had come to
the ship.

The Captain had broken his own rules.

Watching his opportunity, under cover of
the night, he had taken a canoe, and had
secretly crossed the channel to the Holy
Island.   No one had been near him at the
time, but the chief's son.   The lad had
vainly tried to induce him to abandon his
desperate enterprise, and had vainly waited
on the shore in the hope of hearing the
sound of the paddle announcing his return.
Beyond all reasonable doubt, the infatuated
man had set foot on the shores of the
tabooed island.

The one chance for his life was to conceal
what he had done, until the ship could be
got out of the harbour, and then (if no
harm had come to him in the interval) to
rescue him after nightfall.   It was decided
to spread the report that he had really been
taken ill, and that he was confined to his
cabin.   The chief's son, whose heart the
Captain's kindness had won, could be
trusted to do this, and to keep the secret
faithfully for his good friend's sake.

Towards noon, the next day, they
attempted to take the ship to sea, and
failed for want of wind.   Hour by hour,
the heat grew more oppressive.   As the
day declined, there were ominous appearances in the western heaven.   The natives,
who had given some trouble during the day
by their anxiety to see the Captain, and by
their curiosity to know the cause of
the sudden preparations for the ship's
departure, all went ashore together, looking
suspiciously at the sky, and re-appeared no
more.   Just at midnight, the ship (still in
her snug berth inside the reef) suddenly
trembled from her keel to her uppermost
masts.   Mr. Duncalf, surrounded by the
startled crew, shook his knotty fist at the
island as if he could see it in the dark.
' My lads, what did I tell you ?   That was
a shock of earthquake.'

With the morning the threatening aspect
of the weather unexpectedly disappeared.
A faint hot breeze from the land, just

enough to give the ship steerage-way, offered Mr. Duncalf a chance of getting to sea. Slowly the *Fortuna*, with the mate himself at the wheel, half sailed, half drifted into the open ocean. At a distance of barely two miles from the island the breeze was felt no more, and the vessel lay becalmed for the rest of the day.

At night the men waited their orders, expecting to be sent after their Captain in one of the boats. The intense darkness, the airless heat, and a second shock of earthquake (faintly felt in the ship at her present distance from the land) warned the mate to be cautious. 'I smell mischief in the air,' said Mr. Duncalf. 'The Captain must wait till I am surer of the weather.'

Still no change came with the new day. The dead calm continued, and the airless heat. As the day declined, another ominous appearance became visible. A thin line of smoke was discovered through the telescope, ascending from the topmost peak of the mountain on the main island. Was the volcano threatening an eruption? The mate, for one, entertained no doubt of it. 'By the Lord, the place is going to burst up!' said Mr. Duncalf. 'Come what may of it, we must find the Captain to-night!'

V.

WHAT was the lost Captain doing? and what chance had the crew of finding him that night?

He had committed himself to his desperate adventure, without forming any plan for the preservation of his own safety; without giving even a momentary consideration to the consequences which might follow the risk that he had run. The charming figure that he had seen haunted him night and day. The image of the innocent creature, secluded from humanity in her island-solitude, was the one image that filled his mind. A man, passing a woman in the street, acts on the impulse to turn and follow her, and in that one thoughtless moment shapes the destiny of his future life. The Captain had acted on a similar impulse, when he took the first canoe he found on the beach, and shaped his reckless course for the tabooed island.

Reaching the shore while it was still dark, he did one sensible thing — he hid the canoe so that it might not betray him when the daylight came. That done, he waited for the morning on the outskirts of the forest.

The trembling light of dawn revealed the mysterious solitude around him. Following the outer limits of the trees, first in one direction, then in another, and finding no trace of any living creature, he decided on penetrating to the interior of the island. He entered the forest.

An hour of walking brought him to rising ground. Continuing the ascent, he got clear of the trees, and stood on the grassy top of a broad cliff which overlooked the sea. An open hut was on the cliff. He cautiously looked in, and discovered that it was empty. The few household utensils left about, and the simple bed of leaves in a corner, were covered with fine sandy dust. Night-birds flew blundering out of inner cavities in the roof, and took refuge in the shadows of the forest below. It was plain that the hut had not been inhabited for some time past.

Standing at the open doorway and considering what he should do next, the Captain saw a bird flying towards him out of the forest. It was a turtle-dove, so tame that it fluttered close up to him. At the same moment the sound of sweet laughter became audible among the trees. His heart beat fast; he advanced a few steps and stopped. In a moment more the nymph of the island appeared, in her white robe, ascending the cliff in pursuit of her truant bird. She saw the strange man, and suddenly stood still; struck motionless by the amazing discovery that had burst upon her. The Captain approached, smiling and holding out his hand. She never moved; she stood before him in helpless wonderment— her lovely black eyes fixed spell-bound on his face; her dusky bosom palpitating above the fallen folds of her robe; her rich red lips parted in mute astonishment. Feasting his eyes on her beauty in silence, the Captain after a while ventured to speak to her in the language of the main island. The sound of his voice, addressing her in the words that she understood, roused the lovely creature to action. She started, stepped close up to him, and dropped on her knees at his feet.

'My father worships invisible deities,' she said softly. 'Are you a visible deity? Has my mother sent you?' She pointed as she spoke to the deserted hut behind them. 'You appear,' she went on, 'in the place where my mother died. Is it for her sake that you show yourself to her child? Beautiful deity, come to the Temple—come to my father!'

The Captain gently raised her from the ground. If her father saw him, he was a doomed man.

Infatuated as he was, he had sense enough left to announce himself plainly in his own character, as a mortal creature arriving from a distant land. The girl instantly drew back from him with a look of terror.

'He is not like my father,' she said to herself; 'he is not like me. Is he the lying demon of the prophecy? Is he the predestined destroyer of our island?'

The Captain's experience of the sex showed him the only sure way out of the awkward position in which he was now placed. He appealed to his personal appearance.

'Do I look like a demon?' he asked.

Her eyes met his eyes; a faint smile trembled on her lips. He ventured on asking what she meant by the predestined destruction of the island. She held up her hand solemnly, and repeated the prophecy.

The Holy Island was threatened with destruction by an evil being, who would one day appear on its shores. To avert the fatality the place had been sanctified and set apart, under the protection of the gods and their priest. Here was the reason for the taboo, and for the extraordinary rigour with which it was enforced. Listening to her with the deepest interest, the Captain took her hand and pressed it gently.

'Do I feel like a demon?' he whispered.

Her slim brown fingers closed frankly on his hand. 'You feel soft and friendly,' she said with the fearless candour of a child. 'Squeeze me again. I like it!'

The next moment she snatched her hand away from him; the sense of his danger had suddenly forced itself on her mind. 'If my father sees you,' she said, 'he will light the signal fire at the Temple, and the people from the other island will come here and put you to death. Where is your canoe? No! It is daylight. My father may see you on the water.' She considered a little, and, approaching him, laid her hands on his shoulders. 'Stay here till nightfall,' she resumed. 'My father never comes this way. The sight of the place where my mother died is horrible to him. You are safe here. Promise to stay where you are till night-time.'

The Captain gave his promise.

Freed from anxiety so far, the girl's mobile temperament recovered its native cheerfulness, its sweet gaiety and spirit. She admired the beautiful stranger as she might have admired a new bird that had flown to her to be fondled with the rest.

She patted his fair white skin, and wished she had a skin like it. She lifted the great glossy folds of her long black hair, and compared it with the Captain's bright curly locks, and longed to change colours with him from the bottom of her heart. His dress was a wonder to her ; his watch was a new revelation. She rested her head on his shoulder to listen delightedly to the ticking, as he held the watch to her ear. Her fragrant breath played on his face, her warm supple figure rested against him softly. The Captain's arm stole round her waist, and the Captain's lips gently touched her cheek. She lifted her head with a look of pleased surprise. ' Thank you,' said the child of nature simply. ' Kiss me again ; I like it. May I kiss you ?' The tame turtle-dove perched on her shoulder as she gave the Captain her first kiss, and diverted her thoughts to the pets that she had left, in pursuit of the truant dove. ' Come,' she said, 'and see my birds. I keep them on this side of the forest. There is no danger, so long as you don't show yourself on the other side. My name is Aimata. Aimata will take care of you. Oh, what a beautiful white neck you have !' She put her arm admiringly round his neck. The Captain's arm held her tenderly to him. Slowly the two descended the cliff, and were lost in the leafy solitudes of the forest. And the tame dove fluttered before them, a winged messenger of love, cooing to his mate.

VI.

THE night had come, and the Captain had not left the island.

Aimata's resolution to send him away in the darkness was a forgotten resolution already. She had let him persuade her that he was in no danger, so long as he remained in the hut on the cliff ; and she had promised, at parting, to return to him while the Priest was still sleeping, at the dawn of day.

He was alone in the hut. The thought of the innocent creature whom he loved was sorrowfully as well as tenderly present to his mind. He almost regretted his rash visit to the island. ' I will take her with me to England,' he said to himself. ' What does a sailor care for the opinion of the world ? Aimata shall be my wife.'

The intense heat oppressed him. He stepped out on the cliff, towards midnight, in search of a breath of air.

At that moment, the first shock of earthquake (felt in the ship while she was inside the reef) shook the ground he stood on. He instantly thought of the volcano on the main island. Had he been mistaken in supposing the crater to be extinct ? Was the shock that he had just felt a warning from the volcano, communicated through a submarine connection between the two islands ? He waited and watched through the hours of darkness, with a vague sense of apprehension, which was not to be reasoned away. With the first light of daybreak he descended into the forest, and saw the lovely being whose safety was already precious to him as his own, hurrying to meet him through the trees.

She waved her hand distractedly, as she approached him. ' Go !' she cried ; ' go away in your canoe before our island is destroyed !'

He did his best to quiet her alarm. Was it the shock of earthquake that had frightened her ? No : it was more than the shock of earthquake—it was something terrible which had followed the shock. There was a lake near the Temple, the waters of which were supposed to be heated by subterranean fires. The lake had risen with the earthquake, had bubbled furiously, and had then melted away into the earth and been lost. Her father, viewing the portent with horror, had gone to the cape to watch the volcano on the main island, and to implore by prayers and sacrifices the protection of the gods. Hearing this, the Captain entreated Aimata to let him see the emptied lake, in the absence of the Priest. She hesitated ; but his influence was all-powerful. He prevailed on her to turn back with him through the forest.

Reaching the farthest limit of the trees, they came out upon open rocky ground which sloped gently downward towards the centre of the island. Having crossed this space, they arrived at a natural amphitheatre of rock. On one side of it, the Temple appeared, partly excavated, partly formed by a natural cavern. In one of the lateral branches of the cavern was the dwelling of the Priest and his daughter. The mouth of it looked out on the rocky basin of the lake. Stooping over the edge, the Captain discovered, far down in the empty depths, a light cloud of steam. Not a drop of water was visible, look where he might.

Aimata pointed to the abyss, and hid her face on his bosom. 'My father says,' she whispered, ' that it is your doing.'

The Captain started. ' Does your father know that I am on the island ?'

She looked up at him with a quick glance of reproach. 'Do you think I would tell him, and put your life in peril ?' she asked. ' My father felt the destroyer of the island in the earthquake; my father saw the coming destruction in the disappearance of the lake.' Her eyes rested on him with a loving languor. 'Are you indeed the demon of the prophecy ?' she said, winding his hair round her finger. ' I am not afraid of you, if you are. I am a creature bewitched ; I love the demon.' She kissed him passionately. ' I don't care if I die,' she whispered between the kisses, ' if I only die with you !'

The Captain made no attempt to reason with her. He took the wiser way — he appealed to her feelings.

' You will come and live with me happily in my own country,' he said. ' My ship is waiting for us. I will take you home with me, and you shall be my wife.'

She clapped her hands for joy. Then she thought of her father, and drew back from him in tears.

The Captain understood her. ' Let us leave this dreary place,' he suggested. ' We will talk about it in the cool glades of the forest, where you first said you loved me.'

She gave him her hand. ' Where I first said I loved you !' she repeated, smiling tenderly as she looked at him. They left the lake together.

VII.

THE darkness had fallen again ; and the ship was still becalmed at sea.

Mr. Duncalf came on deck after his supper. The thin line of smoke, seen rising from the peak of the mountain that evening, was now succeeded by ominous flashes of fire from the same quarter, intermittently visible. The faint hot breeze from the land was felt once more. ' There's just an air of wind,' Mr. Duncalf remarked. ' I'll try for the Captain while I have the chance.'

One of the boats was lowered into the water—under command of the second mate, who had already taken the bearings of the tabooed island by daylight. Four of the men were to go with him, and they were all to be well-armed. Mr. Duncalf addressed his final instructions to the officer in the boat.

' You will keep a look-out, sir, with a lantern in the bows. If the natives annoy you, you know what to do. Always shoot natives. When you get anigh the island, you will fire a gun and sing out for the Captain.'

'Quite needless,' interposed a voice from the sea. 'The Captain is here!'

Without taking the slightest notice of the astonishment that he had caused, the commander of the *Fortuna* paddled his canoe to the side of the ship. Instead of ascending to the deck, he stepped into the boat, waiting alongside. 'Lend me your pistols,' he said quietly to the second officer, 'and oblige me by taking your men back to their duties on board.' He looked up at Mr. Duncalf and gave some further directions. 'If there is any change in the weather, keep the ship standing off and on, at a safe distance from the land, and throw up a rocket from time to time to show your position. Expect me on board again by sunrise.'

'What!' cried the mate. 'Do you mean to say you are going back to the island—in that boat—all by yourself?'

'I am going back to the island,' answered the Captain, as quietly as ever; 'in this boat—all by myself.' He pushed off from the ship, and hoisted the sail as he spoke.

'You're deserting your duty!' the old sea-dog shouted, with one of his loudest oaths.

'Attend to my directions,' the Captain shouted back, as he drifted away into the darkness.

Mr. Duncalf—violently agitated for the first time in his life—took leave of his superior officer, with a singular mixture of solemnity and politeness, in these words:

'The Lord have mercy on your soul! I wish you good-evening.'

VIII.

ALONE in the boat, the Captain looked with a misgiving mind at the flashing of the volcano on the main island.

If events had favoured him, he would have removed Aimata to the shelter of the ship on the day when he saw the emptied basin of the lake. But the smoke of the Priest's sacrifice had been discovered by the chief; and he had despatched two canoes with instructions to make inquiries. One of the canoes had returned; the other was kept in waiting off the cape, to place a means of communicating with the main island at the disposal of the Priest. The second shock of earthquake had naturally increased the alarm of the chief. He had sent messages to the Priest, entreating him to leave the island, and other messages to Aimata suggesting that she should exert her influence over her father, if he hesitated. The Priest refused to leave the Temple. He trusted in his gods and his sacrifices — he believed they might avert the fatality that threatened his sanctuary.

Yielding to the holy man, the chief sent reinforcements of canoes to take their turn at keeping watch off the headland. Assisted by torches, the islanders were on the alert (in superstitious terror of the demon of the prophecy) by night as well as by day. The Captain had no alternative but to keep in hiding, and to watch his opportunity of approaching the place in which he had concealed his canoe. It was only after Aimata had left him as usual, to return to her father at the close of evening, that the chances declared themselves in his favour. The fire-flashes from the mountain, visible when the night came, had struck terror into the hearts of the men on the watch. They thought of their wives, their children, and their possessions on the main island, and they one and all deserted their Priest. The Captain seized the opportunity of communicating with the ship, and of exchanging a frail canoe which he was ill able to manage, for a swift-sailing boat capable of keeping the sea in the event of stormy weather.

As he now neared the land, certain small sparks of red, moving on the distant water, informed him that the canoes of the sentinels had been ordered back to their duty.

Carefully avoiding the lights, he reached his own side of the island without accident, and guided by the boat's lantern, anchored under the cliff. He climbed the rocks, advanced to the door of the hut, and was met, to his delight and astonishment, by Aimata on the threshold.

'I dreamed that some dreadful misfortune had parted us for ever,' she said; 'and I came here to see if my dream was true. You have taught me what it is to be miserable; I never felt my heart ache till I looked into the hut and found that you had gone. Now I have seen you, I am satisfied. No! you must not go back with me. My father may be out looking for me. It is you that are in danger, not I. I know the forest as well by dark as by daylight.'

The Captain detained her when she tried to leave him.

'Now you *are* here,' he said, 'why should I not place you at once in safety? I have been to the ship; I have brought back one of the boats. The darkness will befriend us—let us embark while we can.'

She shrank away as he took her hand. 'You forget my father!' she said.

'Your father is in no danger, my love. The canoes are waiting for him at the cape. I saw the lights as I passed.'

With that reply he drew her out of the hut and led her towards the sea. Not a breath of the breeze was now to be felt. The dead calm had returned—and the boat was too large to be easily managed by one man alone at the oars.

'The breeze may come again,' he said. 'Wait here, my angel, for the chance.'

As he spoke, the deep silence of the forest below them was broken by a sound. A harsh wailing voice was heard, calling:

'Aimata! Aimata!'

'My father!' she whispered; 'he has missed me. If he comes here you are lost.'

She kissed him with passionate fervour; she held him to her for a moment with all her strength.

'Expect me at daybreak,' she said, and disappeared down the landward slope of the cliff.

He listened, anxious for her safety. The voices of the father and daughter just reached him from among the trees. The priest spoke in no angry tones; she had apparently found an acceptable excuse for her absence. Little by little, the failing sound of their voices told him that they were on their way back together to the Temple. The silence fell again. Not a ripple broke on the beach. Not a leaf rustled in the forest. Nothing moved but the reflected flashes of the volcano on the mainland over the black sky. It was an airless and an awful calm.

He went into the hut, and laid down on his bed of leaves—not to sleep, but to rest. All his energies might be required to meet the coming events of the morning. After the voyage to and from the ship, and the long watching that had preceded it, strong as he was he stood in need of repose.

For some little time he kept awake, thinking. Insensibly the oppression of the intense heat, aided in its influence by his own fatigue, treacherously closed his eyes. In spite of himself, the weary man fell into a deep sleep.

He was awakened by a roar like the explosion of a park of artillery. The volcano on the main island had burst into a state of eruption. Smoky flame-light overspread the sky, and flashed through the open doorway of the hut. He sprang from his bed—and found himself up to his knees in water.

Had the sea overflowed the land?

He waded out of the hut, and the water rose to his middle. He looked round him by the lurid light of the eruption. The one visible object within the range of view was the sea, stained by reflections from the blood-red sky, swirling and rippling strangely in the dead calm. In a moment more, he became conscious that the earth on which he stood was sinking under his feet. The water rose to his neck; the last vestige of the roof of the hut disappeared.

He looked round again, and the truth burst on him. The island was sinking— slowly, slowly sinking into volcanic depths, below even the depth of the sea! The highest object was the hut, and that had dropped inch by inch under water before his own eyes. Thrown up to the surface by occult volcanic influences, the island had sunk back, under the same influences, to the obscurity from which it had emerged!

A black shadowy object, turning in a wide circle, came slowly near him as the all-destroying ocean washed its bitter waters into his mouth. The buoyant boat, rising as the sea rose, had dragged its anchor, and was floating round in the vortex made by the slowly-sinking island. With a last desperate hope that Aimata might have been saved as *he* had been saved, he swam to the boat, seized the heavy oars with the strength of a giant, and made for the place (so far as he could guess at it now) where the lake and the Temple had once been.

He looked round and round him; he strained his eyes in the vain attempt to penetrate below the surface of the seething dimpling sea. Had the panic-stricken watchers in the canoes saved themselves, without an effort to preserve the father and daughter? Or had they both been suffocated before they could make an attempt to escape? He called to her in his

misery, as if she could hear him out of the fathomless depths, 'Aimata! Aimata!' The roar of the distant eruption answered him. The mounting fires lit the solitary sea far and near over the sinking island. The boat turned slowly and more slowly in the lessening vortex. Never again would those gentle eyes look at him with unutterable love! Never again would those fresh lips touch his lips with their fervent kiss! Alone, amid the savage forces of Nature in conflict, the miserable mortal lifted his hands in frantic supplication — and the burning sky glared down on him in its pitiless grandeur, and struck him to his knees in the boat. His reason sank with his sinking limbs. In the merciful frenzy that succeeded the shock, he saw her afar off, in her white robe, an angel poised on the waters, beckoning him to follow her to the brighter and the better world. He loosened the sail, he seized the oars; and the faster he pursued it, the faster the mocking vision fled from him over the empty and endless sea.

IX.

THE boat was discovered, on the next morning, from the ship.

All that the devotion of the officers of the *Fortuna* could do for their unhappy commander was done on the homeward voyage. Restored to his own country, and to skilled medical help, the Captain's mind by slow degrees recovered its balance. He has taken his place in society again— he lives and moves and manages his affairs like the rest of us. But his heart is dead to all new emotions; nothing remains in it but the sacred remembrance of his lost love. He neither courts nor avoids the society of women. Their sympathy finds him grateful, but their attractions seem to be lost on him ; they pass from his mind as they pass from his eyes — they stir nothing in him but the memory of Aimata.

' Now you know, ladies, why the Captain will never marry, and why (sailor as he is) he hates the sight of the sea.'

Mr. Marmaduke and the Minister

I.

September 13*th*.—Winter seems to be upon us, on the Highland Border, already.

I looked out of window, as the evening closed in, before I barred the shutters and drew the curtains for the night. The clouds hid the hilltops on either side of our valley. Fantastic mists parted and met again on the lower slopes, as the varying breeze blew them. The blackening waters of the lake before our window seemed to anticipate the coming darkness. On the more distant hills the torrents were just visible, in the breaks of the mist, stealing their way over the brown ground like threads of silver. It was a dreary scene. The stillness of all things was only interrupted by the splashing of our little waterfall at the back of the house. I was not sorry to close the shutters, and confine the view to the four walls of our sitting-room.

The day happened to be my birthday. I sat by the peat-fire, waiting for the lamp and the tea-tray, and contemplating my past life from the vantage-ground, so to speak, of my fifty-fifth year.

There was wonderfully little to look back

on. Nearly thirty years since, it pleased an all-wise Providence to cast my lot in this remote Scottish hamlet, and to make me Minister of Cauldkirk, on a stipend of seventy-four pounds sterling per annum. I and my surroundings have grown quietly older and older together. I have outlived my wife; I have buried one generation among my parishioners, and married another; I have borne the wear and tear of years better than the kirk in which I minister and the manse (or parsonage-house) in which I live—both sadly out of repair, and both still trusting for the means of reparation to the pious benefactions of persons richer than myself. Not that I complain, be it understood, of the humble position which I occupy. I possess many blessings; and I thank the Lord for them. I have my little bit of land and my cow. I have also my good daughter, Felicia; named after her deceased mother, but inheriting her comely looks, it is thought, rather from myself.

Neither let me forget my elder sister, Judith; a friendless single person, sheltered under my roof, whose temperament I could wish somewhat less prone to look at persons and things on the gloomy side, but whose compensating virtues Heaven forbid that I should deny. No; I am grateful for what has been given me (from on high), and resigned to what has been taken away. With what fair prospects did I start in life! Springing from a good old Scottish stock, blest with every advantage of education that the institutions of Scotland and England in turn could offer; with a career at the Bar and in Parliament before me— and all cast to the winds, as it were, by the measureless prodigality of my unhappy father, God forgive him! I doubt if I had five pounds left in my purse, when the compassion of my relatives on the mother's side opened a refuge to me at Cauldkirk, and hid me from the notice of the world for the rest of my life.

September 14*th.*—Thus far I had posted up my Diary on the evening of the 13th, when an event occurred so completely unexpected by my household and myself, that the pen, I may say, dropped incontinently from my hand.

It was the time when we had finished our tea, or supper—I hardly know which to call it. In the silence, we could hear the rain pouring against the window, and the wind that had risen with the darkness howling round the house. My sister Judith, taking the gloomy view according to custom — copious draughts of good Bohea and two helpings of such a mutton ham as only Scotland can produce had no effect in raising her spirits—my sister, I say, remarked that there would be ships lost at sea and men drowned this night. My daughter Felicia, the brightest-tempered creature of the female sex that I have ever met with, tried to give a cheerful turn to her aunt's depressing prognostication. 'If the ships must be lost,' she said, 'we may surely hope that the men will be saved.'

'God willing,' I put in—thereby giving to my daughter's humane expression of feeling the fit religious tone that was all it wanted—and then went on with my written record of the events and reflections of the day. No more was said. Felicia took up a book. Judith took up her knitting.

On a sudden, the silence was broken by a blow on the house-door.

My two companions, as is the way of women, set up a scream. I was startled myself, wondering who could be out in the rain and the darkness, and striking at the door of the house. A stranger it must be. Light or dark, any person in or near Cauldkirk, wanting admission, would know where to find the bell-handle at the side of the door. I waited awhile to hear what might happen next. The stroke was repeated, but more softly. It became me as a man and a minister to set an example. I went out into the passage, and I called through the door, 'Who's there?'

A man's voice answered — so faintly that I could barely hear him—'A lost traveller.'

Immediately upon this my cheerful sister expressed her view of the matter through the open parlour door. 'Brother Noah, it's a robber. Don't let him in !'

What would the Good Samaritan have done in my place? Assuredly he would have run the risk and opened the door. I imitated the Good Samaritan.

A man, dripping wet, with a knapsack on his back and a thick stick in his hand, staggered in, and would I think have fallen in the passage if I had not caught him by the arm. Judith peeped out at the parlour door, and said, 'He's drunk.' Felicia was behind her, holding up a lighted candle the better to see what was going on. 'Look at his face, aunt,' says she. 'Worn out with fatigue, poor man. Bring him in, father— bring him in.'

Good Felicia ! I was proud of my girl. 'He'll spoil the carpet,' says sister Judith. I said, 'Silence, for shame!' and brought him in, and dropped him dripping into my own armchair. Would the Good Samaritan have thought of his carpet or his chair ? I did think of them, but I overcame it. Ah, we are a decadent generation in these latter days !

'Be quick, father !' says Felicia ; 'he'll faint if you don't give him something !'

I took out one of our little drinking cups (called among us a ' Quaigh '), while Felicia, instructed by me, ran to the kitchen for the cream-jug. Filling the cup with whisky and cream in equal proportions, I offered it to him. He drank it off as if it had been so much water. ' Stimulant and nourishment, you'll observe, sir, in equal portions,' I remarked to him. ' How do you feel now ?'

' Ready for another,' says he.

Felicia burst out laughing. I gave him another. As I turned to hand it to him, sister Judith came behind me, and snatched away the cream-jug. Never a generous person, sister Judith, at the best of times— more especially in the matter of cream.

He handed me back the empty cup. ' I believe, sir, you have saved my life,' he said. ' Under Providence,' I put in— adding, ' But I would remark, looking to the state of your clothes, that I have yet another service to offer you, before you tell us how you came into this pitiable state.' With that reply, I led him upstairs, and set before him the poor resources of my ward-robe, and left him to do the best he could with them. He was rather a small man, and I am in stature nigh on six feet. When he came down to us in my clothes, we had the merriest evening that I can remember for years past. I thought Felicia would have had an hysteric fit ; and even sister Judith laughed—he did look such a comical figure in the minister's garments.

As for the misfortune that had befallen him, it offered one more example of the preternatural rashness of the English traveller in countries unknown to him. He was on a walking tour through Scotland ; and he had set forth to go twenty miles a-foot, from a town on one side of the Highland Border to a town on the other, without a guide. The only wonder is that he found his way to Cauldkirk, instead of perishing of exposure among the lonesome hills.

' Will you offer thanks for your preservation to the Throne of Grace, in your prayers to-night ?' I asked him. And he answered, ' Indeed I will !'

We have a spare room at the manse ; but it had not been inhabited for more than a year past. Therefore we made his bed, for that night, on the sofa in the parlour ; and so left him, with the fire on one side of his couch, and the whisky and the mutton ham on the other in case of need. He mentioned his name when we bade him good-night. Marmaduke Falmer of London, son of a minister of the English Church Establishment, now deceased. It was plain, I may add, before he spoke, that we had offered the hospitality of the manse to a man of gentle breeding.

September 15*th.*—I have to record a singularly pleasant day ; due partly to a return of the fine weather, partly to the good social gifts of our guest.

Attired again in his own clothing, he was, albeit wanting in height, a finely proportioned man, with remarkably small hands and feet ; having also a bright mobile face, and large dark eyes of an extraordinary diversity of expression. Also, he was of a sweet and cheerful humour ; easily pleased with little things, and amiably ready to make his gifts agreeable to all of us. At the same time, a person of my experience and penetration could not fail to perceive that he was most content when in company with Felicia. I have already mentioned my daughter's comely looks and good womanly qualities. It was in the order of nature that a young man (to use his own phrase) getting near to his thirty-first birthday should feel drawn by sympathy towards a well-favoured young woman in her four-and-twentieth year. In matters of this sort I have always cultivated a liberal turn of mind, not forgetting my own youth.

As the evening closed in, I was sorry to notice a certain change in our guest for the worse. He showed signs of fatigue—falling asleep at intervals in his chair, and waking up and shivering. The spare room was now well aired, having had a roaring fire in it all day.

I begged him not to stand on ceremony, and to betake himself at once to his bed. Felicia (having learned the accomplishment from her excellent mother) made him a warm sleeping-draught of eggs, sugar, nutmeg, and spirits, delicious alike to the senses of smell and taste. Sister Judith waited until he had closed the door behind him, and then favoured me with one of her dismal predictions. ' You'll rue the day, brother, when you let him into the house. He is going to fall ill on our hands.'

II.

November 28th.—God be praised for all His mercies ! This day, our guest, Marmaduke Falmer, joined us downstairs in the sitting-room for the first time since his illness.

He is sadly deteriorated, in a bodily sense, by the wasting rheumatic fever that brought him nigh to death ; but he is still young, and the doctor (humanly speaking) has no doubt of his speedy and complete recovery.

My sister takes the opposite view. She remarked, in his hearing, that nobody ever thoroughly got over a rheumatic fever. Oh, Judith ! Judith ! it's well for humanity that you're a single person ! If, haply, there had been any man desperate enough to tackle such a woman in the bonds of marriage, what a pessimist progeny must have proceeded from you !

Looking back over my Diary for the last two months and more, I see one monotonous record of the poor fellow's sufferings ; cheered and varied, I am pleased to add, by the devoted services of my daughter at the sick man's bedside. With some help from her aunt (most readily given when he was nearest to the point of death), and with needful services performed in turn by two of our aged women in Cauldkirk, Felicia could not have nursed him more assiduously if he had been her own brother. Half the credit of bringing him through it belonged (as the doctor himself confessed) to the discreet young nurse, always ready through the worst of the illness, and always cheerful through the long convalescence that followed. I must also record to the credit of Marmaduke that he was indeed duly grateful. When I led him into the parlour, and he saw Felicia waiting by the armchair, smiling and patting the pillows for him, he took her by the hand, and burst out crying. Weakness, in part, no doubt—but sincere gratitude at the bottom of it, I am equally sure.

November 29th.—However, there are limits even to sincere gratitude. Of this truth Mr. Marmaduke seems to be insufficiently aware. Entering the sitting-room soon after noon to-day, I found our convalescent guest and his nurse alone. His head was resting on her shoulder ; his arm was round her waist—and (the truth before everything) Felicia was kissing him.

A man may be of a liberal turn of mind, and may yet consistently object to freedom when it takes the form of unlicensed embracing and kissing; the person being his own daughter, and the place his own house. I signed to my girl to leave us; and I advanced to Mr. Marmaduke, with my opinion of his conduct just rising in words to my lips—when he staggered me with amazement by asking for Felicia's hand in marriage.

'You need feel no doubt of my being able to offer to your daughter a position of comfort and respectability,' he said. 'I have a settled income of eight hundred pounds a year.'

His raptures over Felicia; his protestations that she was the first woman he had ever really loved; his profane declaration that he preferred to die, if I refused to let him be her husband—all these flourishes, as I may call them, passed in at one of my ears and out at the other. But eight hundred pounds sterling per annum, descending as it were in a golden avalanche on the mind of a Scottish minister (accustomed to thirty years' annual contemplation of seventy-four pounds)—eight hundred a year, in one young man's pocket, I say, completely overpowered me. I just managed to answer, 'Wait till to-morrow'—and hurried out of doors to recover my self-respect, if the thing was to be anywise done. I took my way through the valley. The sun was shining, for a wonder. When I saw my shadow on the hillside, I saw the Golden Calf as an integral part of me, bearing this inscription in letters of flame— 'Here's another of them!'

November 30*th.*—I have made amends for yesterday's backsliding; I have acted as becomes my parental dignity and my sacred calling.

The temptation to do otherwise has not been wanting. Here is sister Judith's advice: 'Make sure that he has got the money first; and, for Heaven's sake, nail

him!' Here is Mr. Marmaduke's proposal: 'Make any conditions you please, so long as you give me your daughter.' And, lastly, here is Felicia's confession: 'Father, my heart is set on him. Oh, don't be unkind to me for the first time in your life!'

But I have stood firm. I have refused to hear any more words on the subject from any one of them, for the next six months to come.

'So serious a venture as the venture of marriage,' I said, 'is not to be undertaken on impulse. As soon as Mr. Marmaduke can travel, I request him to leave us, and not to return again for six months. If, after that interval, he is still of the same mind, and my daughter is still of the same mind, let him return to Cauldkirk, and (premising that I am in all other respects satisfied) let him ask me for his wife.'

There were tears, there were protestations; I remained immovable. A week later, Mr. Marmaduke left us, on his way by easy stages to the south. I am not a hard man. I rewarded the lovers for their obedience by keeping sister Judith out of the way, and letting them say their farewell words (accompaniments included) in private.

III.

May 28*th.*—A letter from Mr. Marmaduke, informing me that I may expect him at Cauldkirk, exactly at the expiration of the six months' interval — viz., on June the seventh.

Writing to this effect, he added a timely word on the subject of his family. Both his parents were dead; his only brother held a civil appointment in India, the place being named. His uncle (his father's brother) was a merchant resident in London; and to this near relative he referred me, if I wished to make inquiries about him. The names of his bankers, authorised to give me every information in respect to his pecuniary affairs, followed. Nothing could be more plain and straight-forward. I wrote to his uncle, and I wrote to his bankers. In both cases the replies were perfectly satisfactory—nothing in the slightest degree doubtful, no pre-varications, no mysteries. In a word, Mr. Marmaduke himself was thoroughly well vouched for, and Mr. Marmaduke's income was invested in securities beyond fear and beyond reproach. Even sister Judith, bent on picking a hole in the record somewhere, tried hard, and could make nothing of it.

The last sentence in Mr. Marmaduke's letter was the only part of it which I failed to read with pleasure.

He left it to me to fix the day for the marriage, and he entreated that I would make it as early a day as possible. I had a touch of the heartache when I thought of parting with Felicia, and being left at home with nobody but Judith. However, I got over it for that time; and, after con-sulting my daughter, we decided on naming a fortnight after Mr. Marmaduke's arrival —that is to say, the twenty-first of June. This gave Felicia time for her preparations, besides offering to me the opportunity of becoming better acquainted with my son-in-law's disposition. The happiest marriage does indubitably make its demands on human forbearance ; and I was anxious, among other things, to assure myself of Mr. Marmaduke's good temper.

IV.

June 22nd.—The happy change in my daughter's life (let me say nothing of the change in *my* life) has come : they were married yesterday. The manse is a desert ; and sister Judith was never so uncongenial a companion to me as I feel her to be now. Her last words to the married pair, when

they drove away, were : ' Lord help you both ; you have all your troubles before you !'

I had no heart to write yesterday's record, yesterday evening, as usual. The absence of Felicia at the supper-table completely overcame me. I, who have so often com-forted others in their afflictions, could find no comfort for myself. Even now that the day has passed, the tears come into my eyes, only with writing about it. Sad, sad weakness ! Let me close my Diary, and open the Bible—and be myself again.

June 23rd.—More resigned since yester-day ; a more becoming and more pious frame of mind — obedient to God's holy will, and content in the belief that my dear daughter's married life will be a happy one.

They have gone abroad for their holiday —to Switzerland, by way of France. I was anything rather than pleased when I heard that my son-in-law proposed to take Felicia to that sink of iniquity, Paris. He knows already what I think of balls and playhouses, and similar devils' diversions, and how I have brought up my daughter to think of them — the subject having occurred in conversation among us more than a week since. That he could meditate taking a child of mine to the headquarters of indecent jiggings and abominable stage-plays, of spouting rogues and painted Jezebels, was indeed a heavy blow.

However, Felicia reconciled me to it in the end. She declared that her only desire in going to Paris was to see the picture-galleries, the public buildings, and the fair outward aspect of the city generally. ' Your opinions, father, are my opinions,' she said; ' and Marmaduke, I am sure, will so shape our arrangements as to prevent our passing a Sabbath in Paris.' Marmaduke not only consented to this (with the perfect good temper of which I have observed more than one gratifying example in him), but likewise assured me that, speaking for himself personally, it would be a relief to him when they got to the mountains and the lakes. So that matter was happily settled. Go where they may, God bless and prosper them!

Speaking of relief, I must record that Judith has gone away to Aberdeen on a visit to some friends. ' You'll be wretched enough here,' she said at parting, ' all by yourself.' Pure vanity and self-complacence! It may be resignation to her absence, or it may be natural force of mind, I began to be more easy and composed the moment I was alone, and this blessed state of feeling has continued uninterruptedly ever since.

V.

September 5th.—A sudden change in my life, which it absolutely startles me to record. I am going to London !

My purpose in taking this most serious step is of a twofold nature. I have a greater and a lesser object in view.

The greater object is to see my daughter, and to judge for myself whether certain doubts on the vital question of her happiness, which now torment me night and day, are unhappily founded on truth. She and her husband returned in August from their wedding-tour, and took up their abode in Marmaduke's new residence in London. Up to this time, Felicia's letters to me were, in very truth, the delight of my life—she was so entirely happy, so amazed and delighted with all the wonderful things she saw, so full of love and admiration for the best husband that ever lived. Since her return to London, I perceive a complete change.

She makes no positive complaint, but she writes in a tone of weariness and discontent; she says next to nothing of Marmaduke, and she dwells perpetually on the one idea of my going to London to see her. I hope with my whole heart that I am wrong; but the rare allusions to her husband, and the constantly repeated desire to see her father (while she has not been yet three months married), seem to me to be bad signs. In brief, my anxiety is too great to be endured. I have so arranged matters with one of my brethren as to be free to travel to London cheaply by steamer ; and I begin the journey to-morrow.

My lesser object may be dismissed in two words. Having already decided on going to London, I propose to call on the wealthy nobleman who owns all the land hereabouts, and represent to him the discreditable, and indeed dangerous, condition of the parish kirk for want of means to institute the necessary repairs. If I find myself well received, I shall put in a word for the manse, which is almost in as deplorable a condition as the church. My lord is a wealthy man —may his heart and his purse be opened unto me !

Sister Judith is packing my portmanteau. According to custom, she forebodes the worst. ' Never forget,' she says, ' that I warned you against Marmaduke, on the first night when he entered the house.'

VI.

September 10th.—After more delays than one, on land and sea, I was at last set ashore near the Tower, on the afternoon of yesterday. God help us, my worst anticipations have been realized ! My beloved Felicia has urgent and serious need of me.

It is not to be denied that I made my entry into my son-in-law's house in a disturbed and irritated frame of mind. First, my temper was tried by the almost interminable journey, in the noisy and comfortless vehicle which they call a cab, from the river-wharf to the west-end of London, where Marmaduke lives. In the second place, I was scandalised and alarmed by an incident which took place—still on the endless journey from east to west—in a street hard by the market of Covent Garden.

We had just approached a large building, most profusely illuminated with gas, and exhibiting prodigious coloured placards having inscribed on them nothing but the name of Barrymore. The cab came suddenly to a standstill ; and looking out to see what the obstacle might be, I discovered a huge concourse of men and women, drawn across the pavement and road alike, so that it seemed impossible to pass by them. I inquired of my driver what this assembling of the people meant. 'Oh,' says he, 'Barrymore has made another hit.' This answer being perfectly unintelligible to me, I requested some further explanation, and discovered that 'Barrymore' was the name of a stage-player favoured by the populace ; that the building was a theatre ; and that all these creatures with immortal souls were waiting, before the doors opened, to get places at the show !

The emotions of sorrow and indignation caused by this discovery so absorbed me, that I failed to notice an attempt the driver made to pass through, where the crowd seemed to be thinner, until the offended people resented the proceeding. Some of them seized the horse's head ; others were on the point of pulling the driver off his box, when providentially the police interfered. Under their protection, we drew back, and reached our destination in safety, by another way. I record this otherwise unimportant affair, because it grieved and revolted me (when I thought of the people's souls), and so indisposed my mind to take cheerful views of anything.

Under these circumstances, I would fain hope that I have exaggerated the true state of the case, in respect to my daughter's married life.

My good girl almost smothered me with kisses. When I at last got a fair opportunity of observing her, I thought her looking pale and worn and anxious. Query : Should I have arrived at this conclusion if I had met with no example of the wicked dissipations of London, and if I had ridden at my ease in a comfortable vehicle ?

They had a succulent meal ready for me, and, what I call, fair enough whisky out of Scotland. Here again I remarked that Felicia ate very little, and Marmaduke nothing at all. He drank wine too—and, good heavens, champagne wine !—a needless waste of money surely when there was whisky on the table. My appetite being satisfied, my son-in-law went out of the room, and returned with his hat in his hand. 'You and Felicia have many things to talk about on your first evening together. I'll leave you for a while—I shall only be in the way.' So he spoke. It was in vain that his wife and I assured him he was not in the way at all. He kissed his hand, and smiled pleasantly, and left us.

'There, father !' says Felicia. 'For the last ten days, he has gone out like that, and left me alone for the whole evening. When we first returned from Switzerland, he left me in the same mysterious way, only it was after breakfast then. Now he stays at home in the daytime, and goes out at night.'

I inquired if she had not summoned him to give her some explanation.

'I don't know what to make of his explanation,' says Felicia. 'When he went away in the daytime, he told me he had business in the City. Since he took to going out at night, he says he goes to his club.'

'Have you asked where his club is, my dear?'

'He says it's in Pall Mall. There are dozens of clubs in that street—and he has never told me the name of *his* club. I am completely shut out of his confidence. Would you believe it, father? he has not introduced one of his friends to me since we came home. I doubt if they know where he lives, since he took this house.'

What could I say?

I said nothing, and looked round the room. It was fitted up with perfectly palatial magnificence. I am an ignorant man in matters of this sort, and partly to satisfy my curiosity, partly to change the subject, I asked to see the house. Mercy preserve us, the same grandeur everywhere! I wondered if even such an income as eight hundred a year could suffice for it all. In a moment when I was considering this, a truly frightful suspicion crossed my mind. Did these mysterious absences, taken in connection with the unbridled luxury that surrounded us, mean that my son-in-law was a gamester? a shameless shuffler of cards, or a debauched bettor on horses? While I was still completely overcome by my own previsions of evil, my daughter put her arm in mine to take me to the top of the house.

For the first time I observed a bracelet of dazzling gems on her wrist. 'Not diamonds?' I said. She answered, with as much composure as if she had been the wife of a nobleman, 'Yes, diamonds—a present from Marmaduke.' This was too much for me; my previsions, so to speak, forced their way into words. 'Oh, my poor child!' I burst out, 'I'm in mortal fear that your husband's a gamester!'

She showed none of the horror I had anticipated; she only shook her head and began to cry.

'Worse than that, I'm afraid,' she said.

I was petrified; my tongue refused its office, when I would fain have asked her what she meant. Her besetting sin, poor soul, is a proud spirit. She dried her eyes on a sudden, and spoke out freely, in these words: 'I am not going to cry about it. The other day, father, we were out walking in the park. A horrid, bold, yellow-haired woman passed us in an open carriage. She kissed her hand to Marmaduke, and called out to him, "How are you, Marmy?" I was so indignant that I pushed him away from me, and told him to go and take a drive with his lady. He burst out laughing. "Nonsense!" he said; "she has known me for years—you don't understand our easy London manners." We have made it up since then; but I have my own opinion of the creature in the open carriage.'

Morally speaking, this was worse than all. But, logically viewed, it completely failed as a means of accounting for the diamond bracelet and the splendour of the furniture.

We went on to the uppermost story. It was cut off from the rest of the house by a stout partition of wood, and a door covered with green baize.

When I tried the door it was locked. 'Ha!' says Felicia, 'I wanted you to see it for yourself!' More suspicious proceedings on the part of my son-in-law! He kept the door constantly locked, and the key in his pocket. When his wife asked him what it meant, he answered: 'My study is up there—and I like to keep it entirely to myself.' After such a reply as that, the preservation of my daughter's dignity permitted but one answer: 'Oh, keep it to yourself, by all means!'

My previsions, upon this, assumed another form.

I now asked myself—still in connection with my son-in-law's extravagant expenditure—whether the clue to the mystery might not haply be the forging of bank-notes on the other side of the baize door. My mind was prepared for anything by this time. We descended again to the dining-room. Felicia saw how my spirits were dashed, and came and perched upon my knee. 'Enough of my troubles for to-night, father,' she said. 'I am going to be your little girl again, and we will talk of nothing but Cauldkirk, until Marmaduke comes back.' I am one of the firmest men living, but I could not keep the hot tears out of my eyes when she put her arm round my neck and said those words. By good fortune I was sitting with my back to the lamp ; she didn't notice me.

A little after eleven o'clock, Marmaduke returned. He looked pale and weary. But more champagne, and this time something to eat with it, seemed to set him to rights again—no doubt by relieving him from the reproaches of a guilty conscience.

I had been warned by Felicia to keep what had passed between us a secret from her husband for the present ; so we had (superficially speaking) a merry end to the evening. My son-in-law was nearly as good company as ever, and wonderfully fertile in suggestions and expedients when he saw they were wanted. Hearing from his wife, to whom I had mentioned it, that I purposed representing the decayed con-dition of the kirk and manse to the owner of Cauldkirk and the country round about, he strongly urged me to draw up a list of repairs that were most needful, before I waited on my lord. This advice, vicious and degraded as the man who offered it may be, is sound advice nevertheless. I shall assuredly take it.

So far I had written in my Diary, in the forenoon. Returning to my daily record, after a lapse of some hours, I have a new mystery of iniquity to chronicle. My abominable son-in-law now appears (I blush to write it) to be nothing less than an associate of thieves !

After the meal they call luncheon, I thought it well, before recreating myself with the sights of London, to attend first to the crying necessities of the kirk and the manse. Furnished with my written list, I presented myself at his lordship's residence. I was immediately informed that he was otherwise engaged, and could not possibly receive me. If I wished to see my lord's secretary, Mr. Helmsley, I could do so. Consenting to this, rather than fail entirely in my errand, I was shown into the secretary's room.

Mr. Helmsley heard what I had to say civilly enough ; expressing, however, grave doubts whether his lordship would do any-thing for me, the demands on his purse being insupportably numerous already. However, he undertook to place my list before his employer, and to let me know the result. 'Where are you staying in London ?' he asked. I answered, 'With my son-in-law, Mr. Marmaduke Falmer.' Before I could add the address, the secretary started to his feet, and tossed my list back to me across the table in the most uncivil manner.

'Upon my word,' says he, 'your assur-ance exceeds anything I ever heard of. Your son-in-law is concerned in the robbery of her ladyship's diamond bracelet—the dis-covery was made not an hour ago. Leave the house, sir, and consider yourself lucky that I have no instructions to give you in charge to the police.' I protested against this unprovoked outrage, with a violence of language which I would rather not recall. As a minister I ought, under every pro-vocation, to have preserved my self-control.

The one thing to do next was to drive back to my unhappy daughter.

Her guilty husband was with her. I was too angry to wait for a fit opportunity of speaking. The Christian humility which I have all my life cultivated as the first of virtues sank, as it were, from under me. In terms of burning indignation I told them what had happened. The result was too distressing to be described. It ended in Felicia giving her husband back the bracelet. The hardened reprobate laughed at us. ' Wait till I have seen his lordship and Mr. Helmsley,' he said, and left the house.

Does he mean to escape to foreign parts ? Felicia, womanlike, believes in him still ; she is quite convinced that there must be some mistake. I am myself in hourly expectation of the arrival of the police.

With gratitude to Providence, I note before going to bed the harmless termination of the affair of the bracelet—so far as Marmaduke is concerned. The agent who sold him the jewel has been forced to come forward and state the truth. His lordship's wife is the guilty person ; the bracelet was hers—a present from her husband. Harassed by debts that she dare not acknowledge, she sold it ; my lord discovered that it was gone ; and in terror of his anger the wretched woman took refuge in a lie.

She declared that the bracelet had been stolen from her. Asked for the name of the thief, the reckless woman (having no other name in her mind at the moment) mentioned the man who had innocently bought the jewel of her agent, otherwise my unfortunate son-in-law. Oh, the profligacy of the modern Babylon ! It was well I went to the secretary when I did, or we should really have had the police in the house. Marmaduke found them in consultation over the supposed robbery, asking for his address. There was a dreadful exhibition of violence and recrimination at his lordship's residence : in the end he repurchased the bracelet. My son-in-law's money has been returned to him ; and Mr. Helmsley has sent me a written apology.

In a worldly sense, this would, I suppose, be called a satisfactory ending.

It is not so, to my mind. I freely admit that I too hastily distrusted Marmaduke ; but am I, on that account, to give him back immediately the place which he once occupied in my esteem ? Again this evening he mysteriously quitted the house, leaving me alone with Felicia, and giving no better excuse for his conduct than that he had an engagement. And this when I have a double claim on his consideration, as his father-in-law and his guest !

September 11*th.*—The day began well enough. At breakfast, Marmaduke spoke feelingly of the unhappy result of my visit to his lordship, and asked me to let him look at the list of repairs. ' It's just useless to expect anything from my lord, after what has happened,' I said. ' Besides, Mr. Helmsley gave me no hope when I stated my case to him.' Marmaduke still held out his hand for the list. ' Let me try if I can get some subscribers,' he replied. This was kindly meant, at any rate. I gave him the list; and I began to recover some of my old friendly feeling for him. Alas ! the little gleam of tranquillity proved to be of short duration.

We made out our plans for the day pleasantly enough. The check came when Felicia spoke next of our plans for the evening. ' My father has only four days more to pass with us,' she said to her husband. ' Surely you won't go out again to-night, and leave him ?' Marmaduke's face clouded over directly ; he looked embarrassed and annoyed. I sat perfectly silent, leaving them to settle it by themselves.

' You will stay with us this evening, won't you ?' says Felicia. No : he was not free for that evening. ' What ! another engagement ? Surely you can put it off ?' No ; impossible to put it off. ' Is it a ball, or a party of some kind ?' No answer ; he changed the subject—he offered Felicia the money repaid to him for the bracelet. 'Buy one for yourself, my dear, this time.' Felicia handed him back the money, rather too haughtily perhaps. 'I don't want a bracelet,' she said : 'I want your company in the evening.'

He jumped up, good-tempered as he was, in something very like a rage—then looked at me, and checked himself on the point (as I believe) of using profane language. 'This is downright persecution !' he burst out, with an angry turn of his head towards his wife. Felicia got up, in her turn. 'Your language is an insult to my father and to me !' He looked thoroughly staggered at this : it was evidently their first serious quarrel.

Felicia took no notice of him. 'I will get ready directly, father ; and we will go out together.' He stopped her as she was leaving the room — recovering his good temper with a readiness which it pleased me to see. 'Come, come, Felicia ! We have not quarrelled yet, and we won't quarrel now. Let me off this one time more, and I will devote the next three evenings of your father's visit to him and to you. Give me a kiss, and make it up.' My daughter doesn't do things by halves. She gave him a dozen kisses, I should think —and there was a happy end to it.

'But what shall we do to-morrow evening ?' says Marmaduke, sitting down by his wife, and patting her hand as it lay in his.

'Take us somewhere,' says she. Marmaduke laughed. 'Your father objects to public amusements. Where does he want to go to ?' Felicia took up the newspaper. 'There is an oratorio at Exeter Hall,' she said ; 'my father likes music.' He turned to me. 'You don't object to oratorios, sir ?' 'I don't object to music,' I answered, 'so long as I am not required to enter a theatre.' Felicia handed the newspaper to me. 'Speaking of theatres, father, have you read what they say about the new play ? What a pity it can't be given out of a theatre !' I looked at her in speechless amazement. She tried to explain herself. 'The paper says that the new play is a service rendered to the cause of virtue ; and that the great actor, Barrymore, has set an example in producing it which deserves the encouragement of all truly religious people. Do read it, father !' I held up my hands in dismay. My own daughter perverted ! pinning her faith on a newspaper ! speaking, with a perverse expression of interest, of a stage-play and an actor ! Even Marmaduke witnessed this lamentable exhibition of backsliding with some appearance of alarm. 'It's not her fault, sir,' he said, interceding with me. 'It's the fault of the newspaper. Don't blame her !' I held my peace ; determining inwardly to pray for her. Shortly afterwards my daughter and I went out. Marmaduke accompanied us part of the way, and left us at a telegraph-office. 'Who are you going to telegraph to ?' Felicia asked. Another mystery ! He answered, 'Business of my own, my dear'—and went into the office.

September 12*th.*—Is my miserable son-in-law's house under a curse ? The yellow-haired woman in the open carriage drove up to the door at half-past ten this morning, in a state of distraction. Felicia and I saw her from the drawing-room balcony—a tall woman in gorgeous garments. She knocked with her own hand at the door—she cried out distractedly, 'Where is he ? I must see him !' At the sound of her voice, Marmaduke (playing with his little dog in the drawing-room) rushed downstairs, and out into the street. 'Hold your tongue !' we heard him say to her. 'What are you here for ?'

What she answered we failed to hear; she was certainly crying. Marmaduke stamped on the pavement like a man beside himself—took her roughly by the arm, and led her into the house.

Before I could utter a word, Felicia left me, and flew headlong down the stairs.

She was in time to hear the dining-room door locked. Following her, I prevented the poor jealous creature from making a disturbance at the door. God forgive me—not knowing how else to quiet her—I degraded myself by advising her to listen to what they said. She instantly opened the door of the back dining-room, and beckoned to me to follow. I naturally hesitated. 'I shall go mad,' she whispered, 'if you leave me by myself!' What could I do? I degraded myself for the second time. For my own child—in pity for my own child!

We heard them, through the flimsy modern folding-doors, at those times when he was most angry, and she most distracted. That is to say, we heard them when they spoke in their loudest tones.

'How did you find out where I live?' says he. 'Oh, you're ashamed of me?' says she. 'Mr. Helmsley was with us yesterday evening. That's how I found out!' 'What do you mean?' 'I mean that Mr. Helmsley had your card and address in his pocket. Ah, you were obliged to give your address when you had to clear up that matter of the bracelet! You cruel, cruel man, what have I done to deserve such a note as you sent me this morning?' 'Do what the note tells you!' 'Do what the note tells me? Did anybody ever hear a man talk so, out of a lunatic asylum? Why, you haven't even the grace to carry out your own wicked deception—you haven't even gone to bed!' There the voices grew less angry, and we missed what followed. Soon the lady burst out again, piteously entreating him this time. 'Oh, Marmy, don't ruin me! Has anybody

offended you? Is there anything you wish to have altered? Do you want more money? It is too cruel to treat me in this way—it is indeed!' He made some answer, which we were not able to hear; we could only suppose that he had upset her temper again. She went on louder than ever. 'I've begged and prayed of you—and you're as hard as iron. I've told you about the Prince —and that has had no effect on you. I have done now. We'll see what the doctor says.' He got angry, in his turn; we heard him again. 'I won't see the doctor!' 'Oh, you refuse to see the doctor? I shall make your refusal known—and if there's law in England, you shall feel it!' Their voices dropped again; some new turn seemed to be taken by the conversation. We heard the lady once more, shrill and joyful this time. 'There's a dear! You see it, don't you, in the right light? And you haven't forgotten the old times, have you? You're the same dear, honourable, kind-hearted fellow that you always were!'

I caught hold of Felicia, and put my hand over her mouth.

There was a sound in the next room which might have been — I cannot be certain—the sound of a kiss. The next moment, we heard the door of the room unlocked. Then the door of the house was opened, and the noise of retreating carriage-wheels followed. We met him in the hall, as he entered the house again.

My daughter walked up to him, pale and determined.

'I insist on knowing who that woman is, and what she wants here.' Those were her first words. He looked at her like a man in utter confusion. 'Wait till this evening; I am in no state to speak to you now!' With that, he snatched his hat off the hall table, and rushed out of the house.

It is little more than three weeks since they returned to London from their happy wedding-tour—and it has come to this!

The clock has just struck seven ; a letter has been left by a messenger, addressed to my daughter. I had persuaded her, poor soul, to lie down in her own room. God grant that the letter may bring her some tidings of her husband! I please myself in the hope of hearing good news.

My mind has not been kept long in suspense. Felicia's waiting-woman has brought me a morsel of writing-paper, with these lines pencilled on it in my daughter's handwriting : 'Dearest father, make your mind easy. Everything is explained. I cannot trust myself to speak to you about it to-night—and *he* doesn't wish me to do so. Only wait till to-morrow, and you shall know all. He will be back about eleven o'clock. Please don't wait up for him—he will come straight to me.'

September 13*th.*—The scales have fallen from my eyes ; the light is let in on me at last. My bewilderment is not to be uttered in words—I am like a man in a dream.

Before I was out of my room in the morning, my mind was upset by the arrival of a telegram addressed to myself. It was the first thing of the kind I ever received ; I trembled under the prevision of some new misfortune as I opened the envelope.

Of all the people in the world, the person sending the telegram was sister Judith! Never before did this distracting relative confound me as she confounded me now. Here is her message : 'You can't come back. An architect from Edinburgh asserts his resolution to repair the kirk and the manse. The man only waits for his lawful authority to begin. The money is ready—but who has found it ? Mr. Architect is forbidden to tell. We live in awful times. How is Felicia?'

Naturally concluding that Judith's mind must be deranged, I went downstairs to meet my son-in-law (for the first time since the events of yesterday) at the late breakfast which is customary in this house. He was waiting for me—but Felicia was not present. 'She breakfasts in her room this morning,' says Marmaduke ; 'and I am to give you the explanation which has already satisfied your daughter. Will you take it at great length, sir ? or will you have it in one word ?' There was something in his manner that I did not at all like—he seemed to be setting me at defiance. I said, stiffly, 'Brevity is best ; I will have it in one word.'

'Here it is then,' he answered. 'I am Barrymore.'

Postscript added by Felicia.

If the last line extracted from my dear father's Diary does not contain explanation enough in itself, I add some sentences from Marmaduke's letter to me, sent from the theatre last night. (N.B.—I leave out the expressions of endearment : they are my own private property.)

* * * 'Just remember how your father talked about theatres and actors, when I was at Cauldkirk, and how you listened in dutiful agreement with him. Would he have consented to your marriage if he had known that I was one of the "spouting rogues," associated with the "painted Jezebels" of the play-house ? He would never have consented — and you yourself, my darling, would have trembled at the bare idea of marrying an actor.

'Have I been guilty of any serious deception ? and have my friends been guilty in helping to keep my secret? My birth, my name, my surviving relatives, my fortune inherited from my father—all these important particulars have been truly stated. The name of Barrymore is nothing but the name that I assumed when I went on the stage.

'As to what has happened, since our return from Switzerland, I own that I ought to have made my confession to you. Forgive me if I weakly hesitated. I was so fond of you ; and I so distrusted the Puritanical convictions which your education had rooted in your mind, that I put it off from day to day. Oh, my angel * * *!

'Yes, I kept the address of my new house a secret from all my friends, knowing they would betray me if they paid us visits. As for my mysteriously-closed study, it was the place in which I privately rehearsed my new part. When I left you in the mornings, it was to go to the theatre-rehearsals. My evening absences began of course with the first performance.

'Your father's arrival seriously embarrassed me. When you (most properly) insisted on my giving up some of my evenings to him, you necessarily made it impossible for me to appear on the stage. The one excuse I could make to the theatre was, that I was too ill to act. It did certainly occur to me to cut the Gordian knot by owning the truth. But your father's horror, when you spoke of the newspaper review of the play, and the shame and fear you showed at your own boldness, daunted me once more.

'The arrival at the theatre of my written excuse brought the manageress down upon me, in a state of distraction. Nobody could supply my place ; all the seats were taken ; and the Prince was expected. There was, what we call, a scene between the poor lady and myself. I felt I was in the wrong ; I saw that the position in which I had impulsively placed myself was unworthy of me—and it ended in my doing my duty to the theatre and the public. But for the affair of the bracelet, which obliged me as an honourable man to give my name and address, the manageress would not have discovered me. She, like everyone else, only knew of my address at my bachelor chambers. How could you be jealous of the old theatrical comrade of my first days on the stage ? Don't you know yet that you are the one woman in the world * * * ?

'A last word relating to your father, and I have done.

'Do you remember my leaving you at the telegraph-office ? It was to send a message to a friend of mine, an architect in Edinburgh, instructing him to go immediately to Cauldkirk, and provide for the repairs at my expense. The theatre, my dear, more than trebles my paternal income, and I can well afford it. Will your father refuse to accept a tribute of respect to a Scottish minister, because it is paid out of an actor's pocket ? You shall ask him the question.

'And, I say, Felicia—will you come and see me act ? I don't expect your father to enter a theatre ; but, by way of further reconciling him to his son-in-law, suppose you ask him to hear me read the play ?'

Mr. Percy and the Prophet

PART I. THE PREDICTION.

CHAPTER I.

THE QUACK.

THE disasters that follow the hateful offence against Christianity, which men call war, were severely felt in England during the peace that ensued on the overthrow of Napoleon at Waterloo. With rare exceptions, distress prevailed among all classes of the community. The starving nation was ripe and ready for a revolutionary rising against its rulers, who had shed the people's blood and wasted the people's substance in a war which had yielded to the popular interests absolutely nothing in return.

Among the unfortunate persons who were driven, during the disastrous early years of this century, to strange shifts and devices to obtain the means of living, was a certain obscure medical man, of French extraction, named Lagarde. The doctor (duly qualified to bear the title) was an inhabitant of London ; living in one of the narrow streets which connect the great thoroughfare of the Strand with the bank of the Thames.

The method of obtaining employment chosen by poor Legarde, as the one alternative left in the face of starvation, was, and is still considered by the medical profession to be, the method of a quack. He advertised in the public journals.

Addressing himself especially to two classes of the community, the Doctor proceeded in these words :

'I have the honour of inviting to my house, in the first place : Persons afflicted with maladies which ordinary medical practice has failed to cure—and, in the second place : Persons interested in investigations, the object of which is to penetrate the secrets of the future. Of the means by which I endeavour to alleviate suffering and to enlighten doubt, it is impossible to speak intelligibly within the limits of an advertisement. I can only offer to submit my system to public inquiry, without exacting any preliminary fee from ladies and gentlemen who may honour me with a visit. Those who see sufficient reason to trust me, after personal experience, will find a money-box fixed on the waiting-room table, into which they can drop their offerings according to their means. Those whom I am not fortunate enough to satisfy will be pleased to accept the expression of my regret, and will not be expected to give anything.   I shall be found at home every evening between the hours of six and ten.'

Towards the close of the year 1816, this strange advertisement became a general topic of conversation among educated people in London.   For some weeks, the Doctor's invitations were generally accepted —and, all things considered, were not badly remunerated.   A faithful few believed in him, and told wonderful stories of what he had pronounced and prophesied in the sanctuary of his consulting-room.   The majority of his visitors simply viewed him in the light of a public amusement, and wondered why such a gentlemanlike man should have chosen to gain his living by exhibiting himself as a quack.

CHAPTER II.

THE NUMBERS.

On a raw and snowy evening towards the latter part of January, 1817, a gentleman, walking along the Strand, turned into the street in which Doctor Lagarde lived, and knocked at the physician's door.

He was admitted by an elderly male servant to a waiting-room on the first floor. The light of one little lamp, placed on a bracket fixed to the wall, was so obscured by a dark green shade as to make it difficult, if not impossible, for visitors meeting by accident to recognise each other.   The metal money-box fixed to the table was just visible.   In the flickering light of a small fire, the stranger perceived the figures of three men seated, apart and silent, who were the only occupants of the room beside himself.

So far as objects were to be seen, there was nothing to attract attention in the waiting-room.   The furniture was plain and neat, and nothing more.   The elderly servant handed a card, with a number inscribed on it, to the new visitor, said in a

whisper, ' Your number will be called, sir, in your turn,' and disappeared.   For some minutes nothing disturbed the deep silence but the faint ticking of a clock.   After a while a bell rang from an inner room, a door opened, and a gentleman appeared, whose interview with Doctor Lagarde had terminated.   His opinion of the sitting was openly expressed in one emphatic word— ' Humbug!'   No contribution dropped from his hand as he passed the money-box on his way out.

The next number (being Number Fifteen) was called by the elderly servant, and the first incident occurred in the strange series of events destined to happen in the doctor's house that night.

One after another the three men who had been waiting rose, examined their cards under the light of the lamp, and sat down again surprised and disappointed.

The servant advanced to investigate the matter.   The numbers possessed by the three visitors, instead of being Fifteen, Six-teen, and Seventeen, proved to be Sixteen, Seventeen, and Eighteen.   Turning to the stranger who had arrived the last, the servant said :

' Have I made a mistake, sir?   Have I given you Number Fifteen instead of Number Eighteen?'

The gentleman produced his numbered card.

A mistake had certainly been made, but not the mistake that the servant supposed. The card held by the latest visitor turned out to be the card previously held by the dissatisfied stranger who had just left the room—Number Fourteen !   As to the card numbered Fifteen, it was only discovered the next morning lying in a corner, dropped on the floor !

Acting on his first impulse, the servant hurried out, calling to the original holder of Fourteen to come back and bear his testimony to that fact.   The street-door had been opened for him by the landlady of the house.   She was a pretty woman— and the gentleman had fortunately lingered to talk to her. He was induced, at the intercession of the landlady, to ascend the stairs again.

On returning to the waiting-room, he addressed a characteristic question to the assembled visitors. ' *More* humbug?' asked the gentleman who liked to talk to a pretty woman.

The servant—completely puzzled by his own stupidity — attempted to make his apologies.

' Pray forgive me, gentlemen,' he said. ' I am afraid I have confused the cards I distribute with the cards returned to me. I think I had better consult my master.'

Left by themselves, the visitors began to speak jestingly of the strange situation in which they were placed. The original holder of Number Fourteen described his experience of the doctor in his own pithy way. ' I applied to the fellow to tell my fortune. He first went to sleep over it, and then he said he could tell me nothing. I asked why. "I don't know," says he. "*I* do," says I—"humbug!" I'll bet you the long odds, gentlemen, that *you* find it humbug, too.'

Before the wager could be accepted or declined, the door of the inner room was opened again. The tall, spare, black figure of a new personage appeared on the threshold, relieved darkly against the light in the room behind him. He addressed the visitors in these words :

' Gentlemen, I must beg your indulgence. The accident—as we now suppose it to be —which has given to the last comer the number already held by a gentleman who has unsuccessfully consulted me, may have a meaning which we can none of us at present see. If the three visitors who have been so good as to wait, will allow the present holder of Number Fourteen to consult me out of his turn—and if the earlier visitor who left me dissatisfied with his consultation will consent to stay here a little longer—something may happen which will justify a trifling sacrifice of your own convenience. Is ten minutes' patience too much to ask of you ?'

The three visitors who had waited longest consulted among themselves, and (having nothing better to do with their time) decided on accepting the doctor's proposal. The visitor who believed it all to be ' humbug ' coolly took a gold coin out of his pocket, tossed it into the air, caught it in his closed hand, and walked up to the shaded lamp on the bracket.

' Heads, stay,' he said, ' Tails, go.' He opened his hand, and looked at the coin. ' Heads ! Very good. Go on with your hocus-pocus, Doctor—I'll wait.'

' You believe in chance,' said the Doctor, quietly observing him. ' That is not my experience of life.'

He paused to let the stranger who now held Number Fourteen pass him into the inner room — then followed, closing the door behind him.

CHAPTER III.

THE CONSULTATION.

THE consulting-room was better lit than the waiting-room, and that was the only difference between the two. In the one as in the other, no attempt was made to impress the imagination. Everywhere, the commonplace furniture of a London lodging-house was left without the slightest effort to alter or improve it by changes of any kind.

Seen under the clearer light, Doctor Lagarde appeared to be the last person living who would consent to degrade himself by an attempt at imposture of any kind. His eyes were the dreamy eyes of a visionary ; his look was the prematurely-aged look of a student, accustomed to give the hours to his book which ought to have been given to his bed. To state it briefly, he was a man who might easily be deceived by others, but who was incapable of consciously practising deception himself.

Signing to his visitor to be seated, he

took a chair on the opposite side of the small table that stood between them— waited a moment with his face hidden in his hands, as if to collect himself—and then spoke.

'Do you come to consult me on a case of illness?' he inquired, 'or do you ask me to look into the darkness which hides your future life?'

The answer to those questions was frankly and briefly expressed : ' I have no need to consult you about my health. I come to hear what you can tell me of my future life.'

'I can try,' pursued the Doctor ; ' but I cannot promise to succeed.'

'I accept your conditions,' the stranger rejoined. ' I neither believe nor disbelieve. If you will excuse my speaking frankly, I mean to observe you closely, and to decide for myself.'

Doctor Lagarde smiled sadly.

' You have heard of me as a charlatan who contrives to amuse a few idle people,' he said. ' I don't complain of that ; my present position leads necessarily to mis-interpretation of myself and my motives. Still, I may at least say that I am the victim of a sincere avowal of my belief in a great science. Yes! I repeat it, a great science! New, I dare say, to the genera-tion we live in, though it was known and practised in the days when the pyramids were built. The age is advancing ; and the truths which it is my misfortune to advocate, before the time is ripe for them, are steadily forcing their way to recognition. I am resigned to wait. My sincerity in this matter has cost me the income that I derived from my medical practice. Patients distrust me ; doctors refuse to consult with me. I could starve if I had no one to think of but myself. But I have another person to con-sider, who is very dear to me ; and I am driven, literally driven, either to turn beggar in the streets, or to do what I am doing now.'

He paused, and looked round towards the corner of the room behind him. ' Mother,' he said gently, ' are you ready?'

An elderly lady, dressed in deep mourning, rose from her seat in the corner. She had been, thus far, hidden from notice by the high back of the easy-chair in which her son sat. Excepting some folds of fine black lace, laid over her white hair so as to form a head-dress at once simple and picturesque, there was nothing remarkable in her attire. The visitor rose and bowed. She gravely returned his salute, and moved so as to place herself opposite to her son.

'May I ask what this lady is going to do ?' said the stranger.

'To be of any use to you,' answered Doctor Lagarde, ' I must be thrown into the magnetic trance. The person who has the strongest influence over me is the person who will do it to-night.'

He turned to his mother. ' When you like,' he said.

Bending over him, she took both the Doctor's hands, and looked steadily into his eyes. No words passed between them ; nothing more took place. In a minute or two, his head was resting against the back of the chair, and his eyelids had closed.

'Are you sleeping ?' asked Madame Lagrade.

'I am sleeping,' he answered.

She laid his hands gently on the arms of the chair, and turned to address the visitor.

' Let the sleep gain on him for a minute or two more,' she said. ' Then take one of his hands, and put to him what questions you please.'

'Does he hear us now, madam ?'

' You might fire off a pistol, sir, close to his ear, and he would not hear it. The vibration might disturb him; that is all. Until you or I touch him, and so establish the nervous sympathy, he is as lost to all sense of our presence here, as if he were dead.'

'Are you speaking of the thing called Animal Magnetism, madam ?'

' Yes, sir.'

'And you believe in it, of course ?'

' My son's belief, sir, is my belief in this

thing as in other things. I have heard what he has been saying to you. It is for me that he sacrifices himself by holding these exhibitions ; it is in my poor interests that his hardly-earned money is made. I am in infirm health ; and remonstrate as I may, my son persists in providing for me, not the bare comforts only, but even the luxuries of life. Whatever I may suffer, I have my compensation ; I can still thank God for giving me the greatest happiness that a woman can enjoy, the possession of a good son.'

She smiled fondly as she looked at the sleeping man. 'Draw your chair nearer to him,' she resumed, 'and take his hand. You may speak freely in making your inquiries. Nothing that happens in this room goes out of it.'

With those words she returned to her place, in the corner behind her son's chair.

The visitor took Doctor Lagarde's hand. As they touched each other, he was conscious of a faintly-titillating sensation in his own hand—a sensation which oddly reminded him of bygone experiments with an electrical machine, in the days when he was a boy at school !

'I wish to question you about my future life,' he began. 'How ought I to begin ?'

The Doctor spoke his first words in the monotonous tones of a man talking in his sleep.

'Own your true motive before you begin,' he said. 'Your interest in your future life is centred in a woman. You wish to know if her heart will be yours in the time that is to come—and there your interest in your future life ends.'

This startling proof of the sleeper's capacity to look, by sympathy, into his mind, and to see there his most secret thoughts, instead of convincing the stranger, excited his suspicions. 'You have means of getting information,' he said, 'that I don't understand.'

The Doctor smiled, as if the idea amused him. Madame Lagarde rose from her place, and interposed.

'Hundreds of strangers come here to consult my son,' she said quietly. 'If you believe that we know who those strangers are, and that we have the means of inquiring into their private lives before they enter this room, you believe in something much more incredible than the magnetic sleep !'

This was too manifestly true to be disputed. The visitor made his apologies.

'I should like to have *some* explanation,' he added. 'The thing is so very extraordinary. How can I prevail upon Doctor Lagarde to enlighten me ?'

'He can only tell you what he sees,' Madame Lagarde answered ; 'ask him that, and you will get a direct reply. Say to him : " Do you see the lady ?" '

The stranger repeated the question. The reply followed at once, in these words :

'I see two figures standing side by side. One of them is your figure. The other is the figure of a lady. She only appears dimly. I can discover nothing but that she is taller than women generally are, and that she is dressed in pale blue.'

The man to whom he was speaking started at those last words. 'Her favourite colour !' he thought to himself—forgetting that, while he held the doctor's hand, the doctor could think with *his* mind.

'Yes,' added the sleeper quietly, 'her favourite colour, as you know. She fades and fades as I look at her,' he went on. 'She is gone. I only see *you*, under a new aspect. You have a pistol in your hand. Opposite to you, there stands the figure of another man. He, too, has a pistol in his hand. Are you enemies ? Are you meeting to fight a duel ? Is the lady the cause ? I try, but I fail to see her.'

'Can you describe the man ?'

'Not yet. So far, he is only a shadow in the form of a man.'

There was another interval. An appearance of disturbance showed itself on the sleeper's face. Suddenly, he waved his free hand in the direction of the waiting-room.

'Send for the visitors who are there,' he

said. 'They are all to come in. Each one of them is to take one of my hands in turn—while you remain where you are, holding the other hand. Don't let go of me, even for a moment. My mother will ring.'

Madame Lagarde touched a bell on the table. The servant received his orders from her and retired. After a short absence, he appeared again in the consulting-room, with one visitor only waiting on the threshold behind him.

CHAPTER IV.

THE MAN.

'THE other three gentlemen have gone away, madam,' the servant explained, addressing Madame Lagarde. 'They were tired of waiting. I found *this* gentleman fast asleep; and I am afraid he is angry with me for taking the liberty of waking him.'

'Sleep of the common sort is evidently not allowed in this house.' With that remark the gentleman entered the room, and stood revealed as the original owner of the card numbered Fourteen.

Viewed by the clear lamplight, he was a tall, finely-made man, in the prime of life, with a florid complexion, golden-brown hair, and sparkling blue eyes. Noticing Madame Lagarde, he instantly checked the flow of his satire, with the instinctive good-breeding of a gentleman. 'I beg your pardon,' he said; 'I have a great many faults, and a habit of making bad jokes is one of them. Is the servant right, madam, in telling me that I have the honour of presenting myself here at your request?'

Madame Lagarde briefly explained what had passed.

The florid gentleman (still privately believing it to be all 'humbug') was delighted to make himself of any use. 'I congratulate you, sir,' he said, with his easy humour, as he passed the visitor who had become possessed of his card. 'Number Fourteen seems to be a luckier number in your keeping than it was in mine.'

As he spoke, he took Doctor Lagarde's disengaged hand. The instant they touched each other, the sleeper started. His voice rose; his face flushed. 'You are the man!' he exclaimed. 'I see you plainly, now!'

'What am I doing?'

'You are standing opposite to the gentleman here who is holding my other hand; and (as I have said already) you have met to fight a duel.'

The unbeliever cast a shrewd look at his companion in the consultation.

'Considering that you and I are total strangers, sir,' he said, 'don't you think the Doctor had better introduce us, before he goes any farther? We have got to fighting a duel already, and we may as well know who we are, before the pistols go off.' He turned to Doctor Lagarde. 'Dramatic situations don't amuse me out of the theatre,' he resumed. 'Let me put you to a very commonplace test. I want to be introduced to this gentleman. Has he told you his name?'

'No.'

'Of course, you know it, without being told?'

'Certainly. I have only to look into your own knowledge of yourselves, while I am in this trance, and while you have got my hands, to know both your names as well as you do.'

'Introduce us, then!' retorted the jesting gentleman. 'And take my name first.'

'Mr. Percy Linwood,' replied the Doctor; 'I have the honour of presenting you to Captain Bervie, of the Artillery.'

With one accord, the gentlemen both dropped Doctor Lagarde's hands, and looked at each other in blank amazement.

'Of course he has discovered our names somehow!' said Mr. Percy Linwood, explaining the mystery to his own perfect satisfaction in that way.

Captain Bervie had not forgotten what Madame Lagarde had said to him, when he too had suspected a trick. He now repeated it (quite ineffectually) for Mr. Linwood's benefit. 'If you don't feel the force of that argument as I feel it,' he added, 'perhaps, as a favour to me, sir, you will not object to our each taking the Doctor's hand again, and hearing what more he can tell us while he remains in the state of trance?'

'With the greatest pleasure!' answered good-humoured Mr. Linwood. 'Our friend is beginning to amuse me; I am as anxious as you are to know what he is going to see next.'

Captain Bervie put the next question.

'You have seen us ready to fight a duel—can you tell us the result?'

'I can tell you nothing more than I have told you already. The figures of the duellists have faded away, like the other figures I saw before them. What I see now looks like the winding gravel-path of a garden. A man and a woman are walking towards me. The man stops, and places a ring on the woman's finger, and kisses her.'

Captain Bervie opened his lips to continue his enquiries—turned pale—and checked himself. Mr. Linwood put the next question.

'Who is the happy man?' he asked.

'*You* are the happy man,' was the instantaneous reply.

'Who is the woman?' cried Captain Bervie, before Mr. Linwood could speak again.

'The same woman whom I saw before; dressed in the same colour, in pale blue.'

Captain Bervie positively insisted on receiving clearer information than this. 'Surely you can see *something* of her personal appearance?' he said.

'I can see that she has long dark-brown hair, falling below her waist. I can see that she has lovely dark-brown eyes. She has the look of a sensitive nervous person. She is quite young. I can see no more.'

'Look again at the man who is putting the ring on her finger,' said the Captain.

'Are you sure that the face you see is the face of Mr. Percy Linwood?'

'I am absolutely sure.'

Captain Bervie rose from his chair.

'Thank you, madam,' he said to the doctor's mother. 'I have heard enough.'

He walked to the door. Mr. Percy Linwood dropped Doctor Lagarde's hand, and appealed to the retiring Captain with a broad stare of astonishment.

'You don't really believe this?' he said.

'I only say I have heard enough,' Captain Bervie answered.

Mr. Linwood could hardly fail to see that any further attempt to treat the matter lightly might lead to undesirable results.

'It is difficult to speak seriously of this kind of exhibition,' he resumed quietly. 'But I suppose I may mention a mere matter of fact, without meaning or giving offence. The description of the lady, I can positively declare, does not apply in any single particular to anyone whom I know.'

Captain Bervie turned round at the door. His patience was in some danger of failing him. Mr. Linwood's unruffled composure, assisted in its influence by the presence of Madame Lagarde, reminded him of the claims of politeness. He restrained the rash words as they rose to his lips. 'You may make new acquaintances, sir,' was all that he said. '*You* have the future before you.'

Upon that, he went out. Percy Linwood waited a little, reflecting on the Captain's conduct.

Had Doctor Lagarde's description of the lady accidentally answered the description of a living lady whom Captain Bervie knew? Was he by any chance in love with her? and had the doctor innocently reminded him that his love was not returned? Assuming this to be likely, was it really possible that he believed in prophetic revelations offered to him under the fantastic influence of a trance? Could any man in the possession of his senses go to those lengths? The Captain's conduct was simply incomprehensible.

Pondering these questions, Percy decided

on returning to his place by the doctor's chair. 'Of one thing I am certain, at any rate,' he thought to himself. 'I'll see the whole imposture out before I leave the house!'

He took Doctor Lagarde's hand. 'Now, then! what is the next discovery?' he asked.

The sleeper seemed to find some difficulty in answering the question.

'I indistinctly see the man and the woman again,' he said.

'Am I the man still?' Percy enquired.

'No. The man, this time, is the Captain. The woman is agitated by something that he is saying to her. He seems to be trying to persuade her to go away with him. She hesitates. He whispers something in her ear. She yields. He leads her away. The darkness gathers behind them. I look and look, and I can see no more.'

'Shall we wait awhile?' Percy suggested, 'and then try again?'

Doctor Lagarde sighed, and reclined in his chair. 'My head is heavy,' he said; 'my spirits are dull. The darkness baffles me. I have toiled long enough for you. Drop my hand and leave me to rest.'

Hearing those words, Madame Lagarde approached her son's chair.

'It will be useless, sir, to ask him any more questions to-night,' she said. 'He has been weak and nervous all day, and he is worn out by the effort he has made. Pardon me, if I ask you to step aside for a moment, while I give him the repose that he needs.'

She laid her right hand gently on the doctor's head, and kept it there for a minute or so. 'Are you at rest now?' she asked.

'I am at rest,' he answered, in faint drowsy tones.

Madame Lagarde returned to Percy. 'If you are not yet satisfied,' she said, 'my son will be at your service to-morrow evening, sir.'

'Thank you, madam, I have only one more question to ask, and you can no doubt answer it. When your son wakes, will he remember what he has said to Captain Ber-

vie and to myself?'

'My son will be as absolutely ignorant of everything that he has seen, and of everything that he has said in the trance, as if he had been at the other end of the world.'

Percy Linwood swallowed this last outrageous assertion with an effort which he was quite unable to conceal. 'Many thanks, madam,' he said; 'I wish you good-night.'

Returning to the waiting-room, he noticed the money-box fixed to the table. 'These people look poor,' he thought to himself, 'and I feel really indebted to them for an amusing evening. Besides, I can afford to be liberal, for I shall certainly never go back.' He dropped a five-pound note into the money-box, and left the house.

Walking towards his club, Percy's natural serenity of mind was a little troubled by the remembrance of Captain Bervie's language and conduct. The Captain had interested the young man in spite of himself. His first idea was to write to Bervie, and mention what had happened at the renewed consultation with Doctor Lagarde. On second thoughts, he saw reason to doubt how the Captain might receive such an advance as this, on the part of a stranger. 'After all,' Percy decided, 'the whole thing is too absurd to be worth thinking about seriously. Neither he nor I are likely to meet again, or to see the Doctor again—and there's an end of it.'

He never was more mistaken in his life. The end of it was not to come for many a long day yet.

PART II. THE FULFILMENT.

CHAPTER V.

THE BALL-ROOM.

WHILE the consultation at Doctor Lagarde's was still fresh in the memory of the persons present at it, Chance or Destiny, occupied in sowing the seeds for the harvest of the future, discovered as one of its fit instruments a retired military officer named Major Mulvany.

The Major was a smart little man, who persisted in setting up the appearance of youth as a means of hiding the reality of fifty. Being still a bachelor, and being always ready to make himself agreeable, he was generally popular in the society of women. In the ballroom he was a really welcome addition to the company. The German waltz had then been imported into England little more than three years since. The outcry raised against the dance, by persons skilled in the discovery of latent impropriety, had not yet lost its influence in certain quarters. Men who could waltz were scarce. The Major had successfully grappled with the difficulties of learning the dance in mature life ; and the young ladies rewarded him nobly for the effort. That is to say, they took the assumption of youth for granted in the palpable presence of fifty.

Knowing everybody and being welcome everywhere, playing a good hand at whist, and having an inexhaustible fancy in the invention of a dinner, Major Mulvany naturally belonged to all the best clubs of his time. Percy Linwood and he constantly met in the billiard-room or at the dinner-table. The Major approved of the easy, handsome, pleasant-tempered young man. 'I have lost the first freshness of youth,' he used to say with pathetic resignation, 'and I see myself revived, as it were, in Percy. Naturally I like Percy.'

About three weeks after the memorable evening at Doctor Lagarde's, the two friends encountered each other on the steps of a club.

'Have you got anything to do to-night ?' asked the Major.

'Nothing that I know of,' said Percy, 'unless I go to the theatre.'

'Let the theatre wait, my boy. My old regiment gives a ball at Woolwich to-night. I have got a ticket to spare ; and I know several sweet girls who are going. Some of them waltz, Percy ! Gather your rosebuds while you may. Come with me.'

The invitation was accepted as readily as it was given. The Major found the carriage, and Percy paid for the post-horses. They entered the ballroom among the earlier guests ; and the first person whom they met, waiting near the door, was—Captain Bervie.

Percy bowed, a little uneasily. 'I feel some doubt,' he said, laughing, 'whether we have been properly introduced to one another or not.'

'Not properly introduced !' cried Major Mulvany. 'I'll soon set that right. My dear friend, Percy Linwood ; my dear friend, Arthur Bervie—be known to each other ! esteem each other !'

Captain Bervie acknowledged the introduction by a cold salute. Percy, yielding to the good-natured impulse of the moment, alluded to what had happened in Doctor Lagarde's consulting-room.

'You missed something worth hearing when you left the Doctor the other night,' he said. 'We continued the sitting ; and *you* turned up again among the persons of the drama, in a new character——'

'Excuse me for interrupting you,' said Captain Bervie. 'I am a member of the committee, charged with the arrangements of the ball, and I must really attend to my duties.'

He withdrew without waiting for a reply. Percy looked round wonderingly at Major Mulvany. 'Strange !' he said, 'I feel rather attracted towards Captain Bervie ; and he seems to have taken such a dislike to me, that he can hardly behave with common civility. What does it mean ?'

'I'll tell you,' answered the Major confidentially. 'Arthur Bervie is madly in love—madly is really the word—with a Miss Bowmore. And (this is between ourselves) the young lady doesn't feel it quite in the same way. A sweet girl ; I've often had her on my knee when she was a child. Her father and mother are old friends of mine. She is coming to the ball to-night. That's the true reason why Arthur left you just now. Look at him—waiting to be the first to speak to her. If he could have his way, he wouldn't let another man come near the poor girl all through the evening ; he really persecutes her. I'll introduce you to Miss Bowmore ; and you will see how he looks at us for presuming to approach her. It's a great pity ; she will never marry him. Arthur Bervie is a man in a thousand ; but he's fast becoming a perfect bear under the strain on his temper. What's the matter ? You don't seem to be listening to me.'

This last remark was perfectly justified. In telling the Captain's love-story, Major Mulvany had revived his young friend's memory of the lady in the blue dress, who had haunted the visions of Doctor Lagarde.

'Tell me,' said Percy, 'what is Miss Bowmore like ? Is there anything remarkable in her personal appearance ? I have a reason for asking.'

As he spoke, there arose among the guests in the rapidly-filling ballroom a low murmur of surprise and admiration. The Major laid one hand on Percy's shoulder, and, lifting the other, pointed to the door.

'What is Miss Bowmore like ?' he repeated. 'There she is ! Let her answer for herself.'

Percy turned towards the lower end of the room.

A young lady was entering, dressed in plain silk, and the colour of it was a pale blue ! Excepting a white rose at her breast, she wore no ornament of any sort. Doubly distinguished by the perfect simplicity of her apparel, and by her tall, supple, commanding figure, she took rank at once as the most remarkable woman in the room Moving nearer to her through the crowd, under the guidance of the complaisant Major, young Linwood gained a clearer view of her hair, her complexion, and the colour of her eyes. In every one of these particulars, she was the living image of the woman described by Doctor Lagarde !

While Percy was absorbed over this strange discovery, Major Mulvany had got within speaking distance of the young lady and of her mother, as they stood together in conversation with Captain Bervie. 'My dear Mrs. Bowmore, how well you are looking ! My dear Miss Charlotte, what a sensation you have made already ! The glorious simplicity (if I may so express myself) of your dress is—is—what was I going to say ?—the ideas come thronging on me ; I merely want words.'

Miss Bowmore's magnificent brown eyes, wandering from the Major to Percy, rested on the young man with a modest and momentary interest, which Captain Bervie's jealous attention instantly detected.

'They are forming a dance,' he said, pressing forward impatiently to claim his partner. 'If we don't take our places, we shall be too late.'

'Stop! stop !' cried the Major. 'There is a time for everything, and this is the time for presenting my dear friend here, Mr. Percy Linwood. He is like me, Miss Charlotte — *he* has been struck by your glorious simplicity, and *he* wants words.' At this part of the presentation, he happened to look toward the irate Captain, and instantly gave him a hint on the subject of his temper. 'I say, Arthur Bervie ! we are all good-humoured people here. What have you got on your eyebrows ? It looks like a frown ; and it doesn't become you. Send for a skilled waiter, and have it brushed off and taken away directly !'

'May I ask, Miss Bowmore, if you are disengaged for the next dance?' said Percy, the moment the Major gave him an opportunity of speaking.

' Miss Bowmore is engaged to *me* for the next dance,' said the angry Captain, before the young lady could answer.

'The third dance, then ?' Percy persisted, with his brightest smile.

'With pleasure, Mr. Linwood,' said Miss Bowmore. She would have been no true woman if she had not resented the open exhibition of Arthur's jealousy ; it was like asserting a right over her to which he had not the shadow of a claim. She threw a look at Percy as her partner led her away, which was the severest punishment she could inflict on the man who ardently loved her.

The third dance stood in the programme as a waltz.

In jealous distrust of Percy, the Captain took the conductor of the band aside, and used his authority as committeeman to substitute another dance. He had no sooner turned his back on the orchestra than the wife of the Colonel of the regiment, who had heard him, spoke to the conductor in her turn, and insisted on the original programme being retained. 'Quote the Colonel's authority,' said the lady, 'if Captain Bervie ventures to object.' In the meantime, the Captain, on his way to rejoin Charlotte, was met by one of his brother officers, who summoned him officially to an impending debate of the committee charged with the administrative arrangements of the supper-table. Bervie had no choice but to follow his brother officer to the committee-room.

Barely a minute later the conductor appeared at his desk, and the first notes of the music rose low and plaintive, introducing the third dance.

'Percy, my boy!' cried the Major, recognising the melody, 'you're in luck's way—it's going to be a waltz!'

Almost as he spoke, the notes of the symphony glided by subtle modulations into the inspiriting air of the waltz. Percy claimed his partner's hand. Miss Charlotte hesitated, and looked at her mother.

'Surely you waltz?' said Percy.

'I have learnt to waltz,' she answered modestly; 'but this is such a large room, and there are so many people!'

'Once round,' Percy pleaded; 'only once round!'

Miss Bowmore looked again at her mother. Her foot was keeping time with the music, under her dress; her heart was beating with a delicious excitement; kind-hearted Mrs. Bowmore smiled and said, 'Once round, my dear, as Mr. Linwood suggests.'

In another moment, Percy's arm took possession of her waist, and they were away on the wings of the waltz!

Could words describe, could thought realize, the exquisite enjoyment of the dance?

Enjoyment? It was more—it was an epoch in Charlotte's life—it was the first time she had waltzed with a man. What a difference between the fervent clasp of Percy's arm and the cold formal contact of the mistress who had taught her! How brightly his eyes looked down into hers; admiring her with such a tender restraint, that there could surely be no harm in looking up at him now and then in return. Round and round they glided, absorbed in the music and in themselves. Occasionally her bosom just touched him, at those critical moments when she was most in need of support. At other intervals, she almost let her head sink on his shoulder in trying to hide from him the smile which acknowledged his admiration too boldly. 'Once round,' Percy had suggested; 'once round,' her mother had said. They had been ten, twenty, thirty times round; they had never stopped to rest like other dancers; they had centred the eyes of the whole room on them—including the eyes of Captain Bervie—without knowing it; her delicately pale complexion had changed to rosy-red; the neat arrangement of her hair had become disturbed; her bosom was rising and falling faster and faster in the effort to breathe—before fatigue and heat overpowered her at last, and forced her to say to him faintly, 'I'm very sorry—I can't dance any more!'

Percy led her into the cooler atmosphere of the refreshment-room, and revived her with a glass of lemonade. Her arm still rested on his—she was just about to thank him for the care he had taken of her—when Captain Bervie entered the room.

'Mrs. Bowmore wishes me to take you back to her,' he said to Charlotte. Then, turning to Percy, he added: 'Will you kindly wait here while I take Miss Bowmore to the ballroom? I have a word to say to you—I will return directly.'

The Captain spoke with perfect politeness—but his face betrayed him. It was pale with the sinister whiteness of suppressed rage.

Percy sat down to cool and rest himself.

With his experience of the ways of men, he felt no surprise at the marked contrast between Captain Bervie's face and Captain Bervie's manner. ' He has seen us waltzing, and he is coming back to pick a quarrel with me.' Such was the interpretation which Mr. Linwood's knowledge of the world placed on Captain Bervie's politeness. In a minute or two more the Captain returned to the refreshment-room, and satisfied Percy that his anticipations had not deceived him.

CHAPTER VI.

LOVE.

FOUR days had passed since the night of the ball.

Although it was no later in the year than the month of February, the sun was shining brightly, and the air was as soft as the air of a day in spring. Percy and Charlotte were walking together in the little garden at the back of Mr. Bowmore's cottage, near the town of Dartford in Kent.

' Mr. Linwood,' said the young lady, ' you were to have paid us your first visit the day after the ball. Why have you kept us waiting? Have you been too busy to remember your new friends?'

' I have counted the hours since we parted, Miss Charlotte. If I had not been detained by business——'

' I understand! For three days business has controlled you. On the fourth day, you have controlled business—and here you are? I don't believe one word of it, Mr. Linwood!'

There was no answering such a declaration as this. Guiltily conscious that Charlotte was right in refusing to accept his well-worn excuse, Percy made an awkward attempt to change the topic of conversation.

They happened, at the moment, to be standing near a small conservatory at the end of the garden. The glass door was closed, and the few plants and shrubs inside

had a lonely, neglected look. ' Does nobody ever visit this secluded place?' Percy asked jocosely, ' or does it hide discoveries in the rearing of plants, which are forbidden mysteries to a stranger?'

' Satisfy your curiosity, Mr. Linwood, by all means,' Charlotte answered in the same tone. ' Open the door, and I will follow you.'

Percy obeyed. In passing through the doorway, he encountered the bare hanging branches of some creeping plant, long since dead, and detached from its fastenings on the woodwork of the roof. He pushed aside the branches so that Charlotte could easily follow him in, without being aware that his own forced passage through them had a little deranged the folds of spotless white cambric which a well-dressed gentleman wore round his neck in those days. Charlotte seated herself, and directed Percy's attention to the desolate conservatory with a saucy smile.

' The mystery which your lively imagination has associated with this place,' she said, ' means, being interpreted, that we are too poor to keep a gardener. Make the best of your disappointment, Mr. Linwood, and sit here by me. We are out of hearing and out of sight of mamma's other visitors. You have no excuse now for not telling me what has really kept you away from us.'

She fixed her eyes on him as she said those words. Before Percy could think of another excuse, her quick observation detected the disordered condition of his cravat, and discovered the upper edge of a black plaster attached to one side of his neck.

' You have been hurt in the neck!' she said. ' That is why you have kept away from us for the last three days!'

' A mere trifle,' he answered, in great confusion ; ' please don't notice it.'

Her eyes, still resting on his face, assumed an expression of suspicious enquiry, which Percy was entirely at a loss to understand. Suddenly, she started to her feet, as if a new idea had occurred to her. ' Wait here,' she said, flushing with excitement, ' till I come back : I insist on it !'

Before Percy could ask for an explanation, she had left the conservatory.

In a minute or two, Miss Bowmore returned, with a newspaper in her hand. ' Read that,' she said, pointing to a paragraph distinguished by a line drawn round it in ink.

The passage that she indicated contained an account of a duel which had recently taken place in the neighbourhood of London. The names of the duellists were not mentioned. One was described as an officer, and the other as a civilian. They had quarrelled at cards, and had fought with pistols. The civilian had had a narrow escape of his life. His antagonist's bullet had passed near enough to the side of his neck to tear the flesh, and had missed the vital parts, literally, by a hair's-breadth.

Charlotte's eyes, riveted on Percy, detected a sudden change of colour in his face the moment he looked at the newspaper. That was enough for her. ' You *are* the man !' she cried. ' Oh, for shame, for shame ! To risk your life for a paltry dispute about cards.'

' I would risk it again,' said Percy, ' to hear you speak as if you set some value on it.'

She looked away from him without a word of reply. Her mind seemed to be busy again with its own thoughts. Did she meditate returning to the subject of the duel? Was she not satisfied with the discovery which she had just made?

No such doubts as these troubled the mind of Percy Linwood. Intoxicated by the charm of her presence, emboldened by her innocent betrayal of the interest that she felt in him, he opened his whole heart to her as unreservedly as if they had known each other from the days of their childhood. There was but one excuse for him. Charlotte was his first love.

' You don't know how completely you have become a part of my life, since we met at the ball,' he went on. ' That one delightful dance seemed, by some magic which I can't explain, to draw us together in a few minutes as if we had known each other for years. Oh, dear! I could make such a confession of what I felt—only I am afraid of offending you by speaking too soon. Women are so dreadfully difficult to understand. How is a man to know at what time it is considerate towards them to conceal his true feelings ; and at what time it is equally considerate to express his true feelings? One doesn't know whether it is a matter of days or weeks or months—there ought to be a law to settle it. Dear Miss Charlotte, when a poor fellow loves you at first sight, as he has never loved any other woman, and when he is tormented by the fear that some other man may be preferred to him, can't you forgive him if he lets out the truth a little too soon?' He ventured, as he put that very downright question, to take her hand. ' It really isn't my fault,' he said simply. ' My heart is so full of you, I can talk of nothing else.'

To Percy's deligh.t, the first experimental pressure of his hand, far from being resented, was softly returned. Charlotte looked at him again, with a new resolution in her face.

' I'll forgive you for talking nonsense, Mr. Linwood,' she said ; ' and I will even permit you to come and see me again, on one condition — that you tell the whole truth about the duel. If you conceal the smallest circumstance, our acquaintance is at an end.'

' Haven't I owned everything already?' Percy inquired, in great perplexity. ' Did I say No, when you told me I was the man?'

' Could you say No, with that plaster on your neck?' was the ready rejoinder. ' I am determined to know more than the newspaper tells me. Will you declare, on your word of honour, that Captain Bervie had nothing to do with the duel? Can you look me in the face, and say that the real cause of the quarrel was a disagreement at cards? When you were talking with me just before I left the ball, how did you answer a gentleman who asked you to make one at the whist-table? You said, "I don't play at cards." Ah! You thought I had forgotten that? Don't kiss my hand! Trust me with the whole truth, or say good-bye for ever.'

'Only tell me what you wish to know, Miss Charlotte,' said Percy humbly. 'If you will put the questions, I will give the answers—as well as I can.'

On this understanding, Percy's evidence was extracted from him as follows :

'Was it Captain Bervie who quarrelled with you?'

'Yes.'

'Was it about me?'

'Yes.'

'What did he say?'

'He said I had committed an impropriety in waltzing with you.'

'Why?'

'Because your parents disapproved of your waltzing in a public ballroom.'

'That's not true! What did he say next?'

'He said I had added tenfold to my offence, by waltzing with you in such a manner as to make you the subject of remark to the whole room.'

'Oh! did you let him say that?'

'No ; I contradicted him instantly. And I said, besides, "It's an insult to Miss Bowmore, to suppose that she would permit any impropriety.'"

'Quite right! And what did he say?'

'Well, he lost his temper; I would rather not repeat what he said when he was mad with jealousy. There was nothing to be done with him but to give him his way.'

'Give him his way? Does that mean fight a duel with him?'

'Don't be angry—it does.'

'And you kept my name out of it, by pretending to quarrel at the card-table?'

'Yes. We managed it when the card-room was emptying at supper-time, and nobody was present but Major Mulvany and another friend as witnesses.'

'And when did you fight the duel?'

'The next morning.'

'You never thought of *me*, I suppose?'

'Indeed, I did ; I was very glad that you had no suspicion of what we were at.'

'Was that all?'

'No ; I had your flower with me, the flower you gave me out of your nosegay, at the ball.'

'Well?'

'Oh, never mind, it doesn't matter.'

'It does matter. What did you do with my flower?'

'I gave it a sly kiss while they were measuring the ground ; and (don't tell anybody!) I put it next to my heart to bring me luck.'

'Was that just before he shot at you?'

'Yes.'

'How did he shoot?'

'He walked (as the seconds had arranged it) ten paces forward ; and then he stopped, and lifted his pistol——'

'Don't tell me any more! Oh, to think of my being the miserable cause of such horrors! I'll never dance again as long as I live. Did you think he had killed you, when the bullet wounded your poor neck?'

'No ; I hardly felt it at first.'

'Hardly felt it? How he talks! And when the wretch had done his best to kill you, and when it came to your turn, what did you do?'

'Nothing.'

'What! You didn't walk your ten paces forward?'

'No.'

'And you never shot at him in return?'

'No ; I had no quarrel with him, poor fellow ; I just stood where I was, and fired in the air——'

Before he could stop her, Charlotte seized his hand, and kissed it with an hysterical fervour of admiration, which completely deprived him of his presence of mind.

'Why shouldn't I kiss the hand of a hero?' she cried, with tears of enthusiasm sparkling in her eyes. 'Nobody but a hero would have given that man his life ; nobody but a hero would have pardoned him, while the blood was streaming from the wound that he had inflicted. I respect you, I admire you. Oh, don't think me bold! I can't control myself when I hear of anything noble and good. You will understand me better when we get to be old friends—won't you?'

She spoke in low sweet tones of entreaty. Percy's arm stole softly round her.

'Are we never to be nearer and dearer to each other than old friends?' he asked in a whisper. 'I am not a hero—your goodness overrates me, dear Miss Charlotte. My one ambition is to be the happy man who is worthy enough to win *you*. At your own time! I wouldn't distress you, I wouldn't confuse you, I wouldn't for the whole world take advantage of the compliment which your sympathy has paid to me. If it offends you, I won't even ask if I may hope.'

She sighed as he said the last words; trembled a little, and silently looked at him.

Percy read his answer in her eyes. Without meaning it on either side, their heads drew nearer together; their cheeks, then their lips, touched. She started back from him, and rose to leave the conservatory. At the same moment, the sound of slowly-approaching footsteps became audible on the gravel walk of the garden. Charlotte hurried to the door.

'My father!' she exclaimed, turning to Percy. 'Come, and be introduced to him.'

Percy followed her into the garden.

CHAPTER VII.

POLITICS.

JUDGING by appearances, Mr. Bowmore looked like a man prematurely wasted and worn by the cares of a troubled life. His eyes presented the one feature in which his daughter resembled him. In shape and colour they were exactly reproduced in Charlotte; the difference was in the ex-

pression. The father's look was habitually restless, eager, and suspicious. Not a trace was to be seen in it of the truthfulness and gentleness which made the charm of the daughter's expression. A man whose bitter experience of the world had soured his temper and shaken his faith in his fellow-creatures—such was Mr. Bowmore as he presented himself on the surface. He received Percy politely — but with a pre-occupied air. Every now and then, his restless eyes wandered from the visitor to an open letter in his hand. Charlotte, observing him, pointed to the letter.

'Have you any bad news there, papa?' she asked.

'Dreadful news!' Mr. Bowmore answered. 'Dreadful news, my child, to every Englishman who respects the liberties which his ancestors won. My correspondent is a man who is in the confidence of the Ministers,' he continued, addressing Percy. 'What do you think is the remedy that the Government proposes for the universal distress among the population, caused by an infamous and needless war? Despotism, Mr. Linwood; despotism in this free country is the remedy! In one week more, sir, Ministers will bring in a Bill for suspending the Habeas Corpus Act!'

Before Percy could do justice in words to the impression produced on him, Charlotte innocently asked a question which shocked her father.

'What is the Habeas Corpus Act, papa?'

'Good God!' cried Mr. Bowmore, 'is it possible that a child of mine has grown up to womanhood, in ignorance of the palladium of English liberty? Oh, Charlotte! Charlotte!'

'I am very sorry, papa. If you will only tell me, I will never forget it.'

Mr. Bowmore reverently uncovered his head, saluting an invisible Habeas Corpus Act. He took his daughter by the hand, with a certain parental sternness: his voice trembled with emotion as he spoke his next words:

'The Habeas Corpus Act, my child,

forbids the imprisonment of an English subject, unless that imprisonment can be first justified by law. Not even the will of the reigning monarch can prevent us from appearing before the judges of the land, and summoning them to declare whether our committal to prison is legally just.'

He put on his hat again. 'Never forget what I have told you, Charlotte!' he said solemnly. 'I would not remove my hat, sir,' he continued, turning to Percy, 'in the presence of the proudest autocrat that ever sat on a throne. I uncover, in homage to the grand law which asserts the sacredness of human liberty. When Parliament has sanctioned the infamous Bill now before it, English patriots may be imprisoned, may even be hanged, on warrants privately obtained by the paid spies and informers of the men who rule us. Perhaps I weary you, sir. You are a young man; the conduct of the Ministry may not interest you.'

'On the contrary,' said Percy, 'I have the strongest personal interest in the conduct of the Ministry.'

'How? in what way?' cried Mr. Bowmore eagerly.

'My late father had a claim on Government,' Percy answered, 'for money expended in foreign service. As his heir, I inherit the claim, which has been formally recognised by the present Ministers. My petition for a settlement will be presented by friends of mine, who can advocate my interests in the House of Commons.'

Mr. Bowmore took Percy's hand, and shook it warmly.

'In such a matter as this you cannot have too many friends to help you,' he said. 'I myself have some influence, as representing opinion outside the House; and I am entirely at your service. Come to-morrow, and let us talk over the details of your claim at my humble dinner-table. To-day I must attend a meeting of the Branch-Hampden-Club, of which I am vice-president, and to which I am now about to communicate the alarming news which my letter contains. Excuse me for leaving you—and count on a hearty welcome when we see you to-morrow.'

The amiable patriot saluted his daughter with a smile, and disappeared.

'I hope you like my father?' said Charlotte. 'All our friends say he ought to be in Parliament. He has tried twice. The expenses were dreadful; and each time the other man defeated him. The agent says he would be certainly elected if he tried again; but there is no money, and we mustn't think of it.'

A man of a suspicious turn of mind might have discovered, in those artless words, the secret of Mr. Bowmore's interest in the success of his young friend's claim on the Government. One British subject, with a sum of ready money at his command, may be an inestimably useful person to another British subject (without ready money) who cannot sit comfortably unless he sits in Parliament. But honest Percy Linwood was not a man of a suspicious turn of mind. He had just opened his lips to echo Charlotte's filial glorification of her father, when a shabbily-dressed man-servant met them with a message, for which they were both alike unprepared:

'Captain Bervie has called, Miss, to say good-bye, and my mistress requests your company in the parlour.'

CHAPTER VIII.

THE WARNING.

HAVING delivered his little formula of words, the shabby servant cast a look of furtive curiosity at Percy and withdrew. Charlotte turned to her lover, with indignation sparkling in her eyes and flushing on her cheeks at the bare idea of seeing Captain Bervie again. 'Does he think I will breathe the same air,' she exclaimed, 'with the man who attempted to take your life!'

Percy gently remonstrated with her.

'You are sadly mistaken,' he said.

'Captain Bervie stood to receive my fire as fairly as I stood to receive his. When I discharged my pistol in the air, he was the first man who ran up to me, and asked if I was seriously hurt. They told him my wound was a trifle; and he fell on his knees and thanked God for preserving my life from his guilty hand. "I am no longer the rival who hates you," he said. "Give me time to try if change of scene will quiet my mind; and I will be *your* brother, and *her* brother." Whatever his faults may be, Charlotte, Arthur Bervie has a great heart. Go in, I entreat you, and be friends with him as I am.'

Charlotte listened with downcast eyes and changing colour. 'You believe him?' she asked, in low trembling tones.

'I believe him as I believe You,' Percy answered.

She secretly resented the comparison, and detested the Captain more heartily than ever. 'I will go in and see him, if you wish it,' she said. 'But not by myself. I want you to come with me.'

'Why?' Percy asked.

'I want to see what his face says, when you and he meet.'

'Do you still doubt him, Charlotte?'

She made no reply. Percy had done his best to convince her, and had evidently failed.

They went together into the cottage. Fixing her eyes steadily on the Captain's face, Charlotte saw it turn pale when Percy followed her into the parlour. The two men greeted one another cordially. Charlotte sat down by her mother, preserving her composure so far as appearances went. 'I hear you have called to bid us good-bye,' she said to Bervie. 'Is it to be a long absence?'

'I have got two months' leave,' the Captain answered, without looking at her while he spoke.

'Are you going abroad?'

'Yes. I think so.'

She turned away to her mother. Bervie seized the opportunity of speaking to Percy.

'I have a word of advice for your private ear.' At the same moment, Charlotte whispered to her mother: 'Don't encourage him to prolong his visit.'

The Captain showed no intention to prolong his visit. To Charlotte's surprise, when he took leave of the ladies, Percy also rose to go. 'His carriage,' he said, 'was waiting at the door; and he had offered to take Captain Bervie back to London.'

Charlotte instantly suspected an arrangement between the two men for a confidential interview. Her obstinate distrust of Bervie strengthened tenfold. She reluctantly gave him her hand, as he parted from her at the parlour-door. The effort of concealing her true feeling towards him, gave a colour and a vivacity to her face which made her irresistibly beautiful. Bervie looked at the woman whom he had lost with an immeasurable sadness in his eyes. 'When we meet again,' he said, 'you will see me in a new character.' He hurried out to the gate, as if he feared to trust himself for a moment longer in her presence.

Charlotte followed Percy into the passage. 'I shall be here to-morrow, dearest!' he said, and tried to raise her hand to his lips. She abruptly drew it away. 'Not that hand!' she answered. 'Captain Bervie has just touched it. Kiss the other!'

'Do you still doubt the Captain?' said Percy, amused by her petulance.

She put her arm over his shoulder, and touched the plaster on his neck gently with her finger. 'There's one thing I don't doubt,' she said: 'the Captain did *that!*'

Percy left her, laughing. At the front gate of the cottage, he found Arthur Bervie in conversation with the same shabbily-dressed man-servant who had announced the Captain's visit to Charlotte.

'What has become of the other servant?' Bervie asked. 'I mean the old man who has been with Mr. Bowmore for so many years.'

'He has left his situation, sir.'

'Why?'

'As I understand, sir, he spoke dis-respectfully to the master.'

'Oh? And how came the master to hear of *you?*'

'I advertised; and Mr. Bowmore an-swered my advertisement.'

Bervie looked hard at the man for a moment, and then joined Percy at the carriage door. The two gentlemen started for London.

'What do you think of Mr. Bowmore's new servant?' asked the Captain, as they drove away from the cottage. 'I don't like the look of the fellow.'

'I didn't particularly notice him,' Percy answered.

There was a pause. When the conversa-tion was resumed, it turned on common-place subjects. The Captain looked uneasily out of the carriage window. Percy looked uneasily at the Captain.

They had left Dartford about two miles behind them, when Percy noticed an old gabled house, sheltered by magnificent trees, and standing on an eminence well removed from the high-road. Carriages and saddle-horses were visible on the drive in front, and a flag was hoisted on a staff placed in the middle of the lawn.

'Something seems to be going on there,' Percy remarked. 'A fine old house! Who does it belong to?'

Bervie smiled. 'It belongs to my father,' he said. 'He is chairman of the bench of local magistrates, and he receives his brother justices to-day, to celebrate the opening of the sessions.'

He stopped, and looked at Percy with some embarrassment. 'I am afraid I have surprised and disappointed you,' he resumed, abruptly changing the subject. 'I told you when we met just now at Mr. Bowmore's cottage that I had something to say to you; and I have not yet said it. The truth is, I don't feel sure whether I have been long enough your friend to take the liberty of advising you.'

'Whatever your advice is,' Percy an-swered, 'trust me to take it kindly on my side.'

Thus encouraged, the Captain spoke out.

'You will probably pass much of your time at the cottage,' he began, 'and you will be thrown a great deal into Mr. Bowmore's society. I have known him for many years. Speaking from that knowledge, I most seriously warn you against him as a thoroughly unprincipled and thoroughly dangerous man.'

This was strong language—and, natu-rally enough, Percy said so. The Captain justified his language.

'Without alluding to Mr. Bowmore's politics,' he went on, 'I can tell you that the motive of everything he says and does is vanity. To the gratification of that one passion he would sacrifice you or me, his wife or his daughter, without hesitation and without remorse. His one desire is to get into Parliament. You are wealthy and you can help him. He will leave no effort un-tried to reach that end ; and, if he gets you into political difficulties, he will desert you without scruple.'

Percy made a last effort to take Mr. Bowmore's part—for the one irresistible reason that he was Charlotte's father.

'Pray don't think I am unworthy of your kind interest in my welfare,' he pleaded. 'Can you tell me of any *facts* which justify what you have just said?'

'I can tell you of three facts,' Bervie answered. 'Mr. Bowmore belongs to one of the most revolutionary clubs in England ; he has spoken rank sedition at public meet-ings ; and his name is already in the black book at the Home Office. So much for the past. As to the future, if the rumour be true that Ministers mean to stop the insur-rectionary risings among the population by suspending the Habeas Corpus Act, Mr. Bowmore will certainly be in danger ; and it may be my father's duty to grant the warrant that apprehends him. Write to my father to verify what I have said, and I will forward your letter, by way of satisfying him that he can trust you. In the meantime, refuse to accept Mr. Bowmore's assist-ance in the matter of your claim on Par-liament ; and, above all things, stop him at the outset, when he tries to steal his way into your intimacy. I need not caution you to say nothing against him to his wife and daughter. His wily tongue has long since deluded them. Don't let it delude *you!* Have you thought any more of our evening at Doctor Lagarde's?' he asked, abruptly changing the subject.

'I hardly know,' said Percy, still under the impression of the formidable warning which he had just received.

'Let me jog your memory,' the other continued. 'You went on with the con-sultation by yourself, after I had left the Doctor's house. It will be really doing me a favour, if you can call to mind what Lagarde saw in the trance—in my absence?'

Thus entreated Percy roused himself. His memory of events was still fresh enough to answer the call that his friend had made on it. In describing what had happened, he accurately repeated all that the Doctor had said.

Bervie dwelt on the words with alarm in his face as well as surprise.

'A man like me, trying to persuade a woman like——,' he checked himself, as if he was afraid to let Charlotte's name pass his lips. 'Trying to induce a woman to go away with me,' he resumed, 'and persuading her at last? Pray go on! What did the Doctor see next?'

'He was too much exhausted, he said, to see any more.'

'Surely you returned to consult him again?'

'No ; I had had enough of it.'

'When we get to London,' said the Cap-tain, 'we shall pass along the Strand, on the way to your chambers. Will you kindly drop me at the turning that leads to the Doctor's lodgings?'

Percy looked at him in amazement. 'You still take it seriously?' he said.

'Is it *not* serious?' Bervie asked. 'Have

you and I, so far, not done exactly what this man saw us doing? Did we not meet, in the days when we were rivals (as he saw us meet), with the pistols in our hands? Did you not recognise his description of the lady when you met her at the ball, as I recognised it before you?'

'Mere coincidences!' Percy answered, quoting Charlotte's opinion when they had spoken together of Doctor Lagarde, but taking care not to cite his authority. 'How many thousand men have been crossed in love? How many thousand men have fought duels for love? How many thousand women choose blue for their favourite colour, and answer to the vague description of the lady whom the Doctor pretended to see?'

'Say that it is so,' Bervie rejoined. 'The thing is remarkable, even from your point of view. And if more coincidences follow, the result will be more remarkable still.'

Arrived at the Strand, Percy set the Cap-tain down at the turning which led to the Doctor's lodgings. 'You will call on me or write me word, if anything remarkable happens,' he said.

'You shall hear from me without fail,' Bervie replied.

That night, the Captain's pen performed the Captain's promise, in few and startling words.

'Melancholy news! Madame Lagarde is dead. Nothing is known of her son but that he has left England. I have found out that he is a political exile. If he has ven-tured back to France, it is barely possible that I may hear something of him. I have friends at the English embassy in Paris who will help me to make enquiries; and I start for the Continent in a day or two. Write to me while I am away, to the care of my father, at "The Manor House, near Dartford." He will always know my address abroad, and will forward your letters. For your own sake, remember the warning I gave you this afternoon! Your faithful friend, A. B.'

CHAPTER IX.

OFFICIAL SECRETS.

THERE was a more serious reason than Bervie was aware of, at the time, for the warning which he had thought it his duty to address to Percy Linwood. The new footman who had entered Mr. Bowmore's service was a Spy.

Well practised in the infamous vocation that he followed, the wretch had been chosen, by the Department of Secret Service at the Home Office, to watch the proceedings of Mr. Bowmore and his friends, and to report the result to his superiors. It may not be amiss to add that the employment of paid spies and informers, by the English Government of that time, was openly acknowledged in the House of Lords, and was defended as a necessary measure in the speeches of Lord Redesdale and Lord Liverpool.*

The reports furnished by the Home Office Spy, under these circumstances, begin with the month of March, and take the form of a series of notes introduced as follows:

'MR. SECRETARY:

'Since I entered Mr. Bowmore's service, I have the honour to inform you that my eyes and ears have been kept in a state of active observation; and I can further certify that my means of making myself useful in the future to my honourable employers are in no respect diminished. Not the slightest suspicion of my true character is felt by any person in the house.

FIRST NOTE.

'The young gentleman now on a visit to Mr. Bowmore is, as you have been correctly informed, Mr. Percy Linwood. Although he is engaged to be married to Miss Bowmore, he is not discreet enough to conceal a certain want of friendly feeling, on his part, towards her father. The young lady has noticed

---

* Readers who may desire to test the author's authority for this statement, are referred to 'The Annual Register' for 1817, Chapters I. and III.; and, further on, to page 66 in the same volume.

this, and has resented it. She accuses her lover of having allowed himself to be prejudiced against Mr. Bowmore by some slanderous person unknown.

'Mr. Percy's clumsy defence of himself led (in my hearing) to a quarrel! Nothing but his prompt submission prevented the marriage engagement from being broken off.

'"If you showed a want of confidence in Me" (I heard Miss Charlotte say), "I might forgive it. But when you show a want of confidence in a man so noble as my father, I have no mercy on you." After such an expression of filial sentiment as this, Mr. Percy wisely took the readiest way of appealing to the lady's indulgence. The young man has a demand on Parliament for moneys due to his father's estate; and he pleased and flattered Miss Charlotte by asking Mr. Bowmore to advise him as to the best means of asserting his claim. By way of advancing his political interests, Mr. Bowmore introduced him to the local Hampden Club; and Miss Charlotte rewarded him with a generosity which must not be passed over in silence. Her lover was permitted to put an engagement ring on her finger, and to kiss her afterwards to his heart's content.'

SECOND NOTE.

'Mr. Percy has paid more visits to the Republican Club; and Justice Bervie (father of the Captain) has heard of it, and has written to his son. The result that might have been expected has followed. Captain Bervie announces his return to England, to exert his influence for political good against the influence of Mr. Bowmore for political evil.

'In the meanwhile, Mr. Percy's claim has been brought before the House of Commons, and has been adjourned for further consideration in six months' time. Both the gentlemen are indignant—especially Mr. Bowmore. He has called a meeting of the Club to consider his young friend's wrongs, and has proposed the election of Mr. Percy as a member of that revolutionary society.'

THIRD NOTE.

'Mr. Percy has been elected. Captain Bervie has tried to awaken his mind to a sense of the danger that threatens him, if he persists in associating with his republican friends—and has utterly failed. Mr. Bowmore and Mr. Percy have made speeches at the Club, intended to force the latter gentleman's claim on the immediate attention of Government. Mr. Bowmore's flow of frothy eloquence has its influence (as you know from our shorthand writers' previous reports) on thousands of ignorant people. As it seems to me, the reasons for at once putting this man in prison are beyond dispute. Whether it is desirable to include Mr. Percy in the order of arrest, I must not venture to decide. Let me only hint that his seditious speech rivals the more elaborate efforts of Mr. Bowmore himself.

'So much for the present. I may now respectfully direct your attention to the future.

'On the second of April next, the Club assembles a public meeting, "in aid of British liberty," in a field near Dartford. Mr. Bowmore is to preside, and is to be escorted afterwards to Westminster Hall on his way to plead Mr. Percy's cause, in his own person, before the House of Commons. He is quite serious in declaring that "the minions of Government dare not touch a hair of his head." Miss Charlotte agrees with her father. And Mr. Percy agrees with Miss Charlotte. Such is the state of affairs at the house in which I am acting the part of domestic servant.

'I enclose shorthand reports of the speeches recently delivered at the Hampden Club, and have the honour of waiting for further orders.'

FOURTH NOTE.

'Your commands have reached me by this morning's post.

'I immediately waited on Justice Bervie (in plain clothes, of course), and gave him your official letter, instructing me to arrest Mr. Bowmore and Mr. Percy Linwood.

'The venerable magistrate hesitated.

'He quite understood the necessity for keeping the arrest a strict secret, in the interests of Government. The only reluctance he felt in granting the warrant related to his son's intimate friend. But for the peremptory tone of your letter, I really believe he would have asked you to give Mr. Percy time for consideration. Not being rash enough to proceed to such an extreme as this, he slily consulted the young man's interests by declining, on formal grounds, to date the warrant earlier than the second of April. Please note that my visit to him was paid at noon, on the thirty-first of March.

'If the object of this delay (to which I was obliged to submit) is to offer a chance of escape to Mr. Percy, the same chance necessarily includes Mr. Bowmore, whose name is also in the warrant. Trust me to keep a watchful eye on both these gentlemen; especially on Mr. Bowmore. He is the most dangerous man of the two, and the most likely, if he feels any suspicions, to slip through the fingers of the law.

'I have also to report that I discovered three persons in the hall of Justice Bervie's house, as I went out.

'One of them was his son, the Captain; one was his daughter, Miss Bervie; and the third was that smooth-tongued old soldier, Major Mulvany. If the escape of Mr. Bowmore and Mr. Linwood is in contemplation, mark my words: the persons whom I have just mentioned will be concerned in it —and perhaps Miss Charlotte herself as well. At present, she is entirely unsuspicious of any misfortune hanging over her head; her attention being absorbed in the preparation of her bridal finery. As an admirer myself of the fair sex, I must own that it seems hard on the girl to have her lover clapped into prison, before the wedding-day.

'I will bring you word of the arrest myself. There will be plenty of time to catch the afternoon coach to London.

'Here—unless something happens which it is impossible to foresee—my report may come to an end.'

CHAPTER X.

THE ELOPEMENT.

ON the evening of the first of April, Mrs. Bowmore was left alone with the servants. Mr. Bowmore and Percy had gone out together to attend a special meeting of the Club. Shortly afterwards Miss Charlotte had left the cottage, under very extraordinary circumstances.

A few minutes only after the departure of her father and Percy, she received a letter, which appeared to cause her the most violent agitation. She said to Mrs. Bowmore:

'Mamma, I must see Captain Bervie for a few minutes in private, on a matter of serious importance to all of us. He is waiting at the front gate, and he will come in if I show myself at the hall door.'

Upon this, Mrs. Bowmore had asked for an explanation.

'There is no time for explanation,' was the only answer she received; 'I ask you to leave me for five minutes alone with the Captain.'

Mrs. Bowmore still hesitated. Charlotte snatched up her garden hat, and declared wildly that she would go out to Captain Bervie, if she was not permitted to receive him at home. In the face of this declaration, Mrs. Bowmore yielded, and left the room.

In a minute more the Captain made his appearance.

Although she had given way, Mrs. Bowmore was not disposed to trust her daughter, without supervision, in the society of a man whom Charlotte herself had reviled as a slanderer and a false friend. She took up her position in the veranda outside the parlour, at a safe distance from one of the two windows of the room, which had been left partially open to admit the fresh air. Here she waited and listened.

The conversation was for some time carried on in whispers.

As they became more and more excited, both Charlotte and Bervie ended in unconsciously raising their voices.

'I swear it to you on my faith as a Christian!' Mrs. Bowmore heard the Captain say. 'I declare before God who hears me that I am speaking the truth!'

And Charlotte had answered, with a burst of tears:

'I can't believe you! I daren't believe you! Oh, how can you ask me to do such a thing? Let me go! let me go!'

Alarmed at those words, Mrs. Bowmore advanced to the window, and looked in.

Bervie had put her daughter's arm on his arm, and was trying to induce her to leave the parlour with him. She resisted, and implored him to release her. He dropped her arm, and whispered in her ear. She looked at him—and instantly made up her mind.

'Let me tell my mother where I am going,' she said; 'and I will consent.'

'Be it so!' he answered. 'And remember one thing; every minute is precious; the fewest words are the best.'

Mrs. Bowmore re-entered the cottage by the adjoining room, and met them in the passage. In few words, Charlotte spoke.

'I must go at once to Justice Bervie's house. Don't be afraid, mamma! I know what I am about, and I know I am right.'

'Going to Justice Bervie's!' cried Mrs. Bowmore, in the utmost extremity of astonishment. 'What will your father say, what will Percy think, when they come back from the Club?'

'My sister's carriage is waiting for me close by,' Bervie answered. 'It is entirely at Miss Bowmore's disposal. She can easily get back, if she wishes to keep her visit a secret, before Mr. Bowmore and Mr. Linwood return.'

He led her to the door as he spoke. She ran back, and kissed her mother tenderly.

Mrs. Bowmore called to them to wait.

' I daren't let you go,' she said to her daughter, ' without your father's leave !'

Charlotte seemed not to hear, the Captain seemed not to hear. They ran across the front garden, and through the gate—and were out of sight in less than a minute.

More than two hours passed ; the sun sank below the horizon, and still there were no signs of Charlotte's return.

Feeling seriously uneasy, Mrs. Bowmore crossed the room to ring the bell, and send the man-servant to Justice Bervie's house to hasten her daughter's return.

As she approached the fireplace, she was startled by a sound of stealthy footsteps in the hall, followed by a loud noise as of some heavy object that had dropped on the floor. She rang the bell violently, and opened the door of the parlour. At the same moment, the spy-footman passed her, running out, apparently in pursuit of somebody, at the top of his speed. She followed him, as rapidly as she could, across the little front garden, to the gate. Arrived in the road, she was in time to see him vault upon the luggage-board at the back of a post-chaise before the cottage, just as the postilion started the horses on their way to London. The spy saw Mrs. Bowmore looking at him, and pointed, with an insolent nod of his head, first to the inside of the vehicle, and then over it to the high-road ; signing to her that he designed to accompany the person in the post-chaise to the end of the journey.

Turning to go back, Mrs. Bowmore saw her own bewilderment reflected in the faces of the two female servants, who had followed her out.

' Who can the footman be after, ma'am ?' asked the cook. ' Do you think it's a thief ?'

The housemaid pointed to the post-chaise, barely visible in the distance.

' Simpleton !' she said. ' Do thieves travel in that way ? I wish my master had come back,' she proceeded, speaking to herself; ' I'm afraid there's something wrong.'

Mrs. Bowmore, returning through the garden-gate, instantly stopped and looked at the woman.

' What makes you mention your master's name, Amelia, when you fear that something is wrong ?' she asked.

Amelia changed colour, and looked confused.

' I am loath to alarm you, ma'am,' she said ; ' and I can't rightly see what it is my duty to do.'

Mrs. Bowmore's heart sank within her under the cruellest of all terrors, the terror of something unknown. ' Don't keep me in suspense,' she said faintly. ' Whatever it is, let me know it.'

She led the way back to the parlour. The housemaid followed her. The cook (declining to be left alone) followed the housemaid.

' It was something I heard early this afternoon, ma'am,' Amelia began. ' Cook happened to be busy——'

The cook interposed : she had not forgiven the housemaid for calling her a simpleton. ' No, Amelia, if you *must* bring me into it—not busy. Uneasy in my mind on the subject of the soup.'

' I don't know that your mind makes much difference,' Amelia resumed. ' What it comes to is this—it was I, and not you, who went into the kitchen-garden for the vegetables.'

' Not by *my* wish, Heaven knows !' persisted the cook.

' Leave the room !' said Mrs. Bowmore. Even her patience had given way at last.

The cook looked as if she declined to believe her own ears. Mrs. Bowmore pointed to the door. The cook said ' Oh ?' —accenting it as a question. Mrs. Bowmore's finger still pointed. The cook, in solemn silence, yielded to circumstances, and banged the door.

' I was getting the vegetables, ma'am,' Amelia proceeded, ' when I heard voices on the other side of the paling. The wood is so old that one can see through the cracks easy enough. I saw my master, and Mr. Linwood, and Captain Bervie. The Captain seemed to have stopped the other two on the pathway that leads to the field ; he stood, as it might be, between them and the back way to the house — and he spoke severely, that he did !'

'What did Captain Bervie say ?'

'He said these words, ma'am : "For the last time, Mr. Bowmore," says he, " will you understand that you are in danger, and that Mr. Linwood is in danger, unless you both leave this neighbourhood to-night ?" My master made light of it.   " For the last time," says he, " will you refer us to a proof of what you say, and allow us to judge for ourselves ?"   " I have told you already," says the Captain, " I am bound by my duty towards another person to keep what I know a secret."   " Very well," says my master, " *I* am bound by my duty to my country.   And I tell you this," says he, in his high and mighty way, " neither Government, nor the spies of Government, dare touch a hair of my head : they know it, sir, for the head of the people's friend !"'

'That's quite true,' said Mrs. Bowmore, still believing in her husband as firmly as ever.

Amelia went on :

'Captain Bervie didn't seem to think so,' she said.   'He lost his temper.   "What stuff !" says he ; " there's a Government spy in your house at this moment, disguised as your footman."   My master looked at Mr. Linwood, and burst out laughing.   " You won't beat that, Captain," says he, " if you talk till doomsday."   He turned about without a word more, and went home.   The Captain caught Mr. Linwood by the arm, as soon as they were alone.   " For God's sake," says he, " don't follow that madman's example !" '

Mrs. Bowmore was shocked.   'Did he really call my husband a madman ?' she asked.

'He did indeed, ma'am—and he was in earnest about it too.   "If you value your liberty," he says to Mr. Linwood ; " if you hope to become Charlotte's husband, consult your own safety.   I can give you a passport.   Escape to France and wait till this trouble is over."   Mr. Linwood was not in the best of tempers—Mr. Linwood shook him off.   " Charlotte's father will soon be my father," says he ; " do you think I will desert him ?   My friends at the Club have taken up my claim ; do you think I will forsake them at the meeting to-morrow ?   You ask me to be unworthy of Charlotte, and unworthy of my friends—you insult me, if you say more."   He whipped round on his heel, and followed my master.'

'And what did the Captain do ?'

'Lifted up his hands, ma'am, to the heavens, and looked—I declare it turned my blood to see him.   If there's truth in mortal man, it's my firm belief——'

What the housemaid's belief was, re-mained unexpressed.   Before she could get to her next word, a shriek of horror from the hall announced that the cook's powers of interruption were not exhausted yet.

Mistress and servant both hurried out, in terror of they knew not what.   There stood the cook, alone in the hall, confronting the stand on which the overcoats and hats of the men of the family were placed.

'Where's the master's travelling-coat?' cried the cook, staring wildly at an un-occupied peg.   'And where's his cap to match?   Oh Lord, he's off in the post-chaise ! and the footman's after him !'

Simpleton as she was, the woman had blundered on a very serious discovery.

Coat and cap—both made after a foreign pattern, and both strikingly remarkable in form and colour to English eyes—had un-questionably disappeared.   It was equally certain that they were well known to the footman, whom the Captain had declared to be a spy, as the coat and cap which his master used in travelling.   Had Mr. Bowmore discovered (since the afternoon) that he was really in danger?   Had the necessities of instant flight only allowed him time enough to snatch his coat and cap out of the hall?   And had the treacherous man-servant seen him as he was making his escape to the post-chaise?   The cook's conclusion answered all these questions in the affirmative—and, if Captain Bervie's words of warning had been correctly reported, the cook's conclusion for once was not to be despised.

Under this last trial of her fortitude, Mrs. Bowmore's feeble reserves of endurance completely gave way. The poor lady turned faint and giddy. Amelia placed her on a chair in the hall, and told the cook to open the front door, and let in the fresh air.

The cook obeyed ; and instantly broke out with a second terrific scream ; announcing nothing less, this time, than the appearance of Mr. Bowmore himself, alive and hearty, returning with Percy from the meeting at the Club !

The inevitable enquiries and explanations followed.

Fully assured, as he had declared himself to be, of the sanctity of his person (politically speaking), Mr. Bowmore turned pale, nevertheless, when he looked at the unoccupied peg on his clothes stand. Had some man unknown personated him? And had a post-chaise been hired to lead an impending pursuit of him in the wrong direction? What did it mean? Who was the friend to whose services he was indebted? As for the proceedings of the man-servant, but one interpretation could now be placed on them. They distinctly justified what Captain Bervie had said of him. Mr. Bowmore thought of the Captain's other assertion, relating to the urgent necessity for making his escape ; and looked at Percy in silent dismay ; and turned paler than ever.

Percy's thoughts, diverted for the moment only from the lady of his love, returned to her with renewed fidelity. ' Let us hear what Charlotte thinks of it,' he said. ' Where is she?'

It was impossible to answer this question plainly and in few words.

Terrified at the effect which her attempt at explanation produced on Percy, helplessly ignorant when she was called upon to account for her daughter's absence, Mrs. Bowmore could only shed tears and express a devout trust in Providence. Her husband looked at the new misfortune from a political point of view. He sat down, and slapped his forehead theatrically with the palm of his hand. ' Thus far,' said the patriot, ' my political assailants have only struck at me through the newspapers. *Now* they strike at me through my child !'

Percy made no speeches. There was a look in his eyes which boded ill for Captain Bervie if the two met. ' I am going to fetch her,' was all he said, ' as fast as a horse can carry me.'

He hired his horse at an inn in the town, and set forth for Justice Bervie's house at a gallop.

During Percy's absence, Mr. Bowmore secured the front and back entrances to the cottage with his own hands.

These first precautions taken, he ascended to his room, and packed his travelling-bag. ' Necessaries for my use in prison,' he remarked. ' The bloodhounds of Government are after me.' ' Are they after Percy, too?' his wife ventured to ask. Mr. Bowmore looked up impatiently, and cried ' Pooh!' —as if Percy was of no consequence. Mrs. Bowmore thought otherwise : the good woman privately packed a bag for Percy, in the sanctuary of her own room.

For an hour, and more than an hour, no event of any sort occurred.

Mr. Bowmore stalked up and down the parlour, meditating. At intervals, ideas of flight presented themselves attractively to his mind. At intervals, ideas of the speech that he had prepared for the public meeting on the next day took their place. ' If I fly to-night,' he wisely observed, ' what will become of my speech? I will *not* fly to-night! The people shall hear me.'

He sat down, and crossed his arms fiercely. As he looked at his wife to see what effect he had produced on her, the sound of heavy carriage-wheels and the trampling of horses penetrated to the parlour from the garden-gate.

Mr. Bowmore started to his feet, with

every appearance of having suddenly altered his mind on the question of flight. Just as he reached the hall, Percy's voice was heard at the front-door. 'Let me in. Instantly! Instantly!'

Mrs. Bowmore drew back the bolts, before the servants could help her. 'Where is Charlotte?' she cried; seeing Percy alone on the doorstep.

'Gone!' Percy answered furiously. 'Eloped to Paris, with Captain Bervie! Read her own confession. They were just sending the messenger with it, when I reached the house.'

He handed a note to Mrs. Bowmore, and turned aside to speak to her husband while she read it. Charlotte wrote to her mother very briefly; promising to explain everything on her return. In the meantime, she had left home under careful protection —she had a lady for her companion on the journey—and she would write again from Paris. So the letter, evidently written in great haste, began and ended.

Percy took Mr. Bowmore to the window, and pointed to a carriage and four horses waiting at the garden-gate.

'Do you come with me, and back me with your authority as her father?' he asked sternly. 'Or do you leave me to go alone?'

Mr. Bowmore was famous among his admirers for his 'happy replies.' He made one now.

'I am not Brutus,' he said. 'I am only Bowmore. My daughter before everything. Fetch my travelling-bag.'

While the travellers' bags were being placed in the chaise, Mr. Bowmore was struck by an idea.

He produced from his coat-pocket a roll of many papers thickly covered with writing. On the blank leaf in which they were tied up, he wrote in the largest letters: 'Frightful domestic calamity! Vice-President Bowmore obliged to leave England! Welfare of a beloved daughter! His speech will be read at the meeting by Secretary Joskin, of the Club. (Private to Joskin. Have

these lines printed and posted everywhere. And, when you read my speech, for God's sake don't drop your voice at the ends of the sentences.')

He threw down the pen, and embraced Mrs. Bowmore in the most summary manner. The poor woman was ordered to send the roll of paper to the Club, without a word to comfort and sustain her from her husband's lips. Percy spoke to her hopefully and kindly, as he kissed her cheek at parting.

On the next morning, a letter, addressed to Mrs. Bowmore, was delivered at the cottage by private messenger.

Opening the letter, she recognised the handwriting of her husband's old friend, and her old friend—Major Mulvany. In breathless amazement, she read these lines:

'DEAR MRS. BOWMORE:

'In matters of importance, the golden rule is never to waste words. I have performed one of the great actions of my life—I have saved your husband.

'How I discovered that my friend was in danger, I must not tell you at present. Let it be enough if I say that I have been a guest under Justice Bervie's hospitable roof, and that I know of a Home Office spy who has taken you unawares under pretence of being your footman. If I had not circumvented him, the scoundrel would have imprisoned your husband, and another dear friend of mine. This is how I did it.

'I must begin by appealing to your memory.

'Do you happen to remember that your husband and I are as near as may be of about the same height? Very good, so far. Did you, in the next place, miss Bowmore's travelling coat and cap from their customary peg? I am the thief, dearest lady; I put them on my own humble self. Did you hear a sudden noise in the hall? Oh, forgive me—I made the noise! And it did just what I wanted of it. It brought the spy up from the kitchen, suspecting that something might be wrong.

'What did the wretch see when he got into the hall? His master, in travelling costume, running out. What did he find when he reached the garden? His master escaping, in a post-chaise, on the road to London. What did he do, the born blackguard that he was? Jumped up behind the chaise, to make sure of his prisoner. It was dark when we got to London. In a hop, skip, and jump, I was out of the carriage, and in at my own door, before he could look me in the face.

'The date of the warrant, you must know, obliged him to wait till the morning. All that night, he and the Bow Street runners kept watch. They came in with the sunrise—and who did they find? Major Mulvany snug in his bed, and as innocent as the babe unborn. Oh, they did their duty! Searched the place from the kitchen to the garrets—and gave it up. There's but one thing I regret—I let the spy off without a good thrashing. No matter. I'll do it yet, one of these days.

'Let me know the first good news of our darling fugitives, and I shall be more than rewarded for what little I have done.

'Your always devoted,
'TERENCE MULVANY.'

CHAPTER XI.

PURSUIT AND DISCOVERY.

FEELING himself hurried away on the road to Dover, as fast as four horses could carry him, Mr. Bowmore had leisure to criticise Percy's conduct, from his own purely selfish point of view.

'If you had listened to my advice,' he said, 'you would have treated that man Bervie like the hypocrite and villain that he is. But no! you trusted to your own crude impressions. Having given him your hand after the duel (I would have given him the contents of my pistol!) you

hesitated to withdraw it again, when that slanderer appealed to your friendship not to cast him off. Now you see the consequence!'

'Wait till we get to Paris!' All the ingenuity of Percy's travelling companion failed to extract from him any other answer than that.

Foiled so far, Mr. Bowmore began to start difficulties next. Had they money enough for the journey? Percy touched his pocket, and answered shortly, 'Plenty.' Had they passports? Percy sullenly showed a letter. 'There is the necessary voucher from a magistrate,' he said. 'The consul at Dover will give us our passports. Mind this!' he added, in warning tones, 'I have pledged my word of honour to Justice Bervie, that we have no political object in view in travelling to France. Keep your politics to yourself, on the other side of the Channel.'

Mr. Bowmore listened in blank amazement. Charlotte's lover was appearing in a new character—the character of a man who had lost his respect for Charlotte's father!

It was useless to talk to him. He deliberately checked any further attempts at conversation, by leaning back in the carriage, and closing his eyes. The truth is, Mr. Bowmore's own language and conduct were insensibly producing the salutary impression on Percy's mind, which Bervie had vainly tried to convey, under the disadvantage of having Charlotte's influence against him. Throughout the journey, Percy did exactly what Bervie had once entreated him to do—he kept Mr. Bowmore at a distance.

At every stage, they inquired after the fugitives. At every stage, they were answered by a more or less intelligible description of Bervie and Charlotte, and of the lady who accompanied them. No disguise had been attempted; no person had in any case been bribed to conceal the truth.

When the first tumult of his emotions had in some degree subsided, this strange circumstance associated itself in Percy's mind with the equally unaccountable conduct of Justice Bervie, on his arrival at the manor house.

The old gentleman met his visitor in the hall, without expressing, and apparently without feeling, any indignation at his son's conduct. It was even useless to appeal to him for information. He only said, 'I am not in Arthur's confidence ; he is of age, and my daughter (who has volunteered to accompany him) is of age. I have no claim to control them. I believe they have taken Miss Bowmore to Paris ; and that is all I know about it.'

He had shown the same dense insensibility in giving his official voucher for the passports. Percy had only to satisfy him on the question of politics ; and the document was drawn out as a matter of course. Such had been the father's behaviour ; and the conduct of the son now exhibited the same shameless composure. To what conclusion did this discovery point ? Percy abandoned the attempt to answer that question in despair.

They reached Dover towards two o'clock in the morning.

At the pier-head they found a coast-guardsman on duty, and received more information.

In 1817 the communication with France was still by sailing-vessels. Arriving long after the departure of the regular packet, Bervie had hired a lugger, and had sailed with the two ladies for Calais, having a fresh breeze in his favour. Percy's first angry impulse was to follow him instantly. The next moment he remembered the insurmountable obstacle of the passports. The Consul would certainly not grant those essentially necessary documents at two in the morning !

The only alternative was to wait for the regular packet, which sailed some hours later—between eight and nine o'clock in the forenoon. In this case, they might apply for their passports before the regular office hours, if they explained the circumstances,

backed by the authority of the magistrate's letter.

Mr. Bowmore followed Percy to the nearest inn that was open, sublimely indifferent to the delays and difficulties of the journey. He ordered refreshments with the air of a man who was performing a melancholy duty to himself, in the name of humanity.

'When I think of my speech,' he said, at supper, 'my heart bleeds for the people. In a few hours more, they will assemble in their thousands, eager to hear me. And what will they see ? Joskin in my place ! Joskin with a manuscript in his hand ! Joskin, who drops his voice at the ends of his sentences ! I will never forgive Charlotte. Waiter, another glass of brandy and water.'

After an unusually quick passage across the Channel, the travellers landed on the French coast, before the defeated spy had returned from London to Dartford by stage-coach. Continuing their journey by post as far as Amiens, they reached that city in time to take their places by the diligence to Paris.

Arrived in Paris, they encountered another incomprehensible proceeding on the part of Captain Bervie.

Among the persons assembled in the yard to see the arrival of the diligence was a man with a morsel of paper in his hand, evidently on the look-out for some person whom he expected to discover among the travellers. After consulting his bit of paper, he looked with steady attention at Percy and Mr. Bowmore, and suddenly approached them. 'If you wish to see the Captain,' he said, in broken English, 'you will find him at that hotel.' He handed a printed card to Percy, and disappeared among the crowd before it was possible to question him.

Even Mr. Bowmore gave way to human weakness, and condescended to feel astonished in the face of such an event as this. 'What next !' he exclaimed.

'Wait till we get to the hotel,' said Percy.

In half an hour more the landlord had

received them, and the waiter had led them to the right door. Percy pushed the man aside, and burst into the room.

Captain Bervie was alone, reading a newspaper. Before the first furious words had escaped Percy's lips, Bervie silenced him by pointing to a closed door on the right of the fireplace.

'She is in that room,' he said ; 'speak quietly, or you may frighten her. I know what you are going to say,' he added, as Percy stepped nearer to him. 'Will you hear me in my own defence, and then decide whether I am the greatest scoundrel living, or the best friend you ever had ?'

He put the question kindly, with something that was at once grave and tender in his look and manner. The extraordinary composure with which he acted and spoke had its tranquillising influence over Percy. He felt himself surprised into giving Bervie a hearing.

'I will tell you first what I have done,' the Captain proceeded, 'and next why I did it. I have taken it on myself, Mr. Linwood, to make an alteration in your wedding arrangements. Instead of being married at Dartford church, you will be married (if you see no objection) at the chapel of the embassy in Paris, by my old college friend the chaplain.'

This was too much for Percy's self-control. 'Your audacity is beyond belief,' he broke out.

'And beyond endurance,' Mr. Bowmore added. 'Understand this, sir ! Whatever your defence may be, I object, under any circumstances, to be made the victim of a trick.'

'You are the victim of your own obstinate refusal to profit by a plain warning,' Bervie rejoined. 'At the eleventh hour, I entreated you, and I entreated Mr. Linwood, to provide for your own safety; and I spoke in vain.'

Percy's patience gave way once more.

'To use your own language,' he said, 'I have still to decide whether you have behaved towards me like a scoundrel or a

friend. You have said nothing to justify yourself yet.'

'Very well put !' Mr. Bowmore chimed in. 'Come to the point, sir ! My daughter's reputation is in question.'

'Miss Bowmore's reputation is not in question for a single instant,' Bervie answered. 'My sister has been the companion of her journey from first to last.'

'Journey ?' Mr. Bowmore repeated indignantly. 'I want to know, sir, what the journey means. As an outraged father, I ask one plain question. Why did you run away with my daughter ?'

Bervie took a slip of paper from his pocket, and handed it to Percy with a smile.

It was a copy of the warrant which Justice Bervie's duty had compelled him to issue for the 'arrest of Orlando Bowmore and Percy Linwood.' There was no danger in divulging the secret now. British warrants were waste-paper in France, in those days.

'I ran away with the bride,' Bervie said coolly, 'in the certain knowledge that you and Mr. Bowmore would run after me. If I had not forced you both to follow me out of England on the first of April, you would have been made State prisoners on the second. What do you say to my conduct now ?'

'Wait, Percy, before you answer him,' Mr. Bowmore interposed. 'He is ready enough at excusing himself. But, observe —he hasn't a word to say in justification of my daughter's readiness to run away with him.'

'Have you quite done ?' Bervie asked as quietly as ever.

Mr. Bowmore reserved the right of all others which he most prized, the right of using his tongue. 'For the present,' he answered in his loftiest manner, 'I have done.'

Bervie proceeded : 'Your daughter consented to run away with me, because I took her to my father's house, and prevailed upon him to trust her with the secret of the coming arrests. She had no choice left but to let her obstinate father and her misguided lover go to prison—or to take her place with my sister and me in the travelling-carriage.' He appealed once more to Percy. ' My friend, you remember the day when you spared my life. Have I remembered it, too ?'

For once, there was an Englishman who was not contented to express the noblest emotions that humanity can feel by the commonplace ceremony of shaking hands. Percy's heart overflowed. In an outburst of unutterable gratitude he threw himself on Bervie's breast. As brothers the two men embraced. As brothers they loved and trusted one another, from that day forth.

The door on the right was softly opened from within. A charming face—the dark eyes bright with happy tears, the rosy lips just opening into a smile—peeped into the room. A low sweet voice, with an under-note of trembling in it, made this modest protest, in the form of an inquiry :

' When you have quite done, Percy, with our good friend, perhaps you will have something to say to ME ?'

LAST WORDS.

THE persons immediately interested in the marriage of Percy and Charlotte were the only persons present at the ceremony.

At the little breakfast afterwards, in the French hotel, Mr. Bowmore insisted on making a speech to a select audience of six —namely the bride and bridegroom, the bridesmaid, the Chaplain, the Captain, and Mrs. Bowmore. But what does a small audience matter ? The English frenzy for making speeches is not to be cooled by such a trifle as that. At the end of the world, the expiring forces of Nature will hear a dreadful voice—the voice of the last Englishman delivering the last speech.

Percy wisely made his honeymoon a long

one ; he determined to be quite sure of his superior influence over his wife, before he trusted her within reach of her father again.

Mr. and Mrs. Bowmore accompanied Captain Bervie and Miss Bervie on their way back to England, as far as Boulogne. In that pleasant town, the banished patriot set up his tent. It was a cheaper place to live in than Paris, and it was conveniently close to England, when he had quite made up his mind whether to be an exile on the Continent, or to go back to his own country and be a martyr in prison. In the end, the course of events settled that question for him. Mr. Bowmore returned to England, with the return of the Habeas Corpus Act.

The years passed. Percy and Charlotte (judged from the romantic point of view) became two uninteresting married people. Bervie (always remaining a bachelor) rose steadily in his profession, through the higher grades of military rank. Mr. Bowmore, wisely overlooked by a new Government, sank back again into the obscurity from which shrewd Ministers would never have assisted him to emerge. The one subject of interest left, among the persons of this little drama, was now represented by Doctor Lagarde. Thus far, not a trace had been discovered of the French physician, who had so strangely associated the visions of his magnetic sleep with the destinies of the two men who had consulted him.

Steadfastly maintaining his own opinion of the prediction and the fulfilment, Bervie persisted in believing that he and Lagarde (or Percy and Lagarde) were yet destined to meet, and resume the unfinished consultation at the point where it had been broken off. Persons, happy in the possession of ' sound common sense,' who declared the prediction to be skilled guess-work, and the fulfilment manifest coincidence, ridiculed the idea of finding Doctor Lagarde as closely akin to that other celebrated idea of finding the needle in the bottle of hay. But Bervie's obstinacy was proverbial. Nothing shook his confidence in his own convictions.

More than thirteen years had elapsed since the consultation at the Doctor's lodgings, when Bervie went to Paris to spend a summer holiday with his friend, the chaplain to the English embassy. His last words to Percy and Charlotte when he took his leave were: ' Suppose I meet with Doctor Lagarde?'

It was then the year 1830. Bervie arrived at his friend's rooms on the 24th of July. On the 27th of the month, the famous revolution broke out which dethroned Charles the Tenth in three days.

On the second day, Bervie and his host ventured into the streets, watching the revolution (like other reckless Englishmen) at the risk of their lives. In the confusion around them, they were separated. Bervie, searching for his companion, found his progress stopped by a barricade, which had been desperately attacked, and desperately defended. Men in blouses and men in uniform lay dead and dying together: the tricoloured flag waved over them, in token of the victory of the people.

Bervie had just revived a poor wretch with a drink from an overthrown bowl of water, which still had a few drops left in it, when he felt a hand laid on his shoulder from behind. He turned and discovered a National Guard, who had been watching his charitable action. ' Give a helping hand to that poor fellow,' said the citizen-soldier, pointing to a workman standing near, grimed with blood and gunpowder. The tears were rolling down the man's cheeks. ' I can't see my way, sir, for crying,' he said. ' Help me to carry that sad burden into the next street.' He pointed to a rude wooden litter, on which lay a dead or wounded man, his face and breast covered with an old cloak. ' There is the best friend the people ever had,' the workman said. ' He cured us, comforted us, respected us, loved us. And there he lies, shot dead while he was binding up the wounds of friends and enemies alike!'

' Whoever he is, he has died nobly,' Bervie answered. ' May I look at him?'

The workman signed that he might look.

Bervie lifted the cloak—and met with Doctor Lagarde once more.

Miss Bertha and the Yankee

(PRELIMINARY STATEMENTS OF WITNESSES FOR THE DEFENCE, COLLECTED AT THE OFFICE OF THE SOLICITOR)

I.

No. 1.—*Miss Bertha Laroche, of Nettle-grove Hall, testifies and says :—*

TOWARDS the middle of June, in the year 1817, I went to take the waters at Maplesworth, in Derbyshire, accompanied by my nearest living relative—my aunt.

I am an only child; and I was twenty-one years old at my last birthday. On coming of age I inherited a house and lands in Derbyshire, together with a fortune in money of one hundred thousand pounds. The only education which I have received has been obtained within the last two or three years of my life ; and I have thus far seen nothing of Society, in England or in any other civilized part of the world. I can be a competent witness, it seems, in spite of these disadvantages. Anyhow, I mean to tell the truth.

My father was a French colonist in the island of Saint Domingo. He died while I was very young ; leaving to my mother and to me just enough to live on, in the remote part of the island in which our little property was situated. My mother was an Englishwoman. Her delicate health made it necessary for her to leave me, for many hours of the day, under the care of our household slaves. I can never forget their kindness to me ; but, unfortunately, their ignorance equalled their kindness. If we had been rich enough to send to France or England for a competent governess we might have done very well. But we were not rich enough. I am ashamed to say that I was nearly thirteen years old before I had learnt to read and write correctly.

Four more years passed—and then there came a wonderful event in our lives, which was nothing less than the change from Saint Domingo to England.

My mother was distantly related to an ancient and wealthy English family. She seriously offended these proud people by marrying an obscure foreigner, who had nothing to live on but his morsel of land in the West Indies. Having no expectations from her relatives, my mother preferred happiness with the man she loved to every other consideration ; and I, for one, think she was right. From that moment she was cast off by the head of the family. For eighteen years of her life, as wife, mother, and widow, no letters came to her from her English home. We had just celebrated my seventeenth birthday when the first letter came. It informed my mother that no less than three lives, which stood between her and the inheritance of certain portions of the family property, had been swept away by death. The estate and the fortune which I have already mentioned had fallen to her in due course of law, and her surviving relatives were magnanimously ready to forgive her at last!

We wound up our affairs at Saint Domingo, and we went to England to take possession of our new wealth.

At first, the return to her native air seemed to have a beneficial effect on my mother's health. But it was a temporary improvement only. Her constitution had been fatally injured by the West Indian climate, and just as we had engaged a competent person to look after my neglected education, my constant attendance was needed at my mother's bedside. We loved each other dearly, and we wanted no strange nurses to come between us. My aunt (my mother's sister) relieved me of my cares in the intervals when I wanted rest.

For seven sad months our dear sufferer lingered. I have only one remembrance to comfort me ; my mother's last kiss was mine—she died peacefully with her head on my bosom.

I was nearly nineteen years old before I had sufficiently rallied my courage to be able to think seriously of myself and my prospects.

At that age one does not willingly submit one's self for the first time to the authority of a governess. Having my aunt for a companion and protectress, I proposed to engage my own masters and to superintend my own education.

My plans failed to meet with the approval of the head of the family. He declared (most unjustly, as the event proved) that my aunt was not a fit person to take care of me. She had passed all the later years of her life in retirement. A good creature, he admitted, in her own way, but she had no knowledge of the world and no firmness of character. The right person to act as my chaperon, and to superintend my education, was the high-minded and accomplished woman who had taught his own daughters.

I declined, with all needful gratitude and respect, to take his advice. The bare idea of living with a stranger so soon after my mother's death revolted me. Besides, I liked my aunt and my aunt liked me. Being made acquainted with my decision, the head of the family cast me off, exactly as he had cast off my mother before me.

So I lived in retirement with my good aunt, and studied industriously to improve my mind until my twenty-first birthday came. I was now an heiress, privileged to think and act for myself. My aunt kissed me tenderly. We talked of my poor mother, and we cried in each other's arms on the memorable day which made a wealthy woman of me. In a little time more, other troubles than vain regrets for the dead were to try me, and other tears were to fill my eyes than the tears which I had given to the memory of my mother.

II.

I MAY now return to my visit, in June, 1817, to the healing springs at Maplesworth.

This famous inland watering-place was only between nine and ten miles from my new home called Nettlegrove Hall. I had been feeling weak and out of spirits for some months, and our medical adviser recommended change of scene and a trial of the waters at Maplesworth. My aunt and I established ourselves in comfortable apartments, with a letter of introduction to the chief doctor in the place. This otherwise harmless and worthy man proved, strangely enough, to be the innocent cause of the trials and troubles which beset me at the outset of my new life.

The day after we had presented our letter of introduction, we met the doctor on the public walk. He was accompanied by two strangers, both young men, and both (so far as my ignorant opinion went) persons of some distinction, judging by their dress and manners. The doctor said a few kind words to us, and rejoined his two companions. Both the gentlemen looked at me, and both took off their hats as my aunt and I proceeded on our walk.

I own I thought occasionally of the well-bred strangers during the rest of the day, especially of the shortest of the two, who was also the handsomest of the two to my thinking. If this confession seems rather a bold one, remember, if you please, that I had never been taught to conceal my feelings at Saint Domingo, and that the events which followed our arrival in England had kept me completely secluded from the society of other young ladies of my age.

The next day, while I was drinking my glass of healing water (extremely nasty water, by the way), the doctor joined us.

While he was asking me about my health, the two strangers made their appearance again, and took off their hats again. They both looked expectantly at the doctor, and the doctor (in performance of a promise which he had already made, as I privately suspected) formally introduced them to my aunt and to me. First (I put the handsomest man first) Captain Arthur Stanwick, of the army, home from India on leave, and staying at Maplesworth to take the waters ; secondly, Mr. Lionel Varleigh, of Boston, in America, visiting England, after travelling all over Europe, and stopping at Maplesworth to keep company with his friend the Captain.

On their introduction, the two gentlemen, observing, no doubt, that I was a little shy, forbore delicately from pressing their society on us.

Captain Stanwick, with a beautiful smile, and with teeth worthy of the smile, stroked his whiskers, and asked me if I had found any benefit from taking the waters. He afterwards spoke in great praise of the charming scenery in the neighbourhood of Maplesworth, and then turning away, addressed his next words to my aunt. Mr. Varleigh took his place. Speaking with perfect gravity, and with no whiskers to

stroke, he said :

' I have once tried the waters here out of curiosity. I can sympathize, Miss, with the expression which I observed on your face when you emptied your glass just now. Permit me to offer you something nice to take the taste of the waters out of your mouth.' He produced from his pocket a beautiful little box filled with sugar-plums. ' I bought it in Paris,' he explained. ' Having lived a good deal in France, I have got into a habit of making little presents of this sort to ladies and children. I wouldn't let the doctor see it, Miss, if I were you. He has the usual medical prejudice against sugar-plums.' With that quaint warning he, too, made his bow and discreetly withdrew.

Thinking it over afterwards, I acknowledged to myself that the English Captain —although he was the handsomest man of the two, and possessed the smoothest manners—had failed, nevertheless, to overcome my shyness. The American traveller's unaffected sincerity and good-humour, on the other hand, set me quite at my ease. I could look at him and thank him, and feel amused at his sympathy with the grimace I had made, after swallowing the illflavoured waters. And yet, while I lay awake at night, wondering whether we should meet our new acquaintances on the next day, it was the English Captain that I most wanted to see again, and not the American traveller! At the time, I set this down to nothing more important than my own perversity. Ah, dear! dear! I know better than that now.

The next morning brought the doctor to our hotel on a special visit to my aunt. He invented a pretext for sending me into the next room, which was so plainly a clumsy excuse, that my curiosity was aroused. I gratified my curiosity. Must I make my confession plainer still? Must I acknowledge that I was mean enough to listen on the other side of the door?

I heard my dear innocent old aunt say, ' Doctor! I hope you don't see anything alarming in the state of Bertha's health?'

The doctor burst out laughing. 'My dear Madam! there is nothing in the state of the young lady's health which need cause the smallest anxiety to you or to me. The object of my visit is to justify myself for presenting those two gentlemen to you yesterday. They are both greatly struck by Miss Bertha's beauty, and they both urgently entreated me to introduce them. Such introductions, I need hardly say, are marked exceptions to my general rule. In ninety-nine cases out of a hundred I should have said No. In the cases of Captain Stanwick and Mr. Varleigh, however, I saw no reason to hesitate. Permit me to assure you that I am not intruding on your notice two fortune-hunting adventurers. They are both men of position and men of property. The family of the Stanwicks has been well known to me for years ; and Mr. Varleigh brought me a letter from my oldest living friend, answering for him as a gentleman in the highest sense of the word. He is the wealthiest man of the two ; and it speaks volumes for him, in my opinion, that he has preserved his simplicity of character after a long residence in such places as Paris and Vienna. Captain Stanwick has more polish and ease of manner, but, looking under the surface, I rather fancy there may be something a little impetuous and domineering in his temper. However, we all have our faults. I can only say, for both these young friends of mine, that you need feel no scruple about admitting them to your intimacy, if they happen to please you — and your niece. Having now, I hope, removed any doubts which may have troubled you, pray recall Miss Bertha. I am afraid I have interrupted you in discussing your plans for the day.'

The smoothly eloquent doctor paused for the moment ; and I darted away from the door.

Our plans for the day included a drive through the famous scenery near the town. My two admirers met us on horseback. Here, again, the Captain had the advantage over his friend. His seat in the saddle and his riding-dress were both perfect things in their way. The Englishman rode on one side of the carriage and the American on the other. They both talked well, but Mr. Varleigh had seen more of the world in general than Captain Stanwick, and he made himself certainly the most interesting and most amusing companion of the two.

On our way back my admiration was excited by a thick wood, beautifully situated on rising ground at a little distance from the high-road. 'Oh, dear,' I said, 'how I should like to take a walk in that wood!' Idle thoughtless words ; but, oh, what remembrances crowd on me as I think of them now!

Captain Stanwick and Mr. Varleigh at once dismounted and offered themselves as my escort. The coachman warned them to be careful ; people had often lost themselves, he said, in that wood. I asked the name of it. The name was Herne Wood. My aunt was not very willing to leave her comfortable seat in the carriage, but it ended in her going with us.

Before we entered the wood, Mr. Varleigh noted the position of the high-road by his pocket-compass. Captain Stanwick laughed at him, and offered me his arm. Ignorant as I was of the ways of the world and the rules of coquetry, my instinct (I suppose) warned me not to distinguish one of the gentlemen too readily at the expense of the other. I took my aunt's arm and settled it in that way.

A winding path led us into the wood.

On a nearer view, the place disappointed me ; the farther we advanced, the more horribly gloomy it grew. The thickly-growing trees shut out the light ; the damp stole over me little by little until I shivered ; the undergrowth of bushes and thickets rustled at intervals mysteriously, as some invisible creeping creature passed through it. At a turn in the path we reached a sort of clearing, and saw the sky and the sunshine once more. But, even here, a disagreeable incident occurred. A snake wound his undulating way across the open space, passing close by me, and I was fool enough to scream. The Captain killed the creature with his riding-cane, taking a pleasure in doing it which I did not like to see.

We left the clearing and tried another path, and then another. And still the horrid wood preyed on my spirits. I agreed with my aunt that we should do well to return to the carriage. On our way back we missed the right path, and lost ourselves for the moment. Mr. Varleigh consulted his compass, and pointed in one direction. Captain Stanwick, consulting nothing but his own jealous humour, pointed in the other. We followed Mr. Varleigh's guidance, and got back to the clearing. He turned to the Captain, and said good-humouredly, 'You see the compass was right.' Captain Stanwick answered sharply, 'There are more ways than one out of an English wood ; you talk as if we were in one of your American forests.'

Mr. Varleigh seemed to be at a loss to understand his rudeness : there was a pause. The two men looked at each other, standing face to face on the brown earth of the clearing—the Englishman's ruddy countenance, light auburn hair and whiskers, and well-opened bold blue eyes, contrasting with the pale complexion, the keenly-observant look, the dark closely-cut hair, and the delicately-lined face of the American. It was only for a moment : I had barely time to feel uneasy before they controlled themselves and led us back to the carriage, talking as pleasantly as if nothing had happened. For days afterwards, nevertheless, that scene in the clearing—the faces and figures of the two men, the dark line of trees hemming them in on all sides, the brown circular patch of ground on which they stood—haunted my memory, and got in the way of my brighter and happier thoughts. When my aunt inquired if I had enjoyed the day, I surprised her by saying, No. And when she asked why, I could only answer, ' It was all spoilt by Herne Wood.'

III.

THREE weeks passed.

The terror of those dreadful days creeps over me again when I think of them. I mean to tell the truth without shrinking ; but I may at least consult my own feelings by dwelling on certain particulars as briefly as I can. I shall describe my conduct towards the two men who courted me, in the plainest terms, if I say that I distinguished neither of them. Innocently and stupidly I encouraged them both.

In books, women are generally represented as knowing their own minds in matters which relate to love and marriage. This is not my experience of myself. Day followed day ; and, ridiculous as it may appear, I could not decide which of my two admirers I liked best!

Captain Stanwick was, at first, the man of my choice. While he kept his temper under control, he charmed me. But when he let it escape him, he sometimes disappointed, sometimes irritated me. In that frame of mind I turned for relief to Lionel Varleigh, feeling that he was the more gentle and the more worthy man of the two, and honestly believing, at such times, that I preferred him to his rival. For the first few days after our visit to Herne Wood I had excellent opportunities of comparing them. They paid their visits to us together, and they divided their attentions carefully between me and my aunt. At the end of the week, however, they began to present themselves separately. If I had possessed any experience of the natures of men, I might have known what this meant, and might have seen the future possibility of some more serious estrangement between the two friends, of which I might be the unfortunate cause. As it was, I never once troubled my head about what might be passing out of my presence. Whether they came together, or whether they came separately, their visits were always agreeable to me, and I thought of nothing and cared for nothing more.

But the time that was to enlighten me was not far off.

One day Captain Stanwick called much earlier than usual. My aunt had not yet returned from her morning walk. The Captain made some excuse for presenting himself under these circumstances which I have now forgotten.

Without actually committing himself to a proposal of marriage, he spoke with such tender feeling, he managed his hold on my inexperience so delicately, that he entrapped me into saying some words, on my side, which I remembered with a certain dismay as soon as I was left alone again. In half an hour more, Mr. Lionel Varleigh was announced as my next visitor. I at once noticed a certain disturbance in his look and manner which was quite new in my experience of him. I offered him a chair. To my surprise he declined to take it.

'I must trust to your indulgence to permit me to put an embarrassing question to you,' he began. 'It rests with you, Miss Laroche, to decide whether I shall remain here, or whether I shall relieve you of my presence by leaving the room.'

'What can you possibly mean?' I asked.

'Is it your wish,' he went on, 'that I should pay you no more visits except in Captain Stanwick's company, or by Captain Stanwick's express permission?'

My astonishment deprived me for the moment of the power of answering him. 'Do you really mean that Captain Stanwick has forbidden you to call on me?' I asked as soon as I could speak.

'I have exactly repeated what Captain Stanwick said to me half an hour since,' Lionel Varleigh answered.

In my indignation at hearing this, I entirely forgot the rash words of encouragement which the Captain had entrapped me into speaking to him. When I think of it now, I am ashamed to repeat the language in which I resented this man's presumptuous assertion of authority over me. Having committed one act of indiscretion already, my anxiety to assert my freedom of action

hurried me into committing another. I bade Mr. Varleigh welcome whenever he chose to visit me, in terms which made his face flush under the emotions of pleasure and surprise which I had aroused in him. My wounded vanity acknowledged no restraints. I signed to him to take a seat on the sofa at my side; I engaged to go to his lodgings the next day, with my aunt, and see the collection of curiosities which he had amassed in the course of his travels. I almost believe, if he had tried to kiss me, that I was angry enough with the Captain to have let him do it!

Remember what my life had been—remember how ignorantly I had passed the precious days of my youth, how insidiously a sudden accession of wealth and importance had encouraged my folly and my pride—and try, like good Christians, to make some allowance for me!

My aunt came in from her walk before Mr. Varleigh's visit had ended. She received him rather coldly, and he perceived it. After reminding me of our appointment for the next day, he took his leave.

'What appointment does Mr. Varleigh mean?' my aunt asked, as soon as we were alone. 'Is it wise, under the circumstances, to make appointments with Mr. Varleigh?' she said, when I had answered her question. I naturally inquired what she meant. My aunt replied, 'I have met Captain Stanwick while I was out walking. He has told me something which I am quite at a loss to understand. Is it possible, Bertha, that you have received a proposal of marriage from him favourably, without saying one word about your intentions to me?'

I instantly denied it. However rashly I might have spoken, I had certainly said nothing to justify Captain Stanwick in claiming me as his promised wife. In his mean fear of a fair rivalry with Mr. Varleigh, he had deliberately misinterpreted me. 'If I marry either of the two,' I said, 'it will be Mr. Varleigh!'

My aunt shook her head. 'These two gentlemen seem to be both in love with you, Bertha. It is a trying position for you between them, and I am afraid you have acted with some indiscretion. Captain Stanwick tells me that he and his friend have come to a separation already. I fear you are the cause of it. Mr. Varleigh has left the hotel at which he was staying with the Captain, in consequence of a disagreement between them this morning. You were not aware of that when you accepted his invitation. Shall I write an excuse for you ? We must, at least, put off the visit, my dear, until you have set yourself right with Captain Stanwick.'

I began to feel a little alarmed, but I was too obstinate to yield without a struggle. ' Give me time to think over it,' I said. ' To write an excuse seems like acknowledging the Captain's authority. Let us wait till to-morrow morning.'

IV.

THE morning brought with it another visit from Captain Stanwick. This time my aunt was present. He looked at her without speaking, and turned to me, with his fiery temper showing itself already in his eyes.

' I have a word to say to you in private,' he began.

' I have no secrets from my aunt,' I answered. ' Whatever you have to say, Captain Stanwick, may be said here.'

He opened his lips to reply; and suddenly checked himself. He was controlling his anger by so violent an effort that it turned his ruddy face pale. For the moment he conquered his temper—he addressed himself to me with the outward appearance of respect at least.

' Has that man Varleigh lied ?' he asked; ' or have you given *him* hopes too—after what you said to me yesterday ?'

' I said nothing to you yesterday which gives you any right to put that question to me,' I rejoined. ' You have entirely misunderstood me if you think so.'

My aunt attempted to say a few temperate words, in the hope of soothing him. He waved his hand, refusing to listen to her, and advanced closer to me.

' *You* have misunderstood *me*,' he said, ' if you think I am a man to be made a plaything of in the hands of a coquette !'

My aunt interposed once more, with a resolution which I had not expected from her.

' Captain Stanwick,' she said, ' you are forgetting yourself.'

He paid no heed to her ; he persisted in speaking to me. ' It is my misfortune to love you,' he burst out. ' My whole heart is set on you. I mean to be your husband, and no other man living shall stand in my way. After what you said to me yesterday, I have a right to consider that you have favoured my addresses. This is not a mere flirtation. Don't think it ! I say it's the passion of a life ! Do you hear ? It's the passion of a man's whole life ! I am not to be trifled with. I have had a night of sleepless misery about you—I have suffered enough for you—and you're not worth it. Don't laugh ! This is no laughing matter. Take care, Bertha ! Take care !'

My aunt rose from her chair. She astonished me. On all ordinary occasions the most retiring, the most feminine of women, she now walked up to Captain Stanwick and looked him full in the face, without flinching for an instant.

' You appear to have forgotten that you are speaking in the presence of two ladies,' she said. ' Alter your tone, sir, or I shall be obliged to take my niece out of the room.'

Half angry, half frightened, I tried to speak in my turn. My aunt signed to me to be silent. The Captain drew back a step as if he felt her reproof. But his eyes, still fixed on me, were as fiercely bright as ever. *There* the gentleman's superficial good-breeding failed to hide the natural man beneath.

' I will leave you in undisturbed possession of the room,' he said to my aunt with bitter politeness. 'Before I go, permit me to give your niece an opportunity of reconsidering her conduct before it is too late.' My aunt drew back, leaving him free to speak to me. After considering for a moment, he laid his hand firmly, but not roughly, on my arm. 'You have accepted Lionel Varleigh's invitation to visit him,' he said, 'under pretence of seeing his curiosities. Think again before you decide on keeping that engagement. If you go to Varleigh to-morrow, you will repent it to the last day of your life.' Saying those words, in a tone which made me tremble in spite of myself, he walked to the door. As he laid his hand on the lock, he turned towards me for the last time. 'I forbid you go to Varleigh's lodgings,' he said, very distinctly and quietly. 'Understand what I tell you. I forbid it.'

With those words he left us.

My aunt sat down by me and took my hand kindly. 'There is only one thing to be done,' she said; 'we must return at once to Nettlegrove. If Captain Stanwick attempts to annoy you in your own house, we have neighbours who will protect us, and we have Mr. Loring, our Rector, to appeal to for advice. As for Mr. Varleigh, I will write our excuses myself before we go away.'

She put out her hand to ring the bell and order the carriage. I stopped her. My childish pride urged me to assert myself in some way, after the passive position that I had been forced to occupy during the interview with Captain Stanwick.

'No,' I said, 'it is not acting fairly towards Mr. Varleigh to break our engagement with him. Let us return to Nettlegrove by all means, but let us first call on Mr. Varleigh and take our leave. Are we to behave rudely to a gentleman who has always treated us with the utmost consideration, because Captain Stanwick has tried to frighten us by cowardly threats? The commonest feeling of self-respect forbids it.'

My aunt protested against this outbreak of folly with perfect temper and good sense.

But my obstinacy (my firmness as I thought it!) was immovable. I left her to choose between going with me to Mr. Varleigh, or letting me go to him by myself. Finding it useless to resist, she decided, it is needless to say, on going with me.

We found Mr. Varleigh very courteous, but more than usually grave and quiet. Our visit only lasted for a few minutes; my aunt using the influence of her age and her position to shorten it. She mentioned family affairs as the motive which recalled us to Nettlegrove. I took it on myself to invite Mr. Varleigh to visit me at my own house. He bowed, and thanked me, without engaging himself to accept the invitation. When I offered him my hand at parting, he raised it to his lips, and kissed it with a fervour that agitated me. His eyes looked into mine with a sorrowful admiration, with a lingering regret, as if they were taking their leave of me for a long while. 'Don't forget me!' he whispered, as he stood at the door, while I followed my aunt out. 'Come to Nettlegrove,' I whispered back. His eyes dropped to the ground; he let me go without a word more.

This, I declare solemnly, was all that passed at our visit. By some unexpressed consent among us, no allusion whatever was made to Captain Stanwick; not even his name was mentioned. I never knew that the two men had met, just before we called on Mr. Varleigh. Nothing was said which could suggest to me the slightest suspicion of any arrangement for another meeting between them later in the day. Beyond the vague threats which had escaped Captain Stanwick's lips—threats which I own I was rash enough to despise—I had no warning whatever of the dreadful events which happened at Maplesworth on the day after our return to Nettlegrove Hall.

I can only add that I am ready to submit to any questions that may be put to me. Pray don't think me a heartless woman. My worst fault was ignorance. In those days, I knew nothing of the false pretences under which men hide what is selfish and savage in their natures from the women whom it is their interest to deceive.

No. 2.—*Julius Bender, fencing-master, testifies and says :*—

I am of German nationality; established in England as teacher of the use of the sword and the pistol since the beginning of the present year.

Finding business slack in London, it unfortunately occurred to me to try what I could do in the country. I had heard of Maplesworth as a place largely frequented by visitors on account of the scenery, as well as by invalids in need of taking the waters; and I opened a gallery there at the beginning of the season of 1817, for fencing and pistol practice. About the visitors I had not been deceived; there were plenty of idle young gentlemen among them who might have been expected to patronise my establishment. They showed the most barbarous indifference to the noble art of attack and defence—came by twos and threes, looked at my gallery, and never returned. My small means began to fail me. After paying my expenses, I was really at my wits' end to find a few pounds to go on with, in the hope of better days.

One gentleman I remember, who came to see me, and who behaved most liberally.

He described himself as an American, and said he had travelled a great deal. As my ill luck would have it, he stood in no need of my instructions. On the two or three occasions when he amused himself with my foils and my pistols, he proved to be one of the most expert swordsmen and one of the finest shots that I ever met with. It was not wonderful : he had by nature cool nerves and a quick eye ; and he had been taught by the masters of the art in Vienna and Paris.

Early in July—the 9th or 10th of the month, I think—I was sitting alone in my gallery, looking ruefully enough at the last two sovereigns in my purse, when a gentleman was announced who wanted a lesson.

' A *private* lesson,' he said with emphasis, looking at the man who cleaned and took care of my weapons.

I sent the man out of the room. The stranger (an Englishman, and, as I fancied, judging by outward appearances, a military man as well) took from his pocket-book a fifty-pound bank-note, and held it up before me. ' I have a heavy wager depending on a fencing match,' he said, ' and I have no time to improve myself. Teach me a trick which will make me a match for a man skilled in the use of the foil, and keep the secret — and there are fifty pounds for you.'

I hesitated. I did indeed hesitate, poor as I was. But this devil of a man held his bank-note before me whichever way I looked, and I had only two pounds left in the world !

' Are you going to fight a duel?' I asked.

' I have already told you what I am going to do,' he answered.

I waited a little. The infernal bank-note still tempted me. In spite of myself, I tried him again.

' If I teach you the trick,' I persisted, ' will you undertake to make no bad use of your lesson?'

' Yes,' he said, impatiently enough.

I was not quite satisfied yet.

' Will you promise it, on your word of honour ?' I asked.

' Of course I will,' he answered. ' Take the money, and don't keep me waiting any longer !'

I took the money, and I taught him the trick—and I regretted it almost as soon as it was done. Not that I knew, mind, of any serious consequences that followed ; for I returned to London the next morning. My sentiments were those of a man of honour, who felt that he had degraded his art, and who could not be quite sure that he might not have armed the hand of an assassin as well. I have no more to say.

No. 3.—*Thomas Outwater, servant to Captain Stanwick, testifies and says :*—

If I did not firmly believe my master to be out of his senses, no punishment that I could receive would prevail upon me to tell of him what I am going to tell now.

But I say he is mad, and therefore not accountable for what he has done—mad for love of a young woman. If I could have my way, I should like to twist her neck, though she *is* a lady, and a great heiress into the bargain. Before she came between them, my master and Mr. Varleigh were more like brothers than anything else. She set them at variance, and whether she meant to do it or not is all the same to me. I own I took a dislike to her when I first saw her. She was one of the light-haired, blue-eyed sort, with an innocent look and a snaky waist—not at all to be depended on, as I have found them.

I hear I am not expected to give an account of the disagreement between the two gentlemen, of which this lady was the cause. I am to state what I did in Maplesworth, and what I saw afterwards in Herne Wood. Poor as I am, I would give a five-pound note to anybody who could do it for me. Unfortunately, I must do it for myself.

On the 10th of July, in the evening, my master went, for the second time that day, to Mr. Varleigh's lodgings.

I am certain of the date, because it was the day of publication of the town newspaper, and there was a law report in it which set everybody talking. There had been a duel with pistols, a day or two before, between a resident in the town and a visitor, caused by some dispute about horses. Nothing very serious came of the meeting. One of the men only was hurt, and the wound proved to be of no great importance. The awkward part of the matter was that the constables appeared on the ground, before the wounded man had been removed. He and his two seconds were caught, and the prisoners were committed for trial. Duelling (the magistrates said) was an inhuman and unchristian practice, and they were determined to put the law in force and stop it. This sentence made a great stir in the town, and fixed the date, as I have just said, in my mind.

Having been accidentally within hearing of some of the disputes concerning Miss Laroche between my master and Mr. Varleigh, I had my misgivings about the Captain's second visit to the friend with whom he had quarrelled already. A gentleman called on him, soon after he had gone out, on important business. This gave me an excuse for following him to Mr. Varleigh's rooms with the visitor's card, and I took the opportunity.

I heard them at high words on my way upstairs, and waited a little on the landing. The Captain was in one of his furious rages; Mr. Varleigh was firm and cool as usual. After listening for a minute or so, I heard enough (in my opinion) to justify me in entering the room. I caught my master in the act of lifting his cane—threatening to strike Mr. Varleigh. He instantly dropped his hand, and turned on me in a fury at my intrusion. Taking no notice of this outbreak of temper, I gave him his friend's card, and went out. A talk followed in voices too low for me to hear outside the room, and then the Captain approached the door. I got out of his way, feeling very uneasy about what was to come next. I could not presume to question Mr. Varleigh. The only thing I could think of was to tell the young lady's aunt what I had seen and heard, and to plead with Miss Laroche herself to make peace between them. When I inquired for the ladies at their lodgings, I was told that they had left Maplesworth.

I saw no more of the Captain that night.

The next morning he seemed to be quite himself again. He said to me, ' Thomas, I am going sketching in Herne Wood. Take the paint-box and the rest of it, and put this into the carriage.'

He handed me a packet as thick as my arm, and about three feet long, done up in many folds of canvas. I made bold to ask what it was. He answered that it was an artist's sketching umbrella, packed for travelling.

In an hour's time, the carriage stopped on the road below Herne Wood. My master said he would carry his sketching things himself, and I was to wait with the carriage. In giving him the so-called umbrella, I took the occasion of his eye being off me for the moment to pass my hand over it carefully; and I felt, through the canvas, the hilt of a sword. As an old soldier, I could not be mistaken—the hilt of a sword.

What I thought, on making this discovery, does not much matter. What I did was to watch the Captain into the wood, and then to follow him.

I tracked him along the path to where there was a clearing in the midst of the trees. There he stopped, and I got behind a tree. He undid the canvas, and produced *two* swords concealed in the packet. If I had felt any doubts before, I was certain of what was coming now. A duel without seconds or witnesses, by way of keeping the town magistrates in the dark—a duel between my master and Mr. Varleigh! As his name came into my mind the man himself appeared, making his way into the clearing from the other side of the wood.

What could I do to stop it? No human creature was in sight. The nearest village was a mile away, reckoning from the farther side of the wood. The coachman was a stupid old man, quite useless in a difficulty, even if I had had time enough to go back to the road and summon him to help me. While I was thinking about it, the Captain and Mr. Varleigh had stripped to their shirts and trousers. When they crossed their swords, I could stand it no longer—I burst in on them. 'For God Almighty's sake, gentlemen,' I cried out, 'don't fight without seconds!' My master turned on me, like the madman he was, and threatened me with the point of his sword. Mr. Varleigh pulled me back out of harm's way. 'Don't be afraid,' he whispered, as he led me back to the verge of the clearing; 'I have chosen the sword instead of the pistol expressly to spare his life.'

Those noble words (spoken by as brave and true a man as ever breathed) quieted me. I knew Mr. Varleigh had earned the repute of being one of the finest swordsmen in Europe.

The duel began. I was placed behind my master, and was consequently opposite to his antagonist. The Captain stood on his defence, waiting for the other to attack. Mr. Varleigh made a pass. I was opposite the point of his sword; I saw it touch the Captain's left shoulder. In the same instant of time my master struck up his opponent's sword with his own weapon seized Mr. Varleigh's right wrist in his left hand, and passed his sword clean through Mr. Varleigh's breast. He fell, the victim of a murderous trick—fell without a word or a cry.

The Captain turned slowly, and faced me with his bloody sword in his hand. I can't tell you how he looked; I can only say that the sight of him turned me faint with terror. I was at Waterloo — I am no coward. But I tell you the cold sweat poured down my face like water. I should have dropped if I had not held by the branch of a tree.

My master waited until I had in a measure recovered myself. 'Feel if his heart beats,' he said, pointing to the man on the ground.

I obeyed. He was dead—the heart was still; the beat of the pulse was gone. I said 'You have killed him!'

The Captain made no answer. He packed up the two swords again in the canvas, and put them under his arm. Then he told me to follow him with the sketching materials. I drew back from him without speaking; there was a horrid hollow sound in his voice that I did not like. 'Do as I tell you,' he said: 'you have yourself to thank for it if I refuse to lose sight of you now,' I managed to say that he might trust me to say nothing. He refused to trust me; he put out his hand to take hold of me. I could not stand that. 'I'll go with you,' I said; 'don't touch me!' We reached the carriage and returned to Maplesworth. The same day we travelled by post to London.

In London I contrived to give the Captain the slip. By the first coach the next morning I went back to Maplesworth, eager to hear what had happened, and if the body had been found. Not a word of news reached me ; nothing seemed to be known of the duel in Herne Wood.

I went to the wood—on foot, fearing that I might be traced if I hired a carriage. The country round was as solitary as usual. Not a creature was near when I entered the wood; not a creature was near when I looked into the clearing.

There was nothing on the ground. The body was gone.

No. 4.—*The Reverend Alfred Loring, Rector of Nettlegrove, testifies and says :—*

I.

Early in the month of October, 1817, I was informed that Miss Bertha Laroche had called at my house, and wished to see me in private.

I had first been presented to Miss Laroche on her arrival, with her aunt, to take possession of her property at Nettlegrove Hall. My opportunities of improving my acquaintance with her had not been so numerous as I could have desired, and I sincerely regretted it. She had produced a very favourable impression on me. Singularly inexperienced and impulsive—with an odd mixture of shyness and vivacity in her manner, and subject now and then to outbursts of vanity and petulance which she was divertingly incapable of concealing—I could detect, nevertheless, under the surface the signs which told of a true and generous nature, of a simple and pure heart. Her personal appearance, I should add, was attractive in a remarkable degree. There was something in it so peculiar, and at the same time so fascinating, that I am conscious it may have prejudiced me in her favour. For fear of this acknowledgment being misunderstood,

I think it right to add that I am old enough to be her grandfather, and that I am also a married man.

I told the servant to show Miss Laroche into my study.

The moment she entered the room, her appearance alarmed me : she looked literally panic-stricken. I offered to send for my wife; she refused the proposal. I entreated her to take time at least to compose herself. It was not in her impulsive nature to do this. She said, 'Give me your hand to encourage me, and let me speak while I can.' I gave her my hand, poor soul. I said, ' Speak to me, my dear, as if I were your father.'

So far as I could understand the incoherent statement which she addressed to me, she had been the object of admiration (while visiting Maplesworth) to two gentlemen, who both desired to marry her. Hesitating between them, and perfectly inexperienced in such matters, she had been the unfortunate cause of enmity between the rivals, and had returned to Nettlegrove, at her aunt's suggestion, as the best means of extricating herself from a very embarrassing position. The removal failing to alleviate her distressing recollections of what had happened, she and her aunt had tried a further change by making a tour of two months on the Continent. She had returned in a more quiet frame of mind. To her great surprise, she had heard nothing of either of her two suitors, from the day when she left Maplesworth to the day when she presented herself at my rectory.

Early that morning she was walking, after breakfast, in the park at Nettlegrove, when she heard footsteps behind her. She turned, and found herself face to face with one of her suitors at Maplesworth. I am informed that there is no necessity now for my suppressing the name. The gentleman was Captain Stanwick.

He was so fearfully changed for the worse that she hardly knew him again.

After his first glance at her, he held his hand over his bloodshot eyes as if the sunlight hurt them. Without a word to prepare her for the disclosure, he confessed that he had killed Mr. Varleigh in a duel. His remorse (he declared) had unsettled his reason: only a few days had passed since he had been released from confinement in an asylum.

'You are the cause of it,' he said wildly. 'It is for love of you. I have but one hope left to live for—my hope in you. If you cast me off, my mind is made up. I will give my life for the life that I have taken; I will die by my own hand. Look at me, and you will see that I am in earnest. My future as a living man depends on your decision. Think of it to-day, and meet me here to-morrow. Not at this time; the horrid daylight feels like fire in my eyes, and goes like fire to my brain. Wait till sunset—you will find me here.'

He left her as suddenly as he had appeared. When she had sufficiently recovered herself to be able to think, she decided on saying nothing of what had happened to her aunt. She took her way to the rectory, to seek my advice.

It is needless to encumber my narrative by any statement of the questions which I felt it my duty to put to her, under these circumstances.

My inquiries informed me that Captain Stanwick had, in the first instance, produced a favourable impression on her. The less showy qualities of Mr. Varleigh had afterwards grown on her liking; aided greatly by the repelling effect on her mind of the Captain's violent language and conduct when he had reason to suspect that his rival was being preferred to him. When she knew the horrible news of Mr. Varleigh's death, she 'knew her own heart' (to repeat her exact words to me) by the shock that she felt. Towards Captain Stanwick the only feeling of which she was now conscious was, naturally, a feeling of the strongest aversion.

My own course in this difficult and painful matter appeared to me to be clear.

'It is your duty as a Christian to see this miserable man again,' I said. 'And it is my duty, as your friend and pastor, to sustain you under the trial. I will go with you to-morrow to the place of meeting.'

II.

The next evening we found Captain Stanwick waiting for us in the park.

He drew back on seeing me. I explained to him, temperately and firmly, what my position was. With sullen looks he resigned himself to endure my presence. By degrees I won his confidence. My first impression of him remains unshaken—the man's reason was unsettled. I suspected that the assertion of his release was a falsehood, and that he had really escaped from the asylum. It was impossible to lure him into telling me where the place was. He was too cunning to do this—too cunning to say anything about his relations, when I tried to turn the talk that way next. On the other hand, he spoke with a revolting readiness of the crime that he had committed, and of his settled resolution to destroy himself if Miss Laroche refused to be his wife. 'I have nothing else to live for ; I am alone in the world,' he said. 'Even my servant has deserted me. He knows how I killed Lionel Varleigh.' He paused, and spoke his next words in a whisper to me. 'I killed him by a trick—he was the best swordsman of the two.'

This confession was so horrible that I could only attribute it to an insane delusion. On pressing my inquiries, I found that the same idea must have occurred to the poor wretch's relations, and to the doctors who signed the certificates for placing him under medical care. This conclusion (as I afterwards heard) was greatly strengthened by the fact that Mr. Varleigh's body had not been found on the reported scene of the duel. As to the servant, he had deserted his master in London, and had never reappeared. So far as my poor judgment went, the question before me was not of delivering a self-accused murderer to justice (with no corpse to testify against him), but of restoring an insane man to the care of the persons who had been appointed to restrain him.

I tried to test the strength of his delusion in an interval when he was not urging his shocking entreaties on Miss Laroche.

' How do you know that you killed Mr. Varleigh?' I said.

He looked at me with a wild terror in his eyes. Suddenly he lifted his right hand, and shook it in the air, with a moaning cry, which was unmistakably a cry of pain. ' Should I see his ghost,' he asked, ' if I had not killed him? I know it, by the pain that wrings me in the hand that stabbed him. Always in my right hand! always the same pain at the moment when I see him!' He stopped, and ground his teeth in the agony and reality of his delusion. ' Look!' he cried. ' Look between the two trees behind you. There he is—with his dark hair, and his shaven face, and his steady look! There he is, standing before me as he stood in the wood, with his eyes on my eyes, and his sword feeling mine!' He turned to Miss Laroche. ' Do *you* see him too?' he asked eagerly. ' Tell me the truth. My whole life depends on your telling me the truth.'

She controlled herself with a wonderful courage. ' I don't see him,' she answered.

He took out his handkerchief, and passed it over his face with a gasp of relief. ' There is my last chance!' he said. ' If she will be true to me—if she will be always near me, morning, noon, and night, I shall be released from the sight of him. See! he is fading away already. Gone!' he cried, with a scream of exultation. He fell on his knees, and looked at Miss Laroche like a savage adoring his idol. ' Will you cast me off now?' he asked humbly. ' Lionel was fond of you in his lifetime. His spirit is a merciful spirit. He shrinks from frightening you ; he has left me for your sake ; he will release me for your sake. Pity me, take me to live with you—and I shall never see him again!'

It was dreadful to hear him. I saw that the poor girl could endure no more. ' Leave us,' I whispered to her ; ' I will join you at the house.'

He heard me, and instantly placed himself between us. ' Let her promise, or she shan't go.'

She felt, as I felt, the imperative necessity of saying anything that might soothe him. At a sign from me she gave him her promise to return.

He was satisfied—he insisted on kissing her hand, and then he let her go. I had by this time succeeded in inducing him to trust me. He proposed, of his own accord, that I should accompany him to the inn in the village at which he had been staying. The landlord (naturally enough distrusting his wretched guest) had warned him that morning to find some other place of shelter. I engaged to use my influence with the man to make him change his purpose, and I succeeded in effecting the necessary arrangements for having the poor wretch properly looked after. On my return to my own house, I wrote to a brother magistrate living near me, and to the superintendent of our county asylum, requesting them to consult with me on the best means of lawfully restraining Captain Stanwick until we could communicate with his relations. Could I have done more than this ? The event of the next morning answered that question—answered it at once and for ever.

III.

Presenting myself at Nettlegrove Hall towards sunset, to take charge of Miss Laroche, I was met by an obstacle in the shape of a protest from her aunt.

This good lady had been informed of the appearance of Captain Stanwick in the park, and she strongly disapproved of encouraging any further communication with him on the part of her niece. She also considered that I had failed in my duty in still leaving the Captain at liberty. I told her that I was only waiting to act on the advice of competent persons, who would arrive the next day to consult with me ; and I did my best to persuade her of the wisdom of the course that I had taken in the meantime. Miss Laroche, on her side, was resolved to be true to the promise that she had given. Between us, we induced her aunt to yield on certain conditions.

' I know the part of the park in which the meeting is to take place,' the old lady said ; 'it is my niece's favourite walk. If she is not brought back to me in half an hour's time, I shall send the men-servants to protect her.'

The twilight was falling when we reached the appointed place. We found Captain Stanwick angry and suspicious ; it was not easy to pacify him on the subject of our delay. His insanity seemed to me to be now more marked than ever. He had seen, or dreamed of seeing, the ghost during the past night. For the first time (he said) the apparition of the dead man had spoken to him. In solemn words it had condemned him to expiate his crime by giving his life for the life that he had taken. It had warned him not to insist on marriage with Bertha Laroche : ' She shall share your punishment if she shares your life. And you shall know it by this sign—*She shall see me as you see me.*'

I tried to compose him. He shook his head in immovable despair. ' No,' he answered ; ' if she sees him when I see him, there ends the one hope of release that holds me to life. It will be good-bye between us, and good-bye for ever !'

We had walked on, while we were speaking, to a part of the park through which there flowed a rivulet of clear water. On the farther bank the open ground led down into a wooded valley. On our side of the stream rose a thick plantation of fir-trees, intersected by a winding path. Captain Stanwick stopped as we reached the place. His eyes rested, in the darkening twilight, on the narrow space pierced by the path among the trees. On a sudden he lifted his right hand, with the same cry of pain

which we had heard before : with his left hand he took Miss Laroche by the arm. ' There !' he said. ' Look where I look ! Do you see him there ?'

As the words passed his lips, a dimly-visible figure appeared, advancing towards us along the path.

Was it the figure of a living man ? or was it the creation of my own excited fancy ? Before I could ask myself the question, the man advanced a step nearer to us. A last gleam of the dying light fell on his face through an opening in the trees. At the same instant Miss Laroche started back from Captain Stanwick with a scream of terror. She would have fallen if I had not been near enough to support her. The Captain was instantly at her side again. ' Speak !' he cried. ' Do *you* see it too ?'

She was just able to say ' Yes,' before she fainted in my arms.

He stooped over her, and touched her cold cheek with his lips. ' Good-bye !' he said, in tones suddenly and strangely changed to the most exquisite tenderness. ' Good-bye, for ever !'

He leapt the rivulet ; he crossed the open ground ; he was lost to sight in the valley beyond.

As he disappeared, the visionary man among the fir-trees advanced ; passed in silence ; crossed the rivulet at a bound ; and vanished as the figure of the Captain had vanished before him.

I was left alone with the swooning woman. Not a sound, far or near, broke the stillness of the coming night.

No 5.—*Mr. Frederic Darnel, Member of the College of Surgeons, testifies and says :—*

In the intervals of my professional duty I am accustomed to occupy myself in studying Botany, assisted by a friend and neighbour, whose tastes in this respect resemble my own. When I can spare an hour or two from my patients, we go out together searching for specimens. Our favourite place is Herne Wood. It is rich in material for the botanist, and it is only a mile distant from the village in which I live.

Early in July, my friend and I made a discovery in the wood of a very alarming and unexpected kind. We found a man in the clearing, prostrated by a dangerous wound, and to all appearance dead.

We carried him to the gamekeeper's cottage, on the outskirts of the wood, and on the side of it nearest to our village. He and his boy were out, but the light cart in which he makes his rounds, in the remoter part of his master's property, was in the outhouse. While my friend was putting the horse to, I examined the stranger's wound. It had been quite recently inflicted, and I doubted whether it had (as yet, at any rate) really killed him. I did what I could with the linen and cold water which the gamekeeper's wife offered to me, and then my friend and I removed him carefully to my house in the cart.

I applied the necessary restoratives, and I had the pleasure of satisfying myself that the vital powers had revived. He was perfectly unconscious, of course, but the action of the heart became distinctly perceptible, and I had hopes.

In a few days more I felt fairly sure of him. Then the usual fever set in. I was obliged, in justice to his friends, to search his clothes in presence of a witness. We found his handkerchief, his purse, and his cigar-case, and nothing more. No letters or visiting cards; nothing marked on his clothes but initials. There was no help for it but to wait to identify him until he could speak.

When that time came, he acknowledged to me that he had divested himself purposely of any clue to his identity, in the fear (if some mischance happened to him) of the news of it reaching his father and mother abruptly, by means of the newspapers. He had sent a letter to his bankers in London, to be forwarded to his parents, if the bankers neither saw him nor heard from him in a month's time. His first act was to withdraw this letter. The other

particulars which he communicated to me are, I am told, already known. I need only add that I willingly kept his secret, simply speaking of him in the neighbourhood as a traveller from foreign parts who had met with an accident.

His convalescence was a long one. It was the beginning of October before he was completely restored to health. When he left us he went to London. He behaved most liberally to me; and we parted with sincere good wishes on either side.

No. 6.—*Mr. Lionel Varleigh, of Boston, U.S.A., testifies and says :—*

My first proceeding, on my recovery, was to go to the relations of Captain Stanwick in London, for the purpose of making inquiries about him.

I do not wish to justify myself at the expense of that miserable man. It is true that I loved Miss Laroche too dearly to yield her to any rival except at her own wish. It is also true that Captain Stanwick more than once insulted me, and that I endured it. He had suffered from sunstroke in India, and in his angry moments he was hardly a responsible being. It was only when he threatened me with personal chastisement that my patience gave way. We met sword in hand. In my mind was the resolution to spare his life. In his mind was the resolution to kill me. I have forgiven him. I will say no more.

His relations informed me of the symptoms of insane delusion which he had shown after the duel; of his escape from the asylum in which he had been confined; and of the failure to find him again.

The moment I heard this news the dread crossed my mind that Stanwick had found his way to Miss Laroche. In an hour more I was travelling to Nettlegrove Hall.

I arrived late in the evening, and found Miss Laroche's aunt in great alarm about her niece's safety. The young lady was at that very moment speaking to Stanwick in the park, with only an old man (the Rector) to protect her. I volunteered to go at once, and assist in taking care of her. A servant accompanied me to show me the place of meeting. We heard voices indistinctly, but saw no one. The servant pointed to a path through the fir-trees. I went on quickly by myself, leaving the man within call. In a few minutes I came upon them suddenly, at a little distance from me, on the bank of a stream.

The fear of seriously alarming Miss Laroche, if I showed myself too suddenly, deprived me for a moment of my presence of mind. Pausing to consider what it might be best to do, I was less completely protected from discovery by the trees than I had supposed. She had seen me; I heard her cry of alarm. The instant afterwards I saw Stanwick leap over the rivulet and take to flight. That action roused me. Without stopping for a word of explanation, I pursued him.

Unhappily, I missed my footing in the obscure light, and fell on the open ground beyond the stream. When I had gained my feet once more, Stanwick had disappeared among the trees which marked the boundary of the park beyond me. I could see nothing of him, and I could hear nothing of him, when I came out on the high-road. There I met with a labouring man who showed me the way to the village.

From the inn I sent a letter to Miss Laroche's aunt, explaining what had happened, and asking leave to call at the Hall on the next day.

Early in the morning the Rector came to me at the inn. He brought sad news. Miss Laroche was suffering from a nervous attack, and my visit to the Hall must be deferred. Speaking next of the missing man, I heard all that Mr. Loring could tell me. My intimate knowledge of Stanwick enabled me to draw my own conclusion from the facts. The thought instantly crossed my mind that the poor wretch might have committed his expiatory suicide at the very spot on which he had attempted to kill me. Leaving the Rector to institute the necessary inquiries, I took post-horses to Maplesworth on my way to Herne Wood.

Advancing from the high-road to the wood, I saw two persons at a little distance from me—a man in the dress of a game-keeper and a lad. I was too much agitated to take any special notice of them; I hurried along the path which led to the clearing. My presentiment had not misled me. There he lay, dead on the scene of the duel, with a blood-stained razor by his side! I fell on my knees by the corpse; I took his cold hand in mine; and I thanked God that I had forgiven him in the first days of my recovery.

I was still kneeling, when I felt myself seized from behind. I struggled to my feet, and confronted the gamekeeper. He had noticed my hurry in entering the wood; his suspicions had been aroused, and he and the lad had followed me. There was blood on my clothes, there was horror in my face. Appearances were plainly against me; I had no choice but to accompany the gamekeeper to the nearest magistrate.

My instructions to my solicitor forbade him to vindicate my innocence by taking any technical legal objections to the action of the magistrate or of the coroner. I insisted on my witnesses being summoned to the lawyer's office, and allowed to state, in their own way, what they could truly declare on my behalf; and I left my defence to be founded upon the materials thus obtained. In the meanwhile I was detained in custody, as a matter of course.

With this event the tragedy of the duel reached its culminating point. I was accused of murdering the man who had attempted to take my life!

———

This last incident having been related, all that is worth noticing in my contribution to the present narrative comes to an end. I was tried in due course of law. The evidence taken at my solicitor's office was necessarily altered in form, though not in substance, by the examination to which the witnesses were subjected in a court of justice. So thoroughly did our defence satisfy the jury, that they became restless towards the close of the proceedings, and returned their verdict of Not Guilty without quitting the box.

When I was a free man again, it is surely needless to dwell on the first use that I made of my honourable acquittal. Whether I deserved the enviable place that I occupied in Bertha's estimation, it is not for me to say. Let me leave the decision to the lady who has ceased to be Miss Laroche—I mean the lady who has been good enough to become my wife.

Miss Dulane and My Lord

I.

ONE afternoon old Miss Dulane entered her drawing-room ; ready to receive visitors, dressed in splendour, and exhibiting every outward appearance of a defiant frame of mind.

Just as a saucy bronze nymph on the mantelpiece struck the quarter to three on an elegant clock under her arm, a visitor was announced—'Mrs. Newsham.'

Miss Dulane wore her own undisguised gray hair, dressed in perfect harmony with her time of life. Without an attempt at concealment, she submitted to be too short and too stout. Her appearance (if it had only been made to speak) would have said, in effect: ' I am an old woman, and I scorn to disguise it.'

Mrs. Newsham, tall and elegant, painted and dyed, acted on the opposite principle in dressing, which confesses nothing. On exhibition before the world, this lady's disguise asserted that she had reached her thirtieth year on her last birthday. Her husband was discreetly silent, and Father Time was discreetly silent ; they both knew that her last birthday had happened thirty years since.

' Shall we talk of the weather and the news, my dear? Or shall we come to the object of your visit at once ?' So Miss Dulane opened the interview.

' Your tone and manner, my good friend, are no doubt provoked by the report in the newspaper of this morning. In justice to you, I refuse to believe the report.' So Mrs. Newsham adopted her friend's suggestion.

' Your kindness is thrown away, Elizabeth. The report is true.'

' Matilda, you shock me !'

' Why ?'

' At your age !'

' If *he* doesn't object to my age, what does it matter to *you*?'

' Don't speak of that man !'

' Why not ?'

' He is young enough to be your son ; and he is marrying you—impudently, undisguisedly marrying you—for your money !'

' And I am marrying him—impudently, undisguisedly marrying him—for his rank.'

' You needn't remind me, Matilda, that you are the daughter of a tailor.'

' In a week or two more, Elizabeth, I shall remind you that I am the wife of a nobleman's son.'

' A younger son ; don't forget that.'

'A younger son, as you say. He finds the social position, and I find the money—half a million at my own sole disposal. My future husband is a good fellow in his way, and his future wife is another good fellow in her way. To look at your grim face, one would suppose there were no such things in the world as marriages of convenience.'

'Not at your time of life. I tell you plainly, your marriage will be a public scandal.'

'That doesn't frighten us,' Miss Dulane remarked. 'We are resigned to every ill-natured thing that our friends can say of us. In course of time, the next nine days' wonder will claim public attention, and we shall be forgotten. I shall be none the less on that account Lady Howel Beaucourt. And my husband will be happy in the enjoyment of every expensive taste which a poor man can gratify, for the first time in his life. Have you any more objections to make? Don't hesitate to speak plainly.'

'I have a question to ask, my dear.'

'Charmed, I am sure, to answer it—if I can.'

'Am I right in supposing that Lord Howel Beaucourt is about half your age?'

'Yes, dear; my future husband is as nearly as possible half as old as I am.'

Mrs. Newsham's uneasy virtue shuddered. 'What a profanation of marriage!' she exclaimed.

'Nothing of the sort,' her friend pronounced positively. 'Marriage, by the law of England (as my lawyer tells me), is nothing but a contract. Who ever heard of profaning a contract?'

'Call it what you please, Matilda. Do you expect to live a happy life, at your age, with a young man for your husband?'

'A happy life,' Miss Dulane repeated, 'because it will be an innocent life.' She laid a certain emphasis on the last word but one.

Mrs. Newsham resented the emphasis, and rose to go. Her last words were the bitterest words that she had spoken yet.

'You have secured such a truly remark-able husband, my dear, that I am emboldened to ask a great favour. Will you give me his lordship's photograph?'

'No,' said Miss Dulane, 'I won't give you his lordship's photograph.'

'What is your objection, Matilda?'

'A very serious objection, Elizabeth. You are not pure enough in mind to be worthy of my husband's photograph.'

With that reply the first of the remonstrances assumed hostile proportions, and came to an untimely end.

II.

THE second remonstrance was reserved for a happier fate. It took its rise in a conversation between two men who were old and true friends. In other words, it led to no quarrelling.

The elder man was one of those admirable human beings who are cordial, gentle, and good-tempered, without any conscious exercise of their own virtues. He was generally known in the world about him by a fond and familiar use of his Christian name. To call him 'Sir Richard' in these pages (except in the character of one of his servants) would be simply ridiculous. When he lent his money, his horses, his house, and (sometimes, after unlucky friends had dropped to the lowest social depths) even his clothes, this general benefactor was known, in the best society and the worst society alike, as 'Dick.' He filled the hundred mouths of Rumour with his nickname, in the days when there was an opera in London, as the proprietor of the 'Beauty-box.' The ladies who occupied the box were all invited under the same circumstances. They enjoyed operatic music; but their husbands and fathers were not rich enough to be able to gratify that expensive taste. Dick's carriage called for them, and took them home again; and the beauties all agreed (if he ever married) that Mrs. Dick would be the most enviable woman on the face of the civilised earth. Even the false reports, which declared that he was privately married already, and on bad terms with his wife, slandered him cordially under the popular name. And his intimate companions, when they alluded among each other to a romance in his life which would remain a hidden romance to the end of his days, forgot that the occasion justified a serious and severe use of his surname, and blamed him affectionately as ' poor dear Dick.'

The hour was midnight ; and the friends, whom the most hospitable of men delighted to assemble round his dinner-table, had taken their leave—with the exception of one guest specially detained by the host, who led him back to the dining-room.

' You were angry with our friends,' Dick began, ' when they asked you about that report of your marriage. You won't be angry with Me. Are you really going to be the old maid's husband ?'

This plain question received a plain reply: ' Yes, I am.'

Dick took the young lord's hand. Simply and seriously, he said: ' Accept my congratulations.'

Howel Beaucourt started as if he had received a blow instead of a compliment.

' There isn't another man or woman in the whole circle of my acquaintance,' he declared, ' who would have congratulated me on marrying Miss Dulane. I believe you would make allowances for me if I had committed murder.'

' I hope I should,' Dick answered gravely. ' When a man is my friend—murder or marriage—I take it for granted that he has a reason for what he does. Wait a minute. You mustn't give me more credit than I deserve. I don't agree with you. If I were a marrying man myself, I shouldn't pick an old maid—I should prefer a young one. That's a matter of taste. You are not like me. *You* always have a definite object in view. I may not know what the object is. Never mind! I wish you joy all the same.'

Beaucourt was not unworthy of the friendship that he had inspired. ' I should

be ungrateful indeed,' he said, ' if I didn't tell you what my object is. You know that I am poor ?'

' The only poor friend of mine,' Dick remarked, ' who has never borrowed money of me.'

Beaucourt went on without noticing this. ' I have three expensive tastes,' he said. ' I want to get into Parliament ; I want to have a yacht; I want to collect pictures. Add, if you like, the selfish luxury of helping poverty and wretchedness, and hearing my conscience tell me what an excellent man I am. I can't do all this on five hundred a year—but I can do it on forty times five hundred a year. Moral : marry Miss Dulane.'

Listening attentively until the other had done, Dick showed a sardonic side to his character never yet discovered in Beaucourt's experience of him.

' I suppose you have made the necessary arrangements,' he said. ' When the old lady releases you, she will leave consolation behind her in her will.'

' That's the first ill-natured thing I ever heard you say, Dick. When the old lady dies, my sense of honour takes fright, and turns its back on her will. It's a condition on my side, that every farthing of her money shall be left to her relations.'

' Don't you call yourself one of them ?'

' What a question ! Am I her relation because the laws of society force a mock marriage on us ? How can I make use of her money unless I am her husband ? and how can she make use of my title unless she is my wife ? As long as she lives I stand honestly by my side of the bargain. But when she dies the transaction is at an end, and the surviving partner returns to his five hundred a year.'

Dick exhibited another surprising side to his character. The most compliant of men now became as obstinate as the proverbial mule.

' All very well,' he said, ' but it doesn't explain why—if you must sell yourself—

you have sold yourself to an old lady. There are plenty of young ones and pretty ones with fortunes to tempt you. It seems odd that you haven't tried your luck with one of them.'

'No, Dick. It would have been odd, and worse than odd, if I had tried my luck with a young woman.'

'I don't see that.'

'You shall see it directly. If I marry an old woman for her money, I have no occasion to be a hypocrite; we both know that our marriage is a mere matter of form. But if I make a young woman my wife because I want her money, and if that young woman happens to be worth a straw, I must deceive her and disgrace myself by shamming love. That, my boy, you may depend upon it, I will never do.'

Dick's face suddenly brightened with a mingled expression of relief and triumph.

'Ha! my mercenary friend,' he burst out, 'there's something mixed up in this business which is worthier of you than anything I have heard yet. Stop! I'm going to be clever for the first time in my life. A man who talks of love as you do, must have felt love himself. Where is the young one and the pretty one? And what has she done, poor dear, to be deserted for an old woman? Good God! how you look at me! I have hurt your feelings—I have been a greater fool than ever—I am more ashamed of myself than words can say!'

Beaucourt stopped him there, gently and firmly.

'You have made a very natural mistake,' he said. 'There *was* a young lady. She has refused me — resolutely refused me. There is no more love in my life. It's a dark life and an empty life for the rest of my days. I must see what money can do for me next. When I have thoroughly hardened my heart I may not feel my misfortune as I feel it now. Pity me or despise me. In either case let us say good-night.'

He went out into the hall and took his hat. Dick went out into the hall and took *his* hat.

'Have your own way,' he answered, 'I mean to have mine—I'll go home with you.'

The man was simply irresistible. Beaucourt sat down resignedly on the nearest of the hall chairs. Dick asked him to return to the dining-room. 'No,' he said; 'it's not worth while. What I can tell you may be told in two minutes.' Dick submitted, and took the next of the hall chairs. In that inappropriate place the young lord's unpremeditated confession was forced out of him, by no more formidable exercise of power than the kindness of his friend.

'When you hear where I met with her,' he began, 'you will most likely not want to hear any more. I saw her, for the first time, on the stage of a music hall.'

He looked at Dick. Perfectly quiet and perfectly impenetrable, Dick only said, 'Go on.' Beaucourt continued in these words:

'She was singing Arne's delicious setting of Ariel's song in the "Tempest," with a taste and feeling completely thrown away on the greater part of the audience. That she was beautiful—in my eyes at least—I needn't say. That she had descended to a sphere unworthy of her and new to her, nobody could doubt. Her modest dress, her refinement of manner, seemed rather to puzzle than to please most of the people present; they applauded her, but not very warmly, when she retired. I obtained an introduction through her music-master, who happened to be acquainted professionally with some relatives of mine. He told me that she was a young widow; and he assured me that the calamity through which her family had lost their place in the world had brought no sort of disgrace on them. If I wanted to know more, he referred me to the lady herself. I found her very reserved. A long time passed before I could win her confidence—and a longer time still before I ventured to confess the feeling with which she had inspired me. You know the rest.'

'You mean, of course, that you offered her marriage?'

'Certainly.'

'And she refused you on account of your position in life.'

'No. I had foreseen that obstacle, and had followed the example of the adventurous nobleman in the old story. Like him, I assumed a name, and presented myself as belonging to her own respectable middle class of life. You are too old a friend to suspect me of vanity if I tell you that she had no objection to me, and no suspicion that I had approached her (personally speaking) under a disguise.'

'What motive could she possibly have had for refusing you?' Dick asked.

'A motive associated with her dead husband,' Beaucourt answered. 'He had married her—mind, innocently married her—while his first wife was living. The woman was an inveterate drunkard; they had been separated for years. Her death had been publicly reported in the newspapers, among the persons killed in a railway accident abroad. When she claimed her unhappy husband he was in delicate health. The shock killed him. His widow—I can't, and won't, speak of her misfortune as if it was her fault—knew of no living friends who were in a position to help her. Not a great artist with a wonderful voice, she could still trust to her musical accomplishments to provide for the necessities of life. Plead as I might with her to forget the past, I always got the same reply: "If I was base enough to let myself be tempted by the happy future that you offer, I should deserve the unmerited disgrace which has fallen on me. Marry a woman whose reputation will bear inquiry, and forget me." I was mad enough to press my suit once too often. When I visited her on the next day she was gone. Every effort to trace her has failed. Lost, my friend—irretrievably lost to me!'

He offered his hand and said good-night. Dick held him back on the doorstep.

'Break off your mad engagement to Miss Dulane,' he said. 'Be a man, Howel; wait and hope! You are throwing away your life when happiness is within your reach, if you will only be patient. That poor young creature is worthy of you. Lost? Nonsense! In this narrow little world, people are never hopelessly lost till they are dead and underground. Help me to recognise her by a description, and tell me her name. I'll find her; I'll persuade her to come back to you—and, mark my words, you will live to bless the day when you followed my advice.'

This well-meant remonstrance was completely thrown away. Beaucourt's despair was deaf to every entreaty that Dick had addressed to him.

'Thank you with all my heart,' he said. 'You don't know her as I do. She is one of the very few women who mean No when they say No. Useless, Dick—useless!'

Those were the last words he said to his friend in the character of a single man.

PART II.   PLATONIC MARRIAGE.

III.

'SEVEN months have passed, my dear Dick, since my "inhuman obstinacy" (those were the words you used) made you one of the witnesses at my marriage to Miss Dulane, sorely against your will. Do you remember your parting prophecy, when you were out of the bride's hearing? "A miserable life is before that woman's husband—and, by Jupiter, he has deserved it!"

'Never, my dear boy, attempt to forecast the future again. Viewed as a prophet you are a complete failure. I have nothing to complain of in my married life.

'But you must not mistake me. I am far from saying that I am a happy man; I only declare myself to be a contented man. My old wife is a marvel of good temper and good sense. She trusts me implicitly, and I have given her no reason to regret it. We have our time for being together, and our time for keeping apart. Within our inevitable limits we understand each other and respect each other, and have a truer feeling of regard on both sides than many people far better matched than we are in point of age. But you shall judge for yourself. Come and dine with us, when I return on Wednesday next from the trial trip of my new yacht. In the meantime I have a service to ask of you.

' My wife's niece has been her companion for years. She has left us to be married to an officer, who has taken her to India; and we are utterly at a loss how to fill her place. The good old lady doesn't want much. A nice-tempered refined girl, who can sing and play to her with some little taste and feeling, and read to her now and then when her eyes are weary — there is what we require; and there, it seems, is more than we can get, after advertising for a week past. Of all the " companions " who have presented themselves, not one has turned out to be the sort of person whom Lady Howel wants.

' Can you help us ? In any case, my wife sends you her kind remembrances ; and (true to the old times) I add my love.'

On the day which followed the receipt of this letter, Dick paid a visit to Lady Howel Beaucourt.

' You seem to be excited,' she said. ' Has anything remarkable happened?'

' Pardon me if I ask a question first,' Dick replied. ' Do you object to a young widow?'

' That depends on the widow.'

' Then I have found the very person you want. And, oddly enough, your husband has had something to do with it.'

' Do you mean that my husband has recommended her ?'

There was an undertone of jealousy in Lady Howel's voice—jealousy excited not altogether without a motive. She had left it to Beaucourt's sense of honour to own the truth, if there had been any love affair in his past life which ought to make him hesitate before he married. He had justified Miss Dulane's confidence in him; acknowledging an attachment to a young widow,

and adding that she had positively refused him. ' We have not met since,' he said, ' and we shall never meet again.' Under those circumstances, Miss Dulane had considerately abstained from asking for any further details. She had not thought of the young widow again, until Dick's language had innocently inspired her first doubt. Fortunately for both of them, he was an outspoken man ; and he reassured her unreservedly in these words : ' Your husband knows nothing about it.'

' Now,' she said, ' you may tell me how you came to hear of the lady.'

' Through my uncle's library,' Dick replied. ' His will has left me his collection of books—in such a wretchedly neglected condition that I asked Beaucourt (not being a reading man myself) if he knew of any competent person who could advise me how to set things right. He introduced me to Farleigh and Halford, the well-known publishers. The second partner is a bookcollector himself, as well as a bookseller. He kindly looks in now and then, to see how his instructions for mending and binding are being carried out. When he called yesterday I thought of you, and I found he could help us to a young lady employed in his office at correcting proof sheets.'

' What is the lady's name?'

' Mrs. Evelin.'

' Why does she leave her employment?'

' To save her eyes, poor soul. When the senior partner, Mr. Farleigh, met with her, she was reduced by family misfortunes to earn her own living. The publishers would have been only too glad to keep her in their office, but for the oculist's report. He declared that she would run the risk of blindness, if she fatigued her weak eyes much longer. There is the only objection to this otherwise invaluable person—she will not be able to read to you.'

' Can she sing and play ?'

' Exquisitely. Mr. Farleigh answers for her music.'

' And her character?'

' Mr. Halford answers for her character.'

'And her manners?'

'A perfect lady. I have seen her and spoken to her; I answer for her manners, and I guarantee her personal appearance. Charming! charming!'

For a moment Lady Howel hesitated. After a little reflection, she decided that it was her duty to trust her excellent husband. 'I will receive the charming widow,' she said, 'to-morrow at twelve o'clock; and, if she produces the right impression, I promise to overlook the weakness of her eyes.'

IV.

BEAUCOURT had prolonged the period appointed for the trial trip of his yacht by a whole week. His apology when he returned delighted the kind-hearted old lady who had made him a present of the vessel.

'There isn't such another yacht in the whole world,' he declared 'I really hadn't the heart to leave that beautiful vessel after only three days' experience of her.' He burst out with a torrent of technical praises of the yacht, to which his wife listened as attentively as if she really understood what he was talking about. When his breath and his eloquence were exhausted alike, she said, 'Now, my dear, it's my turn. I can match your perfect vessel with my perfect lady.'

'What! you have found a companion?'

'Yes.'

'Did Dick find her for you?'

'He did indeed. You shall see for yourself how grateful I ought to be to your friend.'

She opened a door which led into the next room. 'Mary, my dear, come and be introduced to my husband.'

Beaucourt started when he heard the name, and instantly recovered himself. He had forgotten how many Marys there are in the world.

Lady Howel returned, leading her favourite by the hand, and gaily introduc-

ing her the moment they entered the room.

'Mrs. Evelin; Lord——'

She looked at her husband. The utterance of his name was instantly suspended on her lips. Mrs. Evelin's hand, turning cold at the same moment in her hand, warned her to look round. The face of the woman more than reflected the inconcealable agitation in the face of the man.

The wife's first words, when she recovered herself, were addressed to them both.

'Which of you can I trust,' she asked, 'to tell me the truth?'

'You can trust both of us,' her husband answered.

The firmness of his tone irritated her. 'I will judge of that for myself,' she said. 'Go back to the next room,' she added, turning to Mrs. Evelin; 'I will hear you separately.'

The companion, whose duty it was to obey—whose modesty and gentleness had won her mistress's heart—refused to retire. 'No,' she said; 'I have been deceived too. I have *my* right to hear what Lord Howel has to say for himself.'

Beaucourt attempted to support the claim that she had advanced. His wife sternly signed to him to be silent. 'What do you mean?' she said, addressing the question to Mrs. Evelin.

'I mean this. The person whom you speak of as a nobleman was presented to me as "Mr. Vincent, an artist." But for that deception I should never have set foot in your ladyship's house.'

'Is this true, my lord?' Lady Howel asked, with a contemptuous emphasis on the title of nobility.

'Quite true,' her husband answered. 'I thought it possible that my rank might prove an obstacle in the way of my hopes. The blame rests on me, and on me alone. I ask Mrs. Evelin to pardon me for an act of deception which I deeply regret.'

Lady Howel was a just woman. Under other circumstances she might have shown herself to be a generous woman. That brighter side of her character was incapable of revealing itself in the presence of Mrs. Evelin, young and beautiful, and in possession of her husband's heart. She could say, ' I beg your pardon, madam; I have not treated you justly.' But no self-control was strong enough to restrain the next bitter words from passing her lips. ' At my age,' she said, ' Lord Howel will soon be free; you will not have long to wait for him.'

The young widow looked at her sadly— answered her sadly.

' Oh, my lady, your better nature will surely regret having said that !'

For a moment her eyes rested on Beaucourt, dim with rising tears. She left the room—and left the house.

There was silence between the husband and wife. Beaucourt was the first to speak again.

' After what you have just heard, do you persist in your jealousy of that lady, and your jealousy of me?' he asked.

' I have behaved cruelly to her and to you. I am ashamed of myself,' was all she said in reply. That expression of sorrow, so simple and so true, did not appeal in vain to the gentler side of Beaucourt's nature. He kissed his wife's hand; he tried to console her.

' You may forgive me,' she answered. ' I cannot forgive myself. That poor lady's last words have made my heart ache. What I said to her in anger I ought to have said generously. Why should she not wait for you? After your life with me—a life of kindness, a life of self-sacrifice—you deserve your reward. Promise me that you will marry the woman you love—after my death has released you.'

' You distress me, and needlessly distress me,' he said. ' What you are thinking of, my dear, can never happen; no, not even if——' He left the rest unsaid.

' Not even if you were free?' she asked.

' Not even then.'

She looked towards the next room. ' Go in, Howel, and bring Mrs. Evelin back ; I have something to say to her.'

The discovery that she had left the house caused no fear that she had taken to flight with the purpose of concealing herself. There was a prospect before the poor lonely woman which might be trusted to preserve her from despair, to say the least of it.

During her brief residence in Beaucourt's house she had shown to Lady Howel a letter received from a relation, who had emigrated to New Zealand with her husband and her infant children some years since. They had steadily prospered; they were living in comfort, and they wanted for nothing but a trustworthy governess to teach their children. The mother had accordingly written, asking if her relative in England could recommend a competent person, and offering a liberal salary. In showing the letter to Lady Howel, Mrs. Evelin had said: ' If I had not been so happy as to attract your notice, I might have offered to be the governess myself.' Assuming that it had now occurred to her to act on this idea, Lady Howel felt assured that she would apply for advice either to the publishers who had recommended her, or to Lord Howel's old friend.

Beaucourt at once offered to make the inquiries which might satisfy his wife that she had not been mistaken. Readily accepting his proposal, she asked at the same time for a few minutes of delay.

' I want to say to you,' she explained, ' what I had in my mind to say to Mrs. Evelin. Do you object to tell me why she refused to marry you? I couldn't have done it in her place.'

' You would have done it, my dear, as I think, if her misfortune had been your misfortune.' With those prefatory words he told the miserable story of Mrs. Evelin's marriage.

Lady Howel's sympathies, strongly excited, appeared to have led her to a conclusion which she was not willing to communicate to her husband. She asked him, rather abruptly, if he would leave it to her to find Mrs. Evelin. 'I promise,' she added, 'to tell you what I am thinking of, when I come back.'

In two minutes more she was ready to go out, and had hurriedly left the house.

V.

AFTER a long absence Lady Howel returned, accompanied by Dick. His face and manner betrayed unusual agitation; Beaucourt noticed it.

'I may well be excited,' Dick declared, 'after what I have heard, and after what we have done. Lady Howel, yours is the brain that thinks to some purpose. Make our report—I wait for you.'

But my lady preferred waiting for Dick. He consented to speak first, for the thoroughly characteristic reason that he could 'get over it in no time.'

'I shall try the old division,' he said, 'into First, Second, and Third. Don't be afraid; I am not going to preach—quite the contrary; I am going to be quick about it. First, then, Mrs. Evelin has decided, under sound advice, to go to New Zealand. Second, I have telegraphed to her relations at the other end of the world to tell them that she is coming. Third, and last, Farleigh and Halford have sent to the office, and secured a berth for her in the next ship that sails—date the day after to-morrow. Done in half a minute. Now Lady Howel!'

'I will begin and end in half a minute too,' she said, 'if I can. First,' she continued, turning to her husband, 'I found Mrs. Evelin at your friend's house. She kindly let me say all that I could say for the relief of my poor heart. Secondly——'

She hesitated, smiled uneasily, and came to a full stop.

'I can't do it, Howel,' she confessed; 'I must speak to you as usual, or I can never get on. Saying many things in few words— if the ladies who assert our Rights will forgive me for confessing it—is an accomplishment in which we are completely beaten by the men. You must have thought me rude, my dear, for leaving you very abruptly, without a word of explanation. The truth is, I had an idea in my head, and I kept it to myself (old people are proverbially cautious, you know) till I had first found out whether it was worth mentioning. When you were speaking of the wretched creature who had claimed Mrs. Evelin's husband as her own, you said she was an inveterate drunkard. A woman in that state of degradation is capable, as I persist in thinking, of any wickedness. I suppose this put it into my head to doubt her—no; I mean, to wonder whether Mrs. Evelin—do you know that she keeps her husband's name by his own entreaty addressed to her on his deathbed?—oh, I am losing myself in a crowd of words of my own collecting! Say the rest of it for me, Sir Richard!'

'No, Lady Howel. Not unless you call me "Dick."'

'Then say it for me—Dick.'

'No, not yet, on reflection. Dick is too short, say "Dear Dick."'

'Dear Dick—there!'

'Thank you, my lady. Now we had better remember that your husband is present.' He turned to Beaucourt. 'Lady Howel had the idea,' he proceeded, 'which ought to have presented itself to you and to me. It was a serious misfortune (as she thought) that Mr. Evelin's sufferings in his last illness, and his wife's anxiety while she was nursing him, had left them unfit to act in their own defence. They might otherwise not have submitted to the drunken wretch's claim, without first making sure that she had a right to advance it. Taking her character into due consideration, are we quite certain that she was herself free to marry, when Mr. Evelin unfortunately made her his wife? To that serious question we now mean to find an answer. With Mrs. Evelin's knowledge of the affair to help us, we have discovered the woman's address, to begin with. She keeps a small tobacconist's shop at the town of Grailey in the north of England. The rest is in the hands of my lawyer. If we make the discovery that we all hope for, we have your wife to thank for it.' He paused, and looked at his watch. ' I've got an appointment at the club. The committee will blackball the best fellow that ever lived if I don't go and stop them. Good-bye.'

The last day of Mrs. Evelin's sojourn in England was memorable in more ways than one.

On the first occasion in Beaucourt's experience of his married life, his wife wrote to him instead of speaking to him, although they were both in the house at the time. It was a little note, only containing these words : ' I thought you would like to say good-bye to Mrs. Evelin. I have told her to expect you in the library, and I will take care that you are not disturbed.'

Waiting at the window of her sitting-room, on the upper floor, Lady Howel perceived that the delicate generosity of her conduct had been gratefully felt. The interview in the library barely lasted for five minutes. She saw Mrs. Evelin leave the house with her veil down. Immediately afterwards, Beaucourt ascended to his wife's room to thank her. Carefully as he had endeavoured to hide them, the traces of tears in his eyes told her how cruelly the parting scene had tried him. It was a bitter moment for his admirable wife. ' Do you wish me dead ?' she asked with sad self-possession. ' Live,' he said, ' and live happily, if you wish to make me happy too.' He drew her to him and kissed her forehead. Lady Howel had her reward.

PART III. NEWS FROM THE COLONY.

VI.

FURNISHED with elaborate instructions to guide him, which included golden materials for bribery, a young Jew holding the place of third clerk in the office of Dick's lawyer was sent to the town of Grailey to make discoveries. In the matter of successfully instituting private inquiries, he was justly considered to be a match for any two Christians who might try to put obstacles in his way. His name was Moses Jackling.

Entering the cigar-shop, the Jew discovered that he had presented himself at a critical moment.

A girl and a man were standing behind the counter. The girl looked like a maid-of-all-work : she was rubbing the tears out of her eyes with a big red fist. The man, smart in manner and shabby in dress, received the stranger with a peremptory eagerness to do business. ' Now, then ! what for you ?' Jackling bought the worst cigar he had ever smoked, in the course of an enormous experience of bad tobacco, and tried a few questions with this result. The girl had lost her place ; the man was in ' possession ;' and the stock and furniture had been seized for debt. Jackling thereupon assumed the character of a creditor, and asked to speak with the mistress.

' She's too ill to see you, sir,' the girl said.

' Tell the truth, you fool,' cried the man in possession. He led the way to a door with glass in the upper part of it, which opened into a parlour behind the shop. As soon as his back was turned, Jackling whispered to the maid, ' When I go, slip out after me ; I've got something for you.' The man lifted the curtain over the glass. ' Look through,' he said, ' and see what's the matter with her for yourself.'

Jackling discovered the mistress flat on her back on the floor, helplessly drunk. That was enough for the clerk—so far. He took leave of the man in possession, with the one joke which never wears out in the estimation of Englishmen ; the joke that foresees the drinker's headache in the morning. In a minute or two more the girl showed herself, carrying an empty jug. She had been sent for the man's beer, and she was expected back directly. Jackling, having first overwhelmed her by a present of five shillings, proposed another appointment in the evening. The maid promised to be at the place of meeting ; and in memory of the five shillings she kept her word.

'What wages do you get ?' was the first question that astonished her.

'Three pounds a year, sir,' the unfortunate creature replied.

'All paid ?'

'Only one pound paid—and I say it's a crying shame.'

'Say what you like, my dear, so long as you listen to me. I want to know everything that your mistress says and does—first when she's drunk, and then when she's sober. Wait a bit ; I haven't done yet. If you tell me everything you can remember—mind, *everything*—I'll pay the rest of your wages.'

Madly excited by this golden prospect, the victim of domestic service answered inarticulately with a scream. Jackling's right hand and left hand entered his pockets, and appeared again holding two sovereigns separately between two fingers and thumbs. From that moment, he was at liberty to empty the maid-of-all-work's memory of every saying and doing that it contained.

The sober moments of the mistress yielded little or nothing to investigation. The report of her drunken moments produced something worth hearing. There were two men whom it was her habit to revile bitterly in her cups. One of them was Mr. Evelin, whom she abused—sometimes for the small allowance that he made to her ; sometimes for dying before she could prosecute him for bigamy. Her drunken remembrances of the other man were associated with two names. She called him 'Septimus'; she called him 'Darts'; and she despised him occasionally for being a 'common sailor.' It was clearly demonstrated that he was one man, and not two. Whether he was 'Septimus,' or whether he was 'Darts,' he had always committed the same atrocities. He had taken her money away from her ; he had called her by an atrocious name ; and he had knocked her down on more than one occasion. Provided with this informa-

tion, Jackling rewarded the girl, and paid a visit to her mistress the next day.

The miserable woman was exactly in the state of nervous prostration (after the excess of the previous evening) which offered to the clerk his best chance of gaining his end. He presented himself as the representative of friends, bent on helping her, whose modest benevolence had positively forbidden him to mention their names.

'What sum of money must you pay,' he asked, 'to get rid of the man in possession ?'

Too completely bewildered to speak, her trembling hand offered to him a slip of paper on which the amount of the debt and the expenses was set forth : £51 12s. 10d.

With some difficulty the Jew preserved his gravity. 'Very well,' he resumed. 'I will make it up to sixty pounds (to set you going again) on two conditions.'

She suddenly recovered her power of speech. 'Give me the money!' she cried, with greedy impatience of delay.

'First condition,' he continued, without noticing the interruption : 'you are not to suffer, either in purse or person, if you give us the information that we want.'

She interrupted him again. 'Tell me what it is, and be quick about it.'

'Second condition,' he went on as impenetrably as ever : 'you take me to the place where I can find the certificate of your marriage to Septimus Darts.'

Her eyes glared at him like the eyes of a wild animal. Furies, hysterics, faintings, denials, threats—Jackling endured them all by turns. It was enough for him that his desperate guess of the evening before, had hit the mark on the morning after. When she had completely exhausted herself he returned to the experiment which he had already tried with the maid. Well aware of the advantage of exhibiting gold instead of notes, when the object is to tempt poverty, he produced the promised bribe in sovereigns, pouring them playfully backwards and forwards from one big hand to the other.

The temptation was more than the woman could resist. In another half-hour the two were travelling together to a town in one of the midland counties.

The certificate was found in the church register, and duly copied. It also appeared that one of the witnesses to the marriage was still living. His name and address were duly noted in the clerk's pocket-book. Subsequent inquiry, at the office of the Customs Comptroller, discovered the name of Septimus Darts on the captain's official list of the crew of an outward bound merchant vessel. With this information, and with a photographic portrait to complete it, the man was discovered, alive and hearty, on the return of the ship to her port.

His wife's explanation of her conduct included the customary excuse that she had every reason to believe her husband to be dead, and was followed by a bold assertion that she had married Mr. Evelin for love. In Moses Jackling's opinion she lied when she said this, and lied again when she threatened to prosecute Mr. Evelin for bigamy. 'Take my word for it,' said this new representative of the Unbelieving Jew, ' she would have extorted money from him if he had lived.' Delirium tremens left this question unsettled, and closed the cigar shop soon afterwards, under the authority of death.

The good news, telegraphed to New Zealand, was followed by a letter containing details.

At a later date, a telegram arrived from Mrs. Evelin. She had reached her destination, and had received the despatch which told her that she had been lawfully married. A letter to Lady Howel was promised by the next mail.

While the necessary term of delay was still unexpired, the newspapers received intelligence of a volcanic eruption in the northern island of the New Zealand group. Later particulars, announcing a terrible destruction of life and property, included the homestead in which Mrs. Evelin was living. The farm had been overwhelmed, and every member of the household had perished.

PART IV. THE NIGHT NURSE.

VII.

Endorsed as follows:—' Reply from Sir Richard, addressed to Farleigh and Halford.'

' Your courteous letter has been forwarded to my house in the country.

' I really regret that you should have thought it necessary to apologise for troubling me. Your past kindness to the unhappy Mrs. Evelin gives you a friendly claim on me which I gladly recognise—as you shall soon see.

' " The extraordinary story," as you very naturally call it, is nevertheless true. I am the only person, now at your disposal, who can speak as an eye-witness of the events.

' In the first place I must tell you that the dreadful intelligence, received from New Zealand, had an effect on Lord Howel Beaucourt which shocked his friends, and inexpressibly distressed his admirable wife. I can only describe him, at that time, as a man struck down in mind and body alike.

' Lady Howel was unremitting in her efforts to console him. He was thankful and gentle. It was true that no complaint could be made of him. It was equally true that no change for the better rewarded the devotion of his wife.

' The state of feeling which this implied embittered the disappointment that Lady Howel naturally felt. As some relief to her overburdened mind, she associated herself with the work of mercy, carried on under the superintendence of the Rector of the parish. I thought he was wrong in permitting a woman, at her advanced time of life, to run the risk encountered in visiting the sick and suffering poor at their own dwelling-places. Circumstances, however,

failed to justify my dread of the perilous influences of infection and foul air. The one
untoward event that happened, seemed to be
too trifling to afford any cause for anxiety.
Lady Howel caught cold.

'Unhappily, she treated that apparently
trivial accident with indifference. Her
husband tried in vain to persuade her to
remain at home. On one of her charitable
visits she was overtaken by a heavy fall of
rain ; and a shivering fit seized her on returning to the house. At her age the results
were serious. A bronchial attack followed.
In a week more, the dearest and best of
women had left us nothing to love but the
memory of the dead.

'Her last words were faintly whispered
to me in her husband's presence : " Take
care of him," the dying woman said, " when
I am gone."

'No effort of mine to be worthy of that
sacred trust was left untried. How could
I hope to succeed where *she* had failed ?
My house in London and my house in the
country were both open to Beaucourt ; I
entreated him to live with me, or (if he preferred it) to be my guest for a short time
only, or (if he wished to be alone) to choose
the place of abode which he liked best for
his solitary retreat. With sincere expressions of gratitude, his inflexible despair
refused my proposals.

'In one of the ancient " Inns," built
centuries since for the legal societies of
London, he secluded himself from friends
and acquaintances alike. One by one, they
were driven from his dreary chambers by a
reception which admitted them with patient
resignation, and held out little encouragement to return. After an interval of no
great length, I was the last of his friends who
intruded on his solitude.

'Poor Lady Howel's will (excepting
some special legacies) had left her fortune
to me in trust, on certain conditions with
which it is needless to trouble you. Beaucourt's resolution not to touch a farthing of
his dead wife's money laid a heavy responsibility on my shoulders ; the burden

being ere long increased by forebodings
which alarmed me on the subject of his
health.

'He devoted himself to the reading of old
books, treating (as I was told) of that
branch of useless knowledge generally
described as " occult science." These un-
wholesome studies so absorbed him, that he
remained shut up in his badly ventilated
chambers for weeks together, without once
breathing the outer air even for a few
minutes. Such defiance of the ordinary
laws of nature as this could end but in one
way ; his health steadily declined, and
feverish symptoms showed themselves. The
doctor said plainly, " There is no chance for
him if he stays in this place."

'Once more he refused to be removed to
my London house. The development of
the fever, he reminded me, might lead to
consequences dangerous to me and to my
household. He had heard of one of the
great London hospitals, which reserved
certain rooms for the occupation of persons
capable of paying for the medical care bestowed on them. If he were to be removed
at all, to that hospital he would go. Many
advantages, and no objections of importance,
were presented by this course of proceeding.
We conveyed him to the hospital without
a moment's loss of time.

'When I think of the dreadful illness that
followed, and when I recall the days of un-
relieved suspense passed at the bedside, I
have not courage enough to dwell on this part
of my story. Besides, you know already that
Beaucourt recovered—or, as I might more
correctly describe it, that he was snatched
back to life when the grasp of death was on
him. Of this happier period of his illness I
have something to say which may surprise
and interest you.

'On one of the earlier days of his convalescence my visit to him was paid later
than usual. A matter of importance,
neglected while he was in danger, had
obliged me to leave town for a few days,
after there was nothing to be feared. Returning, I had missed the train which would

have brought me to London in better time.

'My appearance evidently produced in Beaucourt a keen feeling of relief. He requested the day-nurse, waiting in the room, to leave us by ourselves.

'"I was afraid you might not have come to me to-day," he said. "My last moments would have been embittered, my friend, by your absence."

'"Are you anticipating your death,'' I asked, "at the very time when the doctors answer for your life ?"

'"The doctors have not seen her," he said ; "I saw her last night."

'"Of whom are you speaking?"

'"Of my lost angel, who perished miserably in New Zealand. Twice, her spirit has appeared to me. I shall see her for the third time to-night ; I shall follow her to the better world."

'Had the delirium of the worst time of the fever taken possession of him again ? In unutterable dread of a relapse, I took his hand. The skin was cool. I laid my fingers on his pulse. It was beating calmly.

'"You think I am wandering in my mind," he broke out. "Stay here to-night —I command you, stay!—and see her as I have seen her."

'I quieted him by promising to do what he had asked of me. He had still one more condition to insist on.

'"I won't be laughed at," he said. "Promise that you will not repeat to any living creature what I have just told you."

'My promise satisfied him. He wearily closed his eyes. In a few minutes more his poor weak body was in peaceful repose.

'The day-nurse returned, and remained with us later than usual. Twilight melted into darkness. The room was obscurely lit by a shaded lamp, placed behind a screen that kept the sun out of the sick man's eyes in the daytime.

'"Are we alone?" Beaucourt asked.

'"Yes."

'"Watch the door."

'"Why?"

'"You will see her on the threshold."

'As he said those words the door slowly opened. In the dim light I could only discern at first the figure of a woman. She slowly advanced towards me. I saw the familiar face in shadow ; the eyes were large and faintly luminous—the eyes of Mrs. Evelin.

'The wild words spoken to me by Beaucourt, the stillness and the obscurity in the room, had their effect, I suppose, on my imagination. You will think me a poor creature when I confess it. For the moment I did assuredly feel a thrill of superstitious terror.

'My delusion was dispelled by a change in her face. Its natural expression of surprise, when she saw me, set my mind free to feel the delight inspired by the discovery that she was a living woman. I should have spoken to her if she had not stopped me by a gesture.

'Beaucourt's voice broke the silence. "Ministering Spirit!" he said, "free me from the life of earth. Take me with you to the life eternal."

'She made no attempt to enlighten him. "Wait," she answered calmly, "wait and rest."

'Silently obeying her, he turned his head on the pillow ; we saw his face no more.

'I have related the circumstances exactly as they happened ; the ghost story which report has carried to your ears has no other foundation than this.

'Mrs. Evelin led the way to that farther end of the room in which the screen stood. Placing ourselves behind it, we could converse in whispers without being heard. Her first words told me that she had been warned by one of the hospital doctors to respect my friend's delusion for the present. His mind partook in some degree of the weakness of his body, and he was not strong enough yet to bear the shock of discovering the truth.

'She had been saved almost by a miracle.

'Released (in a state of insensibility) from the ruins of the house, she had been laid with her dead relatives awaiting burial. Happily for her, an English traveller visiting the island was among the first men who volunteered to render help. He had been in practice as a medical man, and he saved her from being buried alive. Nearly a month passed before she was strong enough to bear removal to Wellington (the capital city), and to be received into the hospital.

'I asked why she had not telegraphed or written to me.

'"When I was strong enough to write," she said, "I was strong enough to bear the sea-voyage to England. The expenses so nearly exhausted my small savings that I had no money to spare for the telegraph."

'On her arrival in London, only a few days since, she had called on me at the time when I had left home on the business which I have already mentioned. She had not heard of Lady Howel's death, and had written ignorantly to prepare that good friend for seeing her. The messenger sent with the letter had found the house in the occupation of strangers, and had been referred to the agent employed in letting it. She went herself to this person, and so heard that Lord Howel Beaucourt had lost his wife, and was reported to be dying in one of the London hospitals.

'"If he had been in his usual state of health," she said, "it would have been indelicate on my part—I mean it would have seemed like taking a selfish advantage of the poor lady's death — to have let him know that my life had been saved, in any other way than by writing to him. But when I heard he was dying, I forgot all customary considerations. His name was so well-known in London that I easily discovered at what hospital he had been received. There I heard that the report was false, and that he was out of danger.

I ought to have been satisfied with that— but oh, how could I be so near him and not long to see him? The old doctor with whom I had been speaking discovered, I suppose, that I was in trouble about something. He was so kind and fatherly, and he seemed to take such interest in me, that I confessed everything to him. After he had made me promise to be careful, he told the night-nurse to let me take her place for a little while, when the dim light in the room would not permit his patient to see me too plainly. He waited at the door when we tried the experiment. Neither he nor I foresaw that poor Lord Howel would put such a strange interpretation on my presence. The nurse doesn't approve of my coming back—even for a little while only—and taking her place again to-night. She is right. I have had my little glimpse of happiness, and with that little I must be content."

'What I said in answer to this, and what I did as time advanced, it is surely needless to tell you. You have read the newspapers which announce their marriage and their departure for Italy. What else is there left for me to say?

'There is, perhaps, a word more still wanting.

'Obstinate Lord Howel persisted in refusing to take the fortune that was waiting for him. In this difficulty, the conditions under which I was acting permitted me to appeal to the bride. When she too said No, I was not to be trifled with. I showed her poor Lady Howel's will. After reading the terms in which my dear old friend alluded to her she burst out crying. I interpreted those grateful tears as an expression of repentance for the ill-considered reply which I had just received. As yet, I have not been told that I was wrong.'

Mr. Policeman and the Cook

BEFORE the Doctor left me one evening, I asked him how much longer I was likely to live. He answered : 'It's not easy to say; you may die before I can get back to you in the morning, or you may live to the end of the month.'

I was alive enough on the next morning to think of the needs of my soul, and (being a member of the Roman Catholic Church) to send for the priest.

The history of my sins, related in confession, included blameworthy neglect of a duty which I owed to the laws of my country. In the priest's opinion—and I agreed with him —I was bound to make public acknowledgment of my fault, as an act of penance becoming to a Catholic Englishman. We concluded, thereupon, to try a division of labour. I related the circumstances, while his reverence took the pen, and put the matter into shape.

Here follows what came of it :—

I.

WHEN I was a young man of five-and-twenty, I became a member of the London police force. After nearly two years' ordinary experience of the responsible and ill-paid duties of that vocation, I found myself employed on my first serious and terrible case of official inquiry—relating to nothing less than the crime of Murder.

The circumstances were these :—

I was then attached to a station in the northern district of London—which I beg permission not to mention more particularly. On a certain Monday in the week, I took my turn of night duty. Up to four in the morning, nothing occurred at the station-house out of the ordinary way. It was then spring time, and, between the gas and the fire, the room became rather hot. I went to the door to get a breath of fresh air— much to the surprise of our Inspector on duty, who was constitutionally a chilly man. There was a fine rain falling; and a nasty damp in the air sent me back to the fireside. I don't suppose I had sat down for more than a minute when the swinging-door was violently pushed open. A frantic woman ran in with a scream, and said : 'Is this the station-house?'

Our Inspector (otherwise an excellent officer) had, by some perversity of nature, a hot temper in his chilly constitution. 'Why, bless the woman, can't you *see* it is?' he says. ' What's the matter now?'

' Murder's the matter!' she burst out. ' For God's sake come back with me. It's at Mrs. Crosscapel's lodging-house, number 14, Lehigh Street. A young woman has murdered her husband in the night! With a knife, sir. She says she thinks she did it in her sleep.'

I confess I was startled by this; and the

third man on duty (a sergeant) seemed to feel it too. She was a nice-looking young woman, even in her terrified condition, just out of bed, with her clothes huddled on anyhow. I was partial in those days to a tall figure—and she was, as they say, my style. I put a chair for her; and the sergeant poked the fire. As for the Inspector, nothing ever upset *him*. He questioned her as coolly as if it had been a case of petty larceny.

'Have you seen the murdered man?' he asked.

'No, sir.'

'Or the wife?'

'No, sir. I didn't dare go into the room; I only heard about it!'

'Oh? And who are You? One of the lodgers?'

'No, sir. I'm the cook.'

'Isn't there a master in the house?'

'Yes, sir. He's frightened out of his wits. And the housemaid's gone for the Doctor. It all falls on the poor servants, of course. Oh, why did I ever set foot in that horrible house?'

The poor soul burst out crying, and shivered from head to foot. The Inspector made a note of her statement, and then asked her to read it, and sign it with her name. The object of this proceeding was to get her to come near enough to give him the opportunity of smelling her breath. 'When people make extraordinary statements,' he afterwards said to me, 'it sometimes saves trouble to satisfy yourself that they are not drunk. I've known them to be mad—but not often. You will generally find *that* in their eyes.'

She roused herself, and signed her name —'Priscilla Thurlby.' The Inspector's own test proved her to be sober; and her eyes— of a nice light blue colour, mild and pleasant, no doubt, when they were not staring with fear, and red with crying—satisfied him (as I supposed) that she was not mad. He turned the case over to me, in the first instance. I saw that he didn't believe in it, even yet.

'Go back with her to the house,' he says. 'This may be a stupid hoax, or a quarrel exaggerated. See to it yourself, and hear what the Doctor says. If it *is* serious, send word back here directly, and let nobody enter the place or leave it till we come. Stop! You know the form if any statement is volunteered?'

'Yes, sir. I am to caution the persons that whatever they say will be taken down, and may be used against them.'

'Quite right. You'll be an Inspector yourself one of these days. Now, Miss!' With that he dismissed her, under my care.

Lehigh Street was not very far off—about twenty minutes' walk from the station. I confess I thought the Inspector had been rather hard on Priscilla. She was herself naturally angry with him. 'What does he mean,' she says, 'by talking of a hoax? I wish he was as frightened as I am. This is the first time I have been out at service, sir —and I did think I had found a respectable place.'

I said very little to her—feeling, if the truth must be told, rather anxious about the duty committed to me. On reaching the house the door was opened from within, before I could knock. A gentleman stepped out, who proved to be the Doctor. He stopped the moment he saw me.

'You must be careful, policeman,' he says. 'I found the man lying on his back, in bed, dead—with the knife that had killed him left sticking in the wound.'

Hearing this, I felt the necessity of sending at once to the station. Where could I find a trustworthy messenger? I took the liberty of asking the Doctor if he would repeat to the police what he had already said to me. The station was not much out of his way home. He kindly granted my request.

The landlady (Mrs. Crosscapel) joined us while we were talking. She was still a young woman; not easily frightened, as far as I could see, even by a murder in the house. Her husband was in the passage behind her. He looked old enough to be her father ; and he so trembled with terror that some people might have taken him for the guilty person. I removed the key from the street door, after locking it ; and I said to the landlady : 'Nobody must leave the house, or enter the house, till the Inspector comes. I must examine the premises to see if anyone has broken in.'

'There is the key of the area gate,' she said, in answer to me. 'It's always kept locked. Come downstairs, and see for yourself.' Priscilla went with us. Her mistress set her to work to light the kitchen fire. 'Some of us,' says Mrs. Crosscapel, 'may be the better for a cup of tea.' I remarked that she took things easy, under the circumstances. She answered that the landlady of a London lodging-house could not afford to lose her wits, no matter what might happen.

I found the gate locked, and the shutters of the kitchen window fastened. The back kitchen and back door were secured in the same way. No person was concealed anywhere. Returning upstairs, I examined the front parlour window. There again, the barred shutters answered for the security of that room. A cracked voice spoke through the door of the back parlour. 'The policeman can come in,' it said, 'if he will promise not to look at me.' I turned to the landlady for information. 'It's my parlour lodger, Miss Mybus,' she said, 'a most respectable lady.' Going into the room, I saw something rolled up perpendicularly in the bed curtains. Miss Mybus had made herself modestly invisible in that way. Having now satisfied my mind about the security of the lower part of the house, and having the keys safe in my pocket, I was ready to go upstairs.

On our way to the upper regions I asked if there had been any visitors on the previous day. There had been only two visitors, friends of the lodgers—and Mrs. Crosscapel herself had let them both out. My next inquiry related to the lodgers themselves. On the ground floor there was Miss Mybus. On the first floor (occupying both rooms) Mr. Barfield, an old bachelor, employed in a merchant's office. On the second floor, in the front room, Mr. John Zebedee, the murdered man, and his wife. In the back room, Mr. Deluc ; described as a cigar agent, and supposed to be a Creole gentleman from Martinique. In the front garret, Mr. and Mrs. Crosscapel. In the back garret, the cook and the housemaid. These were the inhabitants, regularly accounted for. I asked about the servants. 'Both excellent characters,' says the landlady, 'or they would not be in my service.'

We reached the second floor, and found the housemaid on the watch outside the door of the front room. Not as nice a woman, personally, as the cook, and sadly frightened of course. Her mistress had posted her, to give the alarm in the case of an outbreak on the part of Mrs. Zebedee, kept locked up in the room. My arrival relieved the housemaid of further responsibility. She ran downstairs to her fellow-servant in the kitchen.

I asked Mrs. Crosscapel how and when the alarm of the murder had been given.

'Soon after three this morning,' says she, 'I was woke by the screams of Mrs. Zebedee. I found her out here on the landing, and Mr. Deluc, in great alarm, trying to quiet her. Sleeping in the next room, he had only to open his door, when her screams woke him. "My dear John's murdered ! I am the miserable wretch—I did it in my sleep !" She repeated those frantic words over and over again, until she dropped in a swoon. Mr. Deluc and I carried her back into the bedroom. We both thought the poor creature had been driven distracted by some dreadful dream. But when we got to the bedside—don't ask me what we saw ; the Doctor has told you about it already. I was once a nurse in a hospital, and accustomed, as such, to horrid sights. It turned me cold and giddy, notwithstanding. As for Mr. Deluc, I thought *he* would have had a fainting fit next.'

Hearing this, I inquired if Mrs. Zebedee had said or done any strange things since she had been Mrs. Crosscapel's lodger.

'You think she's mad?' says the land-lady. 'And anybody would be of your mind, when a woman accuses herself of murdering her husband in her sleep. All I can say is that, up to this morning, a more quiet, sensible, well-behaved little person than Mrs. Zebedee I never met with. Only just married, mind, and as fond of her unfortunate husband as a woman could be. I should have called them a pattern couple, in their own line of life.'

There was no more to be said on the landing. We unlocked the door and went into the room.

II.

HE lay in bed on his back as the Doctor had described him. On the left side of his night-gown, just over his heart, the blood on the linen told its terrible tale. As well as one could judge, looking unwillingly at a dead face, he must have been a handsome young man in his life-time. It was a sight to sadden anybody—but I think the most painful sensation was when my eyes fell next on his miserable wife.

She was down on the floor, crouched up in a corner—a dark little woman, smartly dressed in gay colours. Her black hair and her big brown eyes made the horrid pale-ness of her face look even more deadly white than perhaps it really was. She stared straight at us without appearing to see us. We spoke to her, and she never answered a word. She might have been dead—like her husband—except that she perpetually picked at her fingers, and shuddered every now and then as if she was cold. I went to her and tried to lift her up. She shrank back with a cry that well-nigh frightened me— not because it was loud, but because it was more like the cry of some animal than of a human being. However quietly she might have behaved in the landlady's previous experience of her, she was beside herself now. I might have been moved by a natural pity for her, or I might have been

completely upset in my mind—I only know this, I could not persuade myself that she was guilty. I even said to Mrs. Crosscapel, ' I don't believe she did it.'

While I spoke, there was a knock at the door. I went downstairs at once, and admitted (to my great relief) the Inspector, accompanied by one of our men.

He waited downstairs to hear my report, and he approved of what I had done. ' It looks as if the murder had been committed by somebody in the house.' Saying this, he left the man below, and went up with me to the second floor.

Before he had been a minute in the room, he discovered an object which had escaped my observation.

It was the knife that had done the deed.

The Doctor had found it left in the body —had withdrawn it to probe the wound— and had laid it on the bedside table. It was one of those useful knives which contain a saw, a corkscrew, and other like implements. The big blade fastened back, when open, with a spring. Except where the blood was on it, it was as bright as when it had been purchased. A small metal plate was fastened to the horn handle, containing an inscription, only partly engraved, which ran thus : ' To John Zebedee, from——' There it stopped, strangely enough.

Who or what had interrupted the engraver's work ? It was impossible even to guess. Nevertheless, the Inspector was encouraged.

' This ought to help us,' he said—and then he gave an attentive ear (looking all the while at the poor creature in the corner) to what Mrs. Crosscapel had to tell him.

The landlady having done, he said he must now see the lodger who slept in the next bedchamber.

Mr. Deluc made his appearance, standing at the door of the room, and turning away his head with horror from the sight inside.

He was wrapped in a splendid blue dressing-gown, with a golden girdle and trimmings. His scanty brownish hair curled (whether artificially or not, I am unable to say) in little ringlets. His complexion was yellow; his greenish-brown eyes were of the sort called 'goggle'—they looked as if they might drop out of his face, if you held a spoon under them. His moustache and goat's beard were beautifully oiled; and, to complete his equipment, he had a long black cigar in his mouth.

'It isn't insensibility to this terrible tragedy,' he explained. 'My nerves have been shattered, Mr. Policeman, and I can only repair the mischief in this way. Be pleased to excuse and feel for me.'

The Inspector questioned this witness sharply and closely. He was not a man to be misled by appearances; but I could see that he was far from liking, or even trusting, Mr. Deluc. Nothing came of the examination, except what Mrs. Crosscapel had in substance already mentioned to me. Mr. Deluc returned to his room.

'How long has he been lodging with you?' the Inspector asked, as soon as his back was turned.

'Nearly a year,' the landlady answered.

'Did he give you a reference?'

'As good a reference as I could wish for.' Thereupon, she mentioned the names of a well-known firm of cigar merchants in the City. The Inspector noted the information in his pocket-book.

I would rather not relate in detail what happened next: it is too distressing to be dwelt on. Let me only say that the poor demented woman was taken away in a cab to the station-house. The Inspector possessed himself of the knife, and of a book found on the floor, called 'The World of Sleep.' The portmanteau containing the luggage was locked—and then the door of the room was secured, the keys in both cases being left in my charge. My instructions were to remain in the house, and allow nobody to leave it, until I heard again shortly from the Inspector.

III.

THE coroner's inquest was adjourned; and the examination before the magistrate ended in a remand—Mrs. Zebedee being in no condition to understand the proceedings in either case. The surgeon reported her to be completely prostrated by a terrible nervous shock. When he was asked if he considered her to have been a sane woman before the murder took place, he refused to answer positively at that time.

A week passed. The murdered man was buried; his old father attending the funeral. I occasionally saw Mrs. Crosscapel, and the two servants, for the purpose of getting such further information as was thought desirable. Both the cook and the housemaid had given their month's notice to quit; declining, in the interest of their characters, to remain in a house which had been the scene of a murder. Mr. Deluc's nerves led also to his removal; his rest was now disturbed by frightful dreams. He paid the necessary forfeit-money, and left without notice. The first-floor lodger, Mr. Barfield, kept his rooms, but obtained leave of absence from his employers, and took refuge with some friends in the country. Miss Mybus alone remained in the parlours. 'When I am comfortable,' the old lady said, 'nothing moves me, at my age. A murder up two pairs of stairs is nearly the same thing as a murder in the next house. Distance, you see, makes all the difference.'

It mattered little to the police what the lodgers did. We had men in plain clothes watching the house night and day. Everybody who went away was privately followed; and the police in the district to which they retired were warned to keep an eye on them, after that. As long as we failed to put Mrs. Zebedee's extraordinary statement to any sort of test—to say nothing of having proved unsuccessful, thus far, in tracing the knife to its purchaser—we were bound to let no person living under Mrs. Crosscapel's roof, on the night of the murder, slip through our fingers.

IV.

In a fortnight more, Mrs. Zebedee had sufficiently recovered to make the necessary statement—after the preliminary caution addressed to persons in such cases. The surgeon had no hesitation, now, in reporting her to be a sane woman.

Her station in life had been domestic service. She had lived for four years in her last place as lady's-maid, with a family residing in Dorsetshire. The one objection to her had been the occasional infirmity of sleep-walking, which made it necessary that one of the other female servants should sleep in the same room, with the door locked and the key under her pillow. In all other respects the lady's-maid was described by her mistress as ' a perfect treasure.'

In the last six months of her service, a young man named John Zebedee entered the house (with a written character) as footman. He soon fell in love with the nice little lady's-maid, and she heartily returned the feeling. They might have waited for years before they were in a pecuniary position to marry, but for the death of Zebedee's uncle, who left him a little fortune of two thousand pounds. They were now, for persons in their station, rich enough to please themselves; and they were married from the house in which they had served together, the little daughters of the family showing their affection for Mrs. Zebedee by acting as her bridesmaids.

The young husband was a careful man. He decided to employ his small capital to the best advantage, by sheep-farming in Australia. His wife made no objection ; she was ready to go wherever John went.

Accordingly they spent their short honeymoon in London, so as to see for themselves the vessel in which their passage was to be taken. They went to Mrs. Crosscapel's lodging-house because Zebedee's uncle had always stayed there when he was in London. Ten days were to pass before the day of embarkation arrived. This gave the young couple a welcome holiday, and a prospect of amusing themselves to their hearts' content among the sights and shows of the great city.

On their first evening in London they went to the theatre. They were both accustomed to the fresh air of the country, and they felt half stifled by the heat and the gas. However, they were so pleased with an amusement which was new to them that they went to another theatre on the next evening. On this second occasion, John Zebedee found the heat unendurable. They left the theatre, and got back to their lodgings towards ten o'clock.

Let the rest be told in the words used by Mrs. Zebedee herself.   She said :

' We sat talking for a little while in our room, and John's headache got worse and worse.   I persuaded him to go to bed, and I put out the candle (the fire giving sufficient light to undress by), so that he might the sooner fall asleep.   But he was too restless to sleep.   He asked me to read him something.   Books always made him drowsy at the best of times.

' I had not myself begun to undress.   So I lit the candle again, and I opened the only book I had.   John had noticed it at the railway bookstall by the name of "The World of Sleep."   He used to joke with me about my being a sleep-walker ; and he said, " Here's something that's sure to interest you "—and he made me a present of the book.

' Before I had read to him for more than half an hour he was fast asleep.   Not feeling that way inclined, I went on reading to myself.

' The book did indeed interest me.   There was one terrible story which took a hold on my mind—the story of a man who stabbed his own wife in a sleep-walking dream.   I thought of putting down my book after that, and then changed my mind again and went on.   The next chapters were not so interesting ; they were full of learned accounts of why we fall asleep, and what our brains do in that state, and such like.   It ended in my falling asleep, too, in my armchair by the fireside.

'I don't know what o'clock it was when I went to sleep. I don't know how long I slept, or whether I dreamed or not. The candle and the fire had both burned out, and it was pitch dark when I woke. I can't even say why I woke—unless it was the coldness of the room.

'There was a spare candle on the chimney-piece. I found the match-box, and got a light. Then, for the first time, I turned round towards the bed ; and I saw——'

She had seen the dead body of her husband, murdered while she was unconsciously at his side—and she fainted, poor creature, at the bare remembrance of it.

The proceedings were adjourned. She received every possible care and attention ; the chaplain looking after her welfare as well as the surgeon.

I have said nothing of the evidence of the landlady and the servants. It was taken as a mere formality. What little they knew proved nothing against Mrs. Zebedee. The police made no discoveries that supported her first frantic accusation of herself. Her master and mistress, where she had been last in service, spoke of her in the highest terms. We were at a complete deadlock.

It had been thought best not to surprise Mr. Deluc, as yet, by citing him as a witness. The action of the law was, however, hurried in this case by a private communication received from the chaplain.

After twice seeing, and speaking with, Mrs. Zebedee, the reverend gentleman was persuaded that she had no more to do than himself with the murder of her husband. He did not consider that he was justified in repeating a confidential communication—he would only recommend that Mr. Deluc should be summoned to appear at the next examination. This advice was followed.

The police had no evidence against Mrs. Zebedee when the inquiry was resumed. To assist the ends of justice she was now put into the witness-box. The discovery of her murdered husband, when she woke in the small hours of the morning, was passed over as rapidly as possible. Only three questions of importance were put to her.

First, the knife was produced. Had she ever seen it in her husband's possession ? Never. Did she know anything about it ? Nothing whatever.

Secondly : Did she, or did her husband, lock the bedroom door when they returned from the theatre ? No. Did she afterwards lock the door herself ? No.

Thirdly : Had she any sort of reason to give for supposing that she had murdered her husband in a sleep-walking dream ? No reason, except that she was beside herself at the time, and the book put the thought into her head.

After this the other witnesses were sent out of court. The motive for the chaplain's communication now appeared. Mrs. Zebedee was asked if anything unpleasant had occurred between Mr. Deluc and herself.

Yes. He had caught her alone on the stairs at the lodging-house ; had presumed to make love to her ; and had carried the insult still further by attempting to kiss her. She had slapped his face, and had declared that her husband should know of it, if his misconduct was repeated. He was in a furious rage at having his face slapped ; and he said to her : 'Madam, you may live to regret this.'

After consultation, and at the request of our Inspector, it was decided to keep Mr. Deluc in ignorance of Mrs. Zebedee's statement for the present. When the witnesses were recalled, he gave the same evidence which he had already given to the Inspector —and he was then asked if he knew anything of the knife. He looked at it without any guilty signs in his face, and swore that he had never seen it until that moment. The resumed inquiry ended, and still nothing had been discovered.

But we kept an eye on Mr. Deluc. Our next effort was to try if we could associate him with the purchase of the knife.

Here again (there really did seem to be a sort of fatality in this case) we reached no useful result. It was easy enough to find out the wholesale cutlers, who had manufactured the knife at Sheffield, by the mark on the blade. But they made tens of thousands of such knives, and disposed of them to retail dealers all over Great Britain —to say nothing of foreign parts. As to finding out the person who had engraved the imperfect inscription (without knowing where, or by whom, the knife had been purchased) we might as well have looked for the proverbial needle in the bundle of hay. Our last resource was to have the knife photographed, with the inscribed side uppermost, and to send copies to every police-station in the kingdom.

At the same time we reckoned up Mr. Deluc—I mean that we made investigations into his past life—on the chance that he and the murdered man might have known each other, and might have had a quarrel, or a rivalry about a woman, on some former occasion. No such discovery rewarded us.

We found Deluc to have led a dissipated life, and to have mixed with very bad company. But he had kept out of reach of the law. A man may be a profligate vagabond; may insult a lady ; may say threatening things to her, in the first stinging sensation of having his face slapped—but it doesn't follow from these blots on his character that he has murdered her husband in the dead of the night.

Once more, then, when we were called upon to report ourselves, we had no evidence to produce. The photographs failed to discover the owner of the knife, and to explain its interrupted inscription. Poor Mrs. Zebedee was allowed to go back to her friends, on entering into her own recognisance to appear again if called upon. Articles in the newspapers began to inquire how many more murderers would succeed in baffling the police. The authorities at the Treasury offered a reward of a hundred pounds for the necessary information. And the weeks passed, and nobody claimed the reward.

Our Inspector was not a man to be easily beaten. More inquiries and examinations followed. It is needless to say anything

about them. We were defeated—and there, so far as the police and the public were concerned, was an end of it.

The assassination of the poor young husband soon passed out of notice, like other undiscovered murders. One obscure person only was foolish enough, in his leisure hours, to persist in trying to solve the problem of Who Killed Zebedee ? He felt that he might rise to the highest position in the police-force if he succeeded where his elders and betters had failed—and he held to his own little ambition, though everybody laughed at him. In plain English, I was the man.

V.

WITHOUT meaning it, I have told my story ungratefully.

There were two persons who saw nothing ridiculous in my resolution to continue the investigation, single-handed. One of them was Miss Mybus ; and the other was the cook, Priscilla Thurlby.

Mentioning the lady first, Miss Mybus was indignant at the resigned manner in which the police accepted their defeat. She was a little bright-eyed wiry woman ; and she spoke her mind freely.

' This comes home to me,' she said. ' Just look back for a year or two. I can call to mind two cases of persons found murdered in London—and the assassins have never been traced. I am a person too ; and I ask myself if my turn is not coming next. You're a nice-looking fellow —and I like your pluck and perseverance. Come here as often as you think right ; and say you are my visitor, if they make any difficulty about letting you in. One thing more ! I have nothing particular to do, and I am no fool. Here, in the parlours, I see everybody who comes into the house or goes out of the house. Leave me your address—I may get some information for you yet.'

With the best intentions, Miss Mybus found no opportunity of helping me. Of the two, Priscilla Thurlby seemed more likely to be of use.

In the first place, she was sharp and active, and (not having succeeded in getting another situation as yet) was mistress of her own movements.

In the second place, she was a woman I could trust. Before she left home to try domestic service in London, the parson of her native parish gave her a written testimonial, of which I append a copy. Thus it ran :

' I gladly recommend Priscilla Thurlby for any respectable employment which she may be competent to undertake. Her father and mother are infirm old people, who have lately suffered a diminution of their income ; and they have a younger daughter to maintain. Rather than be a burden on her parents, Priscilla goes to London to find domestic employment, and to devote her earnings to the assistance of her father and mother. This circumstance speaks for itself. I have known the family many years ; and I only regret that I have no vacant place in my own household which I can offer to this good girl.

' (Signed)
' HENRY DERRINGTON, Rector of Roth.'

After reading those words, I could safely ask Priscilla to help me in reopening the mysterious murder case to some good purpose.

My notion was that the proceedings of the persons in Mrs. Crosscapel's house, had not been closely enough inquired into yet. By way of continuing the investigation, I asked Priscilla if she could tell me anything which associated the housemaid with Mr. Deluc. She was unwilling to answer. ' I may be casting suspicion on an innocent person,' she said. ' Besides, I was for so short a time the housemaid's fellow servant——'

' You slept in the same room with her,' I remarked ; ' and you had opportunities of observing her conduct towards the lodgers. If they had asked you, at the examination,

what I now ask, you would have answered as an honest woman.'

To this argument she yielded. I heard from her certain particulars which threw a new light on Mr. Deluc, and on the case generally. On that information I acted. It was slow work, owing to the claims on me of my regular duties ; but with Priscilla's help, I steadily advanced towards the end I had in view.

Besides this, I owed another obligation to Mrs. Crosscapel's nice-looking cook. The confession must be made sooner or later—and I may as well make it now. I first knew what love was, thanks to Priscilla. I had delicious kisses, thanks to Priscilla. And, when I asked if she would marry me, she didn't say No. She looked, I must own, a little sadly, and she said : ' How can two such poor people as we are ever hope to marry ?' To this I answered : ' It won't be long before I lay my hand on the clue which my Inspector has failed to find. I shall be in a position to marry you, my dear, when that time comes.'

At our next meeting we spoke of her parents. I was now her promised husband. Judging by what I had heard of the proceedings of other people in my position, it seemed to be only right that I should be made known to her father and mother. She entirely agreed with me ; and she wrote home that day, to tell them to expect us at the end of the week.

I took my turn of night-duty, and so gained my liberty for the greater part of the next day. I dressed myself in plain clothes, and we took our tickets on the railway for Yateland, being the nearest station to the village in which Priscilla's parents lived.

VI.

THE train stopped, as usual, at the big town of Waterbank. Supporting herself by her needle, while she was still unprovided with a situation, Priscilla had been at work late in the night—she was tired and thirsty. I left the carriage to get her some soda-water. The stupid girl in the refreshment room failed to pull the cork out of the bottle, and refused to let me help her. She took a corkscrew, and used it crookedly. I lost all patience, and snatched the bottle out of her hand. Just as I drew the cork, the bell rang on the platform. I only waited to pour the soda-water into a glass—but the train was moving as I left the refreshment-room. The porters stopped me when I tried to jump on to the step of the carriage. I was left behind.

As soon as I had recovered my temper, I looked at the time-table. We had reached Waterbank at five minutes past one. By good-luck, the next train was due at forty-four minutes past one, and arrived at Yateland (the next station) ten minutes afterwards. I could only hope that Priscilla would look at the time-table too, and wait for me. If I had attempted to walk the distance between the two places, I should have lost time instead of saving it. The interval before me was not very long; I occupied it in looking over the town.

Speaking with all due respect to the inhabitants, Waterbank (to other people) is a dull place. I went up one street and down another—and stopped to look at a shop which struck me; not from anything in itself, but because it was the only shop in the street with the shutters closed.

A bill was posted on the shutters, announcing that the place was to let. The out-going tradesman's name and business, announced in the customary painted letters, ran thus :—*James Wycomb, Cutler, etc.*

For the first time, it occurred to me that we had forgotten an obstacle in our way, when we distributed our photographs of the knife. We had none of us remembered that a certain proportion of cutlers might be placed, by circumstances, out of our reach —either by retiring from business or by becoming bankrupt. I always carried a copy of the photograph about me; and I

thought to myself, 'Here is the ghost of a chance of tracing the knife to Mr. Deluc!'

The shop door was opened, after I had twice rung the bell, by an old man, very dirty and very deaf. He said : 'You had better go upstairs, and speak to Mr. Scorrier —top of the house.'

I put my lips to the old fellow's ear-trumpet, and asked who Mr. Scorrier was.

'Brother-in-law to Mr. Wycomb. Mr. Wycomb's dead. If you want to buy the business apply to Mr. Scorrier.'

Receiving that reply, I went upstairs, and found Mr. Scorrier engaged in engraving a brass door-plate. He was a middle-aged man, with a cadaverous face and dim eyes. After the necessary apologies, I produced my photograph.

'May I ask, sir, if you know anything of the inscription on that knife ?' I said.

He took his magnifying glass to look at it.

'This is curious,' he remarked quietly. 'I remember the queer name — Zebedee. Yes, sir ; I did the engraving, as far as it goes. I wonder what prevented me from finishing it ?'

The name of Zebedee, and the unfinished inscription on the knife, had appeared in every English newspaper. He took the matter so coolly, that I was doubtful how to interpret his answer. Was it possible that he had not seen the account of the murder ? Or was he an accomplice with prodigious powers of self-control ?

'Excuse me,' I said, 'do you read the newspapers ?'

'Never ! My eyesight is failing me. I abstain from reading, in the interests of my occupation.'

'Have you not heard the name of Zebedee mentioned—particularly by people who do read the newspapers ?'

'Very likely ; but I didn't attend to it. When the day's work is done, I take my walk. Then I have my supper, my drop of grog, and my pipe. Then I go to bed. A dull existence you think, I dare say! I had a miserable life, sir, when I was young. A bare subsistence, and a little rest, before the last perfect rest in the grave—that is all I want. The world has gone by me long ago. So much the better.'

The poor man spoke honestly. I was ashamed of having doubted him. I returned to the subject of the knife.

'Do you know where it was purchased, and by whom?' I asked.

'My memory is not so good as it was,' he said; 'but I have got something by me that helps it.'

He took from a cupboard a dirty old scrap-book. Strips of paper, with writing on them, were pasted on the pages, as well as I could see. He turned to an index, or table of contents, and opened a page. Something like a flash of life showed itself on his dismal face.

'Ha! now I remember,' he said. 'The knife was bought of my late brother-in-law, in the shop downstairs. It all comes back to me, sir. A person in a state of frenzy burst into this very room, and snatched the knife away from me, when I was only half way through the inscription!'

I felt that I was now close on discovery. 'May I see what it is that has assisted your memory?' I asked.

'Oh yes. You must know, sir, I live by engraving inscriptions and addresses, and I paste in this book the manuscript instructions which I receive, with marks of my own on the margin. For one thing, they serve as a reference to new customers. And for another thing, they do certainly help my memory.'

He turned the book towards me, and pointed to a slip of paper which occupied the lower half of a page.

I read the complete inscription, intended for the knife that killed Zebedee, and written as follows :

'To John Zebedee.   From Priscilla Thurlby.'

VII.

I DECLARE that it is impossible for me to describe what I felt, when Priscilla's name confronted me like a written confession of guilt. How long it was before I recovered myself in some degree, I cannot say. The only thing I can clearly call to mind is, that I frightened the poor engraver.

My first desire was to get possession of the manuscript inscription. I told him I was a policeman, and summoned him to assist me in the discovery of a crime. I even offered him money. He drew back from my hand. 'You shall have it for nothing,' he said, 'if you will only go away and never come here again.' He tried to cut it out of the page—but his trembling hands were helpless. I cut it out myself, and attempted to thank him. He wouldn't hear me. 'Go away!' he said, 'I don't like the look of you.'

It may be here objected that I ought not to have felt so sure as I did of the woman's guilt, until I had got more evidence against her. The knife might have been stolen from her, supposing she was the person who had snatched it out of the engraver's hands, and might have been afterwards used by the thief to commit the murder. All very true. But I never had a moment's doubt in my own mind, from the time when I read the damnable line in the engraver's book.

I went back to the railway without any plan in my head. The train by which I had proposed to follow her had left Waterbank. The next train that arrived was for London. I took my place in it—still without any plan in my head.

At Charing Cross a friend met me. He said, 'You're looking miserably ill. Come and have a drink.'

I went with him. The liquor was what I really wanted; it strung me up, and cleared my head. He went his way, and I went mine. In a little while more, I determined what I would do.

In the first place, I decided to resign

my situation in the police, from a motive which will presently appear. In the second place, I took a bed at a public-house. She would no doubt return to London, and she would go to my lodgings to find out why I had broken my appointment. To bring to justice the one woman whom I had dearly loved was too cruel a duty for a poor creature like me. I preferred leaving the police force. On the other hand, if she and I met before time had helped me to control myself, I had a horrid fear that I might turn murderer next, and kill her then and there. The wretch had not only all but misled me into marrying her, but also into charging the innocent housemaid with being concerned in the murder.

The same night I hit on a way of clearing up such doubts as still harassed my mind. I wrote to the rector of Roth, informing him that I was engaged to marry her, and asking if he would tell me (in consideration of my position) what her former relations might have been with the person named John Zebedee.

By return of post I got this reply :—

'SIR,—Under the circumstances, I think I am bound to tell you confidentially what the friends and well-wishers of Priscilla have kept secret, for her sake.

'Zebedee was in service in this neighbourhood. I am sorry to say it, of a man who has come to such a miserable end—but his behaviour to Priscilla proves him to have been a vicious and heartless wretch. They were engaged—and, I add with indignation, he tried to seduce her under a promise of marriage. Her virtue resisted him, and he pretended to be ashamed of himself. The banns were published in my church. On the next day Zebedee disappeared, and cruelly deserted her. He was a capable servant ; and I believe he got another place. I leave you to imagine what the poor girl suffered under the outrage inflicted on her. Going to London, with my recommendation, she answered the first advertisement that she saw, and was unfortunate enough to begin her careeer in domestic service in the

very lodging house, to which (as I gather from the newspaper report of the murder) the man Zebedee took the person whom he married, after deserting Priscilla. Be assured that you are about to unite yourself to an excellent girl, and accept my best wishes for your happiness.'

It was plain from this that neither the rector nor the parents and friends knew anything of the purchase of the knife. The one miserable man who knew the truth, was the man who had asked her to be his wife.

I owed it to myself—at least so it seemed to me—not to let it be supposed that I, too, had meanly deserted her. Dreadful as the prospect was, I felt that I must see her once more, and for the last time.

She was at work when I went into her room. As I opened the door she started to her feet. Her cheeks reddened, and her eyes flashed with anger. I stepped forward —and she saw my face. My face silenced her.

I spoke in the fewest words I could find.

' I have been to the cutler's shop at Waterbank,' I said. 'There is the unfinished inscription on the knife, completed in your handwriting. I could hang you by a word. God forgive me—I can't say the word.'

Her bright complexion turned to a dreadful clay-colour. Her eyes were fixed and staring, like the eyes of a person in a fit. She stood before me, still and silent. Without saying more, I dropped the inscription into the fire. Without saying more, I left her.

I never saw her again.

VIII.

BUT I heard from her a few days later.

The letter has been long since burnt. I wish I could have forgotten it as well. It sticks to my memory. If I die with my senses about me, Priscilla's letter will be my last recollection on earth.

In substance it repeated what the rector had already told me. Further, it informed me that she had bought the knife as a keepsake for Zebedee, in place of a similar knife which he had lost. On the Saturday, she made the purchase, and left it to be engraved. On the Sunday, the banns were put up. On the Monday, she was deserted ; and she snatched the knife from the table while the engraver was at work.

She only knew that Zebedee had added a new sting to the insult inflicted on her, when he arrived at the lodgings with his wife. Her duties as cook kept her in the kitchen—and Zebedee never discovered that she was in the house. I still remember the last lines of her confession :

' The devil entered into me when I tried their door, on my way up to bed, and found it unlocked, and listened awhile, and peeped in. I saw them by the dying light of the candle—one asleep on the bed, the other asleep by the fireside. I had the knife in my hand, and the thought came to me to do it, so that they might hang *her* for the murder. I couldn't take the knife out again, when I had done it. Mind this ! I did really like you——I didn't say Yes, because you could hardly hang your own wife, if you found out who killed Zebedee.'

———

Since that past time I have never heard again of Priscilla Thurlby ; I don't know whether she is living or dead. Many people may think I deserve to be hanged myself for not having given her up to the gallows. They may, perhaps, be disappointed when they see this confession, and hear that I have died decently in my bed. I don't blame them. I am a penitent sinner. I wish all merciful Christians good-bye for ever.